Praise for The Annals of the Chosen

The Wizard Lord

"Watt-Evans carries through his tale with a good mix of humor, suspense, and insight into the human condition. Plus, there's a vicious attack by a pack of mind-controlled squirrels. What's not to like?"

—Paul Di Filippo, *Science Fiction Weekly*

"An appealing and entertaining new series."

—*Romantic Times BOOKreviews*

The Ninth Talisman

"Fans of Margaret Weis and Tracy Hickman's Dragonlance saga will find this series much to their taste."

—*Publishers Weekly*

"The deliberately archetypal Chosen are not without individual character, thanks to Watt-Evans's dry wit, and the Wizard Lord isn't a standard magical potentate. But he is treading a classic path for his ilk by introducing technology that may conflict with magic—how deeply [he is treading that path] is the Chosen's current and probably future concern—in the gifted, prolific Watt-Evans's promising new series." —*Booklist*

"Veteran SF and fantasy author Watt-Evans (The Obsidian Chronicles) displays his command of the fantasy genre in this fast-paced, fluidly told sequel to *The Wizard Lord*."

—*Library Journal*

"The second volume in Watt-Evans's appealing and engaging Annals of the Chosen is just as entertaining as the first."

—*Romantic Times BOOKreviews*

THE

SUMMER PALACE

VOLUME THREE OF THE
ANNALS OF THE CHOSEN

LAWRENCE WATT-EVANS

TOR®
fantasy

A TOM DOHERTY ASSOCIATES BOOK
NEW YORK

This is a work of fiction. All of the characters, organizations, and events portrayed in this novel are either products of the author's imagination or are used fictitiously.

THE SUMMER PALACE: VOLUME THREE OF THE ANNALS OF THE CHOSEN

Copyright © 2008 by Lawrence Watt-Evans

A Tor Book
Published by Tom Doherty Associates, LLC
175 Fifth Avenue
New York, NY 10010

www.tor-forge.com

Tor® is a registered trademark of Tom Doherty Associates, LLC.

ISBN 978-0-7653-4903-3

First Edition: June 2008
First Mass Market Edition: August 2009

Printed in the United States of America

0 9 8 7 6 5 4 3 2 1

To William Sanders,
for making my life more interesting

ACKNOWLEDGMENTS

Thanks to Brian Thomsen, Russell Galen, Kristin Sevick, Deborah Wood, and Terry McGarry for making this series better than it might otherwise have been; and again, my thanks to Timothy S. O'Brien for essential aid in world-building.

THE
SUMMER PALACE

[PROLOGUE]

Erren Zal Tuyo, also known as the Chosen Swordsman, or simply Sword, stood in the late afternoon shadows of a Winterhome street, head tilted back, and stared up at the sunlit face of the Eastern Cliffs. He could see a hawk perched on a bit of ledge a few hundred feet up, and a few strands of vine clinging to the rock here and there; rivulets trickled down the stone, leaving streaks of moss and lichen.

Those gray stone cliffs loomed thousands of feet above the town, blocking out almost half the sky. Although they could be seen for a hundred miles or more, Winterhome was built directly under them, at the foot of the one and only crooked path that led from the sheltered realm of Barokan to the vast, windy Uplands above.

Millennia ago, a relatively small triangular portion of that immense, almost vertical face had crumbled, and a few centuries later, human beings had managed to make a trail that led up across those hundreds of feet of fallen stone. It zigzagged up the cliff itself and then turned up the wedge-shaped canyon formed by that long-ago collapse.

That was the only road that connected the warm, wet lowlands of Barokan to the cool, dry plains above, and every year, when the weather turned cold, the several hundred nomadic

Uplanders made their way down that narrow path, to spend the winter in the town of Winterhome, in the great guesthouses the Host People maintained for them.

No one, they said, could survive the harsh winters of the plateau.

No one ever had, at any rate.

And when the spring thaw came, the Uplanders journeyed back up to the plateau to resume their normal life, pursuing the great flightless birds called *ara* across the endless open plain of the highlands.

For centuries, only Uplanders had ever climbed that trail.

Only Uplanders had seen the lands above the cliffs.

But then Artil im Salthir, the Red Wizard, had become the Wizard Lord, the magical protector of Barokan, and he had decided that he wanted to escape the stifling summer heat of Winterhome—heat that had not been so bad under previous Wizard Lords.

For hundreds of years the Wizard Lords had controlled the weather in Barokan, and had kept the summers tolerable, but Artil im Salthir believed that Barokan's magic was fading away, and that people needed to learn to live without it. He had relinquished control of the weather, and now allowed the *ler* of the sky, the spirits that controlled the weather, to do more or less as they pleased; under his reign rain fell in the daytime as often as at night, the winters were colder than his predecessors had permitted them to be, and the summers were hotter than they had ever in mortal memory been before.

Artil did not even use his magic to cool himself or his court; instead he had ordered the building of a Summer Palace in the Uplands, at the cliff's edge a few miles to the north of the trailhead. He took refuge from the heat up there, outside the lands he had sworn to defend.

He did not seem to see anything unreasonable in avoiding the hardships he let befall his fellow Barokanese, or in building one of his palaces in a place where he had no authority and his magic did not operate. Perhaps he felt he had earned this special privilege by the changes he had wrought in Barokan.

Sword could not see the Summer Palace from his present vantage. It was not visible from Winterhome; nothing atop the cliffs could be seen at this angle. One small corner of one terrace of the palace did project out over the edge, and could be seen from the foot of the cliff a couple of miles to the north, around a curve in the cliffs, but not from Winterhome; the palace was not directly above the town.

Still, visible or not, Sword knew it was there. He had visited it once, something over a year ago, and he had seen it from below several times, from points west and north of where he now stood.

The Wizard Lord was not up there now. He had already descended the cliffs for the year and was back at the Winter Palace, in the heart of Winterhome, half a mile north of Sword, at the foot of the trail to the Uplands. The Uplanders would not come down to the guesthouses for at least another two months, but the Wizard Lord did not wait for the snows, only until the worst of the summer heat had passed. He had returned to Barokan a few days ago.

It was hard for Sword to remember just how recently that had been. So much had happened in those few days!

The Leader of the Chosen and the Chosen Scholar—Boss and Lore, as Sword called them—had gone to speak to the Wizard Lord regarding his recent actions, his defiance of tradition, his killing of certain wizards.

Both of them had been taken prisoner, in violation of law and custom.

The Wizard Lord had had no right to do that. The Chosen had simply been doing their job, defending Barokan. It was what the Chosen had been chosen *for*.

Centuries ago wizards had run wild across Barokan, raping and pillaging, fighting each other in staggeringly destructive magical duels, terrorizing the population at every turn. Their magic had enabled them to ignore all restraints.

Some of them, however, had taken it upon themselves to place restraints on their brethren, restraints that could not be ignored. They had formed the grandiosely and inaccurately named Council of Immortals, and chosen one of their number to become the first Wizard Lord. That role brought with it the most powerful magic that the Council could bestow, which the Wizard Lord was charged with using to bring rogue wizards to order; any wizard who refused to cooperate with the Council, any wizard who killed or raped or stole, the Wizard Lord was expected to kill. Other criminals who fled into the wilderness, away from the isolated towns that composed Barokanese civilization, were also considered the Wizard Lord's legitimate prey.

There was no appeal, no refuge, from the Wizard Lord. The Council had deliberately made him too powerful for any other wizard to control.

But they had realized that this power could lead to tyranny. While a single uncontrollable Wizard Lord was preferable to hundreds of lesser wizards running amok, it was still not desirable.

So they had created the Chosen, a band of heroes given limited and specific magic that would permit them, in theory, to kill the Wizard Lord. Originally there had been only three, taking roles now known as the Leader, the Seer, and the Swordsman, but over the centuries others had been added: the Beauty, whose role was to distract any males who might interfere; the Thief, who could pick any lock and find his way into any fortress; the Scholar, who remembered flawlessly every true thing he had ever heard or read; the Archer, who was to missile weapons what the Swordsman was to handheld ones; and the Speaker, who could hear and understand all the *ler* of Barokan.

Ordinarily, the Chosen were to do nothing with their abilities; they were expected to go about their lives, minding their own business. But if a Wizard Lord turned to evil, or went mad, thereby becoming a Dark Lord, the Chosen were to gather and remove him from power, through either abdication or death.

Most Wizard Lords behaved themselves.

Most of the Chosen lived out their lives without ever being called upon to dispose of a Dark Lord.

In seven centuries Barokan had suffered only nine Dark

Lords, three of whom surrendered their role peacefully when confronted by the Chosen.

Six Dark Lords, though, had had to be killed. Most recently, a mere four or five years ago, Sword himself had slain the Dark Lord of the Galbek Hills. He had managed this despite the treachery of the then-Leader of the Chosen, Farash inith Kerra; despite the failure of the then-Chosen Thief to play her role; and despite the last-minute cowardice of the then-Chosen Seer.

He had killed the Dark Lord, and he had demanded that the Council replace the Leader, the Thief, and the Seer, but he had not explained why; he had considered the business finished.

He had thought, when that was done, that he was done with his service. He had thought that Artil im Salthir would be a sensible and harmless Wizard Lord.

The Red Wizard, however, had proved to be a very *untraditional* Wizard Lord. Rather than passively reacting to threats to the peace, as his predecessors had, he had set about actively improving his domain. Where most Wizard Lords avoided contact with the Chosen, he had taken on Farash inith Kerra, the former Leader, as his chief advisor, and had asked Lore, the Chosen Scholar, for advice, as well. He had recruited soldiers—not the two or three dozen guards at most who had sufficed for previous Wizard Lords, but hundreds of eager young men. He had hired builders, and he had set them to work, building a network of roads and canals that were gradually connecting all the heretofore isolated communities that made up Barokan. He had done everything he could to promote trade, and had made the land vastly richer by doing so.

The wild places between towns had been home to various hazards and monsters—soul-eating trees, wild beasts, and semi-sentient mantraps of one sort or another. Artil im Salthir had removed as many of these as he could locate. After all, he was charged with removing criminals from the wilderness; why limit that to humans?

The custom had been for each Wizard Lord to build himself a mansion or tower, using his magic, to demonstrate his mastery of his power. Artil had instead used his construction gangs to build his two immense, elaborate palaces, in Winterhome and atop the cliffs.

That was all to the good, really. This Wizard Lord had made Barokan a richer, safer place, and most of the population idolized him for it; he was a hero, the man who had transformed his society.

The Chosen had observed it all with interest, but somewhat less enthusiasm. The roads and canals seemed an unadulterated good, and no one had any problem with removing hazards. The Summer Palace and Artil's extended stays there were a little worrisome, since it was outside Barokan's borders, but all in all, acceptable.

But then the Chosen learned that Artil had sent his soldiers to find and kill the remaining members of the Council of Immortals.

After centuries of restrictions and poor reputations, wizards were already few, and all of them belonged to the Council; none were considered rogues. That had not stopped Artil's men; apparently innocent wizards were burned, beheaded, or hanged. Still, killing troublesome wizards was the very essence of the Wizard Lord's role, so the Chosen were not certain that they were required to do anything to stop these murders, or to interfere with whatever the Wizard Lord was doing.

Until, that is, it became clear that the wizards were being killed solely because Artil im Salthir believed those wizards had created a ninth member of the Chosen, and were refusing to tell him who this ninth person was.

Although it was indeed true that it was customary to add another member to the Chosen any time a Dark Lord was executed, none of the eight traditional members of the Chosen knew anything about a ninth. Even if Artil was correct, this hardly seemed to justify slaughtering a dozen wizards. In fact, interfering with the Chosen in any way was one of the few things the Wizard Lord was forbidden to do.

So Boss and Lore had gone to discuss the situation—to discuss it, nothing more—and had been taken prisoner.

They had, in fact, walked into a trap. The Wizard Lord had been expecting the Chosen to attack him, and had been waiting for it, with troops specially chosen and trained to handle the specific magic of the eight Chosen. His personal guards had had their ears plugged, so they could not hear the Leader's attempts to persuade them. The moment Boss and Lore were captured, orders had gone out to kill the rest of the Chosen, including Sword—archers to fight the Swordsman, pikemen and swordsmen to fight the Archer, women to kill the Beauty, and so on.

These troops Artil had so diligently recruited and trained had indeed killed the Seer and the Speaker, had cut them to pieces in the street not a mile from where Sword now stood. He had seen the whole thing, and he and the Archer had done what they could to avenge those deaths before fleeing.

The others had scattered, and Sword had no idea what had happened to the Archer, the Beauty, and the Thief. He hoped they were still alive, but he did not know.

He had fled as far as the town of Morning Calm, where the Wizard Lord's troops had found him. He had used the magic of the local *ler* to escape unharmed, but realized that he would never be safe anywhere in Barokan, so long as the Wizard Lord, Artil im Salthir, lived. Flight was pointless.

So he had retraced his steps.

When he had decided to return to Winterhome, he hoped he might catch sight of the other free Chosen, but as yet he had seen no sign of them anywhere. He had listened to a few conversations, hoping for news, but heard nothing relevant, and as a fugitive himself, he did not dare speak directly to anyone to ask. He wore the garb of a man of the Host People, and had done everything he could to match his appearance to that of a Hostman, so he could wander the streets unmolested as long as he kept the sword hidden and let no one see his face clearly enough to recognize him, but he knew he still spoke with the harsher accent of his native Longvale. Anyone who heard him talk would know he was not from Winterhome, and the chances were depressingly good that his face would be recognized. Even if a passing Hostman or foreigner had never seen him in person before, the Wizard Lord's men had been circulating pictures, with captions labeling him a traitor and murderer.

Not so very long ago, being recognized as the Chosen Swordsman would have been a good thing, as almost everyone in Barokan had considered the Chosen to be their protectors, their allies. No more. The Wizard Lord had done a good job of winning the loyalty of his people, and casting the Chosen as outdated relics who wanted to destroy everything Barokan had built in the past few years.

And Sword, in particular, had been labeled a bloodthirsty monster, the man who had slaughtered a dozen innocents in the streets of Winterhome.

Sword regretted now that he had been quite so eager to kill those soldiers, but he still did not consider his victims innocent. All of them had aided in killing the Seer and the Speaker, two harmless, unarmed women.

But hardly anyone knew that, and no one cared. He had seen that when he tried to take refuge in Morning Calm. The townspeople had done nothing to help him when the Wizard Lord's soldiers came looking for him; most of them seemed to take at face value the captain's claim that Sword had butchered the Wizard Lord's troops without cause. No one had asked for his side of the story; they simply wanted him gone.

He had no reason to think that matters would be any different anywhere in Barokan.

And that was why he was here, back in Winterhome, staring up at the cliffs and waiting for dusk. He could not live in Barokan. He knew of no refuge, no place where he could find shelter while he planned how to kill the Wizard Lord—and there was no doubt that he did intend to kill Artil im Salthir; whether he had served Barokan as a whole good or ill, the Wizard Lord had killed Sword's friends, Azir and Babble, the Seer and the Speaker, and Sword intended to see that the Red Wizard paid for it with his own life.

But there was nowhere in Barokan he could find safety, and that meant he must leave Barokan.

[1]

The only land route out of Barokan was that path up the cliff to the Uplands. Escape by sea might be possible, but Sword was no sailor, and knew nothing of where he might find a ship, or where it might take him; he preferred to stay on solid ground. He had doubled back to Winterhome because it was the last place the Wizard Lord's men would expect to find him, and because it was the only way to the Uplands.

Slipping into the town had been surprisingly easy.

It shouldn't have been.

After all, Artil im Salthir, Lord of Winterhome, surely *knew* that Sword intended to kill him. He had ordered the deaths of six of the eight Chosen, and he had taken the other two prisoner. It would be plain to anyone that Sword and any of the others who were still alive and free would now want to kill the Wizard Lord.

There had been half a dozen of the Wizard Lord's guards posted on each of the two roads into town that Sword investigated, and presumably on the other three entry roads as well, but there had been no visible attempt to guard the long border with the wilderness, even though the Wizard Lord knew that the Chosen could travel safely outside the towns, without need of roads. Sword guessed there were two factors at work in leaving the boundaries unmanned—that the Wizard Lord did not think any of the Chosen would be fool enough, having once escaped, to try to reenter Winterhome; and that he simply didn't have enough men to patrol every part of the border.

Whatever the reason, Sword had found it easy to slip across the boundary well away from any guards, and to creep along behind the guesthouses, into the heart of the town, where he made his way up an alley onto the streets.

From there, he had worked slowly and carefully toward the central plaza.

He was not there yet; he had paused here because ahead the crowds were too thick. He could not hope to cross the plaza by daylight without being spotted. He still wore the concealing black garb of the Host People, and could blend in fairly well if he avoided passing too close to anyone else, but even with the hood up and his sword strapped to his back, hidden under the loose black tunic, there was a chance someone might recognize him.

And if anyone spoke to him—well, he had never learned to speak with the lilt of the Winterhome dialect.

He would have to wait until dark.

He wished he could stop in somewhere for something to eat, but the risk of being recognized was too great.

For that matter, standing here staring at the cliff might well draw attention; he lowered his gaze and ambled away, trying to look unconcerned.

The crowds were starting to thin as people headed home for supper, so he risked continuing on to the north, toward the plaza. He made his way safely almost to the edge and looked out at the crowd, and at the front of the Winter Palace.

There in the palace wall was the archway that led to the foot of the trail up the cliffs, and there, also, was a more serious obstacle than the mere possibility of being recognized. Four spearmen stood at the opening, guarding it.

Sword knew he could easily defeat four spearmen. However, he wanted not merely to get to the Uplands, but to do so undetected.

If the Wizard Lord knew where he had gone, it would defeat the whole purpose of going there.

He turned his attention to a merchant's wagon a few steps into the plaza, and began poking through the collection of cutlery and weapons displayed thereon; the proprietor was busy with another customer and merely threw him a quick nod, acknowledging his presence and his right to look through the merchandise.

Studying the blades, holding them up to catch the sinking sun, allowed him plenty of time to think, and an opportunity to get a good look at the guarded gate.

There was no obvious way past the spearmen, who were clustered directly before the arch. He wondered, though, why it was guarded at all. The Uplanders would not be descending for at least another two months, and in any case, to the best of Sword's knowledge they were no threat to anyone or anything the Wizard Lord cared about.

It seemed more likely, given that the guards were facing out into the plaza, that the Wizard Lord did not want any of the people of Barokan slipping through that gate. Had he somehow guessed what Sword intended?

Sword did not see how Artil *could* have guessed.

He looked at the gate, and then up at the cliffs, the upper reaches still brightly lit by the setting sun, and a possibility came to him.

He had noticed when he climbed up once before that from the first diagonal stretch of the trail it would be fairly easy to drop large heavy objects, such as rocks, onto the roof of the Winter Palace. It might be possible to clamber down and lower oneself onto the roof, as well—and just a few days ago Bow, the Chosen Archer, had demonstrated how effective rooftop archery could be.

That was probably what concerned the Wizard Lord, and prompted him to post guards.

It also suggested another possibility to Sword, though. If he could get on the palace roof by some other route, he could slip down onto the loose stone on the other side of the gate, and then go up to the path.

Sword immediately knew what that other route would be; Snatcher, the Chosen Thief, had shown him a way to get onto the palace roof by climbing up a low wall to the north of the palace, jumping across to the roof of a shed, and working upward from there. Sword and Snatcher had used that method to get to the high windows overlooking the Wizard Lord's throne room, and had watched from that unsuspected vantage point as Boss and Lore confronted the Wizard Lord and brought on the open conflict that had ended with the two of them in the dungeons, Azir and Babble dead in the street, and the four remaining Chosen scattered.

Sword had not seen a route across to the back of the palace and down to the stony slope beyond, but surely one could be found, once the roof was gained. He dropped the knife he had been pretending to study, and wandered off, back out of the plaza.

He took his time circling around, through the back streets and alleys; after all, he was not going anywhere until after nightfall. He and Snatcher had climbed the palace roof in broad daylight once without being seen, but Sword saw no reason to assume he would be so fortunate again, and in any case he certainly couldn't climb that exposed trail up the cliffs until darkness had fallen.

That climb had had its frightening moments even in daylight; the prospect of making his way up the narrow path in the dark, without so much as a candle, working largely by touch, was not an attractive one.

But what choice did he have?

By the time the sun's light finally climbed up the cliffs and vanished, and the western sky faded from blue to red to indigo, he had rounded the plaza at a safe distance and then slipped back in toward the north end. There he turned east into a familiar alley.

An ordinary man might have had some difficulty going any farther than that, but Sword was not an ordinary man. He was the world's greatest swordsman, and that meant he was stronger, faster, and more agile than an ordinary man. He was able to vault up the stone barrier, then turn and fling himself up to the top of the palace wall.

When he had come this way before, the Thief had provided a grapple and rope, but Sword managed without them, catching the edge and pulling himself up.

From there he clambered up a window frame, launched himself upward to grab the eaves, and swung himself up onto the edge of the roof; it was more difficult alone and without tools than it had been with Snatcher and his ropes and his enchanted rat, but it was certainly possible.

Once on the roof he crouched down to reduce his visibility, and ran across the tiles, keeping his knees bent and his feet low to minimize the sound of his passage. He made his way from roof to roof and wall to wall until he came to the eastern edge, where the windowless back wall of the palace dropped twenty feet down to the crumbled, mossy gray stone.

But he did not immediately drop down onto the rocks in the shadows side of the palace. There was no hurry. He knew that anyone on the zigzag path up the cliff would be plainly visible to hundreds of people below, especially as the last rays of the setting sun still lit the cliffs while the town below sank into shadow.

He had to wait until dark. He settled carefully to the tile behind a chimney and sat with his back against the masonry, waiting as the light faded from the sky and night fell.

As he waited he listened to the sounds from below, the voices of the people in the plaza, and the sounds from inside the palace itself. He could not make out words, but he caught faint snatches of shouting voices, doors slamming, and other noises loud enough to echo up the chimneys or percolate through the tiles.

As night deepened, though, these sounds faded away, and at last he heard nothing but the wind. That was when he crossed the final few yards of tile and dropped down into the blackness east of the palace.

His landing on the loose stone made more noise than he liked; he froze and waited to see whether any guards would come to investigate the sound.

None did.

After several minutes of silence he felt safe enough to move again; he rose from his crouch and oriented himself.

For the most part, the cliffs were invisible in the blackness, but faint light spilled through the gate from the plaza, enough to make sure he was pointed in the right direction. He aimed himself toward the bit of trail he could see, and began walking—or climbing, as the slope he was on was steep right from the start.

He stumbled almost immediately, but caught himself before falling flat on his face, righted himself and continued, almost creeping. The steep slope and near-total darkness made the climb difficult, but he did not dare wait for daylight—he did not want to be seen. He hoped to reach the canyon at the top of the cliffs before daylight, so that no one in Winterhome would spot him.

He was not worried that he would be recognized at such a distance, but at this time of year, with the Wizard Lord and his retinue settled back into the Winter Palace and the Uplanders still on the plateau, *nobody* would have legitimate business ascending this route. If he was spotted, someone might well be sent to investigate.

With that in mind he moved as swiftly as he dared, feeling his way where necessary, and at last found the packed dirt and smoothed stone of the path. He breathed a sigh of relief as he stood on the trail, looking back down at the arch that led to the plaza, and the backs of the spearmen who still guarded it.

He had reached the path, and from here on, once he was around the first bend and out of sight of the guards, he did not expect to see another human being until he was out on the high plateau.

Of course, he would have to make the long climb in the dark, but he was comforted by the knowledge that so many people had walked this path so often that there were unlikely to be any loose stones to send clattering, or spots where the ground beneath his feet could not be trusted.

In fact, the trail was so well-worn that even in the dark he could follow it without any great difficulty, especially once it curved around to parallel the cliffs and zigzag its way up; at that point it was simply a matter of not falling off the edge and tumbling back down into Winterhome. The town's lights made it easy to see the western edge of the path.

It was still a long and wearisome climb, though, and by the time he finally turned eastward into the triangular canyon, the sky above and ahead was starting to lighten.

And at that point it was as if he had walked smack into a wall. He staggered and fell, catching himself before he could tumble back over the edge.

His hands were twitching, his knees buckling, and he could feel the talisman in his pocket, the talisman that bound him to the *ler* of muscle and steel and gave him the magic of the Chosen Swordsman, as if it were burning hot. He had forgotten, once again, how strong that magic was that tied him to his homeland, and how great the difference was between Barokan and the rest of the world.

"O *ler*," he whispered, "I must do this. I am going to slay a Dark Lord by approaching him where his magic cannot help him. I know I must yield you up to do this, but I see no other way."

You will have no magic past this point, something chided him.

"I know," he murmured. "I know. But am I not the *world's* greatest swordsman? Have I not been practicing every day for years so that I can fight on my own, without magical aid?"

We cannot guide you.

"I understand that. I ask no guidance, no assistance. I must face the Wizard Lord without magic. He is too well guarded in Barokan, but in his Summer Palace he will think himself safe from me."

We cannot protect you.

"I know." Sword swallowed. "His guards will probably kill me—but I hope I can kill him before they do, to free Barokan and avenge my companions. I'll use whatever stealth I can, and try to surprise them."

Go.

And the *ler* were gone. Strength returned to his legs, his

hands were steady once again—but he could feel a yawning, terrible emptiness in his heart and soul as he staggered past the boundary marker. The land around him felt dead and somehow less real than it had just a moment before.

He could also feel a horrible weariness; he no longer had any magical reserves of endurance or strength, and he had had a very long day indeed. He had awakened in Morning Calm, decoyed several of the Wizard Lord's men into the clutches of the *ler* of Morning Calm's earth, then marched swiftly cross-country back to Winterhome; he had spent an hour or two prowling the streets without rest, then had climbed the wall, crossed the roof, and climbed the cliffs. His magic had given him the strength to do all this without pain, without succumbing to exhaustion, but now his magic was gone.

A cold wind blew down from the east, from the plateau, and he shivered. He stumbled on, up the triangular canyon, toward the light of dawn, then paused and looked back. He could see nothing of Winterhome now; all he saw was the star-spattered western sky over Barokan.

And that meant, he thought, that no one in Barokan could see *him*.

There was no need to go farther tonight. He could rest here. He curled up at the side of the canyon, against the rocky wall, and fell instantly asleep.

[2]

A few hours later Sword awoke, stiff from sleeping on the stony ground as he had, and immediately cursed himself for a fool. He should never have yielded to exhaustion as he had. The sun was more than halfway up the eastern sky, filling the canyon with daylight; he had been sleeping here in the open for hours. What if someone had passed by and found him here? Yes, it had been several days since the Wizard Lord left the Summer Palace, but there had presumably been servants left behind to finish closing it up, and he was unsure whether all of them had yet descended to Winterhome.

For that matter, despite what he had told himself the day before, Sword was not really sure what schedule the Uplanders followed. They might already be on their way to Winterhome, as well, though he did not really think it likely. The stories said that they came down the cliffs only at the first snowfall, which was surely at least a month or two away.

He shuddered, stretched, and then got slowly to his feet.

He had gotten this far on half-formed ideas and desperation, but he knew he should formulate some real plans before going farther. He had decided that the Uplands were the only place he could go where the Wizard Lord would not find him, and he still believed that, but he had not really worked out any details beyond getting himself atop the cliffs. At the boundary he had told the *ler* that he intended to ambush the Wizard Lord when he came back up to the Summer Palace, but first he would have to survive until spring.

He would need food and water and shelter. He knew that the Summer Palace could provide shelter, if he could get inside, but there was no reason to think any food or water had been left there.

The Uplanders made their own shelter, and reportedly got most of their food from the *ara,* and obviously had some water source, but he had no idea what it was. He had not thought to ask anyone during his previous brief stay at the Summer Palace. He hadn't even noticed where the palace itself got its water.

Really, he had accomplished very little as the Wizard Lord's guest, and in retrospect he thought he knew part of the reason for that. He felt empty, listless, almost hopeless with his link to the *ler* broken. He had not been fully aware of just how debilitating it was during his previous visit, but now he knew. He had simply drifted through those few days before, unable to summon the will to do more.

He felt the same listlessness now, but if he allowed himself to drift, he knew he would die. This time there was no palace staff to provide him with food and wine hauled laboriously up from Barokan, and he had brought no supplies but his sword and the contents of his pockets. He could already feel the strange thin air weakening him. His throat and eyes felt unnaturally dry, and he had not a drop to drink.

He knew he could not survive for very long up here alone; he didn't know enough about the terrain. He would have to find an Uplander tribe and throw himself on their mercy. He would need to find some way to convince them not merely to feed him, or at least teach him how to feed himself, but also to refrain from telling the Wizard Lord where he was.

And when they went down to Winterhome, he would either have to find some way to survive the infamous Upland winter alone, or convince an Uplander tribe to shelter him in their guesthouse, hidden from the Host People. He had no idea at all how he might manage any of these feats.

But that was getting ahead of himself. Before he could survive the winter he had to survive the autumn.

He stretched, got to his feet, stretched again, then began plodding eastward, up the defile and out onto the plateau.

When he emerged from the canyon, the vast flat land stretched out before him, apparently infinite, and he peered off into the distance, looking for some sign of human life on that immense expanse of grass. A few squarish structures were visible, several miles away, each standing completely isolated on empty prairie; he had seen those on his previous visit, and had no idea what they were. Whatever their purpose, there was no sign of life around them, and he doubted they were worth investigating. He looked on.

It took only a moment more before he spotted a thin trail of smoke winding its way up into the blue, far to the southeast.

That was the most he could hope for, really; he turned his steps toward it and began walking.

The ground beneath his boots was flat and even and hard, with little to distinguish one place from another; tufts of grass were spaced widely enough that he had no trouble walking between them, and one patch of plain looked very much like another. His major sign of progress was the lengthening of the Upland terrain visible behind him as he moved steadily away from the cliffs, and the gradual disappearance of the green hills of Barokan.

The sun crawled upward, across the zenith, and made the long, slow descent toward the western horizon, and still Sword trudged onward, toward that lingering wisp of smoke. He saw no plants he recognized as edible, no open water, just endless grass and occasional unfamiliar weeds struggling up through the hard-packed earth. He sometimes glimpsed motion from the corner of his eye that he was fairly certain was small animals fleeing from him, but he could never locate them afterward. He did spot what appeared to be a rabbit dashing madly away, but then it seemed to vanish utterly in the grass. A moment's quick exploration turned up no evidence it had ever really been there at all, and he decided against looking further; the Uplanders might douse the fire he was tracking at any moment.

He had expected to see flocks of *ara* in the distance, as he had during his previous visit, but he did not.

His throat ached, his lips dried and cracked, his eyes stung from the wind. He could feel the skin on his hands and face drying out, but could think of nothing he might do to relieve the discomfort and lessen the damage. He knew there must be water somewhere, or the Uplanders couldn't live here, but he had no idea how to find it.

He walked the sun down, and dusk was thickening around him, stars spreading overhead, when he finally thought he could make out the tents of an Uplander camp far ahead. He tried to quicken his pace, but his reserves of energy were running very low after three long, weary days of running, climbing, and walking, and all he did was transform his steady walk into awkward stumbling. The thin, dry air seemed to snatch every drop of moisture away.

The light and his strength gave out almost simultaneously, and he collapsed in a heap on the rough grass, still a mile or more away from the camp. His throat was agonizingly dry, his belly painfully empty; he could not gather enough voice to call out. Instead he lay exhausted on the hard ground, and fell asleep, much as he had in the canyon.

He was awakened by something prodding him in the side; he rolled over to find two young men staring down at him, their faces invisible in the darkness, their expressions unreadable. They were little more than dark outlines against the starry splendor of the night sky.

One of the men had just poked him with the butt of a spear.

Sword tried to croak a greeting, but his throat was still much too dry. He forced himself to swallow, hoping to collect enough moisture to speak.

"Are you all right?" one of the young men said, speaking the Winterhome dialect of Barokanese with an odd, breathy accent that was both like and unlike the Winterhome lilt.

Sword nodded.

"Were you looking for us?" the other man asked, gesturing toward the orange glow of the Uplander camp.

Sword nodded again.

"We saw you silhouetted against the sunset, and when you fell, we came to see why," he explained.

"Please take no offense at this question," the first said. "Would you like us to help you?"

Sword nodded a third time.

The young man slung his spear on his back, and he and his companion bent down to help Sword to his feet. It took a moment to find the strength to stand, but once he was upright, Sword was able to walk on his own, while the two Uplanders walked on either side, ready to catch him if he fell.

The darkness and his exhaustion kept them moving slowly, giving Sword time to look at his surroundings.

The plain stretched away in every direction; in the darkness it seemed to vanish into infinity and blend into the black sky above. The stars seemed closer and more numerous here than he had ever seen them before; he wondered if the thinner air had something to with that.

Despite the darkness he had no trouble finding his footing; the plain here was as flat and featureless as anywhere.

Ahead of them was the Uplander camp—a collection of

perhaps two or three dozen tents of various sizes. Sword did
not have enough light to see their true colors, but they were
elaborately patterned in light and dark, and were a variety of
shapes. In addition to the tents there were a few structures he
could see as nothing but black outlines against the firelight. As
they approached he could see that these were frameworks,
with things suspended from them.

Half a dozen campfires burned between the tents, providing
the golden glow that guided his captors, and several lanterns
hung from tent-poles and frameworks here and there, as well.
People were gathered around these fires and sitting or leaning
beneath the lanterns; if any of the Uplanders had retired for
the night, it wasn't obvious.

Sword's escorts had said he had been seen outlined against
the sunset; could all these people have stayed up to see him
brought into camp?

As they drew nearer, Sword could see a little more detail, of
both the people in camp and the pair accompanying him. He
could see that the two men wore hip-length vests over knee-
length tunics, with peculiar headdresses framing their faces.
All these garments were trimmed with feathers; *ara* plumes
curled down behind every ear, while smaller feathers and bits
of polished bone dangled from cords alongside each cheek.
Their vests were patterned like the tents, and now Sword
could see that the patterns were made of black and white
feathers. Pink crest-feathers trimmed their sleeves and
adorned their sandals.

The others in the camp mostly seemed to be dressed in similar barbaric and lushly feathered fashion, though the women
wore ankle-length skirts and had far more elaborate headdresses. Bones and feathers were everywhere.

Even in his exhausted state, Sword marveled at this attire;
in Barokan, this profusion of *ara* feathers would represent gigantic wealth. He wondered why he had never heard stories of
this ostentatious display.

The three of them reached the edge of the camp without incident, where Sword passed near one of those mysterious
frameworks and saw that it was a rack that held several strips

of drying meat—*ara* flesh, presumably. He had eaten that during his stay at the Summer Palace and found it edible, if a bit more strongly flavored than he liked.

He glanced more closely at the framework, and was startled to see that it was not made of wood, as he had assumed, but of bone—long, thin bones lashed together to form the structure. He didn't recognize the species that had produced the bones, but he guessed that those, too, came from the *ara*.

Then they reached the camp proper, and Sword was surrounded by curious faces, many of them weathered, all of them tanned dark. No one spoke to him, though; instead his escort guided him to a central tent, larger than any of the others, where a tribal banner flew from a pole at one corner, just above a lantern that let Sword see that the banner displayed a golden crown and spear on a red background.

The tent was the largest Sword had ever seen, as large as most houses. A pair of tent-flaps hung open, pinned up on either side with clusters of *ara* feathers, and Sword was led directly inside, where he found half a dozen men seated on bright carpets, and one man sitting in a finely carved wooden chair, facing the entrance.

That chair, Sword realized, was almost the only wood in sight. The tent-poles were constructed of bones woven and lashed together; even the spears most of the men carried had bone shafts. Even in his debilitated condition, Sword realized that this must be because wood was so rare, trees so scarce, in the Uplands. Wood probably had to be carried up the long trail from Winterhome. For this man to be sitting in a chair made of so precious a substance, he had to be very important indeed.

The walls of the tent were hung with thick opaque fabric— Sword was not sure whether the hangings were tapestries or mere carpets. They were elaborately patterned, but there were no pictures, no scenes. Lamps hung from the ceiling, and the smell of burning fat was thick in the air.

The man in the chair was broad-shouldered and heavily built, his gray-streaked hair and beard worn long but neatly trimmed, combed, and curled. Pink and white *ara* feathers were woven into both hair and beard in a style that was like nothing Sword had ever seen before, but which managed to be elegant, almost beautiful.

The seated man watched silently as Sword approached, while the eyes of the other men in the big tent flicked back and forth between the two.

Sword knew nothing of Uplander customs or etiquette, but this was obviously either a priest or a chieftain of the clan or tribe; when his escorts stopped and stepped to either side, Sword dropped to one knee and bowed deeply. He kept his head down and waited for his host to speak—and tried to keep from fainting.

He had no idea whether this was the correct way to show respect, but he thought it should at least be recognized as an *attempt* at the proper respect.

He wondered whether the man was a priest, or a purely secular authority. Legend had it that the Uplanders *had* no priests, but Sword did not trust those legends. He could not feel the presence of any *ler* himself, but he knew the Uplands were not truly dead. Lore had told him that there were *ler* here, and Lore would have known, as part of his magic.

Still, if priests were as obviously in charge as this, the no-*ler* legends could hardly have gotten started. Until told otherwise, Sword decided he would consider this man a chieftain, but not a magician.

As he waited, kneeling unsteadily, he realized that the two who had brought him here were whispering to others, and word was being passed from man to man. One of the men rose and hurried to the side of the chieftain to convey whatever news had been brought; Sword could see that much from the corner of his downcast eye.

Finally, as he was beginning to wonder how much longer he could hold his position, and whether he had chosen the right one to begin with, the chieftain said, "They tell me you understand Barokanese. Can you speak it?" His voice was deep and rich, but he spoke with the same odd accent as the other two.

Startled, Sword looked up. "Of course, sir." His voice cracked.

"You aren't a Hostman. You wear their garb, but you aren't one of them, are you?"

"No, sir." He glanced at the faces around him, but could read nothing on them. He swallowed, trying to moisten his throat. "I am from Longvale, far to the north of Winterhome. If I have done anything to offend, I plead ignorance and humbly beg your pardon."

Sword had intended this as mere polite rhetoric, and was horrified by the chieftain's reply.

"Offense?" he said. "Of course you have offended us. Do you honestly claim not to know what you have done? Surely you must know the nature of your crime."

Sword blinked, and groped through his memory, trying to recall everything he had ever heard about Uplanders. At last, just as he sensed the chieftain beginning to shift impatiently, the obvious came to him.

"Oh," he said. "I have come uninvited into the Uplands. The Uplands belong to Uplanders, not Barokanese."

The chieftain nodded, sitting up straight with a pleased expression. "Yes. This land is ours, and ours alone."

"I mean no harm, I swear by my soul."

"Do you know the penalty for your intrusion?"

"No, sir." Sword was not happy to hear that there *was* a set penalty.

"Enslavement," the chieftain said, his tone not so much threatening as satisfied. "Intruders here are bound and beaten, then given to the women to use as they please. You may well spend the rest of your life hauling water and tanning hides."

That was hardly an appealing prospect. Sword thought swiftly, then swallowed and said. "If I may speak boldly, sir, I hope to convince you to pardon my crime—a crime I freely admit to, a crime I could hardly deny or expect you to overlook."

"I confess to some curiosity about what madness brought you here," the chieftain said, leaning back in his chair. "I can see you are no trader hoping to cut the Host People out of their share, since you have no pack. You bear a sword, which we have done you the honor of leaving in your possession, but an attacker would not have come alone and slept in the open. You seem to have no food, no water, no tools, and have done nothing to protect yourself from sun and wind beyond wearing that Hostman's hood, yet you do not speak like a madman or a suicide. You say you have an explanation—speak as boldly as you please, then, and tell us why you have come, and why we should not strip you naked and put you to work."

Sword glanced around, then rose to his feet.

"Thank you," he said. He paused.

Before he could say anything more a man handed Sword a cup of water, in response to a gesture from the chieftain; obviously, his hoarseness had been noticed. Sword accepted the cup without hesitation; he knew he could not afford to show any distrust of the Uplanders' hospitality. He drank the water down, then handed the cup back.

The water barely began to restore the moisture he had lost, but at least it took the edge off the pain in his throat. "Thank you," he said again.

"Speak," the chieftain ordered.

Sword swallowed, cleared his throat, and said, "I have noticed that you have allowed other Barokanese into the Uplands these past few years." He saw the chieftain frown, and hastily continued, "I realize that even here in the Uplands it must be difficult to refuse the Wizard Lord anything—after all, you spend your winters in his domain. Still, you have permitted him to build his Summer Palace, and to bring his household up to staff it. You let his people have free passage up and down the cliffs."

"The clans in council have granted him the use of that one place," the chieftain said. "He and his men are forbidden to roam more than a mile from the cliff's edge, or more than a mile north of his great house, or more than a mile south of the defile."

"Yet surely even that must rankle, sir."

The chieftain shrugged. "Our lands extend a thousand miles to the east. We can spare him his little sliver."

"But still, I suspect that at least some among you would prefer not to allow him even that."

The chieftain did not reply in words, but the expression on his face was enough to confirm for Sword that not only did the Wizard Lord's imposition annoy the chieftain, but that Sword's own insistence on it was also annoying. So far, he was not doing his case any good.

"I think we have a common enemy, sir," Sword continued. "At least, I came here in that hope."

"We have no enemies," the seated man replied. "None who still live. But tell us, then, who *your* enemy is."

"You will see when the snows come and you return to Winterhome's guesthouses, I think. You may find notices there, and my portrait," Sword said. "I am the Wizard Lord's foe, and he has declared me traitor and outlaw. He has sent his men out across the countryside seeking me, and ordering any who see me to notify him at once. I fled here, to the Uplands, because there was nowhere in Barokan I would be safe from him."

"Ah, now that *is* interesting," the chieftain said, leaning forward. "And you carry a sword. Are you the Chosen Swordsman, perhaps? Have the Chosen declared this one a Dark Lord?"

Sword bowed. "You are wise, sir. I regret I do not know a better title to call you by, sir, for such wisdom deserves respect." He hoped that he was not overdoing his politeness; he did not want it to be taken for mockery.

Somehow, though, he didn't think these people would see any sort of flattery or formality as excessive.

"I am the Patriarch of the Golden Spear," the seated man said, as if bestowing a great favor. "You may address me as Patriarch."

"Thank you, Patriarch. I am called the Swordsman, as you guessed."

"And have the Chosen named the Wizard Lord of Winterhome a Dark Lord?"

"I think we must say he is, O Patriarch."

"Yet I have heard much of the benefits he has brought to Barokan, and I have seen with my own eyes the magnificence of the market square in Winterhome. I have tasted the new foods and felt the new fabrics available there. What evil has he done, to counterbalance this?"

"He has violated his oath and turned on the Chosen without cause, O Patriarch."

"Has he? In what manner?"

"Two of us sought to parley with the Wizard Lord," he explained, "regarding certain matters where we were unsure he had acted wisely, whereupon he imprisoned the Leader and the Scholar, and sent soldiers to slay the rest of us. They killed the Seer and the Speaker. I escaped, and I do not know what became of the Thief, the Archer, and the Beauty. We had not yet determined him to be a Dark Lord, and ordinarily it is not my place to make that determination, but under the laws and customs of Barokan, if the Wizard Lord brings about the death of any of the Chosen, then he has broken his oath and become a Dark Lord. Therefore, *I* consider him to be one."

His voice started to give out by the end of this speech, and another cup of water appeared. He drank it quickly.

"What were these matters where your comrades thought the Wizard Lord might have acted unwisely?" the Patriarch asked as Sword handed back the empty cup.

"He had ordered several wizards to be killed, and we did not believe he had sufficient cause for their deaths."

"Ah. Then it was purely a Barokanese matter, and none of our concern here."

Sword bowed again. "As you say, O Patriarch."

The Patriarch tugged at his beard thoughtfully, then straightened a bit of feather he had dislodged. "You are aware, of course," he said, "that we do not owe any allegiance to the Wizard Lord, nor do we consider ourselves bound by the foolish games of you chosen heroes, with your rules and magics and trickery. Ordinarily, we would take no side in your quarrel."

"Of course! You are the masters of the Uplands, you aren't Barokanese," Sword said. "But you spend your winters in the Wizard Lord's domain, and I assume that was the power he held over you to compel you to grant him that bit of land on the clifftop—in exchange for your winters below, he wanted summers above."

"And if it was?"

"Why, then you might have cause to dislike him. No one wishes to be compelled in such matters. And for that reason, I thought you might choose to grant me sanctuary."

"Go on."

"If he were slain, you could reclaim that land. The next Wizard Lord, if there even is one after two such Dark Lords in a row, may well be forbidden to leave Barokan—certainly, I will advise the Council of Immortals, the wizards who determine the rules by which the Wizard Lord is bound, to add that restriction. And in any case, the next Wizard Lord will not live in Winterhome; custom requires that each Wizard Lord choose a home where no other Wizard Lord before him has dwelled. If you found this one's presence uncomfortable during these past few winters, that would cease to trouble you when he dies."

"Then you are suggesting that we should allow you to live freely in the Uplands so that you may kill the Wizard Lord at some future time."

"Yes. Killing him is my duty, as the Chosen Swordsman— and while you, as you say, take no side in our quarrels, I thought you might find his death convenient."

The Patriarch leaned back in his chair and stroked his beard. "Interesting," he said. "Just how would you hope to approach him? I had understood, from the stories and ballads, that the Chosen operate as a team, and that most of the others serve only to get you close enough to perform the actual killing. Yet you say two of you have been captured, two have been killed, and the rest have scattered. How, then, do you expect to manage without your companions?"

Sword dropped down to one knee again, and lowered his eyes. "O Patriarch," he said, "while I recognize you as a man to be trusted, a man whose discretion can be relied upon, I do not know what other, less worthy ears may be listening. I do not question the men you allow to serve you here, for to do so would be to question your own judgment, but could there not be boys, women, or slaves listening outside? Children can have keen ears and loose tongues, women can let slip secrets, and what slave can be entirely trusted? What I say here might be heard by the Wizard Lord months from now in Winter-home, passed from eavesdropper to friendly Hostman, Host-man to guard, and guard to lord, and if the wrong words are spoken and transmitted in such a fashion, all my efforts might be thwarted. I would prefer, then, to say nothing of my plans at this time, and in this place."

The Patriarch frowned. "You ask me to take much on faith."

Sword bowed his head, then raised it and met the Patri-arch's gaze. "I do, I know, and therefore I will say that I spent some time in the Winter Palace, and spoke at length with the Scholar, who had been there much longer and had studied its construction. The Thief is a master at entering guarded homes, and may have taught me a few tricks." While these facts were literally true, the implication that he knew of some secret way in, some way to get past all the Wizard Lord's guards and defenses, was not.

"I see." The Patriarch did not sound entirely convinced.

"I do not ask for your assistance in this," Sword said, drop-ping his gaze again. "I ask only that you allow me to live freely on your lands, and teach me enough of your ways to survive. I know nothing of finding food and water here."

"An interesting proposition. But why, O Chosen Swords-man, should we not keep you as a slave for now, and release you when we make the journey down the cliffs? Regardless of how we treat you, you are still required to kill the Wizard Lord, are you not?"

"I am. But I am a strong man, and skilled with the sword, and will not submit willingly, and if you kill me, I am of no use to you and no danger to the Wizard Lord." He carefully kept his gaze lowered as he said this; the words were defiance enough without showing his face.

"Ha! A good reply. Perhaps you could work for us in cer-tain ways, though?"

"I am glad to earn my keep in any honorable fashion, Patri-arch."

"Then I think an accommodation can be reached. Rise, Swordsman."

Sword rose.

He was given a place to sleep in a tent shared by four of the clan's young men—not a bed, but a patch of ground and a thin bit of carpet. Two of them were the pair who had found him out on the plain and helped him to the camp; they were known as Fist and Dancer. The other two were called Whistler and Bent Ear.

He did not think to ask until days later, but eventually Sword discovered that the Uplanders never used true names, not because they were worried about hostile magic like the people of Mad Oak, but because they had no way of learning their own true names. They had no contact with *ler* who might have informed them; even during their stays in Winterhome, they did not consult the Host People's priests. Instead they used nicknames.

They also had clan names that described their lineage, which were used on formal occasions, but which were unsuitable for everyday use—"Second Son of the Third Daughter of the Eleventh Generation of the Blue Chalk Line of the Dragon Clan, Sired by the Eldest Scion of the Tertiary Honor Line of the Clan of the Golden Spear" did not come so easily to the tongue, in either Barokanese or Uplander, as "Fist."

Fist and Dancer seemed friendly enough at that first meeting; Whistler nodded an acknowledgment when introduced, but said nothing, while Bent Ear merely grunted. That night Sword was too exhausted to do anything more than roll himself up in the tattered scrap of carpet and go to sleep. In the morning, though, he felt sufficiently recovered to begin his education in Uplander life.

The young men whose tent he shared and two wrinkled old women, called Gnaw Gnaw and Stepmother, served as his instructors in the ways of the Clan of the Golden Spear. He began asking questions as soon as he was out of his carpet, and the six of them answered—or four of the six, anyway; Bent Ear and Whistler didn't say much.

"Bent Ear doesn't speak much Barokanese," Dancer explained quietly. "We all learn it during the winters, down in the Lowlands, but among ourselves we have our own tongue. Bent Ear has no knack for languages; he sometimes has trouble understanding the dialects of other clans, let alone Barokanese."

"What about Whistler?" Sword asked.

Dancer shrugged. "He just doesn't talk much, in any tongue."

Sword nodded, and asked about what he should wear— would his Host People garb be acceptable?

"You aren't going to look like one of us in any case, so I can't see that it matters," Fist told him.

"I doubt it will hold up," Gnaw Gnaw said. "And you might want more feathers, to keep your dreams private."

Sword did not mention that his clothes were lined with hidden feathers; instead he said, "I can't sense any *ler* at all here; I doubt dreams will be a problem."

"That may change, when you have been here awhile."

"A change of clothing would be welcome, in any case."

"Then you'll need to make some."

"I hope someone will help me with that."

The Uplanders exchanged glances. "If you can find a way to pay for it, I'm sure someone will," Dancer told him.

Sword persevered, asking more about clothing, about food, about shelter, about everything he could think of. While his ignorance often provoked grins or outright laughter, the six of them patiently answered even his most foolish questions. The Patriarch had told them to teach him, and so they would teach him; no one dared defy the Patriarch.

After he had breakfasted on bits of smoked *ara* and washed himself as well as he could with only a small pot of water and a bit of rag, all under Fist's watchful eye, he presented himself to be trained further, and his designated teachers then led him around the encampment, explaining everything he saw.

Each clan, Sword learned, survived by following a particular flock of *ara*. Each year the Uplanders came up from Barokan just as the great flocks were returning from their own winter homes in the distant south, and the clans would find and claim their flocks for that season. If there were not enough flocks, as sometimes happened, then whatever clan failed to find a flock would be forced to disband, its members finding new homes in other clans. If there were more flocks than clans, as happened somewhat more often, then lost clans might be reconstituted, or young men and women from the largest clans might form an entirely new one.

The camp was maintained at a safe distance from the flock—not so close the birds were panicked, nor so far that the flock might slip away unnoticed. If the flock moved on, nesting too far away, the camp was packed up and relocated, as well.

The men of the clan hunted the *ara*. Whenever the supplies of meat were low, a hunting party would go out and pick off any birds that had strayed from the main body, and if those were not sufficient, they would deliberately startle a group of *ara* and bring down the slowest.

Men and women alike worked at plucking and butchering the catch. Tanning the plucked hide to make tents or clothing, and cleaning the bones to make ornaments and tools, was women's work—or if the clan was fortunate enough to have a few slaves, as the Golden Spear did not just now, it was slaves' work.

Sword was curious about the slaves—he understood the concept, certainly, since several Barokanese towns had slaves, but in those cases the system was imposed by *ler* and their priests, while here in the Uplands the land felt dead, and no one seemed to communicate with *ler* at all. He asked several questions about slavery, and Fist and Dancer explained.

Any lowlander who wandered onto the plateau outside the narrow strip conceded to the Wizard Lord was fair game for enslavement, but that was rare; most slaves were outcast Uplanders, criminals driven away by their own clans. Minor offenses were punished by fines, beatings, or other lesser penalties, as the clan elders might see fit, but each clan had certain crimes that merited exile, and humans being what they were, even so dire a threat was not always enough to keep people in line. These criminals were rare—none of the men could remember one among their own clan, though the old women named a few. Every so often, though, someone would be cast out by his clan, and such exiles could then be enslaved by whoever found them. Anyone living on the plains without a clan was assumed to be an exiled criminal; when Sword asked whether there were ever any Uplander hermits, people who *chose* to live alone, it took him several minutes to explain the concept sufficiently, whereupon Stepmother burst into raucous laughter, Dancer made noises of disgust, and Gnaw Gnaw said simply, "No. There is no such thing in the Uplands."

"Madness," Dancer muttered. "Lowlander madness."

"Please, tell me more of how it is," Sword said, ignoring Dancer.

No clan ever enslaved their own people, he was told. That was considered an abomination, to so debase a man that he would be serving his own kinsmen as a slave. Nor did Uplanders ever deliberately kill their own clansmen except in the heat of anger—to spill a helpless kinsman's lifeblood was unspeakable. No crime, not even the murder of a Patriarch, could justify the cold-blooded execution of a member of the clan. Exile was therefore the worst penalty any clan could inflict on its own members.

Once exiled, though, the criminal was fair game for any unrelated clan that came across him, to be enslaved, tortured, or killed as his captors chose. An exile who spoke convincingly enough in proclaiming his own innocence, or who otherwise demonstrated exceptional worth, might be adopted as a free man, but that was rare, as was torture or execution; slavery was the usual result. Every clan had a few nasty jobs they were eager to turn over to slaves.

A slave who served well would be permitted to accompany the clan down to Winterhome when the snows came, which often meant a chance to slip away and live free among the Barokanese, since the Host People did not keep slaves themselves. A slave who was lazy or argumentative, though, would be more likely to find himself cast out again, forbidden access to the trail down the cliff and left to die of cold or hunger on the plain.

Sword wondered whether any of these doubly outcast criminals might slip down the path alone, after the clans were settled in their guesthouses, but the only response to this suggestion was a shrug.

"It's not our concern if they do," Dancer said.

(That was the first time Sword realized that the Wizard Lord might have had a sound reason all along for posting those guards at the gate down in Winterhome.)

At any rate, slaves were useful for plucking and tanning, for cleaning bone, for disposing of offal, and for hauling water. Those were necessary jobs that no one enjoyed.

Carving the bones and beaks to make tools and ornaments and musical instruments, on the other hand, was what men did between hunts, and was generally considered to be great fun, a chance to display one's skill and imagination. Weaving the delicate fibers from certain feathers, binding and dyeing feathers, that was work the women enjoyed and kept for themselves. Virtually all the cloth the Uplanders used was made from feathers or *ara* hide, even the material that did not appear to be. Feathers that were used intact were generally left their natural hues of black, white, and pink, but those that were spun into thread and woven into cloth might be dyed any color of the rainbow.

This, Gnaw Gnaw explained, was all for their *summer* clothing; they did not wear so many feathers so openly when they made their way down to Winterhome. In winter they wore leather, or clothes purchased in Barokan, and kept their feathered garments packed carefully away. They didn't want the lowlanders to realize just how plentiful the feathers really were, for fear of lowering prices.

In addition to weaving and dyeing, women and children also gathered the greens and mushrooms that added a little variety to the Uplander diet, and even did some gardening. When a few handy specimens of native species were pointed out, Sword tried to learn to recognize which were safe and which were poisonous, but was not very confident of his abilities. *Ara* meat in its various forms, and these women's gleanings, made up virtually the entire Uplander diet.

"We ate *ara* eggs at the Summer Palace," Sword remarked.

"Did you?" Dancer was startled. "I'm sure the Wizard Lord paid a great deal for them. *Ara* eggs are rare and precious here. The birds normally breed in their winter home, far to the south, and we never see those eggs, only the chicks."

"Sometimes, though," Gnaw Gnaw told him, "a hen will lay here in our lands, out of season."

"We take those when we find them," Fist said. "They never hatch."

"But they make excellent eating," Stepmother said, licking her lips.

Sword nodded. "They do," he agreed.

The men stared at him; apparently the fact that he had eaten *ara* eggs raised his status in their eyes. Most of the clan, Fist explained, never got to taste them; when they were found, the Patriarch would dole them out to a favored few clansmen as rewards.

If he had known that they were such a delicacy, Sword thought, he might have paid more attention when he ate them. As it was, he had not really registered them as anything special, merely as very large and tasty eggs. He had thought their excellence had been due to the talent of the Wizard Lord's cooks, but perhaps the eggs themselves had been responsible.

The tour and the lectures continued. The clan's water came from two sources. Wells were not practical here, no one had ever sunk a shaft deep enough to find water, but there were streams and rivers, and the Uplanders also used rainwater cisterns. Sword had not realized there were any rivers on the plateau; he did not entirely understand how they might form when the land was so flat, and he had assumed that if they existed, he would have seen waterfalls spilling over the cliffs, rather than the little trickles he was familiar with.

The clanspeople found this particular ignorance very amusing indeed.

"It does rain here, after all," Dancer said. "The water has to go *somewhere*."

"The rivers all flow to the east and south," Fist explained. "The plateau is flat, yes, but it isn't *level*. It's all very slightly tilted to the east. The western cliff-edge is the highest part of the world. When the rain falls, it all runs to the east, and gradually collects into bigger and bigger streams—water is scarce up in the west, but by the time you get a hundred miles from the cliffs, the biggest rivers are a hundred feet wide and as deep as I am tall."

"You really did a remarkable job of missing them, if you didn't see any on your way here," Dancer said.

"Well, he was walking east," Fist said. "He was probably midway between two streams."

Everyone nodded agreement with this suggestion, which left Sword feeling unreasonably stupid, as if he *should* have seen them. He changed the subject, asking about the other water source Gnaw Gnaw had mentioned.

The cisterns, Sword was told, were the strange squarish structures he had glimpsed in the distance on occasion. Each consisted of a large wooden frame, twice the height of a man, lined with what amounted to an immense bag sewn of *ara* hide; rain fell into the open top and collected in the gigantic waterskin, and plugs along the base allowed water to be drawn off as needed. The plugs were of tarred bone, held in place with rawhide drawstrings.

Sword was somewhat surprised the things didn't leak so much as to be useless, but Gnaw Gnaw explained that whenever the clan passed near a cistern, the children were sent out with buckets of varnish, which they smeared all over everything they could reach, sealing cracks and reinforcing the hides. It was great fun for them, splashing sticky goo everywhere, and it kept the bird-leather cisterns functional.

Of course, getting the children clean again afterward was almost impossible, but no one really cared. Children had a tendency to be sticky and dirty anyway, and varnish was not really any worse than some of the stuff they got into on their own. The hair would grow out in time, the skin wear clean, and the clothes would have been torn or outgrown soon enough in any case.

It all fit together into a rather appealing way of life, Sword thought. It was not, perhaps, as pleasant as his childhood in Mad Oak, but it was certainly better than what he had seen people tolerate without complaint in many towns. The people of the nightmare community of Bone Garden, for example, would probably have considered the Uplander life to be paradisial.

That thought sent Sword into an angry funk as he remembered Azir shi Azir, the Seer. She had been born and raised in Bone Garden, and had escaped and made a new life elsewhere, only to be horribly murdered by the Wizard Lord's soldiers.

Those soldiers had died, killed by Bow and Sword in retaliation, but the man who sent them, the Wizard Lord himself, still reigned down in Barokan.

"Are you all right?" Fist asked him, seeing his grimace.

"Ah," Sword said, remembering himself. "Yes. Perhaps still a little thirsty."

"There's a jug," Gnaw Gnaw said, pointing. "And the river's a mile that way."

Sword glanced at the far-off cistern that the others had pointed out while explaining its construction to him. It stood some distance to the southwest; it was hard to judge exactly how far on the vast level plain of the plateau. "Could I get water there instead?" he asked.

"No!" Fist barked, shocked.

Gnaw Gnaw held up a calming hand. "He doesn't know any better," she told Fist. Then she turned to Sword. "No. The cisterns are too precious to be used when the rivers are flowing and nearby. It's a mile to the river, five or six to the cistern. Use the river."

Sword nodded. "Of course," he said. He took a jug from the row standing alongside one of the tents, then glanced around, unsure whether he was expected to find the river on his own, and whether there was anything more he needed to know—any dangers he might encounter, biting animals or poisonous plants to avoid. In Barokan he would have been concerned about hostile *ler* when venturing outside the settlement, but that didn't seem to be an issue here.

"I'll show you," said Whistler, picking up another jug. "Come on."

Whistler had said nothing up to this point, and Sword glanced at the others, to see their reactions to the man's breaking his silence. They didn't seem to think anything of it.

"Thank you," Sword said.

The two of them ambled southeastward out of the camp, leaving Sword's other five instructors behind. For a few minutes they walked in companionable silence; then Whistler asked, "Why did you come here?"

Sword threw him a quick glance. "You didn't hear what I told the Patriarch?"

"You didn't tell him *why*," Whistler said. "You told him that you were planning to kill the Wizard Lord, but you didn't tell him why you came to the Uplands, instead of staying in Barokan."

"The Wizard Lord has ordered that I be killed," Sword said. "Isn't that reason enough to leave Barokan?"

Whistler shook his head. "No, it isn't. The Chosen have fought Dark Lords before—I don't know how many times, but it's happened. None of them has ever before come to the Uplands. They have always found ways to remain in the Lowlands until they could reach their foe and slay him."

Sword did not answer immediately. They walked perhaps a dozen paces before he said, "You're right. There's something different this time. This time, the people of Barokan support the Wizard Lord."

Whistler frowned. "I don't understand."

"Well, you've been down in Barokan for the winter," Sword said. "Have you talked to any of the Host People lately? Have you been to the market in Winterhome?"

"Well, not very much," Whistler said. "I mostly stay in the guesthouse, where it's warm, or walk in the woods behind it. But I've seen the market, and spoken to a few people. I don't know what you mean."

"You're old enough to remember back before the current Wizard Lord, aren't you?"

"Yes." Whistler frowned again. "Are you talking about how the markets are more crowded now?"

"That's part of it," Sword said. He sighed. "This Wizard Lord isn't like any we've had before, not in all the seven hundred years we've *had* Wizard Lords. All the others seem to have been interested in magic more than anything else—that was why they became wizards in the first place. This one, though, doesn't care about magic for its own sake. He wants to make everything *better,* for everyone in Barokan."

"That sounds like a *good* thing," Whistler said, puzzled. "Why do you say he's a Dark Lord, then?"

"I didn't," Sword said. "Not at first. He was doing things no one had done before, building roads and canals, and clearing away monsters, and so on, and really, it seemed as if he *was* making everything better. Traders and merchants could travel freely and bring their goods everywhere the roads went. Everyone loved the Wizard Lord. *I* liked what he was doing. Some of it made me nervous—building a Summer Palace in the Uplands, for example, didn't seem like a good idea—but all in all, I thought it was wonderful."

He stopped, and the two walked on in silence for a few steps until Whistler said, "Wonderful—but? . . ."

"But there were two things, two related things, that went wrong," Sword said. "Is that the river, then?" He pointed.

"That's it. What two things?"

Sword stared at the "river." It was visible as a wiggling break in the grassy plain, rather than as a body of water. He suddenly felt much less foolish about missing it in the dark the night before.

"What two things?" Whistler repeated.

"Oh. Yes. Well, one thing was that he was obsessed with the idea that the Chosen were going to depose him," Sword explained. "I mean, I can see why he would worry about it, since that's what the Chosen are *for,* but he didn't just worry, he was *convinced* that sooner or later we would come after him just because he was doing new and different things and not following the traditional patterns."

"Would you?"

Sword shrugged. "I don't think so, no—but I'm just the Swordsman; the Leader might have talked us all into it if she decided not to trust him."

"Could . . . *she*? She? The Leader is a woman?"

"Not much more than a girl, really," Sword said, remembering. "Younger than I am, and no taller than my shoulder. The old Leader, the man who picked her for the job, was trying to make a joke of the role." He threw Whistler a glance and saw the youth's baffled expression. "It's a long story," he said. "The old Leader was not happy with how things went when we confronted the Dark Lord of the Galbek Hills, so he tried to pass the title to the most inappropriate person he could find. Some powerful *ler* must have intervened, though, because she was actually a very good Leader, much better than the one who chose her had ever been."

"Was? Not is?"

Sword nodded. "She's a prisoner in the Wizard Lord's dungeon now."

"But she still lives?"

"So far as I know, yes." They were nearing the river now, and the ground underfoot was getting soft.

"The hole's over here," Whistler said, pointing off to the left.

"Hole?"

"Yes."

Sword decided to wait and see what the lad was talking about, rather than asking more questions; he followed along, and it soon became clear what the "hole" was.

The river was little more than a muddy ditch with a trickle in the bottom, perhaps six inches deep and two or three feet across, with no sharp edge. The rivulet at the bottom was not much more than an inch deep, and the only way Sword could see to get water out of it into the jug was with a straw.

But a few feet downstream, someone had dug a hole in the middle of the ditch. If Sword laced his fingers and formed his arms into a circle, that would just about be the size of the hole. The yellow dirt that had been displaced was piled up to one side, several feet away, where it would not easily wash back in.

The water in the hole looked surprisingly clean. A thin streak of brown flowed in on the upstream side, but most of it was clear enough for Sword to see that the hole was roughly waist-deep.

"Fill your jug on the downstream side," Whistler said, stooping to demonstrate.

Sword followed his example, and a moment later both jugs were full.

"If we were sent to fetch water, we'd be expected to use the big vessels, and carry two apiece," Whistler said as Sword lifted his jug out of the pool.

"Of course," Sword said as he set the jug aside and looked at the water. "Is it safe to drink this, straight from the stream? Does it need to be blessed or boiled?"

"We don't bless anything," Whistler said. "We have no priests, and we do not speak to *ler*. Our clothes are all made from *ara* so that the *ler* cannot trouble us."

"I see." Sword was well aware of the magic-blocking properties of *ara* feathers, and the Uplanders used them everywhere; every man and woman in the Clan of the Golden Spear walked around wearing what would have been a fortune in *ara* feathers down in Barokan. "Do you boil it?"

"Sometimes, but if you're healthy, drinking it shouldn't hurt you."

Sword nodded, then bent down and scooped up water with his hands. He still felt dry from his long walk across the plateau, and drank thirstily.

Whistler watched him for a moment, then asked, "What was the other thing?"

Sword looked up and blinked. "What?"

"You said there were two problems with the Wizard Lord. One was that he thought the Chosen would turn on him. What was the other?"

"Oh," Sword said. He took one more drink, then shook the water from his hands and got to his feet. "You said that you have no priests up here?"

"That's right."

"Do you have wizards?" He bent down to retrieve his now-full jug.

"No. Our ancestors came up here partly to escape Lowland magic."

"Ah. That's very much why the Wizard Lord built himself the Summer Palace," Sword said. He turned back toward the Golden Spear camp and started walking. "He believes that Barokan's magic is fading, and that we must learn to live without it."

"*That's* the other thing? The problem?" Whistler walked alongside him, and the two ambled along at a casual pace.

"Oh, not that he thought magic was fading," Sword said. "It was what he did about it."

"What did he do?"

"Several things. He built the Summer Palace, for one. His magic doesn't work there; did you know that?"

Whistler threw a glance to the west, past the camp toward the distant cliffs. "No," he said thoughtfully. "I don't think any of us did."

Sword nodded. "Well, it doesn't. Which meant that when he was living there, he had no direct control over events in Barokan. The weather misbehaved a little, and there was some concern that he wouldn't be able to protect everything effectively."

"I can see how that would be something to worry about," Whistler said.

"Most people didn't worry about it, though," Sword said. "Not really. They were too pleased with the roads and canals and the rest."

"But . . ."

"But building the Summer Palace was only part of it," Sword said. "Because he didn't just want *his* magic gone; he wanted *all* of it gone. So he started killing all the other wizards—or rather, sending his men to kill them, so that the Seer wouldn't know what was happening. He gave the orders while he was up in the Summer Palace, where the Seer couldn't sense what was happening."

"Killing the other wizards?"

Sword nodded again. "He intended to kill all of them, but a few escaped—at least, so far. He may find them eventually."

"But didn't . . . I mean, I know he's allowed to kill wizards who break the law, but didn't anyone . . . he tried to kill them *all*?"

"He came up with an excuse, so the soldiers wouldn't question his orders—at least, I think that's why he did it the way he did," Sword explained. "I told you he was convinced the Chosen would turn on him eventually. Well, he found out that the other wizards had added a ninth member to the Chosen— or at least, he claims they did—and he told his men to kill any wizard who refused to tell him who the ninth Chosen is."

"But then, why didn't the wizards tell him?"

"They couldn't," Sword replied bitterly. "They had put themselves under a spell that prevented them from saying anything about the ninth member of the Chosen. It was deliberate murder, killing them that way."

Whistler nodded, and they walked several paces in silence before the Uplander asked, "*Is* there a ninth member of the Chosen? I mean, I only ever heard of eight—the Swordsman and the Leader and the Beauty and the Seer and the Thief, and . . . uh . . ."

"The Archer, the Scholar, and the Speaker." Sword completed the list for him. "That's all *I* know of, too. But in the past, whenever the Chosen have killed a Dark Lord, another member has been added. The last one was the Speaker of All Tongues, added after the Dark Lord of Goln Vleys was removed. Well, eight years ago I slew the Dark Lord of the Galbek Hills, so a ninth one should have been added."

"Wouldn't they . . . would it have been kept secret? So secret, they used magic to keep themselves from talking about it?"

Sword shrugged. "Who knows? Lore—that's the Scholar, we call him Lore—said that the usual system is to tell the Leader of the Chosen, and no one else, but keeping it completely secret has never been required. The present Leader wasn't told anything, but she took over from the old Leader right about the time news would have reached him, so it may be they told *him,* and he didn't pass the news on to *her.*"

"Or—would she have kept it secret from the rest of you?"

"I don't think so, but I don't really know," Sword admitted. "I haven't known her very long. She certainly *seems* trustworthy, but that's her role."

"So you don't know whether there really is a ninth?"

"That's right."

"I'm still not sure I see how this led to you coming to the Uplands, though."

Sword sighed, and shifted his jug to his other hand.

"He was killing wizards because, he said, they wouldn't tell him who was the ninth member of the Chosen. The Leader and the Scholar went to talk to him about why he was killing wizards, and to ask him to stop. Because he was so certain that sooner or later the Chosen would turn on him, he assumed their request for an audience was the start of a campaign against him, and he determined to strike first. He turned it into a trap. He had soldiers whose ears were plugged, so they couldn't be swayed by the Leader's words or magic, and he took the Leader and the Scholar prisoner and had them thrown into his dungeons. Then he sent more soldiers to kill the rest of us—swordswomen to kill the Beauty, archers to kill me, swordsmen and spearmen to kill the Archer, and so on. They killed the Speaker and the Seer, but I escaped, and I think the Thief, the Beauty, and the Archer may have survived, but we were separated, and without the Seer we have no way to find one another, so I'm alone."

"But why are you *here*?"

"Because all of Barokan is siding with *him,* with the Wizard Lord. Everywhere in the Lowlands I'm a fugitive, a criminal. He's sent drawings of me to all the nearby towns, and soldiers are hunting for me, and I realized the only place I could go where he would never find me would be here, to the Uplands. So here I am."

Whistler nodded. "I see," he said. "And what will you do next?"

Sword grimaced, and shifted the jug again.

"I wish I knew," he said.

[4]

Sword was not permitted to hunt at first; the birds belonged to the clan, and he was not a member of the clan. He was given a fair share of the meat at supper, but not allowed to join the young men in obtaining it. Instead he was kept in or near the camp, where he earned his keep by hauling water, cleaning *ara* leather, and doing various other unpleasant but necessary jobs.

In fact, he quickly realized that it was exactly the work he would have done as a slave. The only real differences in how he spent his days were that he was permitted to keep his sword, he was never chained, and his instructions were usually in the form of polite requests rather than brusque orders.

Those differences were appreciated, though, and his evenings were his own—by the Patriarch's orders, his assigned tasks stopped when the sun sank below the cliffs, where a slave might have found himself working well into the night. He decided to use part of this free time to make himself clothing in the Uplander style—he planned *ara* leather pants, a woven-feather shirt, and a long leather vest, and perhaps, if he had the time and materials, a pair of the soft leather boots the Uplanders wore. A proper Uplander vest would be adorned with elaborate patterns of feathers, but Sword did not expect to have the time needed to do that, and intended to leave his plain.

There were plenty of other things he hoped to do with his evenings, as well—planning his revenge on the Wizard Lord was high on the list. Learning more about the Clan of the Golden Spear, perhaps picking up a little of their language, getting to know some of the young women—he hoped to find time for all of those.

First and foremost, though, he intended to stay in shape. Although he no longer had any magical compulsion requiring him to do so, Sword still had his habits, and he therefore spent the first hour of his free evening every day, beginning almost the moment the sun dropped below the horizon, practicing his swordplay. His ability with a blade was no longer superhuman, but all those years of practice had not vanished with his magic, and his skills were still sufficient to impress the Clan of the Golden Spear. By the fourth day his practice sessions were drawing a crowd—mostly young men and children, but a few women and older men watched, as well. Sword was not entirely sure at first just what they thought of his actions, since most of their conversation was in their own Uplander tongue rather than anything he could understand, but eventually a few began to comment in Barokanese.

"I think I'm glad the Patriarch didn't tell us to take your sword away," one hunter remarked as he watched Sword slice a drifting feather to shreds without seeming to move anything but his wrist. "It wouldn't have been easy."

"I'm glad of it, too," Sword replied, without taking his eye off his target. "I wouldn't want to harm anyone here."

"Wouldn't you?" the hunter asked. "But your role is to kill people, isn't it?"

"My *role*," Sword said as he split the remaining bit of quill lengthwise, "is to see that the Wizard Lord does no great harm to the people of Barokan." He flicked a floating shred of feather upward to provide a fresh target.

"But haven't you slain any number of people?"

Sword paused, and looked at the questioner, letting the bit of feather drift away unmolested. "Why do you ask?"

The man shrugged. "Oh, well, last winter, when we were in Winterhome, I heard stories about how you . . . well, about what you did to a rapist in Dog Pole, and how you cut off the hands of the woman who trapped you in the Dark Lord's dungeon and left her to bleed to death—"

"That didn't happen," Sword said sharply, lowering his blade. "I know nothing of any rapists in Dog Pole—I was in Dog Pole only once, years ago, and I barely spoke to anyone there, I certainly didn't get involved in any local business."

"Well, but the Dark Lord's maids—," the hunter persisted.

"Were all alive and well last I saw," Sword interrupted, wiping his blade with his handkerchief. "I admit to threatening two of them, but I never actually struck them. I never drew blood. As of last winter the only person I had ever killed was the Dark Lord of the Galbek Hills. I regret to say I did slay several of the Wizard Lord's soldiers several days ago, shortly before fleeing up the cliffs, but that's all."

"But the stories—," another man began.

"Lies," Sword said. "Lies spread by the Wizard Lord."

"Is that why you plan to kill him?" Fist asked. "Because he's spreading lies about you?"

"No," Sword said. He slid the sword smoothly into its sheath.

"Because he's changing all the traditions?" another man asked.

"No," Sword replied.

"Because he wants to kill *you*?" Whistler asked.

Sword glanced at him. "Partly," he said.

"Well, don't expect us to believe you're killing him so we can take back the cliff-edge where he built his palace," Fist said. "I wouldn't believe that for a minute."

"Neither would I," Sword agreed.

"To protect Barokan?" someone suggested.

"From what?" Fist asked. "What's he doing to Barokan that's so terrible?"

"Oh, yes, they need to be protected from roads and canals and merchants bringing silks and spices and fancy wines," a hunter said scornfully.

"He killed a lot of wizards, Whistler told me."

"Yes, he did," Sword agreed, "but that's not really why I intend to kill him. Let the wizards look after themselves—they chose the Wizard Lord, and if they chose poorly, let them face the consequences."

"He killed your friends," Whistler said quietly.

"Yes," Sword agreed. "Yes, he did—he ordered the deaths of two innocent women who never harmed him, who had both made the best of unhappy lives. He killed them without provocation, simply because they were two of the Chosen and he could not be bothered to offer them any alternative. He never gave them a chance to surrender. He never tried to capture them alive. He just had them slaughtered."

For a moment the group fell silent. Then Fist said, "So you intend to kill him just for your own personal vengeance? Not because it's your duty as one of the Chosen?"

"Oh, it's my duty, as well," Sword said. "It's very convenient when duty and desire align, don't you think? I don't need to choose between them, I can serve both."

That provoked a round of smiles, and chattering bilingual agreement.

The conversation reminded Sword, though, that he needed to devise a plan to kill the Wizard Lord. He had sought refuge among the Uplanders and he had found it here, but it was only temporary; in roughly another month and a half, when the *ara* migrated south and the first snow fell, the Clan of the Golden Spear would be making the journey down to Winterhome.

He had three choices, as he saw it. He could continue to live among the Uplanders, accompany them down to Winterhome, live in their guesthouse there—and then what? Simply go on like that, hiding and skulking indefinitely? And what if the Wizard Lord's soldiers searched the clan guesthouses? Run and hide again?

Sword did not want to hide. He did want to kill Artil im Salthir for what he had done to the Speaker and the Seer. Poor Babble, constantly barraged by voices only she could hear, had never meant the Wizard Lord any harm. And the Seer, Azir shi Azir, had survived and escaped perhaps the most horrific childhood Sword had ever heard of, in the infamous hell-town of Bone Garden, only to be cut to pieces in the supposedly safe and peaceful streets of Winterhome. Sword wanted more than mere survival; he wanted retribution. If he accompanied the Uplanders down to Barokan for the winter, he wanted to have a plan ready, some way to get at the Wizard Lord and kill him.

Or he could leave the clan before that, and return to Barokan on his own. That path likewise led in two directions of its own—either finding another refuge, or making a bid to slay the Wizard Lord, presumably in the Winter Palace. Again, he had as yet no plan for getting at Artil during the winter.

Or finally, he could remain in the Uplands when the clan left, and try to survive the winter up here. His goal in that case would be to be waiting in or near the Summer Palace when the Wizard Lord returned, to ambush him there and kill him while he had no magic protecting him.

Sword had no interest in hiding indefinitely, either among the Uplanders or anywhere else. He wanted Artil dead. He dismissed the possibility of hiding, either among the Uplanders or on his own.

He did know what he believed to be a relatively safe route into the Winter Palace, if he chose to attack the Wizard Lord there; the Thief had shown him a way up onto the roof, where he could smash in the windows overlooking the Wizard Lord's throne room and drop down unexpectedly.

The problems there were obvious. It was a long drop; if he lowered himself down a rope, that would give the guards time to stop him, and if he simply leapt, he was likely to break a leg or otherwise incapacitate himself before he could slay his foe.

That assumed he *could* kill Artil; the Wizard Lord had plenty of magic at his command. He couldn't use it directly against Sword—that was part of the magic of the Chosen, that they were themselves immune to most magic—but he could use it around anything and anyone *around* Sword. That was one reason there were several Chosen, and not merely a Chosen Swordsman: The Wizard Lord had powerful defenses.

One of them was that he might be able to simply fly away, leaving Sword trapped in the Winter Palace with no way to get out undetected. Jumping down from the roof was only a way *in*.

And once the Wizard Lord was either dead or gone, Sword would be surrounded by enemies. Sword did not think that simply killing Artil im Salthir would end his hold on the hearts of the Barokanese; his guards would almost certainly butcher Sword on the spot, even if the Wizard Lord was already dead. Yes, he would have his magical fighting abilities back, and would be able to hold them off for a long time, perhaps kill several of them, but sooner or later they would be able to get to him—probably with archery.

If it came to a fight, he might be forced to kill any number of guards, which he did not really want to do—it was only the Wizard Lord's death he wanted.

Even if Sword escaped the Palace, he would still be in the middle of Winterhome, and might well face an angry mob.

Sword thought he might be willing to die if he could be sure of taking the Wizard Lord with him, but he certainly wasn't *eager* to do so, and the possibility that the Wizard Lord might use magic to escape him could not be ignored. Sword didn't know just what magic Artil had available. *Some* of it he knew—he knew Artil could fly on the winds he summoned, that he could draw on inhuman reserves of strength, that he was inhumanly persuasive, and so on—but he did not know what other abilities the Wizard Lord might have in reserve.

An attack in the Winter Palace would be a gamble, at best.

Surviving an Upland winter and ambushing the Wizard Lord in the Summer Palace was not likely to be easy, either, of course. Artil would have his guards and other supporters, and Sword's abilities would not include magic. He would be a good swordsman, but not the greatest in the world, not super-human.

But the Wizard Lord would have no magic, either. He kept fewer guards at the Summer Palace—bringing the necessary supplies up the cliff made it impractical to maintain an army there.

Sword would have all winter to set his traps, to learn every nook and cranny of the Summer Palace, to plan his every move.

And if he did manage to kill the Wizard Lord and get out of the Palace alive, he would not be in Winterhome, surrounded by hostile Barokanese; he would be able to flee east, across the Uplands, where the Barokanese would not follow him.

Also, although he could not explain why, Sword thought that the Barokanese were less likely to demand vengeance if Artil were slain while up on the plateau, rather than while in Barokan itself.

An ambush in the Summer Palace really seemed like the best approach. No one would expect him to survive up here. If the Wizard Lord questioned the Uplanders Sword had spoken to, he would almost certainly conclude that Sword intended to slip into the Winter Palace. Everyone thought it was impossible to survive an Upland winter.

Sword thought it well might *be* impossible to survive an Upland winter in the open, or with nothing but tents for shelter, but the Wizard Lord had thoughtfully provided an alternative by building himself a palace atop the cliffs. No one had ever survived an Upland winter before—but no one had ever attempted it in a real, permanent structure, rather than in a tent.

It was worth a try, at any rate—and if it did prove impossible, Sword thought he could still find his way down the cliffs one winter night. Or if he died up here—well, at least he would have tried his best.

But if he intended to spend the winter in the Summer Palace, he would need supplies. He would need food and water, and fuel he could burn for heat.

He frowned. A fire in the Summer Palace might be a problem; smoke would be visible from Barokan. He would need some way to hide the smoke, or some fuel that burned without smoking.

Or he could just let the Wizard Lord see the smoke; after all, what would he be able to do about it?

Water should be easy. Even from his hometown of Mad Oak, one could see the snow blowing from the clifftops in winter; Sword had never heard of a year when the Uplands were *not* covered in snow, and snow could be melted for water.

Food and fuel, fuel and food . . .

He looked around the camp, past the chattering young hunters, thinking.

The Uplanders did not store a great deal of food; when they needed meat, they killed another few *ara* and ate the meat fresh. They did smoke meat for traveling, and simply for variety, but they did not seem to keep any stocks for the winter, since the Host People supplied their food down in Winterhome. Sword would need to find his own way of gathering and preserving food.

And fuel—the Uplanders did not need all that much for heat, since they retreated to Winterhome before the real cold came, but they did cook their food. They usually burned a mixture of dried grass and *ara* dung, but substituted wood or charcoal when they could get it. *Ara* fat fueled their lamps and made their candles, but was not so suitable for cooking or heating.

Sword had been shocked to realize that the *ara* dung the Uplanders burned usually included a generous admixture of feathers, but had to admit that trying to separate out and clean the feathers wasn't practical.

Burning dung, grass, feathers, or fat didn't sound practical for surviving a winter in the palace, but he didn't know enough about what else could be found in the Uplands. . . .

But perhaps someone did. He glanced at the young men who had watched his sword practice. Some of them were drifting away now, toward the campfires, but Whistler and Fist and a few others were still seated nearby.

"Tell me," he said, "what do you eat on the journey to Winterhome? Do you have fresh *ara*?"

"Of course not," Fist said. "The *ara* have all gone south by then—that's how we know it's time to leave. We have roots and jerky." He grimaced. "Which makes it all the better when we get down to the Lowlands and the Winterhome market!"

"Roots?"

"Beets, potatoes, carrots—the women plant gardens in the spring, and we harvest them as we go west. There are markers, saying which clan owns each plot." This came as news to Sword, and he wondered how he had managed to completely miss these garden plots on his long walk east. "They don't taste as good up here as they do down in Winterhome, though—the Uplands aren't good for such things. Ours are small and hard and bitter, nothing like the Lowland crops."

"And jerky?"

"Dried, smoked *ara*. With herbs that keep it from rotting." He looked disgusted. "Nasty stuff, nothing like the usual smoked meat. We only make it for the trip down the cliffs, in case the snow delays us. It's hard to chew, and tastes like leather, but it keeps us alive." He glanced up at the sky. "We'll probably start making this year's supply in a few weeks."

Sword nodded. "Will you teach me how?"

Fist snorted. "Oh, you won't have a choice," he said. "*Everyone* helps with the smoking!"

"Ah." That sounded promising. He might be able to lay in a supply of food, then.

Which still left fuel. Well, he had a few ideas about that. Grass and *ara* dung were not hard to find, after all, and even if he had to dig them out of the snow, he thought he could manage. Besides, the Wizard Lord's staff surely had stocks of wood and charcoal for cooking.

"You're done with the sword for today?" Fist asked.

"Yes," Sword said, expecting Fist to walk away now that he had confirmed that the show was over.

Fist did not walk away. He hesitated.

"Yes?" Sword asked.

"Could I try it?"

Sword smiled.

"If you're careful," he said. He drew the weapon and handed it over, hilt first.

Fist grinned as his hand closed on the worn leather grip. He lifted the weapon and looked it up and down.

"It's lighter than I thought!" he said. "Is that part of its magic?"

"It isn't magical," Sword said. "Just first-rate smithing. It's the finest steel available, stronger than anything else men can make, so it doesn't need to be heavy. A heavy blade would tire my hand and arm."

Fist nodded, and swung the sword tentatively—more as if it were a club than as if he knew what he was doing. Sword resisted the urge to smile; after all, it wasn't that long since he had been almost as clumsy.

"It feels strange," he said. "Are you sure it isn't magical?"

"Even if it were, the magic wouldn't work up here," Sword said.

Fist nodded, staring at the sword. He took a few slashes at

the air. Then he lifted the weapon again and felt the edge with his thumb.

He drew blood. "Sharp!" he exclaimed. He stuck his injured thumb in his mouth and looked at the weapon with new respect.

"I try to keep it ready," Sword replied.

"Let me try it!" Whistler called, stepping forward, hand outstretched.

Fist stepped back, sword raised, and Sword was suddenly afraid that someone was going to get seriously hurt. He called, "Don't move!"

Everyone froze; Fist began trembling, so much that the tip of the sword wavered. *"Is it the magic?"* he whispered loudly.

Sword decided he had had enough of the truth. "Yes," he said. "It must return to me. It doesn't like being handled by strangers." He reached out and pulled the weapon from Fist's reluctant fingers, wiped it ceremoniously, and sheathed it.

The remaining hunters watched this in intense silence. Sword bowed and said, "Excuse me," then turned and walked away, out from the firelit camp onto the dark, open plain.

He glanced back a moment later and saw that the young men had scattered—except for Whistler, who was following him, several paces back. Sword stopped and turned.

Whistler stopped, then smiled bashfully and came forward.

"Did you want something?" Sword asked.

"You said the sword isn't magical," he said.

Sword grimaced. "It's not," he said. "But it *is* dangerous. I was afraid someone would get cut badly."

"I thought that might be it."

"You were right."

For a moment the two men stood silently, facing one another; then Whistler said, "May I try it now, then?"

"If you cut yourself, you'll have to explain it to the others."

Whistler grinned. "I can do that."

"All right, then." Sword drew the weapon and passed it over.

Whistler took it, much as Fist had, but right from the start he handled it more gracefully; when he turned his wrist he shifted his forearm the other way, keeping the blade in front of him, keeping it firmly under control. He, too, tested the edge, but on his thumbnail, not on the flesh.

Then he tried to imitate a few of the motions he had seen Sword make in his practice.

"You must have a strong wrist," he said, after several of his own slashes and thrusts had fallen badly off the intended line.

"Yes," Sword said. "I've been working on it for years." He reached out for the sword. "You handle it well for a beginner, though."

"I watched you." Whistler pretended not to see the waiting hand—or perhaps, in the gathering gloom, he genuinely didn't. Sword couldn't be sure.

"So did Fist, but he still held it like a stick, not a sword."

"Well, Fist . . ." Whistler shrugged. "He can use a spear. He's strong and fast."

The implication that Fist wasn't particularly smart was obvious.

"Listen," Sword said. "Would you like to learn to use a sword?"

Whistler gave him a sideways glance, then looked down at the outstretched hand.

"Yes," he said.

"It's easier to practice with someone else," Sword said. "If you help me out, I'll teach you the basics."

"Just help you practice?"

"And perhaps with a few other little things, now and then."

Whistler looked at the sword, then turned it as he had seen Sword do, and held it out, hilt first.

"That would suit me well," he said.

On his ninth day in the camp the pieces for Sword's leather pants and vest were bought and cut, but he had not yet sewn them; he had not yet managed to obtain fabric for his shirt, as he was paying for his materials by helping several old women with their work, and they were overcharging him shamelessly.

The old women seemed to find him entertaining, and treated him almost like a pet. The nature of the work he was given was such that he spent much of his day in their company, and often found them watching him, giggling and chatting amongst themselves in the Uplander language, rather than tending to their own business.

He knew that much of their amusement came from his ineptitude at the simple tasks they had been doing for years. He needed all day to pluck and scrape a single hide properly; Gnaw Gnaw or Stepmother or almost any of the others could do the same job in less than an hour, and probably do it better.

He never did learn the names of any of the other old women beyond his original teachers; in fact, most of them refused to speak to him at all, beyond gestures and giggling. Whether they genuinely didn't speak Barokanese or simply preferred not to admit it, he could not tell. He considered trying to trick a reaction out of them by saying something shocking or funny or insulting, but thought better of it; his situation was not secure enough to risk being rude in such a fashion.

He had met several of the men in camp, too, though he was not permitted to work with them. In addition to the four whose tent he shared, he had talked with perhaps half a dozen hunters and a handful of men who had retired from that role. Where the old women treated him like a marginally trainable pet, the men seemed to consider him a dangerous curiosity, to be watched intently, but from a respectful distance. They were fascinated with his sword; there were no Uplander swordsmiths, and so far as anyone there knew, the only other swords to be found on all the vast plain were a few ceremonial weapons owned by clan elders of one sort or another, none of them in the Clan of the Golden Spear. Sword's practice sessions always drew a crowd, and a few of the men were visibly envious of Whistler, once the youth began assisting Sword and learning a little swordsmanship of his own.

Young women and children watched, as well. The children seemed to consider it an interesting entertainment and nothing more than that; for the most part they did not share their elders' fascination with Sword's weapon itself, but cared only about what he could do with it. They paid little attention to him when he was not wielding the blade.

The women didn't seem even as interested in the sword as the children were; they watched his arms and shoulders, rather than the blade. Sword was used to that. He did not know whether the legends about the Chosen Swordsman's magical skills in bed had reached the Uplanders, as they had almost everywhere in Barokan, but he recognized here the same wary but definite interest he was accustomed to seeing back home.

Most of the adult clan members were paired off, and at the end of each practice session much of the crowd would drift away in couples, men and women with their arms around one another, but there were a few young women who did not seem to have male companions, and some of them seemed to be among those most interested in Sword's performance.

He would not have had any objection to acting on that interest, but there were no obvious opportunities. His living quarters, sleeping on the floor of a shared tent, did not provide any privacy at night. By day, he was under the constant supervision of the old women. In the evenings, his practice sessions, attempts at sewing, and meals took up much of his time. Back in Barokan he might have managed something, perhaps arranging a rendezvous and slipping out at night, but here he was not sufficiently sure of the customs to attempt it.

He did meet the eyes of a lovely young woman during one practice session and smiled at her, but she did not smile back; she blushed and turned away.

After the session, Whistler mentioned, out of earshot of the others and without preamble, "We do most of our courting in the winter."

"Thank you," Sword said.

That explained why he had heard no mention of dances or other entertainments. Sword thought it unlikely that those young people who had no partners really waited all through the three seasons atop the cliffs without exploring a few possibilities, but apparently he had been a little too open and obvious.

He was mulling that over on his ninth night in camp as he tried to thread the *ara*-bone needle to start sewing his new pants together. He suspected that wearing the same stained and worn black clothing day after day did not make him any more appealing to the Uplander women; he had rinsed the Hostman garments out a couple of times, but hadn't really gotten them clean, since clan custom did not allow him to go naked anywhere except inside his own tent, and it wasn't possible to wash them properly with nothing but his hands, a borrowed basin, and a jug of water, especially not in the poor light in the tent.

Attempts to borrow clothing, so he could go wash his in the stream, had been met with first confusion, then disgust; apparently Uplanders did not share clothing under any circumstances.

Therefore, he needed to make himself a new outfit. It wasn't just a matter of making himself more comfortable, or fitting in better; a change of clothing was a necessity. His present garb would not last forever. He didn't think it would even last until winter.

Cutting the pieces hadn't been too difficult, but assembling them was a challenge. He had learned to use a needle and thread as a boy, so as to repair his own clothing when necessary, but he had never made an entire garment from scratch before, let alone with a bone needle rather than steel.

A shadow fell across his fingers, and he looked up to find Whistler crouching beside him, with Fist and Dancer standing by, blocking the lanternlight.

"We were wondering," Whistler said, "whether you might want a break from Stepmother and her friends."

Puzzled, Sword looked around, but didn't see the old women.

"Tomorrow, I mean," Whistler said.

"Oh," Sword said. "What did you have in mind?"

"Come hunting with us," Fist replied.

"You won't be allowed to actually kill anything," Dancer warned. "But we could use a hand."

"Bent Ear hurt his foot," Fist explained.

"We want you to help carry things," Whistler added with a wry smile.

"Dead birds are heavy," Dancer agreed.

"We'll give you a share of the feathers," Fist said, grinning.

Whistler cast him a disgusted look. "Feathers aren't worth much of anything here," he said. "That's why we've always considered you Lowlanders to be fools, because you'll pay so much for them. We'll give you a share of the meat and bone— say, a leg."

"Not all of one!" Dancer protested. "Just for carrying?"

"Come on, Whistler, don't make him any gifts!" Fist agreed. "We'll give him a fair share, but not an entire leg."

Sword looked up at them, then glanced down at his unfinished trousers.

He needed new garments—but learning how to hunt *ara* might well be necessary to his survival, as well, and this was clearly a social step upward, an opportunity not to be missed.

Especially since he would get a share of the catch. He had been paying for scraps to eat by working for the old women; supplying his own meat for a day or two, and having a few bones to trade, would put him in a much better position.

He looked up. "A thigh, then?" he suggested.

The three Uplanders exchanged glances. "All right," Dancer said. "The smallest thigh, if there's a difference. Meat and bone and feathers, not hide."

Sword glanced at the hides he had already purchased with his efforts. "Fair enough."

"In the morning, then," Fist said.

Sword nodded. Then, as the others turned away, he leaned over and murmured to Whistler, "Thank you."

Whistler nodded in return, but said nothing as he rose and turned to go.

That night, when Sword slipped into the tent, he noticed Bent Ear lying in bed, looking foul-tempered; a thick bandage was wrapped around his left foot. Sword considered saying something sympathetic, then thought better of it—Bent Ear looked in no mood to appreciate sympathy, even if his Barokanese were good enough to recognize it.

In the morning Sword was shaken awake; he unrolled from his carpet to find Fist standing over him. The sky outside the tent's open flap was the dirty gray of pre-dawn.

"Come on," Fist said.

Sword came, tugging his clothes into place and slinging his sword on his back—he did not dare leave it unattended in camp. The Clan of the Golden Spear had strong proscriptions against theft, but Sword saw no reason to provide needless temptation.

"You carry," Dancer told him as he emerged from the tent. The hunter was holding out a leather-wrapped bundle with three spears thrust through it, protruding from either end.

Sword accepted the bundle silently and hoisted it onto one shoulder, giving it only a quick glance.

The spearshafts were polished bone, he noticed, with good steel heads—*barbed* steel heads, razor-sharp and broad. These weren't intended for crowd control, like the spears the Wizard Lord's guards carried; these were designed to kill.

The bundle was lighter than he had expected, and he wondered what else was in it, but he didn't ask; instead he followed the other three as they set out eastward, toward the approaching dawn, at a trot.

They were well clear of the camp when Dancer turned and smiled at him. "I'll wager you're glad to be free of Stepmother for the day."

"I appreciate a little variety," Sword said.

Fist gave a snort of laughter at that. "Variety!"

" 'Freedom' might be a better word," Dancer said.

Sword just smiled in reply; he wasn't sure just how disrespectful he could be without giving offense.

The others seemed disappointed by that response, though, so he asked, "Why is she called Stepmother, anyway?"

"Because that's what she is," Fist answered.

"She's been married four times and widowed four times," Dancer explained. "Each time she married a widowed father, but she never bore any children herself. Sometimes it seems like half the clan is her stepchildren or her stepchildren's children, even though none of us are her blood kin."

"She always married men much older than she was," Fist added.

"Which she can't do anymore," Dancer said. "There aren't any!"

Fist laughed at that, while Whistler and Sword smiled.

"Some people say she just wanted to inherit her husbands' belongings," Whistler said quietly. "But I never believed it. I don't think she *wanted* any of them to die."

"No, she wanted to raise her place in the clan," Dancer said. "Each husband was closer to the Patriarch than the one before. And for that, a live husband is better than a dead one."

"She likes bossing people around," Fist said.

Sword nodded. "I had noticed that," he said.

Dancer laughed.

The conversation waned after that, but still, Sword felt as if he had now been accepted by his tent-mates in a way he hadn't before. He ambled on beside them, enjoying their company.

The sun was just above the horizon when they neared the flock of *ara*, and when they were perhaps thirty paces away Dancer held up a hand to signal a stop. All four men stopped in their tracks.

"Spears," Fist said quietly, staring at the birds.

Sword quickly slipped the bundle from his shoulder and untied the leather cords; the wrapper fell open, and the spears tumbled out, along with a tangle of rope and a few pouches. Each of the three Uplanders snatched up a spear, and Dancer grabbed the rope.

Then the three of them stopped and looked at Sword.

"Have you ever hunted *ara* before?" Fist asked.

"Have you ever *seen* anyone hunt *ara*?" Dancer asked before Sword could reply.

"No," he admitted.

"Do you know how it's done?"

"No."

The three exchanged glances.

"He's with me, then," Fist said.

The others nodded an acknowledgment.

"There are actually several ways to hunt them," Whistler said. "This is ours." He snagged a loose end of the rope Dancer held; Dancer paid out a few yards. Fist hefted his spear, checking the edge on the head with his thumb.

"Are there any prayers we need to say?" Sword asked.

The three Uplanders all turned to stare at him.

"Prayers?" Fist said.

"To the birds' *ler*," Sword explained, feeling foolish. "Asking their forgiveness and asking them to let us kill them."

"Lowlander magic," Dancer said in disgust.

"We don't talk to *ler*," Fist said.

"They couldn't hear us if we did," Whistler said. "They're *ara*. They're immune to magic."

Whistler's logic was irrefutable. "Of course," Sword said.

"Whistler and I are going to circle around the flock," Dancer explained. "We'll wait over there with the rope strung between us." He pointed. "Then you and Fist chase a few birds to us, and we pull up the rope to block them, and we spear them while they're tangled in the rope."

"Any that get away, we let go, unless they're wounded," Fist said. "*Ara* are too fast to run down. If we don't get four the first time, we do it again."

"Four?"

"Yes, four," Fist said, baffled at Sword's question.

"We each carry one back with us," Dancer explained. "That's why you're here. If you weren't, we'd only be able to take three, and it takes four to feed the whole clan a decent meal."

The Clan of the Golden Spear was composed of roughly two hundred people, by Sword's estimate. Four birds didn't seem very many to fill so many mouths—but then, Sword wasn't sure just how big a full-grown *ara* really was. He hadn't been permitted a close look when hunters brought in their catch. He glanced over at the *ara*.

They were grazing peacefully, seemingly untroubled by the presence of the hunters; there were hundreds, perhaps thousands of them in this one huge flock. In fact, Sword could not see the far side of the flock, and the ground beneath them was thick with shed feathers.

Sword had never been this close to live *ara* before, had never had such a good look at them. Each bird stood roughly the height of a man—no, more, Sword realized, with long thick legs and long tapering necks. Each sleek body was covered in gleaming black feathers; the wings, usually tucked up close to the body, were almost entirely white, but with black along the leading edge, and a tuft of pink at the tip. The long, graceful tails had a black triangle at the base, and the rest was bright white, with a few pure-white three-foot plumes reaching almost to the ground.

A white ring circled each slanting neck, and each face was patterned in black and white, with white rings around the eyes, and that amazing, intensely pink crest rising a foot or more from the top of the head. The beaks were perhaps half a foot long, slightly curved, and looked as if they could tear a man's arm off.

"They can't fly over the rope?" he asked.

"They can't fly," Dancer replied. "They can't even jump. I know they look as if they ought to be able to, but they can't."

"But they can run," Fist said. "I mean, *really* run."

"Much faster than a man," Dancer agreed.

"That's why we use a rope," Fist explained. "Understand?"

Sword nodded. It was easy to believe, looking at them, that they could move swiftly; those long necks and bodies were gracefully streamlined, and the strong legs looked powerful indeed.

"Then go on, you two," Fist said, waving at Dancer and

Whistler. Whistler nodded, and he and Dancer turned and trotted away to the south, looping around the immense flock.

"Wouldn't it be easier that way?" Sword said, pointing to the northeast.

Fist shook his head. "*Ara* almost always run south when startled," he said. "No one really knows why."

"Into the sun, maybe, to blind their pursuers?" Sword suggested.

"At this time of day?" Fist said, gesturing at the rising sun, which was clearly in the east, rather than the south.

"Hm." Sword acknowledged this disproof of his theory.

"They spend the winters somewhere far to the south," Fist said. "We think maybe that has something to do with it. Whistler thinks they came from the south thousands of years ago, and still instinctively run for home when they're scared."

"That makes as much sense as anything," Sword said.

Fist shrugged, and peered toward their companions, who were still trotting, the rope strung between them. "They're birds," he said. "Who knows why they do anything?"

Sword blinked.

In Barokan, the priests often knew exactly why birds and beasts did as they did—the *ler* told them. Here in the Uplands, though, there were no priests, and the natural world must be a mystery.

If the Wizard Lord had his way, and magic were stamped out in Barokan, would that mean eliminating the priests, as well? Would people lose touch with the world around them? How would they know where to find game, or when the crops were exactly right for harvest?

The Uplanders seemed to manage, but Sword did not find the idea appealing. Putting an end to wizards and Wizard Lords was one thing, but destroying *all* magic, including priestly magic, seemed like a bad idea. . . .

Or did it? The priests of Bone Garden were monsters who treated their people as mere things, subject to the whims of bloodthirsty *ler.* There were other towns, perhaps half a dozen, where *ler* sometimes required human sacrifices. And even in towns where no one was ever asked to give up his life, or even just a little blood, there might be demands. The High Priestess of Greenwater, for example, the very first priestess Sword had ever met outside his native town, was required to spend much of her time swimming naked in the lake, and was forbidden to take a husband and raise a family in the normal fashion. The *ler* of Mad Oak did not make any such unreasonable demands, but Sword had realized long ago that they were unusually benign.

The Uplanders were free of any priestly requirements at all—but that meant they had none of the benefits. They could not ask anyone about the future, could rely only on their own limited senses to see and understand their surroundings. Here on the plain, Sword's sword was just a lifeless piece of metal, while back in Barokan he could feel its cold hunger, its fierce power; he could tell from the slightest touch whether it needed sharpening or polishing, whether anything was interfering with its pure swordness.

Didn't it *bother* the Wizard Lord, leaving that awareness of the spirit world behind whenever he came up the Summer Palace?

Didn't it bother the Uplanders, to come back up here after spending the winters in the living realm of Barokan?

"That should do," Fist said, breaking into Sword's thoughts. He raised one arm and waved.

Sword turned and looked. Dancer and Whistler had rounded one corner of the flock, but were still well west of the flock's center. "Shouldn't they go all the way around?" he asked.

"No," Fist said, barely hiding his contempt at the question. "We don't want to frighten the entire flock; we just want four. If we scare them all, they may relocate, and then *we'd* have to relocate, and moving camp is far more work than *I* want to do without a better reason than that!"

"Oh," Sword said. He looked, and saw Dancer waving an acknowledgment of Fist's signal. He and Whistler stretched the rope out—Sword could not see the details from where he stood, since there were several *ara* and a few hundred feet of distance in between, but Dancer and Whistler moved with the ease of long practice and obviously knew what they were doing.

"You've never seen this, right?" Fist asked, watching the rope-men.

"That's right."

"Well, the important thing is to make a lot of noise and motion, so the birds don't know what's happening, except that it's scary. I'll be waving my spear around. . . ." He glanced at Sword.

"I could wave my sword," Sword said.

"That would be good," Fist said. "It's shiny and unfamiliar. But don't try to *hit* anything with it—at least, not until we have them tangled in the rope."

Sword nodded. "I understand," he said. He reached up and unsheathed his blade.

"Good. Then let's go!" And with that he let out a wordless bellow and began running full-tilt toward the grazing *ara,* waving his spear above his head.

Caught off guard, Sword took a second to follow, brandishing his own weapon and yelling.

[6]

At first the *ara* ignored the two screaming attackers, but then, as the men came nearer, several heads bobbed up and turned to see what was happening. Then, suddenly, several birds were running, and Sword saw that Dancer and Fist had not exaggerated—they moved with unbelievable speed. They rose up on their toes and sprinted away, their talons tearing up the turf and spraying dirt, dung, and feathers behind them.

"Keep them moving!" Fist called.

Sword did not waste breath replying, but ran harder, waving his sword and shouting.

He realized immediately that he could not possibly catch up with the fleeing *ara*; a man simply couldn't run that fast. *Nothing* Sword had ever seen before could run that fast. The best he could do was to stay close enough to keep them moving until they hit the rope. He tried to force himself to pick up his pace.

And he promptly slipped on a patch of feathers. One foot went out from under him, and he stumbled and fell. He landed rolling, as the Old Swordsman had taught him years ago, and came up quickly, but Fist and the fleeing birds were already far ahead of him.

He started toward them, breaking into a trot; he thought another flat-out run might just end in another fall, perhaps a worse one, because now that he had a moment to look, he could see that the ground ahead was largely covered in a gray carpet of feathers and guano. This was not the dried, hard stuff that the Uplanders burned in their campfires, but fresh, foul, and slippery.

Fist didn't seem bothered by it. Neither were the *ara*. Sword watched as they charged onward, untroubled by the soft, slippery mess underfoot.

And then Dancer and Whistler popped up, pulling the rope taut between them, and the first few birds slammed into it, almost yanking it from their grip. Fist raised his spear and stopped shouting, and Sword forced himself into a run again, despite the treacherous footing.

Dancer and Whistler were moving forward, pulling the rope around the *ara,* letting out enough slack for the birds to entangle themselves as they flapped their wings wildly and tried to brush this obstacle aside. There were at least half a dozen birds, rather than the four the hunters had said they wanted, and Sword found himself running headlong into a fluttering, flapping tangle of screaming birds and shouting men.

Fist's spear thrust out, and blood was added to the chaos of feathers, talons, and rope; one of the *ara* went down, and Fist moved in to finish it off. Meanwhile Dancer was living up to his name, dancing nimbly around another bird, looping rope around its legs and neck and immobilizing it while he readied his own spear. Whistler was standing still now, hanging on to his end of the rope, anchoring it for the others.

And then one of the *ara* freed itself and doubled back, turning north rather than trying to force its way south past the rope, and suddenly Sword found himself face-to-face with a charging bird as big as himself.

He swung his sword, but he had misjudged the bird's speed; he had intended to lop its head right off, but instead the blade struck an upraised wing and caught on the bone. The bird shrieked, a ghastly, ear-piercing sound like nothing Sword had ever heard before today, and for an instant he found himself looking directly into a pair of black, white-ringed eyes; then the bird pulled free and turned away.

For that instant, meeting those dark eyes, Sword felt a sudden shock; for the first time since leaving Barokan he felt the presence of *ler*. He knew he was seeing into the bird's own primitive soul—and it was like no spirit he had ever felt before. It was powerful, dark, and completely alien. Sword shuddered.

Then the contact was broken, and the bird was wheeling away, turning south again.

Sword was no hunter, but he knew better than to let wounded prey get away. He lunged after it, sword thrusting, and this time the blade slid under the injured wing, between layers of sleek black feathers, and into the creature's body.

But apparently not into the heart he had been aiming for; the bird screamed again, pulled itself off the blade, and took a few unsteady steps.

"Fist!" Sword called.

The Uplander turned and took in the situation, then sprinted toward Sword's wounded opponent. The white spear flashed in the sun as Fist brought it around and plunged it into the bird's chest.

This time the *ara* went down, and Fist gave it another blow to ensure that it stayed down.

And that, Sword saw, was the fourth dead bird—Fist had already taken two others down, while Dancer accounted for one. Whistler and Dancer had released the rope, and the remaining *ara* were scattering.

Some, Sword realized, were already looping back around to rejoin the main flock, which had ignored the entire affair.

"What happened to *you*?" Dancer asked, marching up to where Sword and Fist stood. "Where were you?"

"I slipped," Sword said. "And then that one charged at me." He pointed at the bird Fist had just finished off.

"Slipped?" Dancer looked down at the muck of feathers, blood, and excrement that covered the ground, as if noticing it for the first time. "On that?"

"On that," Sword said, mildly annoyed at the man's tone of disbelief. He, too, looked at the ground.

This certainly explained why Uplanders didn't consider *ara* feathers to be valuable; there were thousands, perhaps millions, of them strewn across the plain here. Most seemed to be the short, soft down, rather than the long outer feathers, but still, they were *ara* feathers. Sword knew that a handful of these would be enough to pay for half a month's meals in Mad Oak, or any of a hundred other towns in Barokan.

Here they weren't even worth picking up.

And there were the dead birds. That looked like hundreds of pounds of meat and bone; no wonder the others had wanted a fourth man to help carry. Sword bent over the one he had fought, approaching it cautiously—he knew it was dead, Fist clearly understood what he was doing and had plenty of experience, but still, some part of him didn't entirely accept that conclusion. The thing's eyes . . .

Those eyes were still open, but now they were empty and dead; the spirit he had seen there had vanished.

"It got a look at you, did it?" Dancer said.

Sword looked up, startled. "Yes," he said.

"That's one reason we don't talk to *ler*," Dancer said. "Would *you* want to talk to something like that?"

"But . . ." Sword looked back down. "I've never seen anything like that before. I've looked animals in the eye often enough, and they were never like that. And I've talked to other spirits, in dreams and with magic, and I never saw anything like that."

Dancer shrugged. "Whatever *ler* we have here—they're

nothing. Except *ara*. Some of the old men think they must come from another world entirely, to be what they are. Or maybe it's their breeding ground in the south that makes them what they are."

"There are stories about them," Whistler said.

"Children's tales," Dancer said dismissively. "Moral lessons dressed up with magic and adventure."

Whistler gave his companion a look that Sword would not want directed his way, but Dancer didn't seem to notice.

"What *I* care about is that they're good eating," Fist called, heaving a dead bird up onto his shoulder, staggering slightly under its weight. He looked almost ludicrous carrying it; the dead *ara* was as big as he was, and Fist was not a small man.

Whistler had hefted one of the others onto his back; now Dancer pointed at the one Sword knelt over and said, "That one's yours," and turned to get the last of the four for himself.

Sword nodded, and reached down.

It took a moment for Sword to find a decent grip, and by the time he did, blood from the wounded wing had smeared down his sleeve; it smelled surprisingly foul for so fresh a bleed. Sword heaved.

The bird was lighter than it looked, and the muck underfoot was slick; Sword almost went over backward as the bird came up, but managed to catch himself with the corpse against his chest. Blood from the other wounds was oozing onto his tunic as Sword righted himself and hoisted the carcass onto his shoulder.

Sword realized his clothes were going to be absolutely disgusting by the time they got back to camp—and he had no others. He *really* needed to finish making new ones. And a spear would be good to have—the sword didn't seem to have the reach necessary to deal with *ara* effectively, and the birds were strong enough, he thought they might eventually break the blade, which was irreplaceable in the Uplands.

Besides, he had noticed that the spears were obviously more than just tools to the Uplanders. Every young man carried one, whether hunting or not. Sword's lack of one, as much as his black clothing, marked him as a foreigner.

Rope, too, would be good to have. The hunters' rope was hemp, though, from the look of it, and Sword had seen no sign that hemp grew anywhere up here; that must have come from Barokan.

And a pack to carry his things. Really, he needed to assemble an entire set of proper supplies if he intended to survive up here after the Uplanders had descended the cliffs. He would presumably find some of what he needed in the Summer Palace, but it would be wiser not to rely on that.

"Here," Dancer said, handing him the bundle of spears and rope. The spearheads had been wiped clean and shone silver in the sun; the bone shafts gleamed white. Sword wondered who had found time to clean them and reassemble the bundle—whoever it was had apparently done so while Sword was still trying to maneuver the *ara* carcass onto his shoulder.

He accepted the bundle with one hand, almost losing the carcass in the process, but quickly managed to readjust and steady his burden.

"You've certainly made a mess," Dancer said, pointing a thumb at Sword's tunic. "It doesn't show much on the black fabric, but that's going to be stiff and stinking soon."

"I know," Sword said with a grimace. Then he turned and started trudging toward camp; Fist was already a few steps ahead, and Whistler just behind.

Sword glanced back at the flock of *ara*. A few of them were watching without any sign of interest as the mortal remains of their erstwhile companions were carried off to be butchered. The rest were going about their business, pecking at what little plant life they hadn't trampled, grooming themselves, or wandering aimlessly. There was not the slightest hint of that fierce spirit Sword had seen in the eyes of his attacker.

"*Strange* creatures," he said.

"They're *ara,*" Dancer said, glancing back.

That seemed to sum it all up, really—they were *ara,* and unlike anything else. Sword did not bother to ask any more questions.

The walk back to camp was uneventful, if tiring—Sword estimated that the bird he was carrying weighed a little over a hundred pounds. It was bigger than a man, though much of that was legs and neck, and looked as if it should weigh more, but Sword knew its bones were hollow, and that formidable beak was porous under the hard surface.

Sword followed along as his companions led the way to the clan's butchers, who would reduce the birds to meat, bone, and hide. There he lowered his burden, and asked, "Which leg is mine?"

The others turned to stare at him.

"What does it matter, which one?" Fist asked. "You'll get your share of the meat, along with everyone else."

"Because I want the bones," Sword said. "I intend to use them immediately. I think it's time I had a spear, and a few other tools. And clothes. I ruined my only tunic carrying this thing back here . . ."

He stopped without finishing the sentence as he realized that he was forgetting his place as an unwelcome guest. He was in no position to make demands.

For a minute he stood silently as the butcher and the three hunters stared at him; then Whistler said, "That's sensible."

"A spear won't clean your shirt," Dancer remarked.

"But it will mark me as a man among men, and not a trained animal." Sword had learned that much about his hosts; they did not consider Barokanese "Lowlanders" to be entirely human. So long as he wore Hostman garb, he would be seen as an outsider and inferior. Even dressed as an Uplander, if he had no spear, he would be a child or a woman, not a man.

And if he was a man among men, he could bargain with the old women as an equal, rather than simply accepting their orders and the prices they set. That made a spear an important, even an urgent, necessity.

"We'll need to ask the Patriarch," Fist said. "No one said anything about giving you a spear."

"I will, of course, abide by the Patriarch's wishes."

Fortunately, the Patriarch had no objections. "If he wishes to outfit himself properly, so much the better," was the response Whistler reported.

The meat he had brought back bought him three days'

respite from earning his keep scraping hides and hauling water; the bone provided the material for a spearshaft. He had to work in the tent he shared, with Bent Ear mumbling unpleasantly in the background much of the time, since he could not bring himself to wear the blood-soaked tunic and he was not welcome elsewhere in the camp bare-chested, but he was able to complete his pants and vest that first day.

That stained Host People tunic spent the entire day and the following night soaking in a pot of water mixed with salt and urine, a solution that Gnaw Gnaw assured him was the best way to remove *ara* blood from fabric.

The second day Bent Ear took an interest in his project and taught him, by gestures and demonstration, the proper method of cleaning and shaping *ara* bone and using bird-sinew to bind the bones into a solid shaft. It turned out to be more difficult than Sword had hoped—but then, worthwhile new skills often did.

The tunic was now soaking in clean water; Gnaw Gnaw's formula had indeed removed the worst of the bloodstains, and this second soaking was mostly to remove the stench of urine.

He was unable to complete a full-length spearshaft in a single day—for one thing, Bent Ear insisted that he not try, though Sword was unsure why, and Bent Ear subsided into surly silence when Sword asked for an explanation. Sword left it at that initially, but when Whistler eventually wandered in, Sword asked what the problem was.

Whistler took a glance and said, "You don't have a spearhead."

"I know that," Sword said.

"You need to build the top of the shaft *around* the spearhead. You can't just stick it in later and expect it to hold."

"Oh." Sword felt like a complete idiot for not realizing that himself. "Where do I get a spearhead?"

"We trade for them down in Winterhome. White Eye keeps the reserve supply."

Sword therefore spent the third day of his reprieve from Stepmother and her company working for White Eye, an old man who had lost the sight in his left eye to a growth he called a cataract. Sword wore his tunic, now much the worse for wear; the long soaking had gotten out most of the blood, but had also faded the dye, and done a good deal of damage to the layer of *ara* feathers he had painstakingly sewn into the lining to prevent the Wizard Lord's magic from locating him. The garment smelled very odd indeed, and was still damp in places, but Sword had nothing else to wear under his vest, and the vest itself was not considered sufficient for decency.

However, he also wore his new *ara*-leather pants, and was pleased to find them sturdy and comfortable.

White Eye was a widower, and Sword found himself dealing with a backlog of neglected housework—sweeping out the old man's tent, cleaning his clothes and bedding, and polishing the first traces of rust from the half-dozen steel spearheads that he had stashed away in a small wooden chest.

In exchange, Sword was permitted to keep the smallest of the spearheads—which was still, counting the tang, well over a foot long. Uplanders took their spears seriously.

Upon installing it in the bone-and-sinew staff, however, Sword found that the resulting construction was still not really adequate as a spear—the joints between bones were far too flexible. "You didn't put on any resin," Whistler explained. "It keeps the sinew from drying out, and stiffens everything up. Without resin, the sinews dry out and lose flexibility, and in a year or so, at best, they'll snap and the whole thing will shatter."

"Resin?" Sword asked. "What kind of resin?"

"It's made from the talons," Whistler replied. "Gnaw Gnaw knows how to make it."

Sword sighed.

It took another six days of hard work before his spear was finally finished, all the materials paid for with his labor. Bone, sinew, steel, resin, and varnish had all been properly assembled, the whole thing dried and polished.

With that, Sword had declared himself a man again—but he still needed to earn his keep by cleaning hides, hauling water, and so on, mostly at the behest of the old women.

Still, his treatment improved. When he was finally able to

dress himself properly in trousers, vest, and feather shirt, the old women began to defer to him, even as they gave him his orders. And young women were willing to speak to him; he managed to spend an evening or two talking to a couple of them, out of earshot but within sight of older members of the clan who made sure that it was only talk. He described a few of his adventures, and talked a little about his plans for dealing with Artil im Salthir, then tried to steer the conversation to the possibility of arranging a rendezvous for later that night.

The women just giggled and changed the subject. Sword was not sure whether he was missing some aspect of Uplander courtship, or whether they just didn't want him, but he was never able to do more than talk.

After completing his spear, he began on a second set of clothing, a pack to sling on his shoulder, and assorted other supplies he thought he might need to survive a winter in the Summer Palace, including a thick coat stuffed with *ara* down.

A month slipped away, and most of another, and although he had accompanied his tent-mates on a second hunt and even a third, he had barely equipped himself with all the necessities of everyday life in the Uplands, let alone the supplies he would need for his schemes to defeat the Wizard Lord, when the Clan of the Golden Spear began their own preparations for the journey to Winterhome.

[7]

Making jerky was a messy job.

To begin the process, a rectangular pit, perhaps six feet wide and thirty feet long, was dug and filled with grass and dung—Sword, along with several children, was given the task of gathering this fuel. A thin layer of wood and charcoal was then laid over that. While the pit was being readied, most of the clan's tents were taken down—for the next few days the clan would make do either sleeping in the open, or crowded into the remaining few—and the poles that had supported them, some wood and some *ara* bone, were assembled into a large framework, or rack, about six feet above the fire pit, with coarse fabric over that.

On the next hunt more than a dozen *ara* were speared in quick succession; normally the clan sent only a small party to kill four at a time, since that was enough to feed everyone for a day, but this time all the clan's hunters participated, even Sword, and they brought down as many as they could before the others fled, screeching, across the plateau. Then the wounded birds were finished off, and hauled back to camp to be plucked and gutted.

Then the meat was cut into thin strips, much thinner than the usual roasts, which were thrown into buckets of an herbal brew the women had prepared while the men were hunting, and left to soak while the fire was lit. Some of the offal from the dead birds was thrown into the pit to burn. The entire clan then tended the flames to produce a bed of coals that would generate just the right amount of heat and smoke. The fabric spread across the top of the rack was wetted down, to help hold the heat and smoke in—Sword was called upon to haul much of the water needed for this.

When everything was ready, strips of meat were fished out of the buckets and hung on the frame to smoke.

Sword found himself working at the nastiest jobs— cleaning blood away, spreading the offal on the coals, and so on—because even now, he was the least experienced member of the entire party, with no idea of how the more delicate processes should be done. He watched the others intently as he labored, though, trying to learn as much as he could.

He had had some warning of what to expect, so he wore his battered old Host People clothing, rather than either of his two new outfits. This turned out to be a very wise decision. He hoped that after this he would never have any need to wear the filthy, stained, smoke-saturated garments again.

When the preparation work was done and there was nothing to do but wait for the meat to smoke, he stood by the pit, taking it all in. He was sweating for the first time in days—the weather had been cooling steadily ever since he climbed the cliffs, but the effort he had put in, the heat of the fire-pit, and the smoke that stained his face, hands, and clothing, had more than made up for it, and his blackened skin was slick with perspiration.

"How long will the meat keep?" he asked Gnaw Gnaw, who happened to be nearby.

She shrugged. "Months," she said. "Though it gets tougher the longer you wait, and you have to keep ants and rats away from it."

That was exactly what he wanted, then—enough of this smoked meat to last through the winter. This lot was intended to feed the entire clan for just a few days, while they made their way westward across the plateau and down the path to Winterhome; he would only be one man, but he would need enough to last a hundred days or more—probably more.

In other words, he might need more or less a second batch the same size as this one.

"Where's Whistler?" he asked.

Gnaw Gnaw looked at him curiously, then pointed.

Sword did stop at one of the buckets to clean himself up a little, though the rag was already dirty from a dozen others having used it before him, and did little more than smear the smoke and sweat around. When he could stand the feel of his own skin, he pulled his sleeves back down and headed out in the direction Gnaw Gnaw had indicated.

He found Whistler readily enough, and began asking his questions. He was not especially pleased by the answers.

The clan was not going to leave the frame set up for him; it would be disassembled and cleaned as soon as the meat was ready, and taken down to Winterhome when the clan made their pilgrimage—the *ara*-bone shafts had taken a great deal of work to produce and were not to be discarded easily, while the few long, straight wooden poles were rare and valuable in the sparsely treed Uplands. Yes, they could buy wooden replacements in Barokan, but why should they? These were already cut to length and sized exactly right for their various purposes. And the bone poles, though not as carefully made as spearshafts, still represented a considerable investment of time and effort, and would not be left behind, either.

As for building another fire, grass and dung were easy enough to find, but this one burning had used virtually the clan's entire supply of firewood and charcoal. Again, some things that were cheap and plentiful in Barokan were precious up here.

And while Whistler could find out what went into the herbal broth, he did not already know, and he suspected that they had already used the entire year's supply of that, as well.

"I need you to find out for me what's in it," Sword told him.

"But I don't think there is any more!" Whistler insisted.

"That's why I need to know how to make my own," Sword explained.

"I mean, I don't think we have the herbs."

"So I'll have to find them, and I can't do that until I know what they are."

"But . . ." Whistler grimaced in frustration. "But I think you *can't* find them this time of year!"

"Perhaps not, but I'll worry about that later. You just find out what they are."

Whistler frowned, then glanced at Gnaw Gnaw.

"I'll try," he said. He turned away.

Sword watched him go, then looked back at the pit.

Setting up something like that single-handed, and salting away an adequate supply of meat before winter closed in, would be a huge challenge; he wasn't at all sure he could do it. A thought struck him, and he turned to find Fist.

The young man was sitting by a bucket, wiping his arms with a wet rag, as he talked to a few of his friends. He looked up as Sword approached.

"You said the *ara* go south?"

Fist glanced at his companions, but they offered no guidance in dealing with the crazy Lowlander. Uplanders were not given to rhetorical questions outside formal meetings with the Patriarch, and after almost two months in camp, surely even Sword already knew that the *ara* went south in the winter.

"Yes, of course," Fist replied.

"Where do they go?"

Fist shrugged. "No one knows. When the time comes, they just start running, the entire flock, faster than a man can follow, and they run south. I've heard that long ago a few people *tried* to follow them, but they couldn't do it—they managed to keep the birds in sight for a few days, but they just ran and ran and ran, from the first light of dawn until the last glimmer of twilight, day after day, and no one could ever maintain the pursuit for more than four or five days." He glanced at the others again, then asked Sword, "Why? Were you thinking of going with them?"

"Something like that," Sword muttered, frowning.

Fist shook his head. "Can't be done," he said. "People have tried going south in the summer, but most of them didn't come back, and the ones who did said there was nothing to eat or drink, and the heat was unbearable. There's a desert. The *ara* cross it when they make their great run, but if any man's ever crossed it, I've never heard about it."

"You said the *ara* will be leaving soon, then? They *all* go?"

"Well, the old and sick sometimes die on the way, but other than that, they all go. And they've already started moving—so far they're just making short little runs of maybe a hundred yards at a time, but you can see them preparing. They're stuffing themselves fat, getting ready." He waved at the smoking pit. "That's why we're doing this now; the *ara* could go any day now, and when they do, we head for the cliffs and the climb down to Winterhome."

"*Any* day?"

Fist cocked his head to one side. "Any day, yes." He glanced in the direction of the grazing flock, though they were too far from the camp to see as much more than a haze on the horizon. "I'd guess four or five days; we don't like to cut it too close. Wait too long, and you'll wake up one morning to find the *ara* are gone, and you'll have to starve on the way to Winterhome. That's happened to some clans, and it's bad, it's one way they wind up a bunch of scattered survivors instead of a clan." He held up the wet rag. "But we got our stocks in; we'll be fine."

"I see," said Sword. He also glanced toward the flock of birds, thinking. "Could I perhaps get some rope? Quite a lot of rope, actually."

Fist looked baffled. "Rope?"

"Yes."

"There isn't time to work for it. Don't you *have* rope?"

"Not enough. I was hoping perhaps someone could simply *give* me some."

"You'll have to talk to the Patriarch, I think."

Sword nodded. "I'll do that."

He did. He found the Patriarch chatting with two women about the trip down to Barokan, and waited until they had finished before presenting his request.

The Patriarch was puzzled. "Why do you want rope, Chosen?" he demanded.

"I have a plan to defeat the Wizard Lord, O Patriarch, but it requires capturing a few *ara* alive and preventing them from going south for the winter. I need ropes to catch and hold them."

The Patriarch stared at him thoughtfully for a moment, then said, "They can't be tamed. Many people have tried."

"I don't want to tame them," Sword replied. "I just need to keep them from going south."

"Do you think you can catch them single-handed? A Lowlander like you?"

"Perhaps not," Sword admitted. "I would be grateful for any aid your hunters could give me. Along with the rope."

The Patriarch stroked his beard silently, then shrugged. "Rope is easily had in Winterhaven," he said. "You can have whatever isn't needed to pack the camp for travel."

"Thank you, O Patriarch!" Sword said with a deep bow.

"You'll need to hurry. The flocks are already restless. We'll probably be breaking camp the day after tomorrow."

"Thank you," Sword repeated.

The Patriarch waved a hand in dismissal.

Sword emerged from the tent into the slanting light of late afternoon and frowned. The day after tomorrow? But he still had so much to do! With so little time left, he could hardly afford to waste any; he found Whistler and explained his scheme.

It was simple, really; he couldn't prepare enough jerky to see him through the winter before the *ara* and the Clan of the Golden Spear left, so that meant he had to keep a few *ara* at hand until he could slaughter and smoke them.

After butchering and cleaning, each bird yielded about forty pounds of good meat, before it was dried and smoked, and he had to survive about a hundred days; he thought that three birds ought to be plenty, but intended to capture four, if he could. Then he would drag them to the Summer Palace, and when he was ready, he would kill them and use the palace kitchens to smoke the meat. It wouldn't be true jerky, since he didn't have the herbs and knowledge to make that properly, but it ought to keep well enough in the cold.

It wouldn't be a very entertaining diet, either, living on nothing but smoked *ara* for months, but he thought it would keep him alive.

Whistler had his doubts. "I'm not sure you can get them to the Wizard Lord's palace alive," he said. "Not four of them. *Ara* are *strong,* you know, and they'll fight you."

"That's why I need your help," Sword said. "You know far more about *ara* than I ever will. How can I do this?"

"*I* don't know," Whistler said. "I've never heard of anyone doing anything like this." He hesitated, then added, "In the children's stories, *ara* always die rather than accept captivity."

"Those are just stories, aren't they?"

"Yes," Whistler admitted. "In the stories *ara* can talk, and even fly."

"Then they don't mean anything."

"I suppose not."

"Well, will you help me catch them, then? I'll get them to the palace somehow."

Whistler shrugged. "All right," he said.

"Tonight?"

Whistler snorted. "Tomorrow," he said.

Sword had to admit that was reasonable, with the day almost gone, but at the same time, he hated to wait. The clan would be moving west the day after; he was not leaving himself any margin of error.

And in the event, Whistler had to call in a dozen favors to get friends to cover his duties before he could leave the camp; everyone was preparing for departure, and that would not ordinarily include accompanying the Lowlander on his foolish hunt. Sword left all that to Whistler.

At last, though, all was arranged, and Sword retired for the night with everything in place.

He had trouble sleeping; there was too much to think about, and he did not manage to doze off until very late. Thus the sun was well above the horizon when Whistler shook him awake. "We need to go if we're going to do this!" Whistler told him.

Sword started, then sat up. "Of course," he said, pulling at his clothes. "Who else is coming?"

"No one. They're busy, and they think you're crazy to try this."

That was a disappointment, but not a surprise. It was a good thing, Sword thought, that they would be bringing the captured birds back alive; two men might not be able to carry four *ara*. His prizes would need to walk.

A few minutes later the two men were walking eastward, toward the flock of *ara*. Each of them carried two coils of good rope on one shoulder. Whistler moved with the calm smoothness of an experienced hunter, setting each foot silently in place before he put his weight on it, carefully avoiding anything that might crunch or rustle, but still keeping up a good pace.

Whistler moved faster than on their previous hunts; Sword did not ask, but guessed that this was partly due to their late start, and partly because Whistler wanted to get the whole thing over with. Despite his three hunts, the inexperienced Sword was not able to match Whistler's skillful hurry; his feet thumped, he stumbled over rocks and weeds. He did manage to keep up, though, without falling or dropping anything, and before long the two were crouching by a bush, watching the *ara*.

The birds were restless; they were all eating enthusiastically, preparing for their migration to the south, just as Fist had said, but even as they ate they seemed fidgety, moving their feet in odd little patterns and switching their tail feathers back and forth. They had not behaved this way on any of Sword's previous encounters; it was obvious that the cooling weather—or perhaps the recent killing of better than a dozen of their companions—had disturbed them.

"Now what?" Whistler asked.

Sword hefted the coils of rope he had brought. "Now we catch one," he said.

Whistler frowned, and his hand opened and closed as if adjusting his grip on the shaft of a spear. At Sword's insistence they had not brought a spear, despite Whistler's argument that they might need to defend themselves from angry *ara* at some point—Sword had not wanted to risk killing his prey. He wanted them alive.

Whistler, however, was obviously missing his familiar weapon. "How?" he asked.

Sword considered carefully before replying.

He had actually devised three possible methods, and had not decided which to use. One would be to make a lasso and try to throw it over one of the huge birds; another would be to rig a trip line and chase a few *ara* into it, just as the hunters usually did, but then tie the tangled birds up rather than spear them.

The one that seemed simplest, and most likely to succeed, though, was for each man to take one end of the rope, and then walk in opposite directions around a bird, entangling it. They might even be able to get more than one at a time that way; after all, he wanted at least four.

He dropped one rope to the ground and uncoiled a few yards of the other. "You take that end and walk this way, and I'll go that way," Sword said, pointing. "We'll wind it around."

Whistler looked at the rope, and the birds, and Sword; he did not look convinced, but he nodded. "All right," he said. He dropped his own two coils to the ground and grabbed hold of Sword's rope.

On their first try their chosen *ara* started and ran as the rope approached, and they had to wait until the birds had calmed down and resumed eating before making a second attempt. This time they kept the rope almost slack, so that it would be less noticeable, and the *ara* simply stepped over it.

"We need to move faster," Sword said. So they moved faster, and finally managed to whip the rope around a bird.

Sword had had no idea a bird could be that strong; he was caught off guard by the *ara*'s ferocious struggles, and the rope pulled out of his hands. Whistler held on, and Sword hurried to grab the dropped end and heave.

That knocked the *ara* off its feet, and Whistler jumped on it, throwing a loop of rope around its neck He quickly tied that securely in place, as the captured bird screamed with rage, then threw a loop around its legs as well, and knotted that.

Finally he straightened up, stood panting over the hobbled and furious creature, and looked at Sword. His shirt was torn, his face smeared with dirt, sweat, and *ara* spit. He licked his lips, swallowed, caught his breath, and said, "Now what?"

Sword looked back.

The rest of the flock had fled, and was already perhaps half a mile to the south; meanwhile, the captured bird was not standing calmly, accepting its situation, as Sword had imagined; instead it was on the ground, thrashing about and glaring at him. As in Sword's previous encounters with live *ara*, its dark eyes seemed to gleam with hatred and power—there was no question but that there was a soul in there, a strong one. The bird showed no sign it would ever cooperate with its captor.

But Sword had no better option. "Now we catch another one," he said, picking up another rope and uncoiling it.

Whistler stared at him for a moment, then looked down, first at the hobbled bird, then at his torn shirt. Sword knew now just how precious that shirt was.

"This time," Whistler said, "*you* jump on."

"Right," Sword agreed.

Together they set out toward the flock, leaving their first

captive lying where it was. They had gone perhaps a hundred yards when Sword glanced back and saw the *ara* pecking at the rope that bound its legs.

"Damn," he said, turning back.

It took perhaps half an hour to get the bird so securely bound that Sword was certain it would not escape. It took another half hour to approach the flock without frightening them away. And it took an hour to bring down another bird; although Sword would not have thought it possible, he realized that they had actually been lucky, very lucky, in catching their first as easily as they had.

By the time they had the second bird secured, the flock was far away, running southward—but there was something different about the way they were moving this time. This wasn't the fluttering, disorganized, zigzagging motion of a startled flock fleeing from predators; this was an all-out straight-line run, heading due south at high speed.

Sword, sweating, panting, and bleeding, got to his feet and stared after them. He waited for them to stop, and then realized what was happening.

"They're leaving, aren't they?" he asked Whistler. "I mean, *really* leaving?"

The clansman nodded. "I thought we had another couple of days, but that's a migration. No question."

"Did we do that?"

Whistler frowned. "I don't know. They would have gone soon anyway. We might have disturbed them into leaving a little early."

"We aren't going to catch them, are we?"

Whistler shook his head. "No," he said. "We aren't." He looked down at their panicky second capture. "Are two going to be enough? I know you wanted four."

Sword swallowed, and wiped sweat, dirt, and feathers from his forehead with his sleeve. "Two will *have* to be enough," he said. "Because it's what we have."

"You could come down to Winterhome with us," Whistler said. "We could hide you, I'm sure we could."

Sword shook his head. "No, I can't," he said. "And no, you

couldn't. I'll be fine with just these." He wasn't at all sure that was true, but there was no point in worrying Whistler.

Whistler looked down at the bird again. "How are we going to get these two back to camp?"

Ever since he first came up with the notion of capturing *ara* alive, Sword had envisioned leading them along at the end of a rope, like cattle on the way to market. Now that he had actually handled them, he knew that was never going to happen. Cattle were domesticated; these birds weren't, and never would be. A glance at their eyes made that obvious.

The Patriarch had warned him that they couldn't be tamed, and he had ignored that warning. He sighed.

"Drag them," he said.

[8]

The *ara* were not terribly heavy, perhaps a hundred pounds apiece, but they were astonishingly uncooperative. Slinging a dead one across his shoulders was no great feat for Sword, but moving a live one anywhere was a challenge. Even with four generous lengths of strong rope restraining them, the two continued to struggle, strewing their path with feathers as Sword and Whistler dragged them across the plain.

Sword had started to suggest carrying the *ara* at one point, despite their struggles, but then he looked at the nearer bird's mad dark eyes and thrashing wings, and decided not to say anything. Dragging would do well enough. A cart of some sort would have been better, but he had not thought to bring one.

The sun was far down the western sky by the time they finally hauled the still-squirming birds into the camp—or what was left of the camp; much of it had already been disassembled for transport. A good portion of the Clan of the Golden Spear stopped what they were doing to stare at this arrival.

"What do you want with *those*?" Fist asked.

"They're my winter food supply," Sword explained.

"Just two of them?"

"The flock ran south," Whistler told him. "These two were all we could get."

That got the attention of several listeners who had been staring at the bound birds. "They're gone?" Dancer asked.

"So soon?" Gnaw Gnaw added.

Whistler nodded.

"It doesn't matter," Fist said. "We were leaving tomorrow anyway, weren't we?"

"Yes, but—it may mean something," Gnaw Gnaw told him. "It might be a sign of a hard winter." She glanced at the sky, which was thickly streaked with high clouds. A cold, steady wind was blowing from the east, moving the clouds along.

"I thought we might have disturbed them by capturing these two," Whistler said.

"It's possible," said an old man whose name Sword had never learned. "But I think we should be ready for a long, cold winter."

"If you want them for food, why didn't you just kill them?" Fist asked, looking at the squirming *ara*.

"I won't have any way to preserve the meat until we get to . . . until I . . ." Sword hesitated.

Fist glanced at him. "You'll have to feed them, then. Once the snow falls, that won't be easy. And you'll need to give them water. And two birds won't last you *that* long."

"I know," Sword said unhappily. He was beginning to see several flaws in his scheme.

Of course, he had known there would be difficulties, but he had thought he would see ways to handle them as they arose. Instead, it seemed as if there were more of them than he had expected, and fewer solutions.

But he didn't really have any better choices at this point. If he went down the cliffs to Winterhaven, the Wizard Lord's men would almost certainly find him. If he stayed in the Uplands, he would need food and shelter. The Summer Palace was the only possible shelter, and the *ara* were the obvious food supply.

If there was another, less obvious food supply, he had not discovered it—but it might yet turn up.

He very much hoped it would.

After that exchange he was enlisted to help with the final preparations for departure. By the time the clan retired for the night, everything but the actual tents and bedding was packed up and ready to go. Even the Patriarch's lavish pavilion was stripped down to bare cloth. When Sword finally curled up on his carpet and pulled one edge over himself, he was exhausted, and fell asleep instantly despite the chill.

He was rousted out at dawn, and sent to assist in striking the tents.

He turned aside for a moment before taking up his assigned role, though, to check on his captured birds. He had already noticed that they had finally fallen silent, so he assumed they were asleep, and hoped the ropes had held and they hadn't escaped in the night.

Then he saw them.

The ropes had held; each lay in a broad circle of scattered and broken feathers they had shed in their thrashing about. They were no longer struggling; instead they were both stiff and cold. He could not tell whether they had beaten themselves to death against the hard ground, or burst their hearts in fighting their bonds, or died of cold, but they were clearly dead.

Before he could do anything more than stare, a hunter grabbed his shoulder and shoved him toward a tent-peg he was supposed to be pulling up. Sword stumbled, then caught himself and grabbed the peg. Stunned, unsure what had become of his plans, he did his share of the work mechanically, doing what he was told with neither objection nor enthusiasm.

The sun was scarcely clear of the eastern horizon when the Patriarch gave a final command, and the clan began the march toward the cliffs, more than two hundred souls of all ages trudging westward with their possessions on their backs.

Sword did not join them immediately; first he collected his

dead *ara,* and cut their throats to bleed them out, so that the meat would last longer and he would have that much less weight to carry. Two ordinary dead birds would not keep very well, but he had nothing else; all his efforts at capturing them alive had been wasted.

He had no household belongings to speak of, no family heirlooms, but he had the pack he had made slung on one shoulder, stuffed to bursting with his extra clothing and the tools and supplies he had gathered. His precious spear was strapped across it. On top of that he bore the two dead *ara,* which he slung on his back as soon as the bleeding had slowed. He hurried to join the Uplanders with the last bits of the birds' watery blood still spattering his heels—or hurried as best he could under better than two hundred pounds of burden.

Those two birds were more than enough to weigh him down; although he had started out just a pace or two behind the young hunters who took the lead, he gradually fell back until he was among the mothers and young children at the rear of the procession, stumbling and panting.

Now he had the time to think that he had not when he first awoke.

His birds were dead. While draining the blood would help, he needed to butcher them properly within the next few days if the meat was to be any good to him. He would have to do whatever he could to preserve it, even if he could not find the right herbs to make the traditional jerky. Just finding fuel to smoke the meat would be difficult, if not impossible. There would probably be a fair bit of wastage.

He was not going to have anywhere near as large a food supply as he had hoped.

And with that realization he began seeing any number of flaws in his plans that he had steadfastly ignored until now. He had never denied their reality, but he had put them all off, telling himself he would deal with them later.

Well, this was later, and he would need to deal with them. Water, for example—the Summer Palace had a cistern, he knew that from his previous stay there, but would it be adequate? Would it freeze? Had it been drained for the winter?

He had no idea where the cistern was, or how large, only that it fed taps in the palace.

The palace had been designed to be open to the breeze, for cooling in the summer; while it could be closed up, it wasn't intended to keep out cold.

Would it be warm enough?

He would almost certainly need fires; would the smoke be visible down in Barokan?

Would he be able to find the fuel he needed?

And in the spring there would undoubtedly be servants who would come to prepare the palace for the Wizard Lord; if he was still in the palace when they arrived, he would need to hide somewhere from them, and then a way to get past them to get at Artil im Salthir somehow, when the Wizard Lord finally came up the cliff.

At least there was no magic to worry about. Barokanese magic did not work here—the lowland *ler* had no power here, could not even come up here, and if the Uplands had any *ler* of their own, as they surely must, no one seemed to know how to get their attention. The Uplanders actively avoided acknowledging any *ler.*

Even if there *were* any magic up here, Sword could defend against it easily enough—in addition to the protections already sewn into his garments, he had two dead *ara* to provide him with still more feathers. *Ara* feathers presumably shielded against magic of *all* kinds, not just Barokanese.

Of course, this all meant that he would have no magic of his own to aid him, but he didn't really see how useful swordsmanship would be in surviving a winter here in any case, and his skills were good enough that he thought they would serve his purposes even without any magic.

And he really had little choice. He could not see any hope of safety if he descended back to Barokan, and he did not see any way to survive on the plateau other than by taking shelter in the Summer Palace. He would just have to deal with everything as best he could.

That brought him back to the question of food. Perhaps it

was not too late to turn back, to track down another flock of *ara* that had not yet set out to the south. . . .

But how could he catch them, alone and unaided? How long would it take? He was no expert. Perhaps he should consult with some of the hunters, who *were* experts.

He looked around, and realized that he was surrounded by small children who were staring up at him as they walked, and by the mothers herding those children. Even the children carried tiny packs, he saw, probably holding nothing more than a few favorite toys and perhaps a treat of some kind.

Ahead of him were some of the oldest men and women in the clan; the younger and healthier adults were farther ahead, and the hunters—the young men who would be clearing the campsite and setting up tents so that the children would find their homes waiting for them—were at the front, easily a mile away. They weren't hurrying, really; if he tried, he ought to be able to close the gap, even carrying his dead *ara*.

But was there any point in doing so? Was there anything he could do about it today? He would ask that night around the campfires; that would be soon enough.

He shifted the birds on his shoulders, and trudged on.

Although he never caught up to the young men at the front of the march, at one point Sword and the children found themselves surrounded by other women, who were digging at the hard ground with knives and trowels. They had reached one of the plantings—Sword thought they were too crude to be called gardens, really—where the tribe had planted a few root crops that spring; now they were harvesting the results.

Some of the children ran to help out, scurrying about collecting beets and carrots. Sword slowed, but did not stop to help—he knew nothing about the clan's rules and methods, and no one had requested his assistance, so he simply marched on. He had gone perhaps a mile farther when the throng of cheerful, chattering women caught up with him, bags of vegetables slung on their shoulders alongside their packs, and before much longer he was once again among the mothers and children at the very rear.

The clan stopped for the night while the sun was still well above the western horizon; the oldest and youngest members could not be expected to continue. Some of the youngest children had been whimpering and complaining for some time, though their older siblings mocked them for it.

The young adults had arrived well before the stragglers and had pitched tents and readied fire-pits; by the time the last children stumbled into or were carried into the chosen site, it had become a camp, and water was heating to make stew of the freshly harvested vegetables.

"Are we cooking those?" someone asked, jerking a thumb toward Sword's two *ara.*

"No," Whistler said, looking up from a cookfire. "Those are his, for his magic. We eat jerky."

Several people exchanged glances at that, but no one saw fit to argue.

And a thought struck Sword.

"Actually," he said, "I would trade this meat weight-for-weight for jerky." That would save him the effort of trying to make his own—and would also remove the risk that he wouldn't be able to do it at all.

That drew an enthusiastic response. A butcher was found, and a tradesman's balance was unpacked. By the time he retired that night Sword's two birds were gone, and he had better than fifty pounds of jerky packed away, as well as several pounds of feathers.

Whistler stopped him at the flap of the tent they shared. "That wasn't what you had intended," he said.

"No, it wasn't," Sword admitted. "It was better."

"I'm sure it was, for you. I'm not sure it was wise on the part of those who gave you their jerky, though."

"Perhaps not," Sword admitted. "But the Patriarch didn't forbid it, and you should still have enough to get safely to the guesthouse in Winterhome."

"If we aren't delayed, yes. Trading weight for weight, though—that was not right. Dried meat weighs much less than the equivalent in fresh meat."

"I know," Sword admitted. "Those two birds would probably not have gotten me through the winter, but an equal weight of jerky should."

"Some of those people may be very hungry before we can buy our supplies from the markets in Winterhome."

"I hope not," Sword said sincerely. "And they ate well to-night."

"Hm."

Whistler made no further protest, and there was no more conversation that night.

When Sword awoke the next morning the tent was bitterly cold, the fire long dead, and he thought at first that he had overslept, as the light seeping in through the cracks seemed brighter than it ought to be. He wrapped his carpet around himself as he got to his feet and peered out the flap.

He had not overslept; the sun was barely peeping over the eastern horizon beneath the edge of a broad expanse of cloud. The light *was* bright, though, because the world outside the tent was covered in gleaming, freshly fallen snow that reflected every glimmer of the dawn's light and washed everything in a cold white glare. It was not deep; perhaps an inch had accumulated as he slept.

Sword stood in the tent's mouth for a moment, staring out at the snow. He turned when he heard movement behind him, and found Fist standing there.

"Good thing we started when we did," Fist remarked as he looked over Sword's shoulder at the snow.

Whistler was awake, as well; he said, "First snow came early this year. I hope that's not a sign of what's to come."

"Better get started," Fist said. "The little ones won't be moving very fast in this."

Half an hour later the entire clan had been roused and the tents folded; loads were being packed, and a few of the women had already set out to the west.

The bag of jerky was far less cumbersome than the two birds, and this time Sword was able to keep up with the young men in the lead. He took advantage of this to ask a few questions that had not seemed entirely appropriate after last night's trading. They were far less urgent now that he had a supply of jerky, but he preferred as great a margin of safety as he could manage.

"If I wanted to bring down another *ara* or two . . . ," he began, talking quietly to Whistler.

The hunter turned and stared at him. "What?"

"If I wanted to catch another *ara,* how would I best go about it?"

Whistler stared at him for a moment, then shrugged. "Wait until spring," he said.

"But . . . no, I meant now."

"You can't," Whistler told him. "Not unless you manage to get in front of one of the northern flocks and pick one off as it goes past. They're all running south now."

Sword blinked, then looked up at the low-hanging clouds. "The snow?"

"Yes, the snow. Any flock that hadn't already started south would have begun running this morning, as soon as they saw the snow. *Ara* don't stay where there's snow; what would they eat? And what would they drink when the streams are frozen?"

"I didn't know," Sword said.

Whistler did not bother to respond.

They walked on in silence for a moment, then Whistler said, "I don't think you should have done that, last night."

Sword did not pretend ignorance; he knew what the hunter was referring to. "I meant no harm," he said. "I didn't force anyone to trade."

"Most of them have no sense," Whistler replied.

"It's just a few days to Winterhome."

"If we're lucky." He gestured at the endless white landscape that surrounded them. "If that had been a blizzard, rather than a dusting, you might have deaths on your soul."

Sword had to stop and think about what the word "blizzard" might mean up here. It snowed in Barokan, of course, at least in the Vales, but the Wizard Lord's magic kept the weather from getting out of control. Sword had *heard* of blizzards, but he had never seen a real one—people had sometimes called snowstorms "blizzards" back in Mad Oak, but everyone knew the real thing, as found in the Uplands, was far worse. That was one reason the Uplanders didn't stay on the plateau through the winter.

"But isn't it too early for a blizzard?" he asked.

Whistler shook his head. "This isn't the Lowlands," he said. "It's rare, but storms can come early up here. My grandfather told me stories about one bad one that the clan got caught in when my father was a baby. Half a dozen of us died, frozen to death or lost in the snow."

Sword shuddered. "Oh," he said.

In some ways, spending the winter in the Summer Palace had seemed almost like a game until now; this reminded him that it was a deadly serious one. Winter could kill. Even in Mad Oak there were stories of old people or young children dying of the cold, though not in Sword's lifetime, and there was Blackhand, the old woodcutter, who had lost two fingers to frostbite when Sword was about eight—though that had been the result of a long series of stupidities. Sword had been too young to hear all the details, but he knew that Blackhand's wife had thrown him out after an argument, and Blackhand had then gotten thoroughly drunk and wandered off into the woods with some mad notion of making a carving of some sort as an apology, only to get lost overnight after not properly appeasing the *ler* of the groves.

Sword had seen the ugly stumps of those lost fingers. He had never seen a real blizzard, never seen an Upland winter, but he had seen Blackhand's ruined hand, and that was all he needed to know that cold weather was not something to be taken lightly.

"I'm sorry," he said—but he did not offer to return any of the jerky. He might need it to get through the winter. Just staying alive in cold weather took more food than an active man needed in the summer.

Silently, they marched on through the snow.

9

The stop to dig vegetables took longer in the snow; so did clearing a campsite and raising the tents. By the time the campfires were lit, several of the children were either whining with hunger or sound asleep.

Sword's tent-mates did not seem inclined to speak to him that evening.

On the third day of the journey they began to see other clans in the distance, moving westward toward the cliffs. Sword was walking a little apart from the other young men, so it took him a while to realize that they were discussing which banners they could see. He also failed to notice immediately when the Clan of the Golden Spear unfurled their own banner on the breeze.

He turned his steps closer to the others, and waited for a pause in the conversation before asking, "Why are we flying the banner now, when we didn't yesterday?"

Whistler looked at him, then turned away without replying. Fist, though, looked at him pityingly and said, "Why would we bother with it yesterday, when no one else could see it? *We* all know who we are; it's the *other* clans who need to see the banner."

Sword started to say something about showing the banner so *ler* would know them, then caught himself. No one up here paid any attention to the *ler*.

It wasn't that the land *had* no *ler*; Sword had been in places that had been stripped of their spirit, dead places, and knew the lifeless, empty feel of them. When he had first ascended the cliffs he had thought the Uplands were dead, but that had been by contrast with the vitality of Barokan; now he had stayed long enough to accustom himself to the feel of the high plains, he could recognize the difference. He knew that even though he could not sense any of the *ler* directly, this was a living land, one with its own soul, its own *ler*. He couldn't feel that life, but all the same, now that he had spent time here, it no longer felt *dead;* it was as if the *ler* slept.

But the Uplanders didn't acknowledge that in any way. They made no demands of the *ler,* and the *ler* made no demands of them. There was no contact at all.

That was a mystery to Sword. In Barokan the *ler* did not sleep, and could not be ignored. They made their presence felt everywhere. In the towns, the locals would have made their accommodations with the spirits of the place, and in the wilderness between the towns, the wild *ler* were a constant threat, picking at travelers at every opportunity.

On the roads the Wizard Lord had ordered built, the old *ler* had been uprooted and scrambled, and the new *ler* that formed spontaneously had been tamed, but even there they weren't completely ignored. If the roads were not used, if the people using them did not assert that they belonged there, the *ler* would turn hostile; thanking *ler* for a safe passage, asking for their cooperation, was a habit so firmly established that it was automatic.

Up here on the plateau, though, there was no communication of any sort between human and *ler.* No one felt the presence of any spirits. Even the *ara* hunters did not bother to apologize to their prey; they treated the great birds as if they were soulless, less alive than the sword on Sword's hip, even though a glance into any of those avian eyes made it very clear that the *ara* had strong, fierce, inhuman souls.

How such an unnatural state of affairs had ever come about Sword did not know, and none of the Uplanders he had asked during his sojourn had admitted knowing, either, though there were theories. Perhaps the *ara* themselves were responsible; their feathers blocked magic, blocked *ler,* so completely that perhaps the hunters *couldn't* appease their spirits, and had generalized from that. Certainly, the Uplanders considered dealing with *ler* to be something Lowlanders did, not something that concerned *them.* Any Uplander who found his tools uncooperative, or his sleep troubled by dreams, would simply wear a few more *ara* feathers until the problem went away.

There were old stories, as well, folktales about how people

had dealt with *ler* long ago, only to be betrayed or cheated. The stories always ended with the chastened humans swearing to rely only on themselves in the future, and not listen to *ler.*

Sword had always taken it for granted that the Uplanders knew their own land better than he did, but there were times such disrespect troubled him.

It did explain why Uplanders stayed in Winterhome in the winter, and were never seen elsewhere in Barokan; they probably couldn't deal with the omnipresence of *ler.* In Winterhome the Host People had made them welcome, and had made the *ler* accept them, but elsewhere they would have found it very unwise to ignore the spirits.

The clan made camp that night within sight of three other Uplander camps, and the Patriarch sent envoys to each of them to ensure there would be no unpleasantness as they neared the defile leading down off the plateau, no arguments about who would go first. Fist was sent to the Clan of the Five Stars, amid some laughter and nudging.

"He has a girl there," Whistler explained to Sword. "Or at any rate, he'd *like* her to be his girl."

"So the Patriarch chose him for that? So he could see his beloved?"

"Probably," Whistler acknowledged grudgingly. "I don't care to say why the Patriarch does anything; I won't pretend to his wisdom. And Fist isn't the only one who likes a Five Stars girl."

Sword nodded. "You said you do your courting in the winter?"

"Of course," Whistler replied, startled. "Our own women . . ." He bit off his sentence unfinished, as if realizing he had been about to say something disloyal.

"You want a greater choice," Sword said.

Whistler didn't reply; he turned away.

By the end of the fourth day they were traveling in close company with other groups, to the point that Sword could not tell which of half a dozen clans an unfamiliar face belonged to. There was some confusion as guards kept the marchers from trampling various gardens, but in general the migration was peaceful.

There was one unpleasant incident when a slave, now the property of the Three Hawks clan, was recognized by his family in the Crescent Moon clan as a young fool who had run away the previous spring. Since he had run away on his own, and not been exiled, his mother argued that the Hawks had had no right to enslave him; the Hawk patriarch retorted that if they believed every exile who claimed to be an innocent, not only would there be no slaves to deal with the offal, but the Uplands would be overrun with unpunished thieves and bullies.

In the end an agreement was grudgingly reached, so that there would be no violence where so many clans were gathered; the Moons bought their youth back for a hundredweight of bones and feathers, and a promise to let the Hawks' unbetrothed young men, of whom they had a surplus, visit the Moon women's quarters in the guesthouse in Winterhome—properly chaperoned, of course.

Sword watched this with interest, and noticed that even while the negotiations were going on, everyone involved kept moving toward the cliffs. Clouds were gathering in the east, the temperature, chilly to begin with, was dropping, and more snow seemed likely; no one wanted to wait for it to arrive. That earlier inch or so had largely vanished in the sun and the dry air, and what had not evaporated had been trampled into mud by the passing nomads, but everyone knew that once the snows began in earnest the plateau was not a safe place to be.

That night the camps were so close together that they merged into one sprawling city of tents. It occurred to Sword that this was probably the only time all year that the clans lived in such proximity; the guesthouses in Winterhome were more widely spaced. He was not surprised, therefore, to see many animated conversations as members of the various clans swapped news and gossip, or boasted to one another of their accomplishments over the course of the year. Some children seemed to be playing happily with the children of other clans, while others hung back, shy or even frightened by these strangers. Older children, and young men and women, were clearly taking an interest in members of the opposite sex, regardless of clan.

There were flurries that night, but not enough snow to matter, and in the morning the Clan of the Golden Spear marched on—as did the other clans around it.

By the eighth day the clans no longer pretended to remain distinct; they were all one great migration that would sort itself back out at the foot of the cliff.

Sword found Fist and asked him, "Is it always like this? Every year?"

"No," Fist replied. "We don't usually bunch up *this* much—the snow rushed some clans. But there's always a gathering."

On the ninth day some of the Uplanders claimed they could see the smoke rising up from Winterhome; Sword's eyes were not sharp enough, or not trained enough, to make out anything of the sort.

And finally, on the eleventh day, they came within sight of the Summer Palace, and Sword said his farewells.

No one paid much attention; they were more concerned with the long climb they would be making down the cliffs. Despite his new clothing and his spear, Sword had never really been a part of the Clan of the Golden Spear, and his curiosity value had worn off. The closest thing he had to a friend among the Uplanders was Whistler, and that young man had made plain that he didn't approve of Sword's bartering for jerky during their westward migration.

No one called after Sword or waved as he turned aside to march toward the palace, instead of into the defile at the trailhead.

The plain seemed colder away from the crowds of Uplanders, whether because there was no shared body heat, or because there were no neighbors blocking the easterly wind, or because it was actually colder, Sword could not say. He could not be entirely certain he wasn't simply imagining it. He shivered and pulled his vest and coat more tightly around him, glad that he was wearing the winter coat he had made.

When he reached the palace gate he found it locked, the

lanterns gone from the hooks—that was no surprise. He could not hear the burble of the fountains just inside; they had presumably been shut down.

There was no sign of any guards. Sword had wondered whether Artil might have left a few of his soldiers up here to ensure that the Uplanders did not loot the place in his absence, but apparently he had not bothered, or if he had, the guards must already have left.

Or, perhaps, they were inside the walls somewhere, out of the cold.

Sword paused at the gate and looked back at the line of Uplanders, stretching eastward to the horizon. He wondered how Winterhome could accommodate them all. He had seen the immense guesthouses that lined the roads around the town, but he had never really given much thought to just how many people squeezed into those structures. Thousands, obviously—perhaps tens of thousands. How did the Host People *feed* them all?

Well, the system had operated for centuries, so obviously the Host People had ways. Presumably there were storehouses somewhere to supply them.

Some of the Uplanders were staring back at him, he noticed, pointing out the man at the palace to their comrades.

That wouldn't do. He hadn't tried to keep his plans secret from the Clan of the Golden Spear, since that hadn't seemed practical, but they all knew that their patriarch favored Sword's scheme and would not want it spoiled. Other clans, though, knew nothing of it. Sword did not want someone from one of those other clans casually mentioning to the Wizard Lord that some strange man had been seen breaking into the Summer Palace.

Sword turned east, and marched back out onto the open plain. He was not going anywhere in particular; he just did not want to be seen entering the palace. He could not rejoin the Clan of the Golden Spear, which had already gone down the canyon and was on its way down to Winterhome, and did not see any reasonable way to join another clan at this point. Instead he wandered aimlessly through the remainder of the afternoon, and at dusk he settled down at a random spot, within sight of the westernmost of the great birdskin cisterns.

A few hundred yards away to the south the vast encampment of the migrating Uplanders sprawled across the landscape, tents black against the darkening sky, a myriad campfires gleaming orange in the gathering gloom. Sword wondered whether anyone was cooking over those fires, or whether they were all dining on jerky alone, and making fires for light and warmth only. Had the vegetables run out yet?

He considered building a fire of his own, but then decided it would draw too much attention. Instead he simply sat and waited, dozing lightly.

He awoke suddenly to find himself shivering so hard that he had jarred himself out of his doze. With neither fire nor tent to mitigate it, the night air was *cold*. He got to his feet, stamping and flapping his arms to stir his blood, and looked around.

It was very dark; the sun was long gone, an overcast hid the moon and stars, and almost all the fires had been doused.

It was perfect.

Still shivering slightly, he got his bearings, largely from the fading embers of the Uplander fires that had not yet been completely extinguished, and headed back toward the Summer Palace.

This time he did not stop at the gate, but made his way along the eastern side and clambered over the outer wall, moving as quietly as he could—which wasn't very, unfortunately, since he could not see well enough to avoid stumbling over rocks and other obstacles, and ascending the wall was not something he could do silently. He hoped that anyone hearing the racket would attribute it to normal nocturnal activities. The distance was such that he doubted anyone would be able to recognize the sound's exact nature.

Topping the wall was not particularly difficult, despite the darkness; it had not been intended as a serious barrier to invasion, but only to keep *ara* and straying Uplander children out of the gardens, and to provide a little privacy. There were no spikes or pickets to discourage climbers; he merely had to jump onto a convenient rock and then up, throw his arms across the top of the wall, catch himself there, and swing a leg up. He managed as much by feel as by sight, but he managed it. If he hadn't had his pack, sword, and spear, he could have done it in seconds, and almost silently; as it was it took just a moment or two, and required only a moderate amount of scraping and thumping.

Once he got inside the walls the night was so utterly black that he decided trying to find his way into the palace itself would be a mistake; instead he took shelter in a corner of the garden wall, wrapped himself in his winter coat, and waited for morning, dozing occasionally and hoping he wouldn't freeze to death.

He awoke, shivering, in the gray light of early morning, to find snow falling; the first thing he saw when he opened his eyes was a speckling of white on the backs of his hands, specks that quickly melted away. He shook the flakes from his hands and got stiffly to his feet, struggling to remember where he was and why he was so cold. He looked around.

The scene was nothing like the green and welcoming view he remembered. The palace gardens were brown turning to white, the dead stalks and bare earth gradually vanishing beneath the thickening snow. The skeletal trellises, with their meager burden of lifeless vines, seemed to slump beneath the weight of the leaden sky and white flakes. He shivered anew, and stumbled past the dry, snow-speckled fountains and dead planters to the gate, where he put his eye to a crack and peered cautiously out at the distant Uplanders.

They were still coming, moving across the plain and making their way carefully down the steep trail, but the throng had lessened somewhat. He could see few details through the swirling snow, and the wind that blew through or over the locked gate chilled him, so he turned away and headed for the palace itself, seeking shelter.

The doors were locked, of course—he tried every one on the south side, and the first few around the corner on the west, before concluding he would not find one left open. He didn't let that trouble him—he had known he would probably need to break in. Although he thought he might regret it later, he was too cold to bother with latches or hinges in prying open a locked door; instead he used his sheathed sword as a club to smash in a many-paned window overlooking the terrace, breaking out mullions as well as glass, then clambered in through the hole.

Getting in out of the wind and snow helped; he was still cold, but was able to stop shivering, to stop his teeth from chattering, and to think a little more clearly.

He recognized where he was. He had spent a few days in this palace the first year the Wizard Lord had occupied it, and at that time he had learned his way around. This was a small dining salon, designed for those occasions when the Wizard Lord wanted to be able to wander out onto the terrace overlooking Barokan at a moment's notice. A small table stood in the center, with four chairs set atop it for the winter; against the far wall stood a finely carved sideboard between two doors, and two tall matching cupboards in either corner.

Sword doubted he would be using this room much during his stay here; he hurried across and tried the left-hand door.

That led into a narrow, unadorned, windowless corridor, obviously meant for the palace staff rather than for the Wizard Lord or his guests; since he had been one of those guests, Sword had never seen this passage before. He could not tell how far it ran; the only light came from the salon windows behind him. Those windows faced west, and it was early morning, with clouds and snow obscuring the sky and dimming the sun; the dull gray glow reached barely ten feet past the door.

He had tinder in his pack, but Sword was not inclined to waste it; instead he stepped back into the salon and tried the right-hand door. That opened into a sitting room where several tall windows to the south let in what daylight could penetrate the growing storm; Sword stepped in and closed the door behind him, shutting out the mounting howl of the wind.

It was still cold, but just the common chill of an unheated room in winter, not the biting cold he had faced outside; Sword set his spear against the wall, then unslung his pack and dropped it beside the spear, before sinking into one of the richly upholstered chairs. He looked around the room.

The floor was reddish brown tile; a carpet had been rolled up and set against one wall, to stay clean for next summer, while chairs, tables, and settees had been pushed up against the opposite wall, out of the way, leaving the room bare and unwelcoming.

There was no hearth, no stove, no fireplace, and the half-dozen windows that made up most of the south wall were designed to be stood open to catch the breeze. The awnings that would keep the sun out were rolled up and stowed away for the season, leaving just a thin layer of glass and frame to keep out winter's chill.

That was better than nothing, certainly, and probably better than the tents the Uplanders used, but it wasn't much.

Sword thought back over his previous stay, trying to remember whether he had ever seen a hearth or stove of any kind anywhere in the building. There had been candles, of course, and oil lamps, but he could not recall any other flames. This was, after all, the *Summer* Palace—any time heat was called for, the Wizard Lord would be down in Barokan, not up here at all.

But there were other uses for fire besides light and heat; food had to be cooked somewhere. The kitchens would surely have stoves and ovens and hearths.

That was where he would set up housekeeping for the winter—in the palace kitchens. He merely needed to *find* them. As a guest he had had no business there, so he had never set foot in them, but obviously they existed. That passage from the dining salon undoubtedly led to the kitchens eventually, but he preferred to use what little daylight he had, rather than wasting tinder—especially since he saw no lamps or candles, and he had not brought any of his own.

He would need to do some exploring, he decided.

He glanced at his pack and spear, debating whether or not to bring them along; they must weigh at least sixty pounds, he thought, probably more, with all that jerky in addition to his clothing and other gear, and he had been carrying them almost constantly for the past eleven days. He was alone in the palace; precious as they were, what harm would it do to leave them here, and come back once he had found what he sought?

None at all, he told himself. It wasn't as if anyone else would stumble across his belongings.

But then he paused. *He* was here, after all; how could he be sure no one else was? He knew that the Wizard Lord did not leave guards here over the winter, since it was universally accepted that no one could survive a winter in the Uplands, but what if he had posted a guard or two to stay here just until the Uplanders were gone? Sword had never heard of such a precaution, but it wasn't an absurd speculation. This was not the first time he had considered the possibility, and he had no reason to rule it out.

And for that matter, what if some of the Uplanders out there on the plateau decided to break in and take shelter here from the storm before attempting the long climb down to Winterhome? *He* certainly wouldn't want to try to get down the cliff in this storm.

But if an Uplander, or even an entire clan, did break in here, they would surely find better things to steal than his pack, and they *certainly* wouldn't casually steal another man's spear. At least in the Clan of the Golden Spear, spears were almost sacred—and Uplanders in general seemed to be very honest people. Even though they had no *ler* ordering their lives other than their own souls and the souls of those around them, they maintained their codes of behavior well. He had seen that in his time with the Clan of the Golden Spear. Also, this wasn't the first winter that the palace had stood here, yet he had never heard of any Uplander intruding, or disturbing it in any way. That was the sort of thing that would have been all over gossip-loving Winterhome, had it ever occurred.

Of course, most years the snows didn't start this early, and the migration down to Winterhome didn't usually take place in a snowstorm. Sword didn't think this had happened in any previous year since the palace was built.

He wondered whether the Wizard Lord had any control over the weather up here; could he have prevented this storm if he wanted to? Or could he have *created* it? His magic did not extend beyond the borders of Barokan, but wind and weather paid little heed to borders; if Artil had assembled this storm just west of the cliffs and then pushed it eastward, wouldn't it have arrived here just like this? Previous storms had seemed to come from the east, Sword knew, but this one had arrived in the pre-dawn darkness and could have come from anywhere.

But sending it would have been insane, even by Artil's standards. Surely, he did not want to make life more difficult for the Uplanders! In fact, had *he* been in the Wizard Lord's position, and seen this storm hindering the Uplander migration, Sword would have sent the strongest winds he could to blow it away and keep the trail clear.

But Artil was trying to break magic's hold on Barokan, trying to teach the Barokanese to live without wizardry of any kind. He had presumably let this storm happen naturally.

If any clan *did* break into the palace to take shelter, it was Artil's own fault, for building it where he had and allowing these early snows—but Sword didn't think it would happen. The Uplanders would follow their traditions and obey their laws. They had probably had to travel in the snow before, and probably had rules and customs to deal with it, as they did for every other part of their lives.

The possibility of guards seemed significantly more likely, really, but Sword had seen no sign of any, and surely, if the place were guarded, wouldn't someone have seen him approach the gate yesterday? Wouldn't someone have seen him huddled in the garden this morning?

If Artil *had* posted guards, they had probably left for Winterhome the minute the first snow fell. No Barokanese would want to risk being snowbound up here.

Well, no Barokanese except himself.

His pack and spear would be safe, he was sure. He left them where they were as he rose and started his search for access to the palace kitchens.

10

The kitchens were underground.

It took Sword a surprisingly long time to discover this; several times he followed what looked as if it should be a route to the kitchens, only to turn back whenever he encountered stairs leading down, on the incorrect assumption that he had found an entrance to the cellars, rather than the kitchens.

That was one reason; another was that he still had no light, and all the stairs led down into darkness.

At last, though, it occurred to him that he had circled through almost the entire ground floor without finding any kitchens, and that the cellars would surely connect to the kitchens somewhere. He had found candles in a drawer in the main dining hall; he retrieved flint, steel, and tinder from his pack, and made himself a light, then descended the nearest stairs leading down.

As he neared the bottom of the steps the light from his candle seemed to vanish into emptiness ahead. He marched on, and instead of the racks and shelves of wine and cheese and beer he had expected he found a cavernous space, where four sturdy wooden tables were lined up beneath innumerable iron hooks dangling from great stone arches, and where the walls were lined with ovens, stoves, cabinets, and open fireplaces equipped with spits and more hooks. Copper and iron pans hung on all sides, the copper gleaming warmly in the candle-light while the black iron seemed to soak up the light like a sponge. Some of the white-painted wooden cabinets were closed off with wooden doors, while others were open; many were empty, but a few were stacked full of plates, cups, and glassware. A huge gray stone sink stood along one wall, with a row of pipes descending from the ceiling above it and ending in taps. Stairs opened off the kitchens at each corner, leading down another half-level to the cellars he had expected.

There were no windows, of course, but chandeliers hung from several of the iron hooks, and countless sconces adorned the walls. The howl of the wind, which had varied in volume but always been audible, could not be heard here; the silence was complete whenever Sword stopped and allowed the echoes of his footsteps to fade away.

Sword held his lone candle high and looked about.

The floor was solid stone, without seam or polish, and not entirely even; he supposed that the builders had cut it out of the raw stone of the cliff itself. A thin layer of black greasy dirt appeared to be ground in, while the vaulted ceiling above had been blackened by smoke; the walls between the ovens and behind the cabinets were a mix of white plaster, red brick, and the original gray of the native stone. And while the place was not warm, it was only slightly cool, which was so different from the bitter cold upstairs that it *seemed* warm. He would not need to worry about freezing to death in here.

The lack of windows was a potential problem, but still, Sword thought, this would serve. This would be his home for the next hundred days or so. The lack of windows meant he would need to use lamps or candles, but it also meant his lights would be invisible to anyone outside. The ovens and hearths would allow him to safely produce all the heat he needed, and cook anything he found to cook, without worrying about setting anything afire, or about the glow of his fire being seen.

Of course, he would need fuel, but surely there was some stashed away somewhere. And there would still be smoke—those chimneys came out somewhere, obviously—but he hoped it wouldn't be too visible.

He would need bedding, too. Where had the kitchen staff slept?

After further exploration, he concluded that the kitchen staff had slept upstairs; there was no sign of bedding anywhere in the extensive cellars, nor of anywhere bedding might previously have been. There were empty larders and bare pantries and dry sculleries, locked wine racks, well-drained beer kegs, and to his delight, a small wheel of hard cheese tucked away on a shelf and apparently forgotten, but he discovered no evidence that anyone had ever slept anywhere below ground level.

Nor did he find a decent supply of fuel. Candles, yes, hundreds of them, and dozens of empty lamps, but no oil, no charcoal, no firewood. He found what appeared to be a bin for firewood, but only a few sticks and some chips of bark lay at the bottom. Another bin was clearly intended for charcoal, but held little more than a film of black dust. A paper was tacked to the wall between these two bins; he held the candle high and studied it.

It was an inventory, listing quantities of wood and charcoal delivered, quantities used for cooking, and at the bottom was a notation saying, "Remainder 1½ cords wood sold to Uplanders for 100 *ara* plumes. Remainder 2 bushels charcoal sold to Uplanders, 60 plumes, 1 pound assorted feathers."

So much for his expected fuel supply; he would have to improvise. That was bad news, as were all those empty shelves and kegs.

That cheese would definitely enhance his diet, though—the idea of living all winter on nothing but jerky had been seriously unappealing. He carried the cheese back to the row of tables in the great kitchen with him.

With that, he felt he had given his new quarters a good once-over and that it was time to bring down his pack and his spear, find some bedding, and establish himself. He looked around at the six staircases leading up to various portions of the palace, and chose the one he thought would bring him up closest to the southwest sitting room.

His candle had another good hour to burn, so he felt no great need to hurry, and took his time ascending the stair, looking around at the walls as he went. There were lamps mounted on brackets every few feet, but all of them were dry and wickless. That was no surprise; it wouldn't do to have a servant stub his toe in the dark and drop someone's supper, but wicks and oil might suffer if left out all winter.

The air grew noticeably colder as he climbed, and he was shivering slightly by the time the stair came up in a bare stone corridor running what Sword believed to be east and west. He turned west, and a moment later emerged into the little dining salon by the terrace.

The cold air pouring in through the broken window was like a shower of ice water, and despite the overhang a little snow had drifted in onto the polished floor. The wind was howling through the broken glass and curling around his ankles.

He shivered, pulled his coat more tightly about him, set his candle on the sideboard, and hurried around the corner to fetch his pack and spear.

Everything in the sitting room was just as he had left it, but he had an odd feeling of being watched as he retrieved the heavy bundle and hoisted it onto one shoulder. He paused and looked out the nearest window.

Swirling snow hid the outside world; he could not tell whether anyone was out there or not. The garden wall blocked his view of the trailhead, so he could not have seen the migrating Uplanders in any case, but the snow meant that someone could have been lurking on the palace grounds and he might never know it.

The change in the weather astonished him, when he stopped to think about it.

Yes, it had been growing cooler for weeks, but this intense cold and heavy snow still seemed to have arrived suddenly.

He felt sorry for anyone trying to make their way down the cliff face in this weather.

But then, such storms were probably perfectly normal in the Uplands.

Not in Barokan, though—or at least, they hadn't been. Under the previous few Wizard Lords a snowstorm like this would be permitted in Barokan only at night, if at all, and if one tried to spill over the cliffs, it would have been blown back to the east.

But Artil wanted to put an end to magic. With him holding the eight talismans—no, the *nine* talismans—and with several of the Chosen dead, so that some of the nine didn't work, the snow was free to do as it pleased. If it was snowing this heavily here atop the cliffs, it must be snowing down in Winterhome, as well.

It probably wasn't so cold down there, though.

Sword hadn't expected his stay in the palace to start like this; he had assumed he would have a few days of mild weather while he was settling in. He had planned to look around the grounds, see whether there was anything useful to be gleaned from the gardens or the surrounding plains.

This year's winter, though, had started with a bang. Snow and wind and bitter cold, so early in the season! It couldn't last, could it?

For now, though, it seemed as if the best thing he could do was just hole up and wait for the storm to blow itself out. He adjusted his pack, hefted his spear, then returned to the salon, retrieved his candle, and headed back down to the kitchen.

Once there he set his candle in a sconce, lit a second candle as well, and decided it was time for breakfast—he had been awake and active for hours, but had put off eating. He needed to make his limited supplies last; he couldn't simply eat whenever he chose. Now, though, seemed a reasonable time. He dug a strip of jerky from his pack, then found a mug in one of the cabinets, and tried one of the water taps above the big sink.

The stuff that emerged was fiercely cold and had a faint brownish tinge, but it was water. He couldn't imagine a functioning well on the edge of a cliff like this, and there was no visible pump, so he assumed there was a cistern somewhere—probably on the roof, judging by the water's temperature and the speed with which it flowed. He was relieved that the cistern hadn't been drained.

At least, it hadn't been *completely* drained; that off color and the slight metallic taste to the water might, he thought, indicate that the water was low. He would want to check on that at some point.

He took his first bite of jerky.

As he had discovered on the journey west, the stuff was tough, chewy, and dry, but it wasn't bad. It was much drier than ordinary smoked *ara,* having been kept over the fires much longer, and it was a little spicier than any of the recipes for fresh *ara* he had encountered. He thought stewing it, as some of the Uplanders had for their meals on the trail west, rather than eating it dry, might be a good idea.

Of course, he didn't have any vegetables for stew. He had jerky, cheese, and water, and there might be wine in some of the locked cabinets, but that was all. He was going to eat a very dull menu for the next three months.

But he had food, he had water, he had shelter—he thought he would get by well enough. All those stories about how impossible it was to survive the winters up here had begun to seem absurd; if one lived in a tent, winter *anywhere* would be difficult. If the Uplanders had bothered to build themselves clan houses up here, rather than using the guesthouses down in Winterhome, they could have managed, he was sure.

Of course, if they had built permanent structures, they couldn't have followed the flocks of *ara* very well. Tents could be folded up and carried when a flock decided to relocate in search of better eating; houses could not.

Still, if they had built their own winter housing, instead of relying on the guesthouses in Winterhome . . .

Well, the world would have been very different. Theorizing about it could wait; he had his own survival and comfort to attend to.

His next need, he thought, was bedding, but he was not in any great hurry; it was still morning, so he had plenty of time. Instead of going back upstairs he unpacked his meager possessions; there was no reason to keep everything jammed into his pack. That done, he took an inventory of the candles, so that he could figure out how many he could use at a time.

The results were not particularly encouraging. What had looked like a generous supply for the kitchen in one of the cabinets had turned out to be only about forty candles. There were stubs in some of the sconces and chandeliers, but those were mostly quite short, and not all the various candleholders were occupied.

The stock in the cabinet was serious thick candles, not the

elegant tapers that the Wizard Lord used at his table, but even so, Sword doubted that each would burn for more than two days; if he was going to live a subterranean life here, without the sun, he needed enough candles, or enough lamp oil, to last the entire winter.

He had yet to see any oil anywhere in the palace. There were more candles upstairs, where he had gotten the one he had carried down in the first place, but he didn't know how many were there.

Still, even if his supply proved hopelessly inadequate, it wasn't a crisis. It would just mean he needed to spend some of his time upstairs, taking advantage of natural light. Right now the idea was unappealing, but surely when the weather moderated it would be no great hardship.

Any idea he might have had of setting out a dozen candles and lighting the kitchens properly was out of the question, though; he simply didn't have enough candles.

He had not expected the Wizard Lord's staff to have been so thorough in clearing away supplies at summer's end. He had assumed that most of the unused goods would have been left here, to be used or discarded next summer, but apparently someone in charge had made sure that didn't happen. The consumables had been consumed, or sold, or taken back down to Barokan, leaving many of the palace's bins and cupboards bare.

That made his life more difficult. He sighed, and headed upstairs, past the ground floor to the next level, where the guest bedrooms were.

The cold air on this level seemed to stretch the skin tight across his face, and he could feel his breath condensing in his beard as he walked down the corridor—the Summer Palace was simply not designed to keep cold out. A glance out the window at the end of the passage showed him snow swirling down, and he knew it must be far colder outside, but still, the chill was startling.

He had not come to watch the snow, though; he had come to find himself some bedding. He chose a bedchamber door almost at random; fortunately, it wasn't locked. He opened it and stepped in, to find the mattress bare in its frame.

He frowned, but looked further, and found sheets and blankets neatly folded away in a linen press.

At least, he told himself, no one had taken the linens, as they had the firewood and food.

Before continuing with his housekeeping tasks, he took a moment to look out the bedroom window to the south, a bit more closely than the cursory glance he had given the corridor window. The snow was lessening a little, he thought, though the glass was still cold to the touch and ice was beginning to form along the eastern edge; the wind still whistled around the palace, and a fierce chill seeped into the already-cold room around every edge of the casement.

Peering out through the whiteness, he discovered that he was high enough up to see over the garden wall now. In the distance he could make out figures moving into the triangular canyon that led to the cliff trail, but he could also see that there were still pitched tents nearby; presumably some people were waiting out the storm, while others pressed on.

He would not want to climb down that narrow trail in such weather, but the Uplanders presumably knew what they were doing. Surely, this wasn't the first year the snows had caught them here—in fact, from what Whistler had said when he criticized Sword's trading for jerky, Sword *knew* it wasn't the first time.

He wished them all well—and some part of him wished he were with them, on his way back down to the familiar surroundings of Barokan.

But he couldn't do that while the Wizard Lord still reigned. Here he was, and here he would remain, and he needed to make himself as comfortable as possible. He heaved the bare mattress off the bed, and hoisted it onto his shoulders.

Although it was a very generous mattress, thick and heavy, after carrying the two *ara* this was nothing.

He hauled the mattress down to the kitchen, stopping frequently along the way to adjust his hold. Maneuvering it down the dark stairs had been a challenge, as he had to set his candle in a wall-sconce halfway down to light the way, and then be very careful not to let the mattress get too close to the open flame as he manhandled it down the steps.

He reached the kitchen without incident, and when he was safely in the dim confines of his new home he set the mattress on the floor in a corner that seemed a bit warmer than most of the room.

That done, he yielded to hunger and thirst—he got another cup of water and ate another few bites of jerky, but resisted the temptation to start on the wheel of cheese. Then he went back upstairs for the bedclothes.

He didn't want to waste daylight, so after delivering the sheets and blankets to his chosen corner of the kitchen he went back upstairs, searching for candles and wicks and lamp oil, and anything else that might be useful.

He found the servants' quarters; those were on the top floor. Most were small bare rooms lit by small clerestory windows, furnished with simple beds and nightstands. Each nightstand held two or three candles; he gathered those up and shoved them into the pockets of his vest.

The top floor also provided access to the cistern, which was indeed on the roof. Sword opened what he had thought was a storage closet, and found a narrow ladder in a tiny empty room, leading up to a trapdoor; when he climbed it and pushed up through the trap, he found himself in a narrow walkway between a rough wooden wall and a long row of closed shutters. At one end the walkway was blocked by a huge brick column—a chimney, Sword thought. At the other end it turned a right angle. Grayish daylight leaked in through the slats of the shutters, and bitterly cold air whistled through as well. Several pipes emerged from the wooden wall next to that massive brick chimney, then turned right angles to head directly down through the floor—or really, looking at it, through the roof; Sword was standing on tarred tin.

Shivering, Sword peered into the cracks in the wall, and thought he could see metal—more tin, he guessed, lining what was surely the palace cistern. He rapped on the side of the tin-lined tank; the hollow sound this produced convinced him that it was indeed almost empty. He knelt, tapping his way down the wall, and did not ever find a level where he could be sure he was hearing water, rather than air, on the other side.

That was not good, but it made sense that the cistern would have been drained, as a commonsense precaution; the water in it would undoubtedly freeze, if it hadn't already, and if there had been any significant amount, the expansion of the ice would have strained the entire structure.

A little water obviously still lingered in the pipes, and the warmth from that chimney might help keep some of the remaining water in the cistern from freezing, but all in all, Sword did not think he could rely on that water supply.

But then, he didn't need to, if it kept snowing. He could just collect snow and melt it for his water.

He considered walking on to see what was around the corner, if anything, but thought better of it—the wind blowing through the shutters was vicious. Instead he climbed back down, lowering the trap carefully back into place, and went on with his hunt through the third-floor bedrooms.

When he had finished with the servants' quarters he descended a level and started on the other bedrooms. Each of the elegant bedchambers on the second floor provided a candle or two, and the dining hall drawer he had found earlier held thirty or so, but all of these were beeswax tapers, which gave a good clear light, but which would not last all that very long.

And those candles were all he found, as far as useful supplies went.

No oil.

No food.

No firewood.

No charcoal.

No water supply other than the huge, virtually empty rooftop cistern.

None of the bedrooms or other upstairs rooms had stoves or fireplaces—this was a *summer* palace. None of the windows had proper shutters, either, and the upper floors were uniformly cold.

Still, the palace was shelter.

He would manage, he was sure. He would wait out the winter here, and in the spring he would take shelter with an Uplander clan, so that the staff preparing the palace would not find him, and when summer came around and the Wizard Lord came up here to get away from the heat, Sword would meet him and kill him.

Of course, he would be unable to effectively hide the evidence that someone had been here. The staff would know, and they would tell Artil, and Artil would guess who it was. . . .

Or would he? He wouldn't necessarily know who had been here, or when, or for how long. Things would be out of place, but perhaps Sword could try to make it appear that Uplanders had broken in and done some minor looting, rather than that someone had wintered here.

But the Wizard Lord would be suspicious. That was simply in his nature. He would assume that Sword, or perhaps one of the other surviving Chosen, had been here.

And what if he did? What would he do about it? The Wizard Lord had no magic here, outside Barokan's borders. He would post guards, perhaps have the palace and the surrounding area searched, but what else could he do? He always kept himself guarded anyway; a suspicion that one of his enemies had been here over the winter wouldn't change that.

Sword would need to find a way past the Wizard Lord's guards at some point, but he thought he could manage that. He would find a way to get at the Wizard Lord, here where his magic didn't work, and he would avenge Babble and Azir shi Azir, and all the lesser wizards the Wizard Lord had murdered, and he would free Barokan of the Dark Lord who now ruled.

As he carried a bundle of beeswax candles down to his subterranean lair, though, for the first time Sword found himself thinking seriously about what he would do *after* that.

Up until now he had always put that aside for later, but now he gave it some thought.

When the Wizard Lord, the Dark Lord of Winterhome, was dead, what would happen?

Ordinarily when a Wizard Lord died, the Council of Immortals gathered and chose a successor. That was how it had worked for centuries. *This* Wizard Lord, though, had killed most of the Council, and virtually all his potential successors—and who knew what dying outside Barokan might do to the magic of the Great Talismans?

It seemed likely that there would *be* no successor, no new Wizard Lord. Artil im Salthir would be the last of the Wizard Lords—and what would replace them?

Did *anything* have to replace them? Couldn't the towns and villages govern themselves? There were no more rogue wizards to contend with, after all—not unless the half-dozen survivors of the Council of Immortals turned rogue.

And after all, how much harm could half a dozen wizards, most of them well on in years, do?

Well, quite a bit, really, but was there any reason to think they would? And the remaining Chosen would be around to deal with them. The Chosen, or Artil's soldiers . . .

But that might be a problem in its own right—those soldiers. What if they didn't want to disband and go home?

Sword shook his head. If they were a problem, it wouldn't be *his* problem. The priests and their *ler* could deal with soldiers; the soldiers wouldn't have any magic.

An end to the Wizard Lords would presumably mean an end to the Chosen, an end to the Council of Immortals, an end to the entire system that had united and protected Barokan for the last seven centuries—but Sword thought it was a system that had outlived its usefulness. He would be the last Swordsman; the last Seer and Speaker had probably already been butchered on the streets of Winterhome.

The system had been in place so long, though, that it was hard to imagine Barokan without it.

But then he stopped and thought for a moment. It was easy enough to imagine his home town of Mad Oak without any wizards or Chosen or Wizard Lord; none of those had really impinged upon his awareness for the first nineteen years of his life, except as stories of ancient times and distant places. Mad Oak had gone about its business untroubled by the outside world, and could probably return to that state easily.

Would it really be any different anywhere? *He* had always had to take the Wizard Lord and the Chosen into account in his travels because he was the Swordsman, one of the Chosen, but were ordinary people concerned with such matters?

The roads might make a difference, but he could not see how it would be a very great one, really. There would be traders, yes, but what of it?

Let the system die, then.

Artil im Salthir had wanted to replace it with a non-magical system of centralized rule, but there was no need for that. Let it all just wither away, and the towns could take care of themselves. There might be an unsettled period for a time, but surely it wouldn't last long, or be too disruptive.

So there would be no more Wizard Lord, no more Chosen— and what would he, Erren Zal Tuyo of Mad Oak, do?

Go home and grow barley, most likely. He might be able to find a wife, once there was no more risk that he'd go off adventuring and get himself killed. Raise children, perhaps.

That would be lovely.

All he had to do was survive the winter, and then find a way to kill the Wizard Lord, and do it without the help of the other Chosen, who were dead or imprisoned or scattered.

That was all.

He snorted at his own folly, then lit a fresh candle and once again set about arranging his new home.

[11]

That night Sword slept naked, wrapped in blankets taken from several of the rooms upstairs, on a mattress covered in fine linen sheets, on a corner of the kitchen floor. He had stripped off his clothes and unpacked the others he had brought, then rinsed them all lightly in the brownish tap water, and hung them on various hooks and sconces to dry, well away from the smoke of his candles. He didn't expect to actually get them *clean* until he found a better water source, but he hoped to at least remove the worst of the sweat and grime. He had been unable to wash them at all on the way west, as the limited water supplies available on the march were too precious to be wasted on cleaning, and eleven days of travel had left all three outfits—his new Uplander garb and his battered Hostman attire—in desperate need of attention.

As he had stripped off his clothing, the garments had seemed almost alive; he hoped that was his imagination, and not due to an accumulation of parasites. If there *were* mites and fleas, he hoped the water would discourage them.

He had debated whether to build a fire in one of the hearths and ovens, using the scraps he had found in the wood-bin, and had decided not to bother—the kitchen was not so very cold, as yet, and his fuel supply was very limited. The wind had chilled the upper floors, but that chill had not yet penetrated into the depths where he sheltered. He assumed he would need every scrap of fuel eventually, and therefore could not afford to waste it now. Instead of starting a fire he had wrapped himself in the fine woolen blankets, three or four of them covering almost every inch of his flesh, and curled up on his makeshift bed. That was warm enough, and he dozed off easily, feeling oddly calm.

At first he slept deeply and untroubled, but somewhere in the darkness between midnight and dawn he found himself dreaming strange, uneasy dreams, dreams of flying across endless plains of snow, of plunging through the earth into hidden recesses in the stone beneath, of shrinking down to the size of a worm or a beetle and crawling through dark cracks somewhere.

In these dreams he was unsure of his own identity, whether he was a man named Erren Zal Tuyo and called Sword, or a beetle going about its insectile business, or a swirl of snow, or a gust of wind, or something else, something he had no words for, or some combination of all of these. At times he was not a single soul, but a great gathering of *ler*, of spirits merging and separating in ways beyond mortal understanding.

And somewhere in that maze of dreams he realized that these were not just dreams. He had removed all the *ara* feathers that had guarded him from hostile magic. Feathers were sewn into his clothing, pinned to his cuffs, tied onto his pack—but he had put aside his pack, stripped off his clothes, and left them all a few yards away from where he slept.

But he wasn't in Barokan, where everyone knew *ler* sent dreams. He was in the Uplands, where *ler* did not trouble anyone. He had dreamed a few times during his stay with the Clan of the Golden Spear, but those had been ordinary dreams, stray images and bits of memory tangling randomly in his head; they were nothing like this.

But now, he realized, he was not in a tent of *ara* hide, supported by poles made of *ara* bone, sleeping on ground where generations of *ara* had dwelt; he was wrapped in Barokanese bedding, on a mattress made in Barokan, a mattress that was resting upon the bare stone beneath the prairie, stone that no *ara* had ever touched. He had exposed himself to the *ler* of the Uplands in a way no one ordinarily did.

But the Wizard Lord and his staff had slept here in the Summer Palace, and Sword had heard no stories of strange dreams or visitations.

What was different now?

He tried to wake, to free himself of the dreams. He thought about the feather-lined coat that hung on the far side of the kitchen; if he could awaken . . .

No.

In his dream he now stood naked on the endless plains somewhere far to the east of the Summer Palace, a cold wind whipping his hair out behind him, unable to move, unable even to shiver in the frigid blast that was freezing his breath to ice in his beard, and a voice spoke to him from everywhere and nowhere.

You will not wake until we allow it.

His jaw moved, and he was able to speak. "Why? What do you want of me?" he asked, his gaze still unwillingly fixed on infinity.

At first there was no reply to that that he could put into words, but he felt a sense of bemusement; then the voice replied, *To understand.*

"Understand what?"

Who you are. What you are. Why you are here.

"I'm . . . you must know my true name. . . ."

Yes, Erren Zal Tuyo kam Darig seventh Tirinsir abek Du. A chill ran through his entire body at the sound of that. Sword had the feeling that the rest of his name, or at least much more of it, was somehow implied as well, without being spoken. *But the name is not the whole of the thing. It is the essence, but we are intrigued by what surrounds that essence.*

"And who are you? You are *ler,* I know that, but what *ler*?"

Ler of earth and ice, wind and sky. Ler *of the Uplands.*

Ler of the Uplands—of course they were. The *ler* of his blankets and mattress could hardly have had the power to command his dreams.

But no one spoke with the *ler* of the Uplands. The Uplanders had no priests, no wizards. The presence of *ler* could not be felt clearly anywhere in the Uplands. Some people even thought there *were* no *ler* in the Uplands, though Sword had known better than to believe that. Sword had always assumed that no one had *ever* communicated with the Upland *ler,* but here he was, dreaming of them, and he knew this was no ordinary dream.

But why?

If these *ler* were so easily contacted, why hadn't any of the Uplanders ever become priests or wizards in all the centuries they had lived on the plateau?

Suddenly frightened, he called, "Let me wake!"

A bargain: Swear by your name you will not hide again behind the hides and feathers, and we will let you wake.

He hesitated. "For how long?" he asked.

There was no clear answer to that; instead, after an uncertain pause, he heard a single word.

Swear.

"I swear by my true name that I, Erren Zal Tuyo, will not clothe myself in *ara* feathers for . . . for three days. Is that enough?"

There was no reply; wind howled wordlessly around him, but he found that he could move now, he could turn his face away from the wind, wrap his arms around himself, and crouch down, shivering.

"Let me wake!" he shouted, his voice almost inaudible now against the screaming wind. He closed his eyes and lowered his head. . . .

And awoke in the utter darkness of the palace kitchens.

He could see nothing but blackness, hear nothing but his own heart and breath, but he could feel the blankets that wrapped him, and the mattress beneath him, and he could smell the stone and the smoke and the lingering traces of grease, so he knew where he was, and that he was no longer dreaming.

And the world around him, the darkness itself, felt different now. Ever since passing the boundary between Barokan and the Uplands he had been cut off from the *ler,* from his link to magic, his connection to both the local *ler* and the *ler* that made him one of the Chosen—even the *ler* of his own sword had been quiescent. It was as if his sight had dimmed, his hearing had been muffled, his hands wrapped in thick wool.

That had changed now.

He could see nothing in the utter blackness of the under-ground kitchen, yet he could sense a thousand shades of darkness, could feel the air and the blankets and all the world around him.

The world was alive again—alive and *awake.*

"Oh," he said aloud, to no one in particular.

He lay there in the darkness for a moment. He had carefully laid out flint, steel, and tinder, and set a candle nearby, so that he could make a fresh light when he awoke, but he did not reach for them, not yet. He wanted to think first.

He had sworn an oath—or had he merely *dreamed* that he swore an oath? Was a dream binding? He could not say for certain whether he had been in control of his actions in the dream.

Did it matter, though? Could three days unguarded by *ara* feathers do him any real harm?

That was a stupid question; of course they could! He wasn't safely home in Mad Oak, he wasn't protected by his talisman here; he was in the home of unknown, perhaps hostile *ler,* with no other defense against them. They could destroy him— perhaps not directly, but they could undoubtedly find a way. The intense awareness of his surroundings he now felt removed any possibility that his dream had not truly been sent by the local *ler;* they were real, they were here, and they had taken note of him.

He remembered when he had first left Mad Oak, years before, and had almost been caught by the tree that gave the town its name. For all he knew, there could be things in the earth here that would make the old oak seem as harmless as a kitten. Surely, there was a *reason* the Uplanders had made no attempt to bargain with the *ler* in all these years, but had instead used the feathers to shut them out.

But they hadn't harmed him yet. They had accepted his vow and let him wake.

They knew his true name—they had seen into his unguarded soul.

For all he knew, even *ara* feathers might not be enough to protect him now.

And whether a dreamed oath was truly binding or not, he had given his word.

You did, something said in the darkness.

He had not imagined it; *ler* had truly spoken to him in his dream, and were speaking to him now.

Either that, or he was still asleep and dreaming, or he was going mad.

He did not think he was asleep, or that he had gone insane; the feel and smell of his blankets and the kitchens were too real, too solid and detailed and unchanging, to be a dream, and he had never had any real doubts about his sanity.

And why shouldn't *ler* speak to him? There were no others around for them to address.

"You heard my thoughts?" he asked.

We know you now, Erren Zal Tuyo.

"So I have no secrets? You know who I am and why I'm here?"

We do.

"Then what do you want of me?"

For a moment there was no answer; then something replied, *That we do* not *know. Not yet.*

A different spirit said, *We are not of one mind.*

He lay still for a moment longer, absorbing that; then he asked, "Is the sun up?"

Nothing spoke; no words came to him. Perhaps the local *ler* weren't even aware of the sun, as such. After all, he was underground, and presumably speaking with the spirits of stone and earth; what would they know of lights in the sky?

For his own part, he had no sense of time at all; his dreams had disturbed his normal sleep so badly that he could not say whether he had slept an hour or an entire day, and the darkness was too complete to give him any clue. Carefully, he turned and reached for his flint.

His hand brushed the stone floor, and he gasped and snatched it back. The stone was cold and *alive;* he could feel a solidity and a timeless satisfaction in it, a sense of calm antiquity— there really weren't any words for it in Barokanese, but it seemed as if he had reached into the stone's soul as deeply as any *ler* had reached into his mind.

He had felt *ler* before, of course; as the Swordsman he had been intimately acquainted with the *ler* of muscle and steel, he had felt the hard hunger of his sword, but that had been in Barokan. He had been in the Uplands, cut off from the spirits of his homeland, for months, and he had not anticipated finding such a link to Uplander *ler.*

But apparently that link had been made, and he still needed to make a light and see where he was.

Shuddering, he reached out again, and pressed his fingertips to the stone.

It was as if he had set them into a pool of something a thousand times slower and thicker than water, but just as receptive. The stone floor was welcoming him, in its fashion, allowing his fingers to rest against it. He had the definite feeling that if he kept his fingers where they were, in an eon or two the floor would let them sink in, and ripples would spread outward, too slowly for any human to perceive.

"Thank you," he said, and then he groped for his flint and steel and tinder.

The steel was as cold as the stone, but not so calm, and less yielding. It wanted to strike, to break.

The flint was warmer, not so hard, and it held a knowledge of fire and heat.

The tinder was soft and hot, crumbling with decay, eager for its own destruction.

The candle was slick and soft and young, and almost seemed to squirm in his grasp.

Even when he had had his full magic, down in Barokan, he had not been so receptive as this to every *ler* around him; his perceptions had been filtered through the *ler* bound to his talisman. Was this, he wondered, what things felt like to the priests in Barokan? Once, years ago, he had been magically presented with the memories of an ancient priestess, and those memories had included something of her experience of the *ler* in the world around her, but it had been an old, faded memory, without the intensity, the immediacy of these sensations. He could not say whether she had perceived the *ler* as he was perceiving them now, or whether this was something new and different, something peculiar to the Uplands, perhaps even specific to this palace.

He arranged the tinder, then took up the flint and steel and struck.

The steel in his hand rejoiced, the flint accepted, and sparks leapt out in a burst of fiery creation. Those sparks were almost painfully bright; his eyes had adjusted too well to the blackness. He squinted as he struck flint against steel a second time.

This time the tinder caught, and a moment later he was holding a candle high, careful not to look directly at the flame.

The kitchen looked exactly as it had when he went to sleep—but it *felt* different, more alive, more *real*.

Cautiously, he got to his feet.

He wanted to get dressed, but he had promised the *ler* he

would not wear hides or feathers for three days, and all his outer clothing either had feathers sewn into it somewhere, or was made of *ara* hide, or both. He could not wear any of it without breaking his word.

Instead, he wrapped a lush Barokanese blanket around himself, holding it in place with one hand while raising the candle in the other, and headed for the stairs, the stone floor cold and smooth beneath his bare feet.

Then he stopped. He would not wear the forbidden garments, but there were other things he wanted. He crossed to where he had hung his clothing and spread out several other items, and found what he wanted.

His sword belt had no feathers on it anywhere, and was made of good Barokanese leather; he slung it around himself, belting the blanket in place, thereby freeing a hand.

He poked a finger into the pocket of the breeches he had worn the previous day and fished out something small and sharp, letting it fall to the floor. The silver talisman that made him the Swordsman gleamed brightly in the candlelight, perhaps a little more brightly than could be accounted for naturally; he picked it up and clutched it against the candle, feeling it cut into the wax.

In Barokan, if he was ever more than a few yards from the talisman, he would feel ill and weak; in the Uplands, cut off from his magic, that had not been the case. He was still cut off from all the powers of Barokan, but he had connected with *ler* again, and even if they were entirely different *ler,* he still did not care to take any chances—better to have the talisman and not need it than to suddenly need it after leaving it behind. He had not felt ill lying across the room from it, but now that he held it again he felt stronger, more alert.

Thus equipped, he turned again to the stairs, the candle and talisman in one hand, the other holding a corner of blanket to his shoulder.

When he emerged onto the ground floor, shivering with the cold, and peered out at the windows of the main dining hall, he could see at once why the kitchen had been so totally lightless— the sky outside was still dark, though when he looked to his right he could see a very faint grayness spreading in the east. He had awoken well before dawn.

Ordinarily he might have tried to go back to sleep, but he was thoroughly awake now, after his unexpected contact with *ler,* and saw no point in pretending otherwise.

He also saw no point in freezing; he turned and hurried back down the stairs to his underground retreat.

There he lit a second candle and set both lights on the floor, one on either side, then settled down on his mattress, wrapping a second blanket around himself.

"All right, then," he said to the empty air. "What do you want of me?"

No one answered.

"I know you're here," he said. "You spoke to me before; speak to me now."

Again, nothing.

"I don't have any feathers on me." He reached out and touched the wall; the stone was alive, he could feel it. The air around him was still, but still vital.

"Speak to me!"

Still, no response.

"What, are you done with me already? Should I get dressed, then?"

You swore an oath. Three days.

The reply was so sudden and so clear that Sword started, dropping his talisman onto the mattress. He quickly snatched the bit of metal up again.

"All right," he said. "Three days, then."

There was no answer. He waited, listening, for several more minutes, then shrugged.

"Fine," he said. "Three days. I can do that." He glanced longingly at his clothing, and pulled his blankets tighter.

It was obvious that the *ler* were not ready to speak to him beyond ensuring he would abide by his promise not to shut them out, and he could handle that, he was sure. They would speak when they were ready.

And, he admitted to himself, he did not particularly *want* to wear the hides and feathers again, now that he had experienced

the Uplands without them, and had connected with his surroundings. He felt a part of the world once more, as if he belonged again, and was in no hurry to lose that. Quite aside
from the fact that it simply felt better, he had begun to wonder
whether he might be able to use the *ler* somehow. He was no
wizard, nor a priest, but the Upland *ler* had spoken to him, had
entered his dreams—he might be able to negotiate with them.
They might help him survive the winter.

And they might aid him against the Wizard Lord. After all,
wasn't Artil im Salthir an intruder here? Wasn't his summer
palace an invasion of territory to which he had no claim, a
place where he had no right to be? Sword was an intruder
himself, of course, but he had built no structures, dug no cellars, and he would be happy to return forever to the Lowlands
once the Wizard Lord was dead.

Just what form such aid might take Sword had no idea, but
if the *ler* ever did deign to speak freely with him, he could ask.

Surely, it would do no harm to *ask*.

For now, though, he had more immediate concerns. The
temperature in the kitchens was dropping, he was fairly
certain—presumably the weather outside was turning colder,
and that cold air was leaking into the palace. He had survived
one night well enough with nothing but blankets, but he
thought he really would need to build a fire soon.

Finding something to wear, something not feathered but a
little more convenient than a blanket, would also be good.
He knew some of his garments could be made acceptable; he
had not sewn feathers into *all* his Hostman garb. The under-
clothing should be all right, and he was fairly certain he
could render the breeches acceptable with just a little judi-
cious trimming. His Uplander trousers, vests, and shirt were
hopeless, being made almost entirely of *ara;* his winter coat
was stuffed with *ara* down and probably beyond salvage. Removing all the feathers from his Hostman tunic might be
possible, but would probably damage the fabric beyond repair, and he doubted he had gotten all the *ara* blood out of it,
so that was out.

He glanced down at the sheets he had appropriated from the

bedchambers upstairs, and grimaced. At least he had plenty of fabric to use in making more clothes.

He blew out one candle, picked up the other, and marched to where his clothes hung.

After an hour's work picking at stitches, he was able to dress in breeches and belt, but nothing more; thus attired, he drew his sword and spent his daily hour in practice. There were no *ler* requiring it, so far as he knew; his talisman was no longer lifeless metal, but it did not seem to have its full potency, either. Still, the daily routine was a habit, and he might need the practice when the time came to kill the Wizard Lord.

Besides, the activity served to keep him from feeling the cold too strongly. Even so, when he finally lowered his blade he was shivering in seconds, and quickly wrapped himself in a blanket again.

Thus attired, he sheathed his weapon on his belt and headed upstairs, where the sky beyond the windows was brightening from gray to gold.

[12]

He had been unable to find any proper sewing supplies in the palace, and his *ara*-bone needle had been lost somewhere, but he had found that curtains could be tied into crude cloaks and wraps. Curtains handled more easily than blankets, and would have to do until he could manage something better. His black broadcloth breeches were not enough; the air in the palace was cold enough that he thought frostbite was a real concern. He had never seen real frostbite; he had been considered too young to be allowed to see Blackhand's hand until long after it had healed. He had seen the effects, though, and clearly remembered the ugly stumps where those missing fingers had been. He did not want to risk any firsthand experience with such a phenomenon. He wasn't sure just what it involved, really, what it felt like, how long it took, whether there was any warning he might watch for—Blackhand hadn't exactly liked to talk about it, since it had been his own stupidity that allowed it to happen—but Sword knew his fingers and ears might turn black and die, even if literally falling off was some storyteller's exaggeration.

He had improvised a double-layered velvet cloak out of a set of drapes, and wore it over a blanket wrapped around his shoulders, atop his few acceptable ordinary clothes. He had stripped the *ara*-feather ornaments from his Hostman boots, so that he could wear them and keep his feet protected from the cold, as well.

He had not heard any more *ler* voices, but he did not doubt the reality of his earlier experiences; he could *feel* the *ler* in the air around him, and in any exposed stone he touched. Their presence was much less noticeable in other objects; his clothes, the curtains, the blankets all seemed relatively lifeless—not dead, by any means, but not so vigorous. He supposed that that was because these manufactured things had been brought up from Barokan, and therefore had no native Uplander *ler*. Their own Barokanese *ler* were still present, but relatively weak here.

Why that should be so, when up until his arrival in the Summer Palace it had been Uplander *ler* that seemed weak and almost imperceptible, he had no idea.

And why the weather had turned so very intensely cold so very quickly, he did not know, either. Surely, it was not like this *every* winter!

Or perhaps it was. That would certainly explain why the Uplanders fled so swiftly and completely to Winterhome every year. If the weather on the plateau regularly changed from cool and dry to snowy and bitterly cold in a matter of two or three days, and stayed cold all winter, that would seem like a very sound reason to get down the cliffs as rapidly as possible once the *ara* left and the weather started to turn.

He was on the top floor stealing curtains when that thought occurred to him, and he took a moment to look out a window to the south. A few Uplanders were still clustered at the head of the trail down the cliff, but only a few, no more than a single clan, and even these were in the process of vanishing down into the canyon, leaving a muddy campsite behind.

That patch of gray mud was the only visible interruption of any size in a vast expanse of white stretching to the south and east. A few scattered trees and cisterns were faintly visible in the distance through the glare of sunlight on snow, but for the most part, when he looked out across the plateau, all the world seemed to be white snow beneath a gray sky, with a band of intense blue separating the two in the east, where the clouds were clearing.

But when he turned to the west the world fell away at the edge of the cliff, and what lay beyond, in the distance, was green and brown; no snow covered Barokan.

At least, not yet. He supposed that winter would reach the Lowlands soon enough.

How strange, though, that the weather could be so very different above and below the cliffs. Sword did not know whether it was simply because of the altitude, or because the *ler* of the two lands were so different, but he found it hard to comprehend. Up here it was winter; down in Barokan it was still autumn. He could step back in time by climbing down the cliffs.

Except, of course, that he did not dare enter Barokan. He was here, in the Summer Palace, for good reason; if he set foot in Barokan, the Wizard Lord would try to find him and kill him.

Of course, once the Wizard Lord found out he was here, Artil would try to have him killed anyway. He wouldn't care that it wasn't Barokan. His magic wouldn't work here, but he would still have his soldiers.

And it wasn't as if Sword could stay hidden in the palace and take the Red Wizard by surprise. There would undoubtedly be servants coming up here at least a few days in advance, bringing supplies and getting the palace ready, and there was no way that Sword could possibly avoid their notice. Even if he managed to hide somewhere, they would see that someone had been here; he realized now that it simply wasn't possible to spend an entire winter here without leaving obvious evidence. He would never be able to get all the curtains and blankets back where they belonged, or replace the candles he had burned.

Especially, he thought, since sooner or later he was going to need to build a fire, and he had gradually come to accept that the only real fuel he had on hand was the palace furnishings. He hated to do it, to destroy these lovely things, but he would almost certainly need to burn *something*. Venturing outside to find fuel—well, there simply wasn't much wood up here, and the grass and dung the Uplanders used were buried under the snow.

No, he wouldn't be able to just hide in the palace until Artil arrived. For one thing, his food supply would run out before that. Once the Uplanders returned from Winterhome, he would try to rejoin the Clan of the Golden Spear, so that he would have food and shelter. And when the Wizard Lord came to the Summer Palace, Sword would need to get back inside the walls somehow to kill him.

Getting back inside when the gates were guarded would be a challenge, but not insuperable, by any means. He could climb the wall late at night, or simply fight his way in. If there were any secret entrances, he had all winter to find them.

Or, he realized, to *make* them.

He looked thoughtfully out at the snowy plain.

He was going to be trapped in this palace for months, without much to do—he had his food supply, scanty as it was, and his only fuel would be the furniture, and for water he would collect and melt snow, so his needs were largely met. He would probably want to rework his wardrobe, if the Upland *ler* continued to speak to him, but that shouldn't take very long. Arranging some surprise for the Wizard Lord would be a good way to fill the long hours. Not only would he see about finding or creating a secret entrance, so that he could slip back inside unseen, but he could also rig traps—though, of course, he'd need to be careful not to set them off himself.

But on the other hand, traps might well wind up injuring or killing innocent servants, rather than harming the Wizard Lord himself. That needed more thought. A secret entrance, though, would be very welcome.

There might already be one, as it seemed like the sort of thing Artil would do. So far, though, Sword had found no evidence of one.

The local *ler* would know, though. If Sword could speak to them somehow and ask, they might tell him. Perhaps in his dreams?

Or even openly?

"O *ler* of the Uplands," he said aloud, "I beseech you to aid me."

Though nothing spoke, he felt the air stir; the spirits were listening, then.

"I need to know if there are hidden ways in and out of this palace," he continued. "A tunnel, perhaps? A secret door?"

He could *feel* them listening.

"Tell me what you would have of me. Let us bargain. Aid me, and I will do what I may to please you in return."

The curtains he had not taken down fluttered, though he felt no wind.

"Tonight when I sleep, then, perhaps you will speak to me in my dreams?"

Perhaps.

Although he had hoped for a response, he started. "You *can* talk to me when I'm awake," he said.

Yes.

That had been foolish of him; something had spoken to him that morning. He had known that they could speak to him at any time—but they didn't. "But you don't want to?" He hesitated, then shrugged. "As you will, then. I will wait."

There was no reply to that—and why should there be? He smiled at himself. He was no wizard, to force *ler* to speak, or a priest, to plead or bargain with them; getting *any* response was more than he had any right to expect.

It would make his life easier, though, if he could convince them to answer his questions, and perhaps even to do a little more. They might conceivably help him survive the cold somehow. He knew he didn't have the talent, experience, or knowledge to work real weather magic, but just diverting the worst of the winds around the palace might be useful.

He shivered. It was *cold* up here. The snow might have stopped, the clouds might be thinning, but the wind was still howling around the eaves, and was still, judging by the ice thickening on the windows, bitterly cold.

How odd, he thought again, that the temperature had plummeted so swiftly! Just a few days ago, it seemed, he had not even needed a coat out on the open plain, yet now he was worried about freezing to death even in the cozy palace cellars, well out of the wind.

He had heard Uplanders talk about how much more extreme the weather was on the plateau than down in Barokan, but he had just put that down to the Wizard Lord's regulation of the skies of Barokan. Now, though, he was not so sure. Perhaps the thinner air was responsible somehow? Or the lack of trees to break the wind and hold in the warmth? Or the drier air?

Or all of those, and more?

That was something else he could ask the *ler.* He doubted there was anything to be done about it, or that knowledge of the reasons would do anything more than alleviate his curiosity, but he *was* curious, and asking could do no harm.

For now, though, he would put all those questions aside. He had come upstairs to find fuel and clothing, and to take a good look at what was happening outside the Summer Palace, not to interrogate a bunch of whimsical spirits. He had his improvised cloak, and he had seen the last of the Uplanders descending into the canyon, and that left fuel. He wanted to find things that he could burn, if he had to. He looked around the bedroom he was in.

The gilding on the vanity table would not burn well, but the chest of drawers ought to be fine once he broke it up into pieces that would fit into a fireplace. The bedframe would probably serve, as well, but it was big and awkward, and could wait. The bureau he would take right now.

He dumped its meager contents on the floor, drawer by drawer, then stopped as he pulled out the fourth, final, fullest drawer.

The half-dozen light cotton shirts and linen girdles in the drawer would probably burn just fine, he realized. There was no reason to dump them; they were potential fuel, just as much as the wooden bureau itself was, and what's more, some of them might fit him. They were intended for summer wear, of course—that was probably why their owner had left them here—but they would still be better than nothing. He might not need to improvise so much as he had thought in making up his new wardrobe.

Carrying the entire bureau down the stairs would be awkward, but he could carry two drawers at a time easily enough, and make a third trip for the frame.

When he started down the stairs to the kitchen with the first two drawers in his arms, he felt the nearness of the Uplander *ler;* here at the entrance into the earth itself they were much stronger than up in the man-made heights above. He had not felt this when he had been wearing his feather-filled coat and *ara*-hide clothing, but now it was obvious. He was unsure whether the absence of his protective garments was the only difference, or whether he had been sensitized by his dreams, or whether the *ler* were somehow growing stronger—or perhaps some combination of those.

Whatever the reason, the intense presence of *ler* was unmistakable, and he responded as he had been taught all his life. He said, "I ask your pardon, O spirits, for intruding into your home, and I hope you will make me welcome." He bowed his head in respect as he descended into the darkness.

He did not venture far into the gloom, but set the drawers to one side at the foot of the stairs, then turned to go back for the others.

"Thank you for allowing me here," he said as he set his foot on the first step.

The air stirred, but he heard no words.

He shrugged, and headed up.

After his third trip he took a break and ate a candlelight lunch consisting of a strip of jerky, a few ounces of dirty ice water, and a sliver of cheese.

The remaining unfrozen water from the cistern was getting nasty, he thought, so instead of returning to the third floor, he found himself a few pots and a ladle, wrapped more blankets under his makeshift cloak, and ventured out onto the terrace to collect snow.

The wind whipped his cloak around, and blew his hair across his eyes; he knelt on the paving stones and said, "O *ler* of the wind, spare me your wrath, and let me gather the snow you have given me. Do not pull the warmth from my skin, I pray."

The wind dropped as he rose again, but whether in response to his entreaty or merely by coincidence he could not tell. He didn't worry about it; the important thing was that it *had* dropped. He quickly ladled snow into the pots.

The snow wasn't deep enough to simply scoop it up with the pots themselves; there wasn't much more than an inch on the terrace. The ladle worked fairly well, though.

He was aware that even if he filled every pot and packed the snow in as tightly as he could, it would melt down to a small fraction of its volume. He didn't really see any better alternative, though.

As he shoveled snow into the pots he looked out across the terrace—and across the world; beyond the terrace rail was a vast emptiness, and beyond that he could see blue-green hills in the distance, somewhere far to the west, down in Barokan.

Down there his countrymen were bringing in the last of the harvest, clearing the fields, and preparing for winter.

If he had had any sense, he told himself, he would have doubled back to the Summer Palace sooner and laid in supplies, rather than staying with the Clan of the Golden Spear until the last minute. He would have found a way to refill the cistern. He would have stored firewood, or at least a heap of dried dung. Instead here he was, snow already covering the ground, a bitter wind tearing at his cloak, trying to scrape up enough water to get through the next two or three days.

Though the wind was not so bitter as it had been, certainly.

"Thank you, spirits of the air," he said. "You are being kind to me."

And of course, he hadn't realized how sudden the onset of winter would be. He had thought he would have time, a few days at the very least.

Why, he wondered again, *had* the cold come so suddenly?

Was it only because there was no Wizard Lord moderating the weather here? Did the sheer altitude have something to do with it? The thinner air, perhaps?

"O spirits of the Uplands," he said, "help me understand your land better. Tell me why the winter came so quickly."

The wind gusted at that, snow swirling up in white spirals on either side of him, but he heard no voice; no words or images formed in his mind.

Well, he was no priest, and despite centuries of human habitation, the Uplands were still effectively a wilderness, their *ler* untamed. He couldn't expect open communication. Really, it was amazing the *ler* had been as attentive and cooperative as they had. Even in Barokan, even as one of the Chosen, he had only rarely gotten such direct responses to entreaties as he had received here, today.

He supposed it was because he had no other humans competing for their attention; he was probably the only creature larger than a rabbit left in this part of the plateau. In fact, he might be the only human on the entire plain; there might not be a single person for a thousand miles or more to the east, north, and south.

To the west there were hundreds of thousands of people, down below the cliffs, and there were undoubtedly still Uplanders making their way down the trail. Up here, though, he was alone.

He shuddered at the thought.

Thousands of miles of empty prairie!

No people, and no *ara*.

But there were *ler* everywhere, of course, and if any of them wanted to talk to a human, well, he was *it*. He was their only option.

But he had never heard of them *wanting* to talk before.

Well, he had all winter to figure it out, and right now the cold was seeping through his cloak and blankets, filling his boot-tops and spilling up past his breech-cuffs. His fingers were freezing, and handling the metal ladle and the metal pots was becoming painful. He stacked up the snow-filled pots and hurried back into the palace.

Closing the door behind him shut out the wind, but the air in the palace was almost as cold now as the air outside. He shivered and headed for the stairs, wishing he had somehow contrived a pair of gloves, or at least brought some bits of rag to put between flesh and metal.

Moments later he sat in the dim kitchen, warming his hands over a candle and trembling with the cold. The pots of snow were arranged nearby, and so far showed no signs of melting. He hadn't wanted to start a fire, not so soon, not when he had not even been in the palace for a second night, but the chill was intense, and he glanced longingly at the bureau and drawers he had brought down earlier.

It was still so early in the season!

While he could not remember ever experiencing cold much worse than this, he had never before spent a winter in the Uplands. For all he knew this was nothing, just a cool spell, and the real cold was yet to come.

He shuddered and pulled his cloak and blankets more tightly about him.

If he was still shivering when the candle was half-gone, he told himself, he would start a fire . . . Or if the snow hadn't started to melt by then . . . Or if he thought he might be freezing to death.

He tried to remember how one knew he was freezing to death. No one in Mad Oak had frozen to death in decades, perhaps centuries; the Wizard Lord wouldn't allow the winters to be really bad, and not even poor stupid drunken Blackhand had been *that* careless. He knew that fingers and toes went numb, and he seemed to remember something about getting sleepy. . . .

But how would anyone know what it felt like to freeze to death? Obviously, anyone who reported on the sensations had survived! He shook his head.

His ears felt strange—the lobes and the top edge were tingling and felt hot. He reached up and touched one. He had felt this once before, as a young boy, he realized. His ears had partially frozen and gone numb while he was out gathering snow, and now that he was in the warmer confines of the kitchen, with his candle warming his hands, they were thawing out. And it was going to hurt, he remembered. He bit his lower lip.

He should have wrapped something around his head, even if he didn't have a proper hat or hood that wasn't feathered.

Still, his ears were *thawing,* now that he was in here and out of the wind. The numbness wasn't spreading. He didn't need a fire, not yet.

But if he was already freezing his ears, then the cold was serious. He wasn't just being weak and soft, as he had feared. And it would probably get much colder. He glanced at the bureau again.

There were plenty of rooms full of furniture up there. The carpets and draperies would probably burn, as well. He could last out the winter, and he could afford a fire tonight, if he thought it necessary. It would mean the palace's furnishings would be in ruins by the time the Wizard Lord's staff returned in the spring, but he had already known he couldn't keep his presence a secret.

"Forgive me, O *ler,* for what I must do to survive," he murmured.

The candle flame flickered, then flared up more brightly, and the pain in his ears began.

[13]

In the end, he decided he did not need a fire yet. His ears returned to normal, and the pans of snow did begin to melt eventually, though only very slowly. He spent hours doing little more than huddling over a candle, thinking.

He ate another half-strip of jerky and sipped a little snow-melt for his supper, and then decided there was nothing more to be accomplished until he could coax a few answers out of the *ler*. He stripped off his clothes and curled up on the mattress under a stack of blankets.

He did not fall asleep quickly; he couldn't decide whether that was entirely a bad thing or not, given his vague memory that an early sign of freezing to death was sleepiness. He found himself thinking too much, and worrying too much, to doze off easily, and the very question of why he was not falling asleep merely added to those concerns.

He was unsure whether he had enough food, or enough fuel, or even enough water, to survive the winter—what if there wasn't enough snow? Gathering and melting it required so much time, effort, and heat that he could not easily build up a reserve, and water evaporates.

How would he ever actually get at the Wizard Lord? Artil was cautious, and constantly guarded.

What did the *ler* want? Why had they spoken to him in his dreams, but then refused to answer questions when he was awake? Why had they demanded he remove his protective hides and feathers if they did not have something specific in mind that they wanted of him? He lay awake for what seemed like hours, worrying about all these questions.

And there was a thin thread of fear, as well—what if the *ler* answered all his questions in his dreams, and he didn't like the answers? What if his dreams were to be nightmares?

In the end, though, he did finally sleep.

And in time, dreams came.

At first it seemed to him that they were just ordinary dreams—not pleasant ones, but the sort he would expect after a day such as the one he had had. He dreamed he was running through endless corridors as ice formed on the walls and snow drifted from nowhere onto the carpeted floor; he dreamed he was digging up snow with his bare hands, desperate to find something buried beneath the white powder, but more snow appeared as quickly as he could move it; he dreamed he was walking across the Uplands of late autumn searching for water, and a sparkling stream glittered in the morning sun ahead of him, but no matter how fast he walked, it came no closer, and when he began to run, it slid away even faster, receding into the distance.

And then he saw the Leader and the Scholar standing on the far side of the stream, calling a warning to him that he could not understand, and then the stream was not water but blood, spilling from the mangled corpses of the Seer and the Speaker, and the Archer was running alongside him saying, "I could have killed him long ago, if you'd let me."

Sword had had many dreams like this since the Wizard Lord's soldiers had killed or captured half the Chosen; he needed no *ler* to send them, or to interpret them.

But then the dream-Archer said, "You have questions to ask, don't you?"

Sword stopped running. "Yes," he said, unsure whether this was still an ordinary dream, or whether the Uplander *ler* might be starting to intrude.

Suddenly Lore and Babble, miraculously restored to life, were standing beside Bow, and Lore said, "Then ask them."

"Is this real, then? Are you . . . are you avatars of Uplander *ler,* or are you just figments of my imagination?"

"Does it matter very much?" Bow asked.

"Oh, yes," Sword said. He looked up at an infinite blue sky. "O *ler,* if you hear me, whatever spirits there are who wish me well, I need to know whether this is a vision of truth, or just my own thoughts playing tricks on me. I need to know whether I can depend on what I'm told here."

"Can you ever know?" the dream-Babble asked. "Ask and appeal and answer can all be illusion. Every day, when you think you walk the waking world, how do you know you do not dream it?"

"I know," Sword replied. "When I'm awake, I trust my eyes, I know that what I see is really there. I trust my ears, and I know what I hear. I may not always know what it means, or whether someone is lying to me, but I know I'm not just making it up myself."

And if we say to you, this is a true vision?

The words came from everywhere and nowhere, entering his mind with no need for sound.

"I don't know for sure," Sword said unhappily. "I *think* you are Uplander *ler*, talking to me while I sleep, but I don't *know*."

You did not doubt us last night.

Lore and Babble and Bow had vanished now, and he was once again standing naked on the snowy plain, talking to empty sky.

"I know," Sword said. "I believed you, and I didn't wear hides or feathers, and it *felt* as if I had really spoken with *ler*, but now I'm not so certain. Maybe I fooled myself. Or perhaps that was real, but I'm fooling myself now."

Why are you so unsure?

"I have no proof! Maybe I'm just dreaming you, because I so desperately want help against the Wizard Lord, because I don't want to be completely alone in the Uplands."

We do not understand doubt. What is, is, and what is not, is not, and we are aware of what concerns us and do not perceive that which does not.

"You're spirits. I'm a man."

Speaking to you when you are awake is more difficult, but if you cannot believe us without it, perhaps we can accommodate you.

"Or just a sign, to let me know this was real," Sword said. "Something to tell me I didn't imagine it."

A light, perhaps?

"That would be perfect," Sword said, remembering the light of *ler* playing in the trees along the riverbank in Mad Oak at twilight.

Then you will see light when you awaken, seven lights in seven colors. Now, ask your questions.

Sword hesitated.

He was fairly certain now that this was a vision, rather than just a dream, and that he was really conversing with *ler*, but he didn't know *which ler*, or how patient they would be with his questions. Where, then, to start?

"Are there any hidden entrances to the Summer Palace?" he asked. "Ways in and out that aren't obvious? Tunnels, or concealed doors?"

No.

Well, that was definite, anyway. "Could I make one?"

You know your own capabilities, surely.

"But . . . is there anything that would prevent me from digging a tunnel? Can you help me dig one safely, or advise me in the best way to go about it?"

There was a moment of near-silence, when the only sound was the wind; then the reply came.

There are spirits in the earth who will guide you.

"Thank you!" That was perfect; that was all he could hope for. He quickly asked his next question. "Can you aid me in surviving the cold?"

We can. Whether we will do so remains to be seen.

That was disappointing, but not surprising. "Why . . ." He paused, then continued, "Why is it so cold, so soon? It doesn't get this cold this fast down in Barokan."

The birds have gone, and we are free to act.

"I don't understand."

Our strength lies in the winter, when the birds are gone, when the sky is cold and the winds are free.

"You *made* it turn cold?"

As we do every year, as soon as we are free to do so.

"Free?"

The birds have gone south, and we are free to speak and to act.

"The birds?" Realization dawned. "You mean, the *ara* don't just shield the birds, or the people wearing their hides and feathers?"

The birds trample the life from our land. Their feathers ward us off. The hot sun of summer burns us away. Our strength lies in the winter, when the birds are gone, when the sky is cold and the winds are free.

"You're only powerful in the winter? Only when the birds are gone?"

Yes.

"The *ler* of Barokan aren't like that."

We are not the ler *of Barokan.*

"I know that. I know." He stared out at the empty sky and shivered. "And when you're free, each year, you turn the air cold, and bring snow and wind, as quickly as you can?"

Yes.

"And do you keep it cold until the *ara* return?"

Until the sun grows warm, and the birds come, yes.

Sword stood silently for a timeless dream moment—it seemed like years, but he knew it was probably just a few seconds. Then he asked, "Are the *ler* of Barokan growing weaker, as Artil im Salthir says?"

Barokan is not our concern.

"But they might be?"

We know nothing of Barokan.

"Could it be because the Uplanders bring *ara* feathers down every year, and sell them to the Barokanese? Are the feathers weakening the *ler*?"

We know nothing of Barokan.

Sword could not be sure, but he thought he detected a trace of irritation in that response, and quickly switched topics. "Why did you speak to me? Why did you come to me in my dreams, last night and tonight?"

You interest us. We have not spoken with a human for a thousand years.

"A thousand years?" Sword knew it had been a long time, but a *thousand*?

Yes.

"In all that time, no Uplander has ever slept naked, or conjured you somehow?"

Not in winter. Not when the birds were gone south, and we were free to speak.

"Who are you, exactly? I know you are Uplander *ler,* but are you the spirits of this particular place?"

We are the ler.

"In Barokan, there are *ler* of each place, and *ler* that move about freely—which are you?"

We are not the ler *of Barokan. We are what we are.*

"So if I walked a hundred miles east . . ."

We would be there.

That was interesting, very interesting. It was *different.*

And it bore more thought than Sword could manage in his

confused, dreaming state, so he put it aside and went on to matters of more direct, personal importance.

"The man who ordered this palace to be built is the Wizard Lord of Barokan," he said. "I want to kill him. Can you help me accomplish this? *Will* you help me?"

You speak of Artil im Salthir dor Valok seth Talidir?

"I do. I intend to kill him next summer, when he returns to this palace." He hesitated, then asked, "Does that trouble you, that I'm planning murder?"

Not in the slightest.

Sword remembered that he was speaking to untamed *ler*. Of course they wouldn't care if one foreigner killed another. "Will you help me slay him?"

Will his death benefit us?

"I don't know," Sword admitted. "It will benefit *me*."

You have dealt with us thus far honestly and respectfully. We may aid you. We may not. We promise nothing.

That was better than an outright refusal, but not by much. "Have you ever promised anything to *anyone*?" he asked. "I've never heard of any Uplander magic."

No one treats with us. No one commands us. We serve no man, neither by choice nor compulsion.

Before he could stop himself, Sword asked, "Why?"

There was no answer; instead the wind rose into a howl and he was swept off his feet and borne through the air like a leaf on the wind, and the world spun around him until he could no longer tell snow from sky.

And then he woke up.

He lay for a moment looking up at the arched stone ceiling, and gradually became aware that something was wrong. How could he see anything? Colored light was flickering across the stone. . . .

He sat up, pushing aside the blankets despite the cold air.

Lights were moving in the gloom of the kitchen—not candlelight, or lanternlight, but hazy patches of glowing color that sometimes seemed to be moving across the wall, and at other times appeared to be drifting in midair.

They were all different. Blue, and gold, and red, and a pale pink, and a dark rich purple, and the intense green of leaves in springtime, and a watery blue green . . .

And that was all. Seven of them.

These were not the glittering firefly sparkles he used to see in the trees around Mad Oak, which was why he had not immediately recognized them as *ler*-light, but now he knew they could be nothing else. These were the seven colors he had been told he would see, to attest to the reality of the vision he had just seen.

So the *ler* could do more than just talk. How *much* more remained to be seen, as did whether or not he could make any use of them.

The Wizard Lord had no magic in the Uplands, and thought none of the Chosen had any magic here, either; what would happen if he found himself facing a real Uplander wizard, the first one in a thousand years, perhaps the first ever?

That was a very tempting possibility. Sword had never particularly wanted to be a wizard; like most Barokanese, he had grown up thinking of wizards as horrible, callous old brutes who couldn't be trusted. The Uplands, though, were a different realm. Wizards here might be something else entirely, something new.

And besides, thinking back on what he had done in Winterhome to avenge Azir shi Azir and Babble, remembering the bloody corpses he had left sprawled on the street, Sword could hardly claim *not* to be a horrible brute. He had already been corrupted by this mad system of wizards, Wizard Lord, and Chosen, and there was no point in pretending otherwise. He had killed the Dark Lord of the Galbek Hills, he had killed those soldiers in Winterhome, and he intended to kill the Dark Lord of Winterhome, and if these Uplander *ler* could help him do that, he would happily use them, no matter what further damage it might do to his own already-polluted soul. He had become a killer, despite what he had told his mother when he first accepted the role of the Chosen Swordsman. He hoped he had not become a monster, but he had definitely become a killer.

And now he wanted to corrupt these mysterious new *ler,* to turn *them* into killers for the sake of his vengeance.

But they had said that no man commanded or coerced them.

"Why?" he asked the air, looking at those eerie colored lights. "Why have you not spoken to anyone in so long? Is it just the *ara*?"

The lights flickered and danced, but no words came.

Sword sighed. Uncooperative *ler* were nothing new, but back in Mad Oak he had been able to talk to the priestesses, to ask them to intervene. Here there were no priestesses.

Here, *he* was as close to being a priest as anyone had ever been. There had never been Uplander priests or wizards—and the *ler* weren't telling him why. Could it really have just been the *ara*?

They had also mentioned the hot summer sun, but Sword had never before heard of the sun suppressing spirits—well, except the spirits of darkness and cold. Were all the *ler* up here *ler* of darkness and cold?

That made no sense. *Everything* had a spirit. In humans they were called souls, but they were all spirits, all *ler*.

Well, perhaps things were different up here, in the thinner air, on the endless open plain so unlike the wooded hills where Sword had grown up.

"I can see you're there," he said to the lights. "I wish you would answer my questions."

Ask the right ones, then.

Sword grimaced. How was he supposed to know which were the right questions, if the *ler* didn't tell him?

"Is it morning?"

No answer came.

He sighed. He got to his feet, wrapping himself in the blankets, and headed for the stairs.

Then he stopped. What did it matter whether it was day or night? He could keep any schedule he chose while he was down here beneath the ground. He wasn't sleepy, so why should he bother going back to sleep even if the dawn was still hours away?

"Where would be the best place to dig a tunnel?" he asked the air.

That is a good question.

The lights moved, then gathered together to form an arrowhead, pointing him toward one of the stairways leading down to a cellar storeroom.

"In there?" he said, following.

In there.

He took a moment to pull on his breeches and boots, and don his velvet cloak, before following the glowing indicator, and took a lit candle, in case the *ler* did not give enough light. At the foot of the steps he pushed open the storeroom door and peered in.

The *ler* were now clustered on the rear wall of the storeroom, circling an area on the lower left corner. Sword approached cautiously, set his candle on a nearby shelf, then knelt and prodded at the stonework.

Sure enough, he found two large blocks were loose. Guided by the shimmering *ler*-light, he used a knife to pry them out, revealing a small hollow in the stone beyond—and at the back of that hollow were cracks.

Dig here. We will guide you.

He sat down and began thoughtfully exploring the hollow with his fingertips, trying to judge how many more blocks he would need to remove from the wall, and what tools would be best for the job.

[14]

Day by day the weather grew steadily colder, quickly becoming colder than anything Sword had ever experienced before, and every few days more snow fell. He gave in and started his first fire in the kitchen hearth on his fourth day in the palace, burning scraps and the fragments of a bureau drawer.

He spent little time above ground; instead he focused his attention on digging his tunnel, talking to *ler* both while waking and asleep, and keeping a careful eye on his limited supplies of food, water, and fuel. He made expeditions out to the terrace or garden to gather snow to melt roughly every other day, and collected flammable furnishings from the upstairs rooms to keep his fire burning, but otherwise he stayed down in the kitchens and cellars. Much of the time *ler* gave enough light that he was able to conserve his supply of candles.

Gathering water grew steadily easier as more snow accumulated outside; after a month or so he was able to just scoop each pan or bucket full and hurry back down to his warm little haven. Snow also drifted into the rooftop cistern—Sword was never sure whether it was open on top, or whether there was a system of gutters feeding into it, but every so often he would try the taps and find the supply renewed. Sometimes after a big storm he could get by with the trickle from those, and go several days without going outside to collect snow.

Most of his waking hours were devoted to the tunnel, which gradually extended out from the cellar storeroom. Since he had found no actual picks or shovels, he worked on it using whatever tools came to hand—a fireplace poker, a butcher knife, an iron spoon. Most of all, though, he worked on it by coaxing the *ler* of stone and earth to help him.

This turned out to be easier than he had expected, and he gradually wormed the reasons for that out of the spirits that were aiding him.

The Barokanese workmen who had dug out the palace cellars in the first place had not asked the *ler* for help; instead they had simply hacked away at the earth without any acknowledgment at all that it was a living thing worthy of respect. They had worked only in warm weather, when *ara* were everywhere and *ler* could do little to defend themselves, and furthermore they had all worn heavy protective clothing layered with *ara* feathers. From the descriptions, Sword got the impression that the whole operation had been similar to the road crews that had cut paths straight through the wilderness between the towns of Barokan.

This had been disruptive and even painful for the *ler,* and they did not want a repetition.

Sword had been polite and respectful so far, which they found a very welcome change, but they also knew that he could probably wrap himself in feathers and start hacking at his tunnel anyway if they did not cooperate. Better, from their point of view, to help him than to fight him, so the stone and earth sometimes seemed to crumble at his slightest touch.

That they might have killed him by bringing the unfinished tunnel down on his head did not seem to occur to them, and Sword was not about to bring this oversight to their attention.

He did talk to them about what they wanted, what the palace workmen had done to them, what form their revenge might take if they ever had an opportunity, and as they conversed the stone seemed to almost melt away before him, as the *ler* guided his every blow and caused every crack and fracture to spread wildly.

Unless everything they said was exaggeration and lies, they obviously *could* collapse the tunnel at any time, and eventually Sword could not resist asking, "Could you break the palace foundations if you wanted to?"

Of course. We could shake the earth itself. We could shatter stone and tumble the walls. We could break the cliff and send this place falling to the lands below.

"Why haven't you?"

There was no immediate reply; instead a *ler* guided his hand to strike at a rock just so, and another section of tunnel wall tumbled in at his feet.

After a moment, though, words came.

What would they do in response, if we did?

"I don't know," Sword admitted, as he used both hands to shovel debris into a bucket, to be hauled back out and dumped.

Neither do we, and we fear what might happen.

Sword nodded. "I understand."

He discussed other matters with the various *ler* as well, whether in the tunnel, or in the kitchens, or out in the open gathering snow. He was never able to simply sit down, ask all his questions, and get direct answers, but over the course of the winter he gradually pieced together most of it.

The Uplander *ler* really were different from Barokanese *ler* in several ways—almost none of them were tied to specific places, and the *ler* of living things here, other than humans and *ara,* were weak and vague, while the land itself was powerful. And where most land in Barokan wanted to put forth life, the Uplands considered life to be an aberration, something barely to be tolerated.

That the dominant life on the high plains was the bird called *ara* probably had something to do with that; Sword learned that not only did *ara* feathers block magic, but the *ara* themselves, and everything about them, served to weaken and quiet *ler* by their mere presence. When entire flocks were running across the land, the land was beaten insensible.

And as for humans, they lived with the *ara,* they ate *ara* meat and wore *ara* feathers and made tools from *ara* bone and clothes from *ara* hide.

Long ago, when *ler* had tried to speak to the Uplanders, they had asked that the humans put aside their feathers and hides and bones, and the Uplanders had taken this as a sign of weakness. They had built their entire culture around exploiting *ara,* and were not inclined to give up these proofs of their mastery over their environment. Instead, they had rejected magic, or any other dealings with *ler,* as weak and unmanly. The Barokanese had their priests and wizards, and to the Uplanders this became one more demonstration of their own superiority, that they had not stooped to dealing with these feeble spirits as the Lowlanders had.

But it was only when the *ara* were present that the Upland *ler* were weak. When the birds migrated south, the *ler* flourished anew, and did what they could to assert their power. Neither humans nor *ara* liked cold or wind or snow, so each year, as soon as the *ara* were gone, the *ler* plunged the Uplands into the deepest, coldest, bitterest winter they could create. They chased the humans from the plains, drove them to take shelter down in Winterhome, and kept them away until the returning *ara* disrupted the spell.

"Why did you talk to *me,* then?" Sword asked.

You put aside the feathers. You were here after we brought the snow down. You were alone in this alien structure. We were curious.

Not all of us thought it wise, said another "voice."

Sword decided not to pursue that line of questioning, since his relationship with these *ler* was still delicate. Instead he concentrated his attention on digging his tunnel, attending to essentials—digging, keeping himself warm and fed, and of course his daily hour of sword practice. Sometimes when he could not face another hour of toiling in the tunnel, and more urgent needs were met for the moment, he would also work on expanding his wardrobe, making himself new clothes from draperies and linens, or from the few garments left in bedroom drawers, using a broken bit of a paring knife as his needle.

The days wore on. He was always cold, even when huddled by the hearth, as he did not dare build a really big fire—the smoke might draw unwanted attention, and he hated seeing the fine palace furnishings burned, so the kitchens were never truly warm, and the rest of the palace was always bitterly cold. Begging the *ler* to relive the chill only annoyed them; that was one topic on which they were not willing to listen to him at all. They wanted the world as cold as they could make it.

The tunnel was relatively warm, though, even without a fire; the stone and earth kept out the wind and cold, and his candles and his own body heat warmed the tunnel air somewhat. Still, even there, he was never actually *warm*.

He was always hungry, because he needed to ration out his cheese and jerky carefully if he intended to survive until the *ara* returned.

He was often thirsty; it was really astonishing how little water a pot of melted snow yielded, and the trickle from the pipes was inadequate, at best.

The tunnel grew, slowly but steadily, winding out from the storeroom wall, following the path the *ler* of stone and earth assured him was the easiest digging while being safe against collapse. It varied in size and direction; sometimes he could barely squeeze along it, wiggling on his belly, and had to back out on his belly as well, pulling each new load of broken stone, as there wasn't room to turn around. In other parts he could stand upright, as long as he kept his head bent. Usually he brought a candle in with him; in places where he was unsure there was enough good air for both himself and a flame, or where there was nowhere to place a candle that was not at risk of being knocked over by his tools or elbows as he worked, he would ask the *ler* to light the way for him, and if they agreed, he would work in their faint and eerie glow.

When a candle would not fit and the *ler* did not cooperate, he worked in the dark, by feel, letting the spirits in the stone guide his hands.

As he dug he wondered where the tunnel would come out, and whether his creation would really be any use to him. If the palace staff looked in the cellars and found the inside end, blocking it would be easy—the narrow parts were so very narrow! Despite what the *ler* told him, he also suspected that some stretches would be easy to cave in.

And just getting inside the palace would hardly ensure access to the Wizard Lord. He would be in the cellars, and would need to somehow get through the kitchens and up into the staff corridors without being stopped.

But it was something to do, and it *might* be useful. It kept him busy, and it kept him fit, as sitting huddled in the kitchen, picking at draperies with his improvised needle, would not.

More sword practice would probably have served these purposes just as well, but he preferred working on the tunnel to increasing his daily workout; it gave his life a little variety.

One day, after he had done his hour of swordwork and added another few inches to the tunnel, he looked at his supper.

The wheel of cheese was slightly more than half gone. The jerky had turned black and tough as it aged, and needed to be gnawed for several minutes now, and he was fairly certain he had consumed more than half of that, as well. The diet had long since become so monotonous that eating lost almost all its pleasure, and Sword suspected that the lack of variety was damaging his health, as well.

"How long have I been here?" he asked. "How long until the birds return?"

Forty days have gone; at least fifty, perhaps sixty remain. Perhaps more.

That was what Sword had feared. He stared down at his food. "I don't have enough," he said.

Nothing answered.

He looked up at the arched ceiling. "I need more food," he said.

No words came, but he sensed a vast indifference.

He looked down again.

There was no other food in the Summer Palace; he knew that. This was everything. He might perhaps get a little nourishment by chewing leather or candle wax, but probably not enough to matter.

The plains outside were covered by about two feet of snow. The *ara* were gone. Whatever other animals lived here—he knew there were some—were holed up for the winter, probably hibernating, and he had no idea how to find their lairs. There were undoubtedly any number of edible plants under the snow, but he didn't know how to find them or recognize them; all he had seen in the immediate area were trees and grass, and he couldn't eat those.

If he stayed here, there was a very real possibility he would starve.

Anywhere else in the Uplands would be even worse; not only would he have no more food, but he would freeze to death well before he could die of hunger.

Down in Barokan there was plenty of food, he was sure. He remembered cakes and cheese and dried fruits of every sort, thick rich barley bread, foamy beer, bacon and beef; his mouth watered at the thought of all that food, all that glorious food he had taken for granted every year of his life. Even pickled cabbage, a winter favorite of his mother's that he had never liked, seemed wonderful in retrospect—how could he have ever turned up his nose at anything so delicious?

It was all waiting for him, down at the bottom of the cliffs.

And so were the Wizard Lord's guards.

He frowned, and walked away from the table, his hands clutching at each other behind his back.

If he starved to death up here, and the Wizard Lord's staff
found his frozen remains, that would be an ignominious and
pointless end to it all. If he were to fight his way through the
guards, he might at least have a *chance* of killing Artil im
Salthir. And back in Barokan he would have his magic again,
the magic that had let him defeat two dozen soldiers at once.
He *might* get through the guards, if he caught them by surprise, and if the Wizard Lord was home. Artil could fly, could
order wind spirits to carry him aloft, so Sword would need to
catch him somewhere he couldn't just fly away, but . . .

But what?

This was madness, he knew. He had thought this all out in
the autumn, when he was well fed and thinking clearly, and he
knew that descending the cliffs was suicidal—but there was
all that *food* down there, and nothing up here but dry cheese
and stringy, tasteless jerky.

He pulled on a woolen vest he had made from a blanket,
and donned his velvet cloak over that. Then he stopped, looking at the down-filled coat he hadn't worn in months.

"I need more food," he said again, and again, there was no
response. He could feel *ler* nearby, listening; he could feel the
life in the thin air and the stone walls, but nothing answered
him.

If he tried to leave, tried to climb down to Barokan, what
would the Upland *ler* do? Perhaps he should wear his *ara*-hide
clothes, and his *ara*-down coat. Especially since, once he got
down to Barokan, he would need to worry about the Wizard
Lord's magic.

Of course, with the Seer dead, the Talisman of Warding no
longer functioned, and the Wizard Lord would not instantly
know where all the Chosen were, even without any *ara*-
feather protection—but Artil had other magic. Not only might
he have devised ways to find the Chosen using the other Great
Talismans, but he had been a wizard long before he was Wizard Lord.

Sword peeled off the velvet cloak and donned his *ara*-down
coat.

He could feel himself separate from his surroundings. The

air around him was still alive, but it was as if he were watching it through glass, instead of seeing it directly, or as if he were listening through thick cloth instead of bare ears. He hesitated.

Yes, he might need this protection. He pulled the coat around him and buttoned it. Then he picked up the single candle that lit the kitchen, and started up the western stair.

When he emerged from the windowless passage into the little dining salon by the terrace he blew out the candle and tucked it into an inside pocket; it was dusk, the sky darkening swiftly, but there was still more than enough light for his dark-adjusted eyes. He pulled his cloak tightly around himself, and stepped out onto the terrace.

The overhanging eaves had provided some shelter here, but the snow had drifted everywhere; his boots sank into a foot or so of fine powder as soon as he was past the door. A fierce dry wind pressed him back, snatching the moisture from his face; he felt as if his skin were being drawn taut over his cheekbones, and the tears were sucked from his eyes.

For an instant he wondered whether the wind was directed at him, trying to keep him inside the Summer Palace, but then he decided he didn't care. He blinked, and pushed on, out toward the railing, where the palace overlooked Barokan.

He had not been out here lately, he realized. He had not looked down at his homeland in some time.

It was gray and white, like the Uplands. Winter had arrived later down there, but arrive it obviously had, some time ago. A few tiny flickers of orange indicated life and warmth, where people had lit fires, but most of Barokan lay beneath a thick carpet of snow, every detail blurred and softened, or hidden entirely.

But there were those flickers. Warmth and food and friendly voices were all waiting for him down there.

Along with the Wizard Lord and his army.

Sword grimaced, then blinked, trying to restore a little moisture to his eyes.

If he was going to give up and go down the trail, he told himself, he had to do it soon, while he still had the strength.

He would want his sword, of course, and his spear, but he didn't need to take anything more than that; whatever happened when he reached Winterhome would probably happen quickly.

If he left *now,* he thought, he would arrive at the plaza gate long after midnight, in the dead hours before dawn, when the guards would be least alert, least ready to fight, and when the Wizard Lord would probably be asleep in his bed, thinking himself safe.

Not that Sword knew exactly where that bed was, but he thought he could find it.

It would mean climbing down the cliff in the dark, but he had spent so much of his time in darkness lately that the idea did not particularly trouble him. He turned and marched back into the palace to retrieve his weapons.

[15]

An hour later he was fighting his way through a six-foot snowdrift in the surreal landscape of a winter night on the plateau, where the endless expanse of snow seemed to capture and magnify every trace of light. It was as if the snow itself were glowing, rather than merely reflecting the moon and stars; the sky was dark, and all color had been leached from the world. His boots were full of powdery snow that was melting and soaking his feet; his coat was frosted with snow that had been blown from the drifts, and the butt of the spear he had slung on his back dragged across the mounded snow wherever the drifts came much above his knees, tugging at him every so often.

He was having second thoughts. The chances of getting to the Wizard Lord before an alarm was raised were not really good, he knew, and anywhere in Barokan, Artil would have his magic. He could fly away and leave Sword facing a hundred guardsmen. He could fly out of reach and send animals or weapons at Sword. He could summon storms. The Dark Lord of the Galbek Hills had used beasts and storms against the Chosen, and while Artil had never done so, had instead relied on his soldiers, there was no reason to think that would last. If Sword became a real threat, then Artil would surely resort to magic, as Wizard Lords always did.

Before, the Chosen had always fought Dark Lords as a group. Sword had intended to take him on alone, unsupported.

True, he had been acting alone when he killed the Dark Lord of the Galbek Hills, but he had gotten close enough only as part of the team, and had caught that Dark Lord completely by surprise at a time when he had thought Sword was imprisoned. Catching Artil that way was very, very unlikely; the Red Wizard had taken his predecessor's fate to heart, and created his army largely to prevent exactly that sort of surprise.

Even if the guards served as nothing more than a warning that Sword was on his way, that ought to be enough. The warning would allow Artil to prepare magic Sword could not defeat.

If Beauty were with him, she might be able to persuade the soldiers to let Sword in, so that he could catch Artil off guard. If Bow were with him, the Archer would able able to shoot the wizard out of the air as he tried to fly to safety. If Snatcher were available, he might be able to open the door to the Wizard Lord's bedchamber and slip Sword inside. Lore might know of some means of attack Sword had not thought of, and Boss might inspire Sword somehow.

But they were not here. Sword was alone. When he reached Winterhome he would need to find and kill Artil, and he would need to do it unaided.

He was not at all sure that was possible.

Simply climbing down that long, narrow, winding trail in the snow to *get* to Winterhome would not be easy.

Then he caught his first sight of the long triangular canyon that was the start of the descent, and realized "not easy" was an understatement. The canyon was full of snow; its walls had served to trap the blowing powder, and sheltered it from the sun, and now, instead of a steep trench cutting down into the cliff, there was nothing but a gentle depression in the unbroken snow.

Sword crouched, tugging at the collar of his coat, and stared at that snow-filled ravine.

He could not just walk down the path; he would need to tunnel, just as he had in the cellar, though here it would be through snow rather than stone. Or at the very least, he would need to dig a trench.

That was impossible. It would take days, days of working out here in the cold and wind. His fingers were already going numb even now; what would happen to them after he spent hours out here?

And what was the rest of the trail like? That narrow path down the cliff face—was it, too, covered in snow? Shivering, Sword turned westward and began trudging along the northern rim of the canyon to take a look.

An hour later he found himself approaching the edge on his hands and knees, so that the howling wind could not blow him over the precipice. He watched great swirling plumes of snow blow out from the clifftop, like white-speckled spiraling banners a hundred feet long, gleaming in the moonlight, and he knew that if he were to stand too close, he would be swept off the edge as well.

He, however, would not glitter and swoop gracefully in the night air; instead he would tumble down the cliffs to a horrible painful death.

He fell to his belly and crept forward through the snow, so low to the ground that each time he brought up a knee the opposite end of the spear on his back would slap against the snow to the side. Despite this, in time he found himself peering over the top of that final snowbank.

He could not look straight down; there was no way to safely get *that* close to the edge. Instead he was looking along the curve of the cliff face, toward where the trail doubled back on itself two miles south and half a mile down from where he lay.

He blinked snow from his eyes and squinted, trying to interpret what he saw in the colorless moonlight. At first the white and gray and black seemed mere meaningless lines and shapes, but at last he managed to resolve the image into stone, snow, and ice. He found the trail, and followed it with his gaze.

The path was not lost beneath drifting snow, as he had feared; snow had not clung to the sheer cliffs and piled up on the trail. No, it was worse.

It was covered in *ice.*

He could see how it would happen; the afternoon sun shining on the snowpack atop the cliffs produced a thin trickle of meltwater, which ran down the cliffs and pooled on the first horizontal surface it struck—which would usually be the trail. And there most of it froze again, building up over time into the thick sloping layer of slick gray ice he now saw shimmering glassily in the moonlight.

The entire route down the cliff was utterly impassable. He could not possibly hope to climb down mile upon mile of ice without sooner or later slipping over the edge and plummeting to a bloody death.

Whether going down to Winterhome to confront the Wizard Lord was a good idea or not no longer mattered. It wasn't possible. He was trapped in the Uplands until that ice melted in the spring thaw.

He was trapped—and he didn't have enough food.

He would just need to eat less, he told himself. He would need to make what he had left last. He would reduce the size of his meals.

Although perhaps that would just be prolonging the inevitable. Might it be better to just get it over with, and die now? Perhaps if he started down the trail, and fell to his death, his ghost would haunt Artil.

But then, he might just as well haunt the Summer Palace.

A thought struck him. If he started down the trail, he would be back in Barokan, and would have his magic again. He would have the superhuman reflexes of the world's greatest swordsman, the gifts of *ler* of muscle and bone and steel. Perhaps he *could* somehow climb down that path.

He looked down the cliff again, and shook his head. No,

his magic was not *that* strong. The trail was simply gone, buried beneath the ice, and even the Chosen Swordsman could not run down the face of a sheer cliff for thousands of feet and live.

Shivering, he pushed himself back from the edge, turned around, and began shuffling through the snow; when he was fifty feet from the cliffs he arose, bent against the wind, and started the long, weary walk back to the palace.

He would eat less, he told himself as he slogged through the colorless world of snow and wind and night. He would make his food last, somehow. He would ignore the grumbling of his belly.

He would probably die all the same, he knew that. He would die, and his ghost would haunt the palace. . . .

Or would it? In Barokan the soul of someone who had suffered an untimely and unjust death lingered, and could be felt, but in the Uplands? This land was so different that he could not be sure. He had never heard any of the Clan of the Golden Spear mention ghosts, and as it happened no one in the clan had died during his stay with them. Perhaps ghosts dissipated in the thin air.

He did not like that thought at all.

And if he died, Artil im Salthir would reign untroubled over Barokan. The spirits of Babble and Azir would linger unavenged and unappeased in the streets of Winterhome, while Lore and Boss rotted in the Wizard Lord's dungeons.

Barokan as a whole might be happy, he knew—all the lesser wizards were gone, dead or in hiding, while the Wizard Lord presided over expanded trade, safer travel, lesser hazards everywhere. Magic was fading away, and that made life more comfortable for most people.

Much as he hated to admit it, Sword thought that might be a good thing. When Artil finally died, the system of Wizard Lords would presumably be at an end forever.

Or would it? What did Artil plan? Perhaps he intended to train a successor and pass on his amulets and talismans.

And while he lived—yes, he was suppressing other magic, and improving everything he could think of, but he was a tyrant, allowing no threat to his rule. He had destroyed the Council, and broken the Chosen; would he really stop there?

Sword shivered as he pressed on through the snow toward the gate he had left standing open. Artil had found and destroyed potential enemies before they actually threatened him; why would he stop? Anyone and everything was a potential enemy, after all; anything might turn against him in time. The Dark Lord of the Galbek Hills had exterminated his own hometown, innocent and guilty alike, rather than take the trouble to sort them out, or risk leaving witnesses alive—once he began killing, it was easier. Why would Artil be any different?

If he turned his attention to Bone Garden, for example, might he simply wipe out the entire community, guilty and innocent alike?

Perhaps, perhaps not. Perhaps his own better judgment would prevent it—though it hadn't when he went after the Council and the Chosen. If it didn't, well, nothing *else* could stop him.

The Council of Immortals had created the Chosen for good and convincing reasons, Sword thought, and now Artil im Salthir had defeated the Chosen.

He had to be killed.

Sword remembered a conversation he had had with Farash inith Kerra, then Leader of the Chosen, in Winterhome, years ago. They had been arguing about whether the Dark Lord of the Galbek Hills had to be removed. Sword and old Seer had pointed out that the man had killed the entire town of Stoneslope, and Farash had argued that there was no reason to think he would ever do anything like that again.

Sword had been horrified at that. He had done it *once;* that was all the evidence they needed that he might do it again and could not be trusted. Sword had been astonished that Farash could even question the necessity.

Later, of course, it had all made sense, when he learned that Farash had secretly been conspiring with the Wizard Lord to betray the Chosen and rule Barokan.

Artil was a different Wizard Lord, a better one; he had done many good things, and had greatly improved the lot of the ordinary people of Barokan. All the same, he had already murdered innocents not once, but twice—first the Council, then the Chosen. The principle was the same as it had been with Galbek Hills.

He had to be killed.

And if Sword did not give his best efforts toward that end, he was no better than Farash had been—than Farash *was,* since Old Boss was now serving as Artil's chief advisor.

If Sword allowed himself to die of cold or hunger, he was betraying the ghosts of Azir and Babble, betraying the imprisoned Lore and Boss. He could not let himself die.

He staggered up to the open gate and caught himself against the frame, gazing in at the ghostly fountains and trellises, gleaming white in the moonlight, their outlines blurred into soft shapelessness by the snow.

He would survive the winter, Sword promised himself. Somehow, he would live through it—by eating less, by whatever it took. And when first the spring and then the summer came back to the Summer Palace, and the Wizard Lord came back with it, Sword would kill him. He didn't know how he would survive, and he didn't know how he would kill Artil, but he would do it.

He had to.

[16]

He did eat less, and within just a handful of days gnawing hunger became a constant distraction. As Sword practiced with his blade he imagined himself carving up *ara,* or hogs, or cattle; as he hacked and scraped in the tunnel he thought about chopping vegetables, or scooping barley. He tried to fill his belly with water, but the melted snow was cold and sat heavily in his gut. As the days slipped away and his supplies dwindled, he began to feel weaker, and his hands were less steady. His vision seemed blurry, and his thoughts, too, lost focus. His teeth hurt, and chewing the jerky became steadily more difficult.

He tried not to think about it. Instead he thought about anything and everything that might distract him from his present situation.

He thought about his mother, back in Mad Oak, and wondered how much of the Wizard Lord's lies about him had reached her, and how much of them she believed. She had tried to talk him out of accepting the role of Swordsman; she had asked him whether he wanted to be a killer.

He had said no, that he wanted to be a hero.

Some hero he was. He had killed a Dark Lord, yes, but not in some epic battle suitable for a ballad; he had simply caught the man off guard and run him through. The whole thing had been over in a second.

And when another Wizard Lord had gone bad, Sword had been unable to stop it. He had been unable to prevent the murder of two of his friends, and the capture of two others. He hadn't killed *that* Dark Lord. Oh, he had killed more than a dozen soldiers *working* for the Dark Lord, but what good did that do anyone? Artil im Salthir had his magic and his position, and could recruit all the men he needed.

And Sword had sworn to kill Artil despite that.

He had become the killer his mother had feared he would be. Did she know that?

Was she safe, back there in Mad Oak? Were her daughters, Sword's sisters, taking care of her?

How were the townspeople treating her? They all probably believed the Wizard Lord's tales of how the Chosen had rebelled, how they had tried to stop him from improving Barokan. Sword hoped they weren't taking any of that out on a poor old widow.

And Harp, and Fidget, and Spider—what did they think of their brother now? Spider had been so proud that her own brother was one of the Chosen; would it hurt her that the Chosen were now seen as traitors trying to prevent Artil im Salthir from building roads and slaying monsters?

Of course it would hurt her, Sword told himself—but how much? Would she be heartbroken, or just annoyed? Would she believe the lies?

Would Harp still sing the old ballads about the Chosen Heroes? Would her brother's supposed treason have soured her marriage to Smudge the blacksmith? Were their children being teased about their murderous uncle?

At least their father wasn't around to hear anything bad about his only son.

At that thought, Sword's eyes welled with tears.

He had never really wept over his father's death; he had come home from his adventures, from slaying the Dark Lord of the Galbek Hills, to find the old man dead and gone. It had been over and done, and Sword's entire world had changed so much that his father's death had been just one more aspect of his new life, to be accepted and lived with, like his new name or the fact that he had killed a man. Grumbler's son had been a youth named Breaker, a common barley farmer given to bouts of daydreaming and brief fits of ill temper; Sword, the world's greatest swordsman, Chosen Defender of Barokan, slayer of Dark Lords, was someone else, someone who had no father.

But right now, as Sword sat in the cold palace kitchen chewing on a leathery bit of blackened bird-flesh, he wished more than anything else that he could go back to being that ordinary youth, that Grumbler was still alive, that father and son were living peacefully with White Rose in their little house in Mad Oak, a quarter-mile north of the town's pavilion.

Breaker had never been very close to his father; the old man had been ill so much of the time, and even when he was healthy he had never been a very attentive parent. Still, Grumbler had always been there when Breaker was young, always a comforting part of the background.

And now he wasn't.

The Dark Lord of the Galbek Hills was dead and gone, as well, and Sword doubted whether anyone missed *him* very much—he had been an orphan who had wiped out his native village, deliberately killing everyone who had known him before he went off to become a wizard. But everyone knew he had lived and died, and who, now, remembered that Grumbler had ever existed? No one outside of Mad Oak, most likely.

That thought led to another, and another, and as he readied himself for bed that night Sword found himself wondering what had become of the Dark Lord's serving girls. His tentmates in the Clan of the Golden Spear had heard that Sword had lopped the hands off one of them, which was untrue and absurd and insulting, but what *had* happened to them? The Chosen and the Council of Immortals had sent them back to their homes in Split Reed—what happened to them there? What sort of lives did they lead? Were they happier, with their former master dead?

He would probably never know. If he somehow survived this winter, and killed Artil im Salthir, and returned to Barokan a free man, he might want to visit Split Reed and ask.

Or perhaps he would be happier not knowing. If he had somehow ruined their lives, did he really want to be told?

He might never know what had happened to *many* people whose lives he had affected, many of them in far more direct ways. What had become of the Beauty, or the Archer, or the Thief? He had lost all contact with them after fleeing from the slaughter in Winterhome. Were any of them still alive?

Snatcher had probably escaped. He was, after all, the world's greatest thief, the master of stealth and disguise, able to defeat almost any lock or bar. He was probably still free, somewhere down in Barokan. He might be infiltrating the Wizard Lord's guard even now. He might have already cut the Wizard Lord's throat, for all Sword knew.

More likely, though, he was hiding in some obscure coastal village, waiting for his comrades to do the dirty work.

Bow had probably tried to kill the Wizard Lord. He had always wanted to, to go down in legend as the first Archer to do so. But Sword doubted he had succeeded; Artil had always kept the possibility in mind, and would have taken precautions against getting shot. In fact, he would have done everything he could to see Bow dead.

Which did not mean Bow *was* dead, any more than Sword

was, but Sword had no idea where he could be and still be alive. At sea somewhere, perhaps?

As for the Beauty, Sword was unsure what the Wizard Lord might think of her, but *he* certainly didn't think she would try to kill anyone on her own. If she had friends supporting her, perhaps, but not on her own. She had probably simply gone into hiding somewhere—and she had spent much of her life more or less in hiding, so she would probably do a good job of it.

As he lay on his mattress waiting for sleep, Sword thought about the Beauty—and wished he hadn't. There was nothing abstract about her beauty; like his ability with a sword, it had a direct and simple purpose. His skill let him kill people; her magical beauty was intended to provoke lust in any normal adult male who saw her. Men would do what she asked, would let her distract them, because they desired her, plain and simple.

That magic did not work on her fellow Chosen, but she had been chosen in the first place because that magic had plenty to work with. Sword had not been so overcome as other men would be, but for that very reason she had allowed him to see her face often, and to sometimes glimpse more. He had been alone for months, and before that he had been among Uplanders whose women did not consider him suitable for their attentions; the memory of Beauty's face and voice was anything but relaxing. Sleep would not come easily while he thought about her. The curve of her cheek, the flow of her hair . . .

He wondered what she was doing. Hiding, yes—but where? Doing what? Was she alone? Had she found women who would help her, women she could trust, women who would not be envious of her appearance?

Or had she used her magic to get men to aid her? What had it cost her, if she had?

He tried to stop thinking about it, but he couldn't make his imagination let go. Was she safe? Had she been forced into some horrible situation by the combination of her magic and the Wizard Lord's search for the remaining Chosen?

If he survived and returned to Barokan, Sword told himself, finding the Beauty and making sure she was safe and well was far more important than any visit to Split Reed to see what had become of the Dark Lord's maidservants.

He had hoped, years ago, that his friendship with Beauty might develop into something more; she had told him to stop being silly, that she was much too old for him. He wondered whether she would still think so, now that they had both lived a little longer. The eighteen-year difference had seemed huge when he was only twenty or so, but it didn't appear quite so important now.

And once the Wizard Lord was dead, they would both still have their magic, magic that made them curiosities, almost outcasts. He had to practice his swordsmanship for an hour every day, and had to live with the odd combination of fear and fascination that most people felt toward someone chosen to be a killer, while Beauty could not go out in public with her face uncovered without risking rape or riot; why not share their burdens, rather than bear them alone?

Sword admitted he did not actually love Beauty, in the way the old songs described it, or the way he had seen some of his townsfolk moon after one another, but she was a fine person, and of course, even though he was immune to the magical exaggeration, she was very, very beautiful.

Why shouldn't they make a marriage of convenience? Not everyone married for love.

But that assumed she was still alive, and that he would survive this winter and somehow kill the Wizard Lord, and right now that didn't seem very likely. He was probably more likely to starve to death than to ever marry the Beauty.

But still, he couldn't help remembering her face and voice, and imagining what it might be like to share her bed.

His stomach growled, and for once thinking about food was a welcome distraction, at least at first. He was able to fall asleep, at any rate.

In the days that followed he thought about Beauty and the others several times. He wondered what had become of Boss and Lore. The Wizard Lord had almost certainly tried to keep Boss alive, since her death would have rendered his own Talisman of Glory inert and made it that much more difficult for him to recruit supporters and demand obedience, but had he succeeded? Sword thought it was possible, if unlikely, that she might have chosen suicide over continued captivity. Artil claimed he did not need magic, but was it true? If the Leader was dead, and the Wizard Lord's own persuasive magic gone, would the people of Barokan still follow Artil? Would his army still obey him?

Sword reluctantly concluded that yes, they would—after all, centuries of habit aside, this was the ruler who had built roads and canals and bridges that made trade easy, who had slain monsters and dispersed hauntings and made Barokan safer.

He didn't need magic.

Boss would almost certainly realize that, so suicide did not seem likely at all.

And despite his claims to want an end to magic, Sword did not think Artil would throw away the power of the Talisman of Glory by killing her; he would prefer having that power in reserve. After all, if he had wanted Boss dead, he could have killed her in the first place, rather than taking her prisoner at all.

Was Lore essential to Artil's plans? Sword was quite certain that the Scholar would never consider suicide, that his mind simply didn't operate that way, but might Artil have decided to discard Lore after a certain point?

Probably not, but Sword could not be sure. Certainly, the Wizard Lord had no qualms about killing some of the Chosen. Sword remembered very well how the Seer and the Speaker had died. At least two were dead, and it might be more.

In the very worst case, Artil might have killed *all* the Chosen except Sword.

And presumably, except the mysterious ninth member of the Chosen, whoever and whatever that might be, if the ninth even existed.

Sword wondered about that—which was a welcome distraction from thoughts of food, or memories of the Beauty's curves. What might a ninth role be? A male equivalent of the Beauty, perhaps? A Hider, like the Seer but in reverse, who could conceal things from the Wizard Lord? But that was nothing that *ara* feathers couldn't accomplish, so it seemed unlikely, unless the power included invisibility. *That* would be useful.

Might the ninth be something to do with names or spirits? But Sword could not think of any role there that the Speaker did not already fill. A Healer? The Beauty's magic did include some modest healing ability, but more might have been useful. A Poisoner, perhaps? But Lore's knowledge and the Speaker's abilities should have provided the Chosen with all the poisons they needed, which the Beauty or the Thief might administer.

A Flyer, to bring things quickly from one place to another? Someone who could hear the Wizard Lord's thoughts, and know what he was planning? Sword had no idea whether that would be possible, but it would certainly be *useful*.

But if any of these existed, why hadn't any of the eight Chosen known about it? Why hadn't this ninth come to join them? That made Sword think that there *was* no ninth—but then, why had the wizards given Artil that talisman, and told him there *was* a ninth? The more Sword thought about it, the more convinced he became that it was all an elaborate bluff, an attempt to keep the Wizard Lord in line by making him think he had a mysterious, undetectable foe watching him.

If so, it had backfired horribly, by prompting Artil im Salthir to order most of the Council of Immortals slain. And that, in turn, had led to the Wizard Lord attempting to destroy the Chosen.

If it was all a lie, then some would-be trickster among the wizards had effectively destroyed the foundation of Barokanese society with his little ploy, because Sword could not see how the old system could survive with so many wizards dead.

Not that that was necessarily a bad thing. Artil wanted to destroy the old system by removing the Chosen and the Council of Immortals, but keep the role of Wizard Lord for himself, while Sword thought that if the old system was going to go, then *all* of it should go. He intended to kill the Wizard Lord if he could.

But with each meal, it seemed less likely that he could.

Finally, one day as Sword knelt in the tunnel and let the spirits guide the poker in his hand, and when it had become unmistakable that the tunnel had turned upward, something spoke.

There are roots beneath the snow. The people who planted them did not take them all. The snows came before they could.

"What?"

Your body is not meant to live on nothing but meat and cheese.

"It's food. It's what I have." He hacked at the stone again, jabbing the poker into a crevice, and a chunk cracked and fell free, tumbling down the sloping floor past his foot.

It is not enough. We can guide your steps as we guide your hands.

"Can you?" Sword looked up at the stone above him, though he knew the *ler* weren't any more present there than anywhere else. "To one of the Uplander gardens?"

Yes.

"And what would you want in return?"

For a moment there was no reply; then the words came.

If we keep you alive, you must use that life for us. You must serve our ends.

"What, enslave myself?" He hacked at the stone again. "I don't think so."

Your life will remain your own wherever that does not harm us.

"I don't . . ." Sword stopped to think, and the poker slipped from his clumsy fingers. He looked down at it, and when he lowered his head his vision swam, and he thought for a moment he might faint.

He knelt motionless for a long moment, trying to gather his thoughts and his strength, and after a time—a time he was unable to judge—he realized he had little to gather.

"All right," he said. "All right, then. I swear I'll help you when I can, if it doesn't mean doing anything I think is wrong, or *not* doing something I think I should. Now, lead me to this food."

As you wish.

The wind was cold and howled around the palace eaves as Sword stepped out onto the terrace half an hour later, but it dropped as he stumbled away from the door. He pulled his velvet drapery cloak and a couple of blankets more tightly around himself as he looked up at the sky and demanded, "Now what?"

There were no words, but the wind pressed at him, and he turned, trying to shelter his face, and found himself facing the palace gate.

"All right," he muttered. Then he shuddered, and set out.

Almost two hours later he reached down into the hole he had dug in the snow and chipped at the frozen ground with the knife he had brought, trying to free the half-grown and thoroughly frozen turnip he had exposed.

It came up at last, and he moved on quickly to the next spot the *ler* indicated—by now, rather than using wind to guide him, a faint golden glow was leading him to the precise location of each vegetable.

He worked at chipping vegetables from the hard earth for as long as the daylight allowed; the first clan garden yielded a surprisingly large harvest, but not enough, and as the sun sank toward the cliff-edge in the west he moved on to a second garden.

When the sun vanished below the cliffs and the sky turned to fading gold he gathered up his precious finds and headed back toward the palace, floundering through the snow. By the time he staggered down the kitchen stairs the layer of ice on his beard and mustache was easily half an inch thick, his eyebrows were frosted thick with ice as well, and his fingers were trembling despite being numb with cold, but he held an armful of frozen carrots, turnips, beets, radishes, and vegetables whose exact nature he could not name—a feast, it seemed to him, even though every one of his prizes was undersized or severely misshapen.

That was probably why the Uplanders had left them, he thought—these hadn't been overlooked so much as rejected.

But he didn't care. He was in no position to reject anything edible.

Working only by a faint polychrome glow of *ler,* it took

what seemed like an eternity to get a fire burning; his frozen hands could not readily manage the necessary actions. More than once he had to bend stiff, reluctant fingers around a tool or a scrap of wood with his teeth before he could maneuver it into place. Even then, his hands shook so badly that he was not always able to maintain his hold.

At last, though, orange flame flickered up dimly, then caught and spread. The gentle warmth sent a ferocious prickling through his skin as he began to thaw, and cold water trickled down his neck from the melting ice in his beard.

For about an hour he didn't try to do anything but warm up. The numbness passed, the ice melted, the uncontrollable shivering came and went, and finally he simply lay on his mattress, a few feet from the fire, feeling himself relax.

And when he had relaxed enough, he arose and sorted through his still-cold booty, then made himself dinner.

It was astonishing how wonderful a radish tasted after months of nothing but meat, cheese, and water—even a small, bitter radish felt cold and sharp and clean in his mouth, like a flash of early springtime, and helped make yet another scrap of leathery jerky seem edible.

In better times, he thought he could have eaten the entire collection of vegetables in two or three meals; with his shrunken stomach he could easily make them last for weeks, filling out his last bits of jerky and cheese.

He completed the tunnel eleven days later; when he thrust the poker up into the wall where the glow of *ler* indicated, a shower of stone and dirt crumbled in on him, as had often happened before, but this time there was snow mixed in. Blinding sunlight and freezing wind burst in on him, and he tumbled backward, blinking madly in the bright light of a cloudless winter afternoon.

When he had recovered somewhat, he turned and peered shivering out the opening, then thrust himself forward, despite the cold and glare, to see where he was.

The tunnel had emerged in a rocky area just beyond the outer walls, northeast of the palace, out of sight of every window, well away from the top of the canyon.

It was perfect. The outside entrance would be hidden by the wall and the rocks, and he could see no reason anyone would ever wander into that area and find it, while the inside end was in the back of a storage cellar, and could easily be hidden by pushing a few stones back into place and setting a shelf or two in front of them. He had his secret way in and out of the palace.

It wasn't straight; instead it twisted and wound through the earth, following the natural shape of the stone and earth. And it wasn't finished. He still had a month or more before the *ara* returned, and he intended to clean out the debris, widen the narrow spots, and shore up the weak ones, so that his underground passage would be easier and more convenient. But it was open from end to end.

He sat in the hole among the rocks, shivering as he looked out at the snow-covered landscape. He had not been dressed for the cold of the outside world, since generally working in the tunnel had been close work, and his exertions had been more than enough to keep him warm.

When he had thrust his fireplace poker upward, to be greeted by that shower of rocks and snow, the dirt, snow, and wind had put out his candle. That was going to make the trip back through the tunnel to the cellars that much more interesting, as he doubted he could strike a fresh light in the wind.

He had enlarged the opening just enough to climb out and see where he was, and had then slid back down, out of the worst of the cold.

After the initial shock, though, he realized that the wind didn't feel quite so cold as usual. Yes, he was shivering, but he was out in the open without his cloak, without any blankets, yet he was not going numb, and no ice had formed in his beard.

"Is it warmer today?" he asked.

No answer came.

That didn't mean anything; the *ler* answered when they chose, and said nothing when they chose, and he had no way to coax or compel them.

Warmer or not, it was still cold; he took one last look, then ducked back down into the tunnel and started back toward the palace cellars, finding his way by feel, by the faint glimmer of daylight that leaked in behind him, and by the occasional faint flicker from *ler*.

[17]

One day, as he leapt up onto a couch brandishing his sword, just to prove to himself that he *could* still leap, Sword glanced out a nearby window just in time to see a glittering drop of meltwater fall from the tip of one of the great icicles that hung from the palace eaves.

He stopped, balanced on the arm of the couch, blade upraised, and stared.

Another drip fell, sparkling in the morning sun.

"It's melting?" he asked. He lowered the sword, his daily practice forgotten for the moment.

In his half-starved state he had become resigned to the idea that he would probably not survive the winter, the promises he had made to himself while out on the snow that moonlit night notwithstanding. His supply of jerky was gone; only a sliver of cheese remained; in three trips he had stripped bare every garden that the Uplanders themselves had not cleaned out, and had nothing left of his harvest but three half-rotten beets and a shriveled carrot. He had lost track of the days, and the *ler* had not spoken to him lately, but until this very moment the snow and ice outside had seemed as permanent as the stone on which the palace was built.

He had considered taking another look at finding a way down the cliffs to Winterhome, thinking he had little left to lose, but even assuming he could somehow get down the icy trail, he was more likely to be killed at the bottom than fed. Better, he thought, to die up here, so that Artil could not be *sure* he was dead, than to let the Wizard Lord know he had triumphed.

Of course, that would mean he would want to leave the palace, go somewhere his body wouldn't be found, while he still had the strength to do so, and he had been thinking about that, in a rather desultory fashion, but had not yet decided on a definite course of action.

The belief that he was going to die a slow and horrible death from hunger had been oddly liberating; he no longer worried about maintaining any sort of pattern to his days, or minimizing the damage he did to the palace and its furnishings. He had tried to stretch his food supply as much out of habit as any real hope of staying alive until spring, but had stopped keeping track of how much remained, or how many days he had been here.

But now the icicles were melting.

He jumped down from the couch and crossed to the window, staring out.

"It *is* melting!" he announced; the surface of the nearest icicle was slick and wet, glistening in the sun. He looked around, and realized that the film of frost on the inside of the glass was retreating, as well. He touched the windowpane; it was wet.

The evidence had been around him all morning, he realized, but he had not noticed it. He had very little energy these days, and did not devote much of it to observing his surroundings. Now, though, he could see signs of melting everywhere.

"It's real," he said. He looked up. "Is this spring, or just a freak thaw?"

The birds are returning, adults and hatchlings. They are less than a hundred miles south of this place.

"The *ara*?"

The sun has been coming north for many days, but we were able to hold off the warmth until the birds approached.

"So it's spring? Spring is coming?" Sword stared out the window.

He had made it after all—or at least, he knew he could. He had lost a great deal of weight, he was gaunt and weak, but he was not actually dying yet.

The birds are coming. We will hold them as far from this place as we can. . . .

"What? No! I need them! What am I supposed to eat?"

Go to them, if you will.

"I will! I . . ." He looked around, trying to think. He would need weapons, and tinder. . . .

And his coat, the one with feathers sewn into it. His makeshift velvet cloak was too bulky and clumsy for hunting, and Whistler had thought feathers helped to keep *ara* from sensing the hunters' approach.

"A hundred miles?"

Less.

That was at least five days' journey—perhaps less in good weather, but the plains were still deeply covered with snow—and that was assuming he could find them readily. He could not rely on the *ler* to guide him, not once he retrieved his feathers.

"Are they coming nearer?"

There was no answer. Sword stared out the window, watching water drip, seeing the sun glinting from the ice.

"When will the Uplanders return? How do they know where to find the *ara*?"

Again, he received no reply.

Well, if the Upland *ler* wouldn't help him, he would just have to rely on himself. He had done that often enough before, after all.

But there was no need to rush off precipitously. His sword practice forgotten, he headed thoughtfully for the stairs.

Three days later he set out to the southwest, hunting *ara*. He had not eaten for two of the three days, after finishing the last crumb of cheese and the last of the vegetables. The *ler* had not spoken to him at all in those three days; he was unsure whether this was simply their usual perversity, or whether the proximity of the *ara* was affecting them.

Certainly, the weather had abruptly turned warmer. The snow was melting rapidly, and he had been startled a few times by the sound of shattering as oversized icicles lost their grip on the palace eaves. The thaw was happening with astonishing speed.

He wondered how long it would be before the Uplanders came back up from Winterhome. He had gone out on the terrace and peered over the cliff, trying to judge whether spring was coming to Barokan as suddenly as it was arriving up on the plateau, but he had been unable to tell. The trail had still been hopelessly iced over, but there was certainly less snow down there in the towns below than there had been—he could see chimneys and exposed bits of roof where only white had shown before. He could not readily estimate how *much* less, though.

It didn't matter, he told himself as he trudged southward through the snow and slush; he would need to fend for himself for a time, but he could manage that. He could hunt *ara* himself. He had his spear, he had ropes, and his sword, and all the other supplies he thought he would need. He had even made himself a small tent; it had kept him busy after the tunnel was completed, and had been one more thing to keep his mind off his hunger.

For the first time it occurred to him that it might have been clever to have practiced with his spear as well as with the sword, but he had not done so, and it was too late now.

He was leaving the Summer Palace a mess, with half the furnishings torn up and burned, and the remains of his camp in the kitchens, but he couldn't bring himself to care. The Wizard Lord would know someone had been there, certainly, but he would not know for certain who, or whether he had survived or wandered out to die in the snow.

His only worry in that regard was that Artil might decide not to bother cleaning up the mess. He might give up his summer home and stay down in Barokan, where he belonged—and where Sword had no real hope of getting at him.

If that happened, though, Sword had totally misjudged the Wizard Lord's character. He did not think for a minute that Artil would ever give up anything without a fight.

He might not come up *this* summer, though. He might let the repairs take a year. If that happened, Sword would need to spend another winter in there, and he doubted Artil would make that easy. There would be no wheel of cheese next time, no easily burned furniture, no water in the cistern.

But Sword didn't think that would happen. He thought Artil would make a point of using the Summer Palace this year, no matter how damaged. He would not let the Chosen be seen to have inconvenienced him.

There would be workmen, then. Perhaps Sword could slip inside as one of them, and await the Wizard Lord. He knew the palace very well indeed now, after his months there, and thought he might be able to find safe places to hide.

He knew the structure, but of course, he didn't know the people—their numbers, their habits, their routine. That would make hiding a challenge.

But he could think about that later. Right now, he needed to find some *ara*.

He had found the Uplanders the previous year by following their smoke, but of course, birds didn't have campfires. Surely, though, there was some way to locate them. He scanned the horizon, squinting against the glare of sun on snow.

There was nothing immediately obvious.

He marched on, heading south and east, until sunset, when he made camp. He built himself a campfire from the limbs of a nearby tree; even though the sap was not yet running, the wood was damp and green, and getting the fire started took almost an hour. The result was a low, smoky fire that snapped and spat constantly.

If there was anyone else anywhere on this vast plain, he thought, they would be able to find him from a hundred miles away by following that smoke.

He had no food left, none at all; he resisted the temptation to chew on tree bark, since he did not recognize the species of tree and knew some bark was toxic. He did not care to have survived the long, cold winter only to succumb to accidental poisoning. He was able to melt snow in a stolen saucepan for drinking water, but there was nothing he could do for his gnawing hunger. He was used to it by now, but even so, it still hurt.

On the fourth day after leaving the palace he suddenly understood how to find a flock of *ara*, and wondered why it had taken him so long to realize it. The snow was vanishing rapidly, but it was not gone, and even where patches of bare ground showed through, it was not hard-packed turf that was revealed, but mud.

And where hundreds of man-sized birds had run across the plain, the snow was churned into muddy slush, leaving a trail a blind idiot could easily follow. Sword turned his steps to the north again, following the broad swath of cold muck, and the sun was still above the cliffs when he spotted the *ara* ahead.

Hunting *ara,* he discovered, was much more difficult alone than with a partner, and being weak and tired did not help. Hunger and desperation, though, *did* help, and with rope and spear, one end of the rope tied to a scraggly tree, at last he managed to bring down a smallish male, which he quickly beheaded with his sword.

The rest of the *ara* fled, of course, and Sword let them go. He had more meat here than he could eat in several days, and it would be easy enough to follow the flock's trail. He stood over the dead bird, exhausted, panting, sweaty despite the still-cool air; the smell of blood and death was simultaneously nauseating and appetizing. He stared down at his prey.

Those distinctive black, white, and pink feathers could shield a person from *ler.* The flocks of *ara* forced the *ler* of earth and winter into quiescence. How had such a thing ever come to be?

It didn't matter, he told himself. What mattered was that he had food again. He knelt and began the unpleasant job of butchering his kill, and when that was done he set up camp and built himself a fire. Waiting for the meat to cook, when he could smell its savory odor, was hard, but he was used to hardship.

When he could wait no more he tried to restrain himself and not eat too much, but as he had expected, the fresh, half-cooked meat was too rich for his shrunken stomach; he spent an unhappy hour curled into a ball in the mud as cramps twisted his guts. When he finally vomited, that helped; he was able to relax, and even eat a little more before settling to sleep for the night.

In the morning his belly seemed to have made its peace with him; he ate a good breakfast of *ara* thigh, and it stayed down without discomfort.

After that, he squatted by the fire and tried to plan.

He did not want to go too far from the palace; he needed to know when the Wizard Lord came up from Winterhome. On the other hand, he needed to eat, which meant staying near the *ara,* which did not seem inclined to go too near the cliffs. He also needed to decide whether he was going to try to live on his own, or rejoin the Clan of the Golden Spear, or perhaps find a temporary home with some other clan.

For now, he decided, he would expect to live on his own— after all, he didn't know when the Uplanders would return. If he encountered any of the nomads, though, he would try to join them; it would be safer to live in a group. He would stay near the *ara,* but not too near, and would make trips back to the Summer Palace every so often, to reconnoiter.

And sooner or later Artil im Salthir would come, and Sword would kill him, and there would be an end to the whole system of Wizard Lords and Chosen—or else Sword would die, and what became of the world would no longer be his concern.

The possibility of *not* killing the Wizard Lord occurred to him, but after surviving the winter, he dismissed it. He could not hear the ghosts of Babble and Azir shi Azir calling out for vengeance, not up here on the plateau, but he knew they were there, all the same. Lore and Boss were in the Wizard Lord's dungeons, and Snatcher, Beauty, and Bow might still be out there somewhere trying to find him. He could not let them all down. He could not leave the Wizard Lord to rule Barokan in peace. He *would* try to kill Artil im Salthir.

What would become of him if he succeeded, what he would do after he killed the Wizard Lord, he had no idea. Artil's guards might kill him in revenge, he supposed.

Or he might just go home to Mad Oak, raise barley and beans for the rest of his life, and let the rest of Barokan look after itself. That was certainly what he hoped for. Perhaps he might even find a wife—with no Wizard Lord, there would be no need for the Chosen, and he could give up his magic.

At least, he hoped he could; he wasn't sure just how that would work. He knew that when any of the Chosen died, the Wizard Lord's matching talisman stopped working, but the reverse wasn't true. When he had slain the Dark Lord of the Galbek Hills, his own magic hadn't been interrupted. He might remain the Swordsman even if there was no Wizard Lord.

And there would be no new Wizard Lord. Artil's men had slain almost all the remaining wizards, and the handful of survivors surely wouldn't be stupid enough to try to choose one of their number to take on the role.

If they *did* try it, Sword decided, he would finish the job Artil had begun, and kill them all.

His own thirst for blood startled him; after all, it wasn't so very long ago that he had told his mother that he never wanted to kill anyone, and more than once during the winter he had wept over what he had become. He had never thought of himself as a killer, yet he had slaughtered a dozen or more of the Wizard Lord's soldiers, and here he was, calmly considering the murder of every surviving wizard in Barokan.

He did not weep this time; he had food in his belly and hope for the future. Yes, he was a killer. That was what the Wizard Lords had done to him, he told himself. And that was why there could be no more Wizard Lords.

He glanced at his supply of meat, and reached for his knife. He had gotten out of the habit of eating whenever he chose, but now, he told himself, he was free to regain it; if he didn't eat, most of the bird's flesh would spoil and go to waste.

Eight days later, when the snow had shrunk to scattered patches, the first Uplanders appeared on the western horizon; a day after that three armed men approached Sword's camp, bearing a small banner emblazoned with a dragon.

It seemed very strange to see other human beings again, and Sword met them with his hand on his sword hilt and his spear on his back.

"Who are you, and what are you doing here?" one of them asked.

"I am the Chosen Swordsman of Barokan," Sword replied. "I have taken refuge from the Dark Lord of Winterhome as a guest of the Clan of the Golden Spear."

The three men exchanged glances.

"The vanguard of the Clan of the Golden Spear is five days behind us, and is reported to be heading north of this area," the spokesman said. "Why are you *here,* then?"

"I did not return to Winterhome with them," Sword explained. "I took shelter where I could, and stayed in the Uplands through the winter, and am now awaiting their return."

"You're waiting in the wrong place," the dragon-clan spokesman told him. "North, on Blue Toad Creek." He pointed.

"This was where I found food," Sword said, pointing at the remains of the *ara* carcass.

"Why would the Golden Spear give shelter to one of the Chosen?" another man asked before the spokesman could say anything more. "While we were in Winterhome we all heard what you did there."

"You called the Wizard Lord a *Dark* Lord?" the third man asked.

"He killed some of the Chosen," Sword said. "That's not permitted."

"But he built the roads and canals—the markets in Winterhome are *amazing* now!"

"The same man can do both good and evil," Sword replied.

"Enough," the spokesman said, raising a hand to silence his comrade. "You claim to be a guest of the Golden Spear, and we want no quarrel with them. Go to them, then. If we find you wandering about again, it will not go well with you."

"Is that a threat?"

"If you wish it to be."

"Your companion said you had heard what I did in Winterhome," Sword said. "You know I am the Chosen Swordsman, and that I fought a score of the Wizard Lord's men and defeated them. If you are threatening to kill or enslave me, consider well what you are attempting." He pulled his sword a few inches out of its scabbard.

"You are not in Winterhome now, Lowlander," the spokesman said. "This flock is our clan's flock for this year, and this is *our* land."

Sword looked at him thoughtfully. "Yet you cannot hear its spirits, can you?"

"What spirits? This is the Uplands, where we do not truckle to *ler.* Here we rely on muscle and bone and our wits, not dickering with every little spirit."

"Your lands have *ler,* just like any other," Sword said.

"What would you know of it?"

Sword started to reply, then thought better of it. Really, what did he hope to accomplish by arguing with these people? He had not come here to talk to them, but to kill Artil im Salthir.

And if they wanted him to rejoin the Clan of the Golden Spear, well, wasn't that just what he had intended to do in any case?

"Nothing," he said. He pointed. "You say the Clan of the Golden Spear is over there?"

"Roughly. It was agreed in council last month that they would follow Blue Toad Creek."

Sword nodded. "Then I will find them there. Thank you." He started to turn away.

"Wait," the spokesman said.

Sword turned back. "Why?"

"You said . . . you stayed up here all winter?"

"Yes."

"In that?" He gestured at Sword's makeshift little tent.

"Of course not," Sword replied.

"But then—"

"I am the Chosen Swordsman of Barokan," Sword said. "I have magic."

"Yes, but—"

"You told me I wasn't welcome here," Sword interrupted. "Let me break camp and begone, then."

"But—"

Sword turned away and began gathering up his belongings as the spokesman struggled for words. He did not find them, and Sword offered no help.

By the time Sword had the tent down, the three Uplanders had given up and headed back toward their clan's camp.

[18]

The looks on the faces of the Clan of the Golden Spear, when at last Sword found them, were not welcoming; some were astonished, while others were hostile. Sword ignored them as he trudged into the camp.

He had been careful to dress entirely in Uplander clothing—*ara*-hide trousers and vest over an *ara*-cloth shirt, his pack on one shoulder and his spear on his back—but there was still no chance he would ever be mistaken for an Uplander.

And then Fist, Dancer, and Whistler were there with spears pointed at him.

"What are you doing here?" Fist demanded.

"Seeking shelter," Sword replied, "as I did last year."

"You really are the Swordsman?" Whistler asked.

"Yes." Sword wondered whether he had really lost that much weight, or otherwise changed so drastically. He had done his best to keep his hair and beard in check and maintain himself; the Summer Palace had no shortage of mirrors and blades. Perhaps some changes had been so gradual, he hadn't noticed them.

"Where have you been?" Dancer asked. "Where did you hide in Winterhome?"

Sword looked from one to another. "I didn't hide anywhere in Winterhome," he said. "I stayed in the Uplands, as I said I would."

"But you're alive!" Fist said.

"Yes, I am aware of that," Sword said dryly.

"You really . . . ," Fist began, then stopped, as if suddenly realizing how admiring he sounded.

"I really survived a winter in the Uplands," Sword affirmed. "I took shelter in the Summer Palace."

"That can't be," Dancer said. "No one can live in such cold!"

Sword shrugged. "I did. In the cellars."

"What did you *eat*?" Fist asked.

"Was that jerky enough?" Whistler asked.

"No," Sword said. "I found other food."

"How?"

"The *ler* led me to it."

All three looked baffled at that. "What *ler*?" Fist said. "The *ler* in your sword? How did they know where to find food?"

"Uplander *ler*," Sword said.

The three exchanged glances.

"He was probably hallucinating from cold and hunger," Dancer suggested.

"Or loneliness," Whistler murmured.

"The *ler* don't talk to anyone," Dancer added.

"But he's alive," Fist said.

Dancer shrugged.

"What should we do with him?" Fist asked.

"Why should you do anything?" Sword demanded. "The Patriarch granted me the right to live freely on your clan's lands; that's all I ask. I have my own tent now, and have learned to hunt my own *ara;* I need nothing from you but to be left alone."

"But . . . ," Dancer began.

"But then why are you here?" Whistler asked.

"Because when I tried living on my own, without Uplander comrades, the Clan of the Great Dragon chased me away. There are no unclaimed flocks of *ara,* are there? So I need a clan that will allow me to stay."

Again, the three men exchanged baffled looks.

"Take him to the Patriarch, then," Fist said.

The others accepted this. Dancer reached for Sword's arm. Sword stepped back. "I will come freely," he snapped.

"As you will, then," Dancer said, dropping his hand back to his spear.

Fist led the way, while Whistler and Dancer followed behind Sword, spears at the ready.

The Patriarch's tent was just as Sword remembered it. It seemed odd to see it untouched by the winter. The relatively luxurious surroundings were, in their way, reminiscent of the Summer Palace—but of the palace as it had been before Sword repurposed the draperies, and smashed and burned much of the furniture.

"Then you survived the winter," the Patriarch said as Sword bowed before him.

"Yes, O Patriarch."

"And you have come to live among us again?"

"Only until such time as the Wizard Lord comes to the Uplands. When that happens, either he or I will die—or perhaps both. Should I survive that, I will return to Barokan and trouble you no more."

"You still hope to slay him?"

"I do, O Patriarch."

"In Winterhome they speak of the Wizard Lord as a hero who has brought new wealth and freedom to Barokan. They call you and the other Chosen arrogant monsters, slaughtering innocents in a failed attempt to maintain the old system that raised you up to a privileged position you did not deserve."

"We harmed no one until the Wizard Lord turned on us, O Patriarch. When I killed, I killed in self-defense, or to avenge my murdered comrades, and I did not kill innocents."

"That is not how the story is told now."

"The Wizard Lord's people tell the story as their master would have it known. I tell it as I saw it."

"And how am I to know which version lies closer to the truth?"

"You will interpret the words of others as your experience and wisdom guide you, I am sure."

"Meaning I will believe what I think best suits my own people, eh?"

Sword did not reply, but suppressed a small grimace. He

thought the Patriarch would profess to believe whatever best suited *him,* not his people as a whole.

"You understand that if I give you shelter, and the Wizard Lord's faction is triumphant in the end, I will have made myself unwelcome in Winterhome?"

"I cannot deny the possibility," Sword admitted.

"Why, then, should I take that risk?"

Sword raised his head and looked the Patriarch in the eye. "Because, O Patriarch, I am the only limit on the Wizard Lord's power. For seven hundred years the Chosen have kept the Wizard Lords in check, and prevented them from tyranny; now Artil im Salthir has broken that system beyond repair, and I am all that might prevent him from becoming a tyrant such as Barokan has never known. Would you see your young men recruited into his army, your young women taken for a harem? Were I gone, what would prevent the Wizard Lord from extending his rule into the Uplands? You have no magic to protect you, and no way to survive the Upland winters if he bans you from Winterhome. Keep me alive, and he will never be secure enough to threaten you; let me die, and you take your chances with his benevolence, for there will be nothing else to restrain him."

"And for that reason we will not kill you, or deliver you into his hands, but to take you in as our guest. . . ." He spread his hands.

"I do not ask for a place in your tents," Sword replied. "I have learned much since I first came to you. Allow me to camp on your lands and hunt the *ara* of your flock, and I need nothing more."

The Patriarch leaned back in his seat. "Indeed?"

"Indeed."

He considered that for a long moment, tugging at one corner of his beard. Then he said, "I think that can be permitted. One must make allowances for madmen, after all, and surely, given how you spent the winter and that you choose to defy the Wizard Lord, you can be considered mad."

"Surely," Sword bitterly replied.

"Well, then, we are in agreement."

"So it would seem."

And with that, the matter was settled. Sword made camp fifty yards from the nearest tents of the Clan of the Golden Spear.

He had assumed the separation would be a mere formality, but he discovered that was not the case; none of the Uplanders would speak to him, or come near his tent. Whenever he chanced to encounter one, that individual would hurry silently away.

Sword found this surprisingly irritating. He had not expected much from the Uplanders as a whole, after the three Dragoners had spoken of the tales they heard in Winterhome, but he had thought some of them, Fist perhaps, and certainly Whistler, would at least acknowledge his presence and perhaps renew their acquaintance from last year. That even Whistler avoided him came as an annoyance.

The one Uplander he came across who did not flee at the sight of him was old Gnaw Gnaw, the crone who had taught him how jerky was made, how the cisterns worked, and a great deal more about Uplander life. When he approached her she simply sat, paying him no heed, going about her business.

That was hardly a warm welcome, but even this sad excuse for human company was immensely comforting after his long, lonely, miserable months in the palace. He stopped by often, just watching her do her everyday tasks.

Finally, one day he sat down beside her as she worked at carving needles from *ara* wing bones.

"You don't avoid me," he said.

"Why should I?" she said with a shrug. "No one's going to bother an old woman about whom she talks to."

"Then the others have been told to stay away from me?"

"Not in so many words, but the Patriarch made it clear that you were being tolerated, not welcomed, and we had all heard the stories down in Winterhome. No one wants to be taken for your friend when the Wizard Lord's soldiers come for you."

"You think they'll come for me?"

She shrugged again. "Who knows? They came for the wizards, didn't they? And the other Chosen? And I know word got around in Winterhome that we took you in."

Sword glanced up, toward the western horizon. "I hadn't thought about that," he admitted.

"Seems to me you don't think about much."

Stung, Sword retorted, "I think about what matters to me."

"And what's that, then?" She looked up from her work and met his gaze.

"The Wizard Lord. My duties. My friends."

"Not a long list," she observed.

"It's been enough to occupy my mind," Sword said.

"All winter? You were alone all those months, and you never thought about what might happen to us because we sheltered you?"

"No," Sword admitted. "I . . . well, I thought the Wizard Lord would leave you alone because you aren't Barokanese. But now I don't know why I thought that would stop him." He shook his head. "I was too busy thinking about food and water, and the cold and the snow, and the Chosen, and the wizards, and my family, and the *ler*."

"Well, most of those were reasonable concerns," Gnaw Gnaw admitted. "The *ler*, though—who cares about them? Up here, we leave them alone, and they leave us alone. It's not like Barokan."

"They kept me alive," Sword said. "I would have starved if not for them."

Gnaw Gnaw frowned. "What are you talking about?"

"The *ler*. I talked to them, got them to help me."

"You *did* sneak down to Barokan?"

"No, I stayed in the Summer Palace. The *ler* of the Uplands spoke to me there."

Her eyes narrowed. "You were alone in that place too long, weren't you? Loneliness can make one hear voices, I'm told."

"No, I heard them the very first night."

"Upland *ler* don't talk to anyone."

"They can't, in the summer. Only in winter, when the *ara* are gone."

"Is that what the voices told you?"

"It's what the *ler* told me."

She put down her awl and bone. "While I know there are

just as many nature spirits here in the Uplands as anywhere else, Swordsman, they don't talk to anyone. You imagined it."

"I did not!"

"As you will, then." She picked up her tools and turned her attention to her work.

For a moment Sword sat in irritated silence; then he got up and stalked away.

A few days later he found her boiling some foul-smelling mess in a small cauldron, well away from camp, where the stench would not trouble her clansmen.

"Is there any word of the Wizard Lord?" he asked. "Has he learned of the damage to the Summer Palace?"

She shrugged. "I haven't heard," she said. "Gossip does not travel quickly in the Uplands." She prodded her brew with an *ara*-bone spoon.

Sword frowned. He was beginning to become concerned that Artil might make a visit to the palace to inspect the damage, and that he might miss it.

He was also worried that Artil might indeed come looking for him, or send a squad of soldiers, and that that might bode ill for the Clan of the Golden Spear.

"You haven't heard *anything*?"

"Not about the Wizard Lord himself," Gnaw Gnaw said, stirring. "I've heard Crookthumb suggest that your tales of talking to the *ler* are part of some scheme to recruit our young men into helping you murder the Wizard Lord, that you're going to claim our own *ler* want them to help you, but I doubt that's what you wanted to hear."

"That's ridiculous!" Sword protested. "The *ler* . . . I wouldn't . . . It's ridiculous."

She shrugged. "Talking to *ler* is ridiculous in itself. If we believe that, why wouldn't we believe the rest?"

"Because it's nonsense!"

"Mmm."

"The *ler* didn't say anything about your people. They don't *know* anything about you, not with all the *ara* feathers and bones and hides everywhere."

"Just so," Gnaw Gnaw murmured.

Sword stared at her in frustrated annoyance. "You still don't believe me, do you?"

She looked up from her pot. "Why should I?"

"Because I am an honest man!"

"You're Barokanese, and not even a Hostman. Why would I trust you?"

"Why would I lie?"

"You heard Crookthumb's theory."

"I don't even *know* Crookthumb!"

"She knows *you,* she says. She claims she spent time with you last year, and that you're just a-bubble with schemes and plots."

"I don't remember her by that name," Sword said defensively. He remembered his few failed attempts at courting, but honestly could not attach the name Crookthumb to any of them. Perhaps she had claimed a more flattering name.

"So you can't be bothered to learn our names?"

"I know *yours,* Gnaw Gnaw. And Whistler's, and Dancer's, and Fist's, and Stepmother's."

"You saw a lot of us."

For a moment Sword sat silently. Then he asked, "What happened when the Wizard Lord found out that your clan had sheltered me?"

Gnaw Gnaw shrugged. "Nothing. Not really. After all, we could reasonably claim not to know what had happened in Winterhome. But it was made clear that we should have known better than to take in one of the Chosen, under any circumstances."

"Yet here I am again."

Gnaw Gnaw grimaced. "The Patriarch does not *like* the Wizard Lord. Still, he's taking a great risk."

"I'm sorry. I didn't mean to endanger you."

"The Patriarch does as he pleases. He chose not to send you away. And he can claim he did this so he would know where you were, and could keep the Wizard Lord informed."

"*Has* he kept the Wizard Lord informed?"

She looked up from her pot. "Would you believe my answer, if I gave one?"

"Yes, I would, Gnaw Gnaw. What do you care about the Wizard Lord or his plans? You're an honest woman, and I would believe you."

She looked him in the eye for a moment before giving another shrug and turning her attention back to her work. "If anything has been done to tell the Wizard Lord anything, I haven't heard about it."

Sword nodded.

After a brief pause, Gnaw Gnaw added, "You asked what happened to *us* when the Wizard Lord heard about your stay. You haven't asked what we told him about *you*."

"I assume you told him the truth," Sword said.

"That's exactly what we did. Including the fact that we left you up here to die."

"Oh?"

"After all, everyone knows no one can survive an Upland winter. If you were mad enough to attempt it, was it not all for the best that we let you try? *That* was why he did not trouble us over taking you in in the first place."

"I see," Sword said. "But you can't use that excuse twice, can you?"

"No. If you and the Wizard Lord are both alive when we next retreat to Winterhome, I expect our stay there to be unpleasant."

"I see," Sword repeated. "Thank you, Gnaw Gnaw."

He turned and ambled away, thinking deeply.

He could not stay here and endanger the Clan of the Golden Spear, not after they had done so much for him. Besides, he needed to know what was happening at the Summer Palace. Had anyone come up from Barokan to check on its condition?

When he reached his tent he immediately began to break camp.

He had gone to the cliffs, where he had looked long-ingly down at the distant green of spring in Barokan, and he had explored the Summer Palace, where he had found no sign that anyone had set foot inside since he had last been there. He had tried to call on the *ler,* and had received no response but silence.

And there were no *ara* near the palace. After a few days he had to travel east again to find food.

He tried at first to find a clan that would allow him to stay on their lands as a guest, but that had failed. The Clan of Five Rings warned him off with a line of spears. The Clan of the Broken Tree allowed him to speak with a man called Guard, who asked him to leave as soon as he learned Sword's identity; Sword obliged them.

Most of the others he encountered attempted to kill or enslave him. He was forced to injure a few men in defending himself, though he did his best to limit the damage to shallow, painful slashes on arms and chest, and he was fairly certain that, barring an unusually bad infection, he had not killed anyone.

He survived by taking *ara.* After the first few encounters with hostile Uplanders he did his best to approach each flock from the side farthest from the encampment of the clan that claimed it. His skill as a solo hunter rapidly improved with practice; no longer being weak with hunger helped.

The last traces of snow vanished into the dry air; the mud left behind hardened. The *ara* fledglings that had accompanied their parents from the south grew rapidly, becoming less and less obvious among their adult kin. The sun seemed to grow larger and hotter every day.

A day came when Sword realized he was sweating even though it was still morning, and he had not yet exerted himself in any significant way. It wasn't summer yet, but spring was past its peak.

Time, he thought, to return to the Summer Palace and see whether the Wizard Lord's servants had begun to put it right. He had become so settled into his lonely existence, the days spent hunting, butchering, curing, or cooking *ara,* the evenings in tending to other chores, that he had lost track of the date, and not thought about when he should make his move, but the right moment was obviously close. He turned his steps westward again, trudging across the plain, staying well clear of any Uplander camp.

He did not have a marked route to follow; he simply headed into the afternoon sun. That brought him to the cliffs in good time, but well south of the canyon and palace—he knew it was south, rather than north, by the view of Barokan. He turned again, heading north.

When Sword looped eastward around the end of the canyon he saw footprints on the trail—not just the old marks left by the returning Uplanders, but fresh steps that turned north. He frowned. Had he missed his foe? He picked up his pace.

The moment he came within sight of the palace's outer walls, he knew that the Wizard Lord had indeed sent people up the cliffs. There were guards at the palace gate. He stopped some distance away, hoping he looked enough like an ordinary Uplander that they wouldn't notice him, and tried to think this through.

If there were guards there, then there was someone in the palace—not necessarily the Wizard Lord, but somebody. It might be workmen, or the palace staff, trying to repair the damage Sword had done, or it might be Artil im Salthir himself.

The Wizard Lord would not have come up the cliff for the summer yet; it was still spring, far too soon for the heat to be seriously uncomfortable down in Winterhome. He might have come to inspect the damage, though, or even to hunt Sword down.

No, Sword corrected himself, not to hunt him down. The Wizard Lord had no magic in the Uplands, and would not have come himself. He wouldn't take that risk. He would have sent his soldiers, just as he did when he slaughtered most of the Council of Immortals.

So Artil might or might not be in the palace.

Well, there was a way to find out, Sword told himself. This was, after all, exactly what he had spent much of the winter preparing for. He circled around, away from the gates, and then, once he was out of sight of the guards, he cautiously approached the rocky corner where his tunnel came out. He had never done this before, really; he had seen the outer end of the tunnel only when he emerged from it, and he had not done that since the snow melted. He was not at all sure he would recognize the place immediately.

In fact, at first, he did not—but then he felt something, almost as if he had heard a distant voice.

He was being guided, he realized. The *ler* were not so dormant as he had thought. They were subtly directing him, he knew, even though the weather had turned warm, even though he was wearing feathers and *ara* hide.

He was surprised they *could* reach him, under the circumstances, but he was not about to refuse their aid. He let his feet go as they would.

And then he was at the little outcropping behind the wall, and there was the opening, looking like just another little hollow in the rocks. He took a final look around, then stepped in and crouched down.

The darkness between the rocks had no bottom, and he could feel a cool movement of air. The tunnel was still there.

He took off his pack and spear and set them aside; he doubted they would fit through the narrower parts. He had no light, and he briefly considered making one—he had the necessary equipment in his pack—but decided against it. The tunnel had no branchings to lead him astray, and a light might be visible in the cellar at the far end; if a servant happened to see it, his secret would be lost. He would make his way by feel.

He wondered whether any *ler* might provide light, and caught himself. They wouldn't while he was wearing *ara* hide, he knew. He retrieved his pack, then sat down and dug out some of the clothes he had made during the winter. He undressed quickly, and then pulled on the *ara*-free attire.

The air felt different in his new garb, more alive—not so

much as it had in winter, or like the air of Barokan, but more vibrant than it had a moment before. Pleased, he stuffed everything he could back into the pack and set it aside again, hoping no one would stumble across it, or his spear, while he was in the tunnel.

No, he told himself, he could do better than that. First he carefully lowered the spear into the tunnel and laid it against one wall; then he lifted the pack over his head and sank down into the tunnel, filling the entrance with the pack and leaving his belongings to block the way as he crawled into the darkness.

The faint glow that leaked around his pack at the mouth of the tunnel faded quickly, but he found himself oddly untroubled by the utter blackness. The tunnel was *familiar.* He had spent much of the winter in here, and wiggling his way through its cool darkness now was almost like coming home again. The earth and stone around him felt comfortable and welcoming. He made far better time traversing its sixty yards or so than he had any right to expect, and quickly found himself behind the cellar wall, listening closely.

There were people moving around—not in the storeroom where the tunnel began, but not far beyond. He could hear the shuffle of feet, the rattle of tools, the murmur of voices. He knelt and listened, his ear pressed to a crack between the loose stones that closed off the tunnel's mouth, trying to make out words.

He caught snatches of conversation, some meaningless without context, some clear but of no importance. His knees were getting stiff, and he was beginning to think he would need to sneak out into the kitchen, when he heard this:

". . . just enough for supper."

"He's definitely coming?"

"So they tell me. And he wants to see how we found it, so don't move anything you don't need to."

"But you said—"

"Yes, he'll want his supper. So do what you need to to handle that, but leave the rest."

"All right . . ."

Then the voices had moved away, and Sword sat up.

Luck had been with him.

That was what he had needed.

The Wizard Lord wasn't here yet, but he was on the way, and intended to eat his evening meal in the palace.

That meant he was on the path up the cliffs even now. Once he was past the boundary of Barokan, at the lower end of the canyon, he would no longer have his magic. If Sword could catch him there, Artil would be relatively defenseless. An ambush might be possible.

Once again, Sword wished he had practiced more with his spear. He twisted around, and began crawling back out.

At the tunnel's mouth he paused to fish his spear out of the hole, pull on his winter coat, and sling the pack on his shoulder; he did not want to leave anything behind. Once everything was in place he set out southward at a brisk trot.

An hour later he had removed his coat again and was creeping up toward the south edge of the canyon, trying to stay out of sight of the guards at the palace gate. He had circled around, perhaps more widely than necessary, to avoid attracting their attention, hoping that the Wizard Lord would not arrive before he got into position. Here on the south rim he was far enough away that if any of the guards did see him—which seemed unlikely—he doubted they would be able to even identify him as a person, let alone recognize that he posed a threat to their master. Still, there was no need to take any chances.

He could hear voices from below. The procession was on its way up.

He peered over the edge, down into the long triangle of the canyon, where the path sliced up from the cliff face to the plain. No one was in sight yet.

He had set his belongings to one side; now he reached over and grabbed his spear, then swung the weapon into position.

He wished he had a bow and arrow—or even better, that the Archer were here with him. He had learned a little about how to use a spear during his stay in the Uplands, but he still wasn't very good with it. All that sword practice in the palace, and never so much as a single spear-toss—what a fool he had been! Spearing *ara* that were tangled in a rope did not really help much with throwing at a human target a dozen paces away.

If he met the Wizard Lord on the path somewhere, of course, all he would need was his sword, but Artil would undoubtedly be accompanied by guards wherever he went. Here, outside Barokan, Sword could not be sure of dealing with those guards, and even if he did, the Wizard Lord would almost certainly have time to retreat back across the boundary. Once Artil had his magic again, he could escape by flying away.

That was why Sword was not going to cross the boundary himself; yes, he would have his own magic as well, but the Wizard Lord could simply step off the path, over the edge of the cliff, and let the wind *ler* catch him. Sword knew he had to strike when the Wizard Lord was well past the boundary, with no magic to help him escape.

Then a soldier appeared, turning the corner and peering warily up the canyon. Sword ducked back, and pulled back his spear.

The soldier trudged up into the canyon, giving no sign he had seen anything but bare rock.

Behind him were more soldiers—*many* more soldiers, all in the familiar red and black of the Wizard Lord's guards. Sword frowned, and crouched lower, until his nose was pressed to the stone.

The soldiers marched past, dozens of them; Sword did not think to count, but estimated it at thirty or more. They were followed by servants carrying bundles, carters hauling supplies, and workmen with tools slung on their belts and leather sacks on their backs.

Then came another small cluster of guards, and in the center of this group was the Wizard Lord, riding in a contrivance like nothing Sword had ever seen before, a sort of chair on poles, carried by two brawny soldiers, one in front and one behind, with a square framework supporting curtains of some sort. Artil sat in the chair, leaning on one elbow, as if he were in his own throne room.

Sword wondered how they had gotten that thing around some of the corners in the path. Artil had probably had to dismount while the apparatus was wrestled around.

It didn't matter, though; what mattered was that here was his target, approaching at a steady pace. Those two bearers would not be able to dodge or maneuver quickly without dropping the entire chair-thing. Sword reached for his spear.

And just then Artil, blinking in the sun, straightened up and reached behind himself. He tugged at the curtains, which slid along the frame, blocking him from Sword's sight.

Sword froze.

He had already been concerned about throwing a spear well enough to kill the Wizard Lord, and now he would need to strike him through a drawn curtain.

He couldn't do it. He knew how good he was with a spear—and more important, how good he *wasn't*. He was not going to inflict a fatal wound through that drapery, not unless he was fabulously lucky.

Of course, sometimes luck could be provided. Fortune had favored him already, in putting him here in time to catch the Wizard Lord; perhaps it could be coaxed to do more.

"O *ler*," he whispered, "will you guide my aim? Will you see that my spear strikes him down?"

There was no answer.

"Of course you won't," he said. "This is the Uplands, where all *ler* are wild, but weak."

Only weak when the birds have come, something reminded him. It was very faint.

So *ler* were listening, just not cooperating—and that might not be their choice, given the shaft of the spear he was holding, how near his feathered coat was to his right arm, and how many other factors were weakening their power. And since the spear itself was made of *ara* bone and sinew, *ler* probably *couldn't* guide it.

The Wizard Lord's chair was approaching, and behind it Sword could see more people—more guards, and others. He recognized one face immediately.

Farash inith Kerra.

Farash the traitor, who had betrayed the Chosen to the Dark Lord of the Galbek Hills.

Farash, who had enslaved the town of Doublefall.

Farash, who had mocked Zrisha oro Sal thir Karalba by naming her as the new Leader of the Chosen.

Farash, chief advisor to the Wizard Lord.

Sword tightened his grip on the spear. Farash wasn't hidden by curtains, or riding in a chair that made him a smaller target, and he certainly deserved to die. . . .

But if Sword killed Farash, he would be letting everyone know he was here, and his chances of ever getting at the Wizard Lord would be lessened. He lowered the spear again. Perhaps, if he survived killing Artil, he could then go after Farash, but Artil's death was the higher priority.

He looked over the others following the Wizard Lord's chair, and saw several familiar faces, but no one he could attach a name to, no one he considered especially important. The captain of the guard was there, Sword recognized him, but Boss wasn't there, nor was Lore; he had hoped that perhaps Artil might have brought them along, and that he, Sword, might have a chance to free them.

Snatcher wasn't there, so far as he could see, but the Thief was a master of disguise; he could easily be one of those soldiers or courtiers or servants, so thoroughly changed in appearance that Sword had not spotted him.

Beauty couldn't disguise herself unless she hid her face entirely, and Sword could see no sign of her in the procession, no one who might have been her. If she was still alive and free, she wasn't here.

Although Bow had no great skill at disguises, he did have the knack of not being noticed. It didn't work as well on Sword and the other Chosen as it did on ordinary folk, and for that matter it might not work at all here, outside the borders of Barokan, but Sword could not be absolutely certain the Archer wasn't here somewhere. He had heard Uplanders say that the Archer was dead, but he did not necessarily believe it; the Wizard Lord was very good at spreading lies.

Still, it seemed unlikely that Bow could be there. He was a

man fond of direct and simple action; if he were able to get this close to the Wizard Lord, he would have already shot him, he wouldn't be carrying out any sort of stealth or deception.

So if any of the Chosen were here, other than himself, it would be Snatcher, the Thief—or perhaps the mysterious holder of the ninth talisman, if there really was one.

Sword had wondered often about that ninth talisman during the long, cold winter. He had no idea what role the Council of Immortals might have thought up, if they actually had devised a ninth member of the Chosen; his attempts to guess at one had never been convincing. Sword really didn't see any other role that needed to be filled; the eight Chosen had every talent they needed.

Was the ninth talisman simply a ruse, then? Artil had said he had been unable to use the Talisman of Trust effectively, even though he knew it was powerful; perhaps it *wasn't* really powerful. Its power might be an illusion, an attempt to convince the Wizard Lord that he had an unknown enemy with unknown abilities, to discourage him from turning against the Chosen. Perhaps it wasn't really linked to another talisman at all.

Perhaps it *was* just a trick that had backfired. Artil had killed most of the Council, and had done so in part because of the ninth talisman. But if there really *was* a ninth member of the Chosen, he or she might be among the party marching up the canyon, and Sword would have no way of knowing.

If poor Azir, the Seer, were still alive, she might know. She had never been able to sense a ninth member of the Chosen clearly, but she hadn't been certain there wasn't one, either. *Ara* feathers could have hidden the ninth from her, or if not feathers, then some other magic might have been responsible.

But Azir shi Azir was dead, cut to pieces on the streets of Winterhome, and it was Sword's job to avenge her, with or without the aid of any theoretical and mysterious ninth Chosen.

And it was clear now that he was not going to manage it here, from ambush, as he had hoped. That curtained chair protected the Wizard Lord from his spear as effectively as any armor.

But he would not stay in the chair forever. In an hour or so he would be at the Summer Palace, presumably inspecting the damage Sword had inflicted on the place.

Sword knew every inch of the palace—all the servants' corridors and hidden stairs, every niche and corner. And he had a way in that the Wizard Lord didn't know about.

He watched for a moment longer as the parade of Barokanese trudged past; then he slid silently back from the canyon edge. He had not been spotted yet, but there was no need to take any further risks.

He could not go back to the tunnel immediately; there were too many people on the way from the canyon to the palace. He would need to wait until everyone had arrived at the gates. That would probably not happen until dusk.

He sank to his belly and lay quietly on the sandy soil of the Upland, aware that only a thin layer separated him from the solid stone of the plateau and the cliffs, stone that had been alive with *ler* all winter, but which slept now. He lay there, and thought about the Wizard Lords, and about the Chosen, and about the Council of Immortals.

Maybe the Uplanders had the right idea, eschewing magic entirely. No rogue wizards to worry them, no Wizard Lord, no Chosen to keep the Wizard Lord in check. Sword remembered poor little Azir shi Azir, the Chosen Seer, who had grown up in Bone Garden with the horribly simple and descriptive name "Feast." There could never be a nightmare like Bone Garden among the Uplanders; they would never allow their *ler* to demand the horrors that the *ler* of Bone Garden did, and surely, no human beings would ever create such a place on their own.

That had been priests who told Azir shi Azir that she was destined to be eaten by her fellow townsfolk, priests serving as the link between humans and *ler*.

It had been one of the Chosen, their former Leader, Farash inith Kerra, who now walked behind the Wizard Lord, who had ensorcelled the entire town of Doublefall and taken several of its most beautiful young women as his harem. He had later freed them, and even chosen one of them as his successor, but still—one of the *Chosen,* the sworn *defenders* of Barokan, had enslaved a town with his magic.

And both Azir and Boss had been slain on the orders of Artil im Salthir, the Wizard Lord of Winterhome.

The Wizard Lords had prevented rogue wizards from running roughshod over the ordinary people of Barokan for seven hundred years, but even so, magic had still been abused. Wizards had been restrained, but the priests, the Wizard Lords, the Chosen, had all, at one time or another, done shameful, disgraceful things with their magic-derived power.

The Uplanders used no magic, and they seemed to do well enough without it. They kept slaves sometimes, but surely, there was nothing in all the Uplands to compare to what had happened in Bone Garden or Doublefall or Winterhome.

Artil said that magic was weakening throughout Barokan; the Upland *ler* had implied that this was because so many *ara* feathers and things made of *ara* bones and hide had been brought down by the Uplanders and traded to the Barokanese. The magic-dampening effects of *ara* were spreading throughout Barokan, little by little, and accumulating over time. Artil wanted to speed up the process, and eliminate magic from Barokan, and the more Sword thought about it, the more he thought that would be a good thing—but the way the Wizard Lord was going about it was anything *but* good.

The memory of Babble and Azir lying dead in the street came to him again.

An end to magic would be a good thing—but that end did not justify the means Artil was using. Artil had to die for his crimes. Sword would see to it that he did.

And after that, there would be no more Wizard Lords. The Council of Immortals was broken, the handful of survivors scattered. The Chosen, too, were scattered, some of them dead. The old system was destroying itself.

And when it was gone, what then?

The various towns would presumably govern themselves, as they always had. Who would maintain the roads, though? Who would tend the canals and the other structures Artil's men had built? What would become of his hundreds of soldiers?

What would become of the surviving Chosen?

What would become of Sword?

He didn't know—and right now, he didn't care. He just wanted Artil dead.

He lay on the sand, waiting for dark.

[20]

His second trip inbound through the tunnel in utter darkness was even easier than the first; his body remembered the twists and turns surprisingly well. He had once again carefully removed his feather-laden coat, and checked every other garment he wore for any obvious traces of *ara,* and this time he remembered to pull the *ara*-feather rosettes from his boots. He stashed the coat with his pack and spear at the tunnel entrance. He made sure that from the skin out, he was dressed entirely in the *ara*-free clothing he had worn during the winter, when he had been in communion with the Uplander *ler.* Whether the *ler* were guiding him, or whether it was simply experience, he didn't know; he knew only that he was able to slip through the narrow passage even more quickly than before.

He had brought his sword, even though it was sometimes awkward to maneuver it through the tunnel.

As he neared the end he could hear voices and footsteps.

He paused, still in total darkness, and listened.

This time there was no single conversation that told him what he needed to know, but snatches of several exchanges— shouted orders, shouted responses, the clatter of doors, the thump of boots.

The Wizard Lord's soldiers were searching the palace.

He could not judge whether they actually expected to find him still hiding somewhere, or whether they were just seeing whether he had left any traps, or interesting evidence of what he might have planned for their master. The commands, questions, and answers were not detailed enough to be certain.

Two soldiers were searching the cellar storeroom where his tunnel emerged. He held his breath, hoping they would not be thorough enough to find the loose stones that closed off his access.

"Does that wall look right to you?" one of them asked.

Carefully, Sword reached out his hands and pressed on the stones, holding them in place. Faint candlelight flickered through one of the cracks, blindingly bright after the utter blackness that filled the tunnel.

"One of the masons was a little sloppy, perhaps," his companion said.

Then Sword felt a tug on one of the stones, and he pressed down hard to keep it from moving.

"I suppose," the first agreed.

"Can you influence them?" Sword whispered silently. "Please, O *ler*? Make them not find the tunnel."

We cannot ensure that, but we can make it less likely. The words were surprisingly strong and clear, much stronger than those he had sensed on the canyon rim—but then, he was no longer wearing feathers, or carrying an *ara*-bone spear.

"Anything. Please."

Done.

"Someone should touch up the mortar there," one of the voices said.

"It's the back of a larder," the other retorted. "Who *cares* if it's a bit crooked? If we weren't poking around here with lanterns, we'd never have noticed a thing!"

The light retreated; Sword blinked. The glow faded, then cut off entirely as the storeroom door closed.

"Are they gone?" he whispered.

There was no answer.

"Are they still in the . . . the larder?"

No.

"Are they still in the kitchens beyond?"

Yes.

That was not what Sword had wanted to hear. "Are they leaving? Heading for the stairs?"

No.

"It's just the two men, though?"

No. Men are everywhere in the palace, many men.

"Oh." He smothered a sigh. "And they're all looking for me?"

Yes. Most to destroy you. One to aid you.

Sword started. "What?"

There is one who seeks to aid you. An ally.

That was a pleasant surprise; Sword lay on the stone of the tunnel floor and thought.

It had to be Snatcher, the Thief. Nothing else made sense. . . .

No, Sword corrected himself. It might be the ninth Chosen, whoever and whatever that was.

But the ninth Chosen had not revealed himself—or herself—before, had not come to the aid of the others; why would he be here now, seeking to help the Swordsman? No, Sword told himself, it must be Snatcher. "Where is he?" he asked.

He is walking with Artil im Salthir dor Valok seth Talidir through a corridor just above you.

With the Wizard Lord? He must be disguised as one of the guards, then—or perhaps he *was* one of the guards; perhaps he had enlisted and worked his way into the Wizard Lord's personal escort.

Another possibility occurred to him.

"Is Artil still riding in that chair thing?"

No.

Then Snatcher wasn't one of the bearers—and thinking about it, Sword realized he hadn't needed to ask. The Thief wasn't big enough for that role, and no matter how good he might be at disguise, he couldn't add fifty pounds of muscle at whim.

One of the guards, then. That was good to know.

But why, then, hadn't he already killed the Wizard Lord? Slit his throat while he slept, perhaps?

And how had he managed to infiltrate the guards? Surely,

anyone trusted so close to the Wizard Lord would have been questioned and tested somehow. When Sword had been granted an audience, he had had to strip naked to prove he had no weapons before he was allowed into Artil's presence. Wouldn't the Wizard Lord have used his magic to make sure that none of his guards were that mysterious ninth Chosen he was so worried about?

Perhaps Snatcher wasn't a guard after all, but some other official—he might be anything from a palace architect to an errand boy.

He is hoping to find you and aid you. He seeks to get away from Artil im Salthir so that he might look for you.

"Can you talk to him? Give him a message?" Sword knew it was unlikely—but on the other hand, the guards' uniforms didn't include any *ara* feathers.

Perhaps. He is . . . receptive.

That was encouraging. Did the Thief's own long experience with magic make him more accessible, even up here where his magic didn't work? "Tell him where I am. Tell him I can't get into the palace while the kitchens are full of soldiers. If there's anything he can do to make them withdraw, ask him to do it."

For a long moment there was no response, and Sword began to think about what he could do if Snatcher couldn't help him. He could go back through the tunnel and try to find another way in, perhaps one where he could smash through a window and take the Wizard Lord by surprise; how well guarded were the palace grounds?

Given how many men the Wizard Lord had brought, probably very well guarded indeed. That plan didn't look promising.

The expedition he had watched come up the canyon had not seemed heavy-laden; presumably they had not brought supplies for a long stay. This was not Artil's annual return to the Summer Palace, after all, but only an inspection trip. Could Sword ambush him on his way back down, perhaps?

That idea seemed promising. . . .

He will do what he can, the *ler* informed him.

"Hm," Sword said. Now he had to decide whether to stay where he was and hope Snatcher, or whoever his ally was, could do something useful, or whether to head out to the canyon to arrange an ambush.

He would give his friend a few minutes, anyway.

"All right, all of you," someone bellowed, loud enough to be heard through the storeroom door and the stone wall. "Upstairs, now. He's not down here, and Old Boss wants us all ready in case the Swordsman has recruited an Uplander army to attack us."

Old Boss? Sword blinked. Farash inith Kerra was giving the orders, rather than Artil himself?

It probably didn't mean anything. The order to withdraw, though, was just the break Sword had hoped for. Once he was out of the tunnel and loose in the palace he could use the servants' corridors to get anywhere in the place. There might be guards in some of them, even with much of their attention turned outward against an assault that wasn't coming, but he surely knew his way around better than the soldiers did.

Your way has been cleared.

Then this was his ally's doing. He didn't know whether Snatcher had impersonated Farash, or whether the Thief had Farash's ear, and he didn't much care—however he had done it, his hidden compatriot had given him the chance he needed. He slid forward quickly, and began pushing and lifting out the stone blocks that obstructed the entrance.

A moment later he got carefully to his feet, sword drawn and ready, his other hand brushing dirt and dust from his clothing. He listened at the storeroom door, but heard nothing, and no light leaked around the edges.

He took a moment to push the stones back in place; he might need the tunnel again. Then he once more approached the door, and carefully lifted the latch.

The door swung in easily, revealing the short staircase that led up to the main kitchens; a faint glow from somewhere above illuminated the steps well enough for him to ascend, bent in a wary crouch.

The kitchens were deserted, but someone had lit four of the

candle stubs on the central chandelier and left them to burn, so that the great room was not entirely dark. Sword looked around.

His bedding still lay more or less where he had left it, but had been torn to pieces; the mattress had been slashed, its woolen stuffing strewn in all directions. His little store of candles was gone. The various pots and pans he had kept close at hand all winter were scattered and spilled.

It was evident that no one was planning to do any cooking in these kitchens tonight, despite what he had overheard earlier. Sword supposed that everyone would make do with a cold supper brought up from Winterhome.

"The Wizard Lord is upstairs?"

Yes.

"What's he doing?"

Preparing to depart. He has seen what he came to see.

That wasn't good. "Where is he?"

The answer came not in words, but in an odd awareness of direction, not unlike the guidance Sword had received from the earth-*ler* while digging his tunnel. The Wizard Lord was upstairs, to the north—in the main dining hall, Sword judged.

This was probably the best chance he was going to get. Artil thought the palace had been searched, and that Sword was nowhere in it; he was apparently expecting an attack, but an attack from outside. If Sword came bursting into the room from one of the servants' entrances, he might well be able to get to the Wizard Lord and kill him before anyone could react.

And once the Wizard Lord was dead, surely the soldiers would see their cause was lost, and would drop their weapons—and if they did not, well, he would have fulfilled his duties as the Chosen Swordsman, and he would have avenged his fallen comrades. If he died in carrying out his assigned role, that was simply his fate. He did not *want* to die, but he was ready to risk it, so long as he could take Artil im Salthir with him.

He started up the steps, moving as stealthily as he could, listening for any sound from ahead.

The candlelight was behind him here, which was unfortunate; his own shadow hid much of the stairway before him. The corridor above was completely unlit—but then he saw faint gray daylight ahead. Someone had left a door open.

He had never done that when he lived here; he had done everything he could to keep out the cold. The soldiers were obviously not so careful. And why should they be? The cold was gone, the snow melted, winter's hold broken and lost. He crept toward the door.

It was indeed a door to the large dining hall on the north side of the palace, a room designed to shelter its inhabitants from the hot sun of summer while allowing cooling breezes to enter; several tall casement windows looked out northward, on the cliffs and the high plains. The center of the room was taken up by a long, broad trestle table, surrounded by a dozen finely carved chairs; a few sideboards lined the walls to east and west, with several gaps where smaller serving tables had once been, while the southern wall held no fewer than three doors that led to the passage down to the kitchen.

Sword had never used the table for firewood because it was too large and heavy to fit down the stairs, and too strong to be worth breaking up where it stood when there were still lighter, more fragile pieces to be had. He had smashed and burned one of the chairs, but the thick varnish had flared up dangerously and stank horribly, so he had left the others. The sideboards had been finished with what appeared to be the same varnish, and thus they, too, had survived. The missing serving tables, on the other hand, had burned very nicely.

Sword found himself peering cautiously around the jamb of the most westerly of the three servants' doors.

The room was full of soldiers, dozens of them, all looking northward. And there, standing before the windows, looking out at the plateau, was Artil im Salthir, the Lord of Winterhome, Wizard Lord of Barokan.

He looked much as Sword remembered him. His ankle-length red robe was embroidered in green and gold, and his straight black hair reached halfway down his back; gold rings gleamed from his fingers and his ears. Sword could not see his face, as he was turned away.

Farash inith Kerra was standing beside him, also looking out the window, but Sword paid no attention to him. He needed to kill the Wizard Lord; any other revenge could wait.

If Sword could get to him, this was a perfect opportunity to strike him down. The only problem was that the Wizard Lord was on the far side of a large room, and the huge table, several chairs, and several guards stood between the two men.

Sword hesitated, but then told himself this was probably the best chance he was ever going to get. The Dark Lord of Winterhome was smarter than the Dark Lord of the Galbek Hills had been, and would never be caught so completely defenseless as Galbek Hills had been. Sword could see that no one was looking at him, there in the kitchen door; no one was ready for an attack from behind.

The biggest obstacle was that table, but Sword thought he could handle that.

He braced himself, naked sword in his right hand, and then, with his left hand, he flung the door wide. He started across the room at a run.

He did not bother to yell, or call threats; he already had the element of surprise, and he doubted anything he could say would be enough of a distraction to be worth his breath.

Soldiers turned at the sound of the door hitting the wall, and Sword's boots hitting the floor; jaws dropped, hands reached for weapons. A dozen voices all started to shout at once.

Sword leapt for the tabletop—and realized in midair that he had made a mistake. He had no magical assistance, no strength or dexterity beyond the ordinary. He was tired and stiff from his passages through the tunnel and his running back and forth to the canyon, and he had not yet fully recovered from the long winter's semi-starvation. He was, he thought, only just barely going to clear the table's edge, and he would not be surprised if he landed so off-center that the whole table might tip under him. He tried to tuck his feet up, so that at worst he might land on his knees—just as an amazingly alert guardsman reached up to block him.

The move was too little, too late, to stop him entirely, but a hand brushed against one leg, and instead of landing smoothly atop the heavy table, Sword's left toe caught on the edge and he stumbled, sprawling across the wood. His left hand went down to catch him; his right hand, holding the sword, flew upward, struggling for balance, as he landed awkwardly on one knee.

The Wizard Lord had heard the commotion, and was whirling to face his attacker. Sword's gaze locked on to Artil's face.

The man had aged badly in less than a year, and he looked terrified. Defeating and scattering the Chosen and murdering most of the Council of Immortals had apparently not made his life easier. Sword doubted anyone so obviously frightened could think clearly. If he could just reach him, Sword was sure he could kill this Wizard Lord. He was obviously in no condition to defend himself.

But he had others to defend him. The guards in the room were reacting as well, moving to block his path, weapons raised. A dozen voices were shouting contradictory orders or simple exclamations—"Stop him!" "Look out!" "It's the Swordsman!"

Sword sprang to his feet—he was not so far gone he couldn't manage that—and strode across the table, but then stopped. His stumble had given the soldiers time to respond, and if he jumped off, he would be flinging himself onto raised spears. They were the simple wooden spears of Barokan, not the elaborate bone-shafted spears of the Uplands, but they were still effective enough.

A spear jabbed at him, and he slashed with his sword, knocking it aside.

In Barokan he would not just have knocked it aside, but he would have sliced it apart, or sent it flying from the soldier's hands—but he was not in Barokan, and he had no magic here. He still had his years of training and practice, but he was facing a score of foes.

"Stand aside!" he bellowed, hoping that the guardsmen were still sufficiently startled to obey without thinking.

A few spears wavered, but no more than that.

"Get me out of here," Artil said loudly, tugging at Farash's sleeve. Sword heard him clearly.

"Wait," Farash said, raising a hand and staring at Sword. "He's alone, and you have two dozen soldiers!"

"How do you know he's alone?" Artil screamed. "Why would he be mad enough to come here alone? No, he has a scheme, he must!"

Farash turned his gaze from Sword to the Wizard Lord. "But, my lord—"

"Kill him!" Artil shouted. "All of you, honors and gold to whoever kills him!"

With that, a dozen spears thrust forward, and Sword stepped back, his blade flashing from side to side as he deflected their jabs. Fortunately, they were hopelessly disorganized; this was not a situation they had been trained for. Sword recognized the captain of the guard, standing near Artil and Farash, who should have been taking charge; fortunately for Sword, he was instead listening to his superiors argue, and looking around as if expecting more attackers.

Presumably the captain had heard the Wizard Lord's suggestion that there were others, and had taken it to heart.

"But—" Farash began.

"It's a trap, I'm *certain* of it! Now, get me out of here, before his trap is sprung!" Artil demanded.

"I am the Chosen Swordsman, defender of Barokan!" Sword called, in the deepest, loudest, most commanding voice he could summon. "I am here to remove a Dark Lord—who would stand against me in this?"

Most of the soldiers hesitated, but their leaders paid no attention; they were still talking amongst themselves. "My lord, how would it look, to flee while your men fight against the world's greatest swordsman?" Farash said. Sword did not think he had really intended the question to be heard by everyone, but in order to be heard over the clatter of spears, the thump of boots, and the shouting of a dozen guards, Old Boss had had to speak quite loudly. "If he kills them—"

"Why would he kill *them*?" Artil interrupted. "*I'm* the one he wants!"

"But they're the ones fighting him; you just ordered them to kill him."

The hesitation had passed. A spear narrowly missed Sword's foot, and he decided he could no longer simply wait here atop the table, deflecting the spears; sooner or later the soldiers would gather their nerve and do something more than jab ineffectually. He stamped down on the spearhead, slamming it to the table, then stooped and thrust with his sword, jabbing it through the spearman's shoulder. He still did not want to kill any of the soldiers if he could help it, but he could not just stand and wait. He needed to get through the crowd and strike at the Wizard Lord.

The wounded soldier screamed and dropped his spear, then fell back against two of his companions.

Another guardsman struck at Sword from behind, thinking he would be distracted, but Sword somehow heard the creak of leather and whirled, his bloodied sword slashing at this new attacker. The tip of his blade drew a bloody line across the man's cheek, missing his eye by a fraction of an inch.

"Get me out of here, *now,*" Artil growled. "If you won't lead the way, Farash, then you will, Captain. I want to get back to Barokan!"

That made sense to Sword; in Barokan the Wizard Lord would have his magic back, and however much he might say he wanted to rule without it, the man obviously put more trust in his magic than in anything else.

"What about the men, my lord?" the captain asked.

"Hold him off until we're clear. Kill him if you can." Artil threw a glance at Farash.

"Don't be stupid about it," Farash added. "There's no sense in getting killed."

With that, Artil and Farash turned and began moving quickly along the north wall toward the door, on their way out of the palace.

Sword watched his target trying to escape, and felt fury and frustration welling up in his heart. When another spear jabbed at him, he reached down with his left hand and grabbed it, tearing it from the surprised spearman's hand. Then he stood, spun the spear around, and flung it at Artil's departing back.

He missed. He had never tried throwing with his left hand at all, and hadn't had time to swap sword and spear. The missile passed close enough to the Wizard Lord's ear to rustle his hair, but did not touch flesh.

Given how little he had practiced with spears, Sword knew that was closer than he deserved.

Artil screamed, though he was untouched, and ducked as he grabbed for the door.

Growling at his own mistake, Sword tossed his sword to his left hand and reached for another spear, but it was too late— Farash had opened the door and hustled his master out of the dining hall. The captain of the guard had followed them to the door, and was now tapping several soldiers and sending them after the Wizard Lord, as his guards.

Sword transferred the sword back to his right hand just in time to counter a fresh flurry of blows from the guards surrounding his perch. Most jabbed at his feet and ankles, trying to bring him down, and as long as he kept moving, he could dodge most of those, but sometimes a spearpoint was thrust up at him and had to be avoided or parried, and some of the attacks on his feet were sweeps, rather than jabs, or aimed well enough that they had to be turned.

His boots received a few slashes, but as yet the flesh within was undamaged.

Sword watched in furious frustration as the captain passed a few final orders to some of his men, too quietly for Sword to hear over the clangor of combat, then vanished through the door, closing it behind him.

Sword desperately wanted to pursue the fleeing Wizard Lord, but for the next several minutes he was kept very busy, much too busy to escape the table. While some of the guards had followed the Wizard Lord, and others were hanging back and leaving the fighting to their comrades, eight or nine of the group seemed determined to bring down the Chosen Swordsman any way they could.

Sword could understand that; after all, even if the Wizard Lord reneged on his promise of honor and wealth, it would be something to brag about to be the man who brought down the world's greatest swordsman. He was determined to discourage them as quickly as possible, though, and to chase after Artil. He might yet catch up to him before he reached the boundary.

And right now, he thought, would be a good time for this mysterious ally the *ler* had mentioned to do something. If the Thief *was* here, wasn't there something he could do to help?

Apparently not.

"Any time, O *ler*," Sword said, but there was no answer, from *ler* or Chosen or anyone else.

Sword slashed at hands and arms and faces, stabbed at shoulders, trying to inflict wounds as bloody and painful as possible without killing anyone. Outnumbered as he was, though, he could not afford to be *too* fastidious, and did not hesitate to lop off one man's hand at the wrist when no alternative other than being skewered presented itself.

The man's screams and the blood spurting from the stump of his arm were very effective in discouraging the others, and at last Sword was able to jump down off the table and start making his way toward the door.

The guards in his path took a few halfhearted jabs at him, but kept outside his reach, so that he was able to get to the door uninjured, and without inflicting anything worse than a few superficial scratches. He turned, groping for the latch with his left hand while defending himself with the sword in his right.

A half-circle of wary guards surrounded him, but did nothing to prevent him from opening the door. He thanked whatever *ler* or fate might be responsible for the good fortune that the captain had not locked it behind himself, or otherwise blocked it—Sword knew it did have a lock, but perhaps the captain had not had the key.

He looked at the guards, trying to judge whether they would follow him, or try to spear him in the back when he slipped through the door. Was one of these men the Thief in disguise? He didn't recognize any faces. Where was this supposed ally who the *ler* had told him had been so eager to help?

Not in the dining hall, apparently, nor, when he made his move through the door, in the corridor beyond. The passage was empty. Sword ran toward the door to the gardens—there was nowhere else Artil and Farash and their handful of guards could have gone.

"Where's my ally?" he muttered, not really expecting a response here, above ground.

With your quarry.

Startled, Sword almost stumbled. "He is?"

Yes.

"Can't he do something? Can't *he* kill the Wizard Lord?"

Not yet.

Sword slammed through the next door, out of the palace, and saw the last of the guards jogging through the palace gate, with the captain calling something to them. He sprinted after them.

"Well, if he doesn't do something soon, it'll be too late," Sword told the *ler*. "If the Wizard Lord reaches Barokan, he'll have his magic back, and we won't have a chance."

There was no reply. Sword tore open the gate the captain had just closed, and charged through; Artil and Farash were some distance away, and had broken into a run, with the little band of soldiers running close behind them.

Sword ran hard across the plain after them, along the trail toward the head of the canyon, and Artil's party ran as well, staying ahead of him—though he was, very slowly, closing the distance.

The absurdity of the situation did not escape him, that more than half a dozen armed men were fleeing one tired man with a sword, but absurd or not, that was the situation. Yes, he was the world's greatest swordsman, at least when he was in Barokan, but he was not in Barokan, he had no magic, and if it came to a pitched battle, as he hoped it would, he would be severely outnumbered. His success was hardly assured, but he had no other option.

And he didn't need to defeat all of them. He just needed to get past them and kill the Wizard Lord. After that, if they wanted to, he supposed they could kill him—but they would have nothing left to fight for, so he hoped they would see reason.

He was closing with them—but much too slowly, and he was growing very tired indeed. Remembering what had happened to his pursuers in Morning Calm, where the local *ler* had softened the ground beneath them until they were almost sucked into the earth, Sword gasped out, "Can't *you* do something? Can't you stop them somehow?" The ground here was rocky, and sucking Artil and company down was probably impossible, but perhaps there was a way. . . .

Stop them? The tone of the response carried an air of wonder and confusion that Sword had never heard before, as if the spirit that spoke had never imagined the possibility of intervening among humans.

Perhaps it hadn't.

"Yes!" Sword shouted. "Can't you keep them from going down the trail through the canyon?"

For a moment he thought the *ler* would not answer, but then came the reply.

Yes.

"Then do it!"

As you will.

For a few seconds nothing more happened, save that the men continued to race across the plateau; the Wizard Lord's party had reached the head of the canyon and was turning west, down the defile. Sword thought the *ler* had misunderstood him somehow, or misjudged their own abilities.

But then a rumble sounded, and the ground shook. Sword stumbled, tottered, and then regained his footing as the ground stilled and a roar and a cloud of dust rose up from the canyon.

Artil and Farash did not slow; if anything, they accelerated, vanishing down into the canyon. Sword tried to quicken his own pace. The earthquake, impressive though it was, had not stopped them. Sword bit his lip, resisting the urge to shout imprecations at the *ler* that had so misjudged its capabilities. It had *tried,* at any rate.

But then he made the turn into the canyon, and saw what the earthquake had accomplished. The *ler* had done more than try.

A hundred yards ahead the stone sides of the canyon had crumbled. A wall of fallen rock closed off the trail. Artil and Farash and their guards were running down into a dead end.

And not being blind, they knew it. They slowed.

Sword slowed as well. He did not need to run anymore; his prey was trapped.

"Prey." Sword smiled bitterly to himself at his choice of words. By his best count, made during the pursuit, they still outnumbered him eight to one—ten, if he counted Artil and Farash. All of them were tired from the long run, but he was still suffering the aftereffects of his winter deprivations, and had already fought his way through their companions.

And he was fairly certain those companions were following him, though not in any great hurry, so that in time, perhaps half an hour, he would be surrounded by dozens of foes.

Still, these eight were turning at bay, ready to defend themselves and their masters. They were clearly disinclined to attack, though; they were taking up purely defensive postures, making no move to escape the canyon. Artil and Farash had their backs to the rock wall; the soldiers had formed up into two lines of four in front of them.

Sword crouched a little and began stalking forward, sword raised, in a pose intended solely to intimidate. "Anything more you can do for me?" he asked the Uplander *ler* as he marched toward his enemies. "Bring down more rocks, on their heads this time?"

No. Our strength is gone. The rockslide used it all.

"Well, thank you for that much," Sword said. "It's more than I'd hoped for."

There was no answer.

"Who is he talking to?" Artil shrieked, loudly enough that Sword could understand him perfectly. "He has allies! Invisible ones, perhaps—or Uplander magic!"

"My lord, he can't—"

"Uplander magic! That's how he survived the winter, how he brought down these walls—he's an Uplander wizard, come to punish me for intruding on their land!"

"My lord, he's the Chosen Swordsman, not any sort of wizard."

"But not up here! In Barokan he's Chosen, but the Chosen have no magic here, any more than I do."

Judging by their faces, that admission startled several of the soldiers. A few were clearly unhappy to hear that their master had no magic to call on; a couple made the jump to understanding that the eight of them were facing an ordinary man, not the infamous magical monster who had single-handedly defeated twenty-five men, and smiled fiercely.

"Stand ready," the captain said quietly.

"Are you sure of that?" Sword called. "Just because *your* magic doesn't work here, why do you assume *mine* doesn't?"

"Because the Scholar *told* me that!" Artil shouted back.

"You think the Chosen Scholar wouldn't lie to the Dark Lord of Winterhome?"

"But he didn't! Any magic you have is Uplander magic! *Your* magic couldn't have caused that rockfall!"

"Oh, *I* didn't cause it at all!"

Artil threw Farash a terrified glance.

Sword felt a twinge of pity; what had *happened* to the man in the months since they had last seen one another? Artil had always been obsessively worried about dying at the hands of the Chosen, but he hadn't been panicky, hadn't been openly scared like this.

"Who else is with you, then? The Thief? The Ninth? The Archer and the Seer and the Speaker are all dead, the Leader and the Scholar are secure in my dungeons, and the Beauty could do little for you here, but I never found the Thief or the Ninth. What is the Ninth, then—the Destroyer?"

"Do you think I'm fool enough to tell you?" Sword snapped back, doing his best to hide his anger and dismay at learning of Bow's death. He had suspected as much, the Uplanders had said as much, but he had still hoped the reports were wrong.

The Wizard Lord, though, would know, and if he was lying, if his apparent panic was an act, then Sword had completely misjudged him. No, the Archer was surely dead.

The Thief and the Beauty still lived, though—that was good to know.

Was Snatcher one of the eight men guarding the Wizard Lord? Sword didn't see anyone who looked anything like the Thief; all these men were bigger, heavier than Snatcher. But then where was the ally the *ler* had promised him? Was there really a ninth Chosen after all?

He had closed most of the distance between himself and the soldiers now; he stopped and called, "You men! I don't want to harm any of you. I'm charged by my oath as one of the Chosen Protectors of Barokan to kill the Dark Lord of Winterhome, but I wish no one else ill. Step aside now, and I will let you go unscathed."

"Don't listen to him!" Artil shouted. "He's lying! He'll kill you all!"

"I am not the liar here!"

"Swordsman, wait, wait!" Artil called. "Listen to me! You don't need to do this!"

Sword's eyes narrowed. "Are you offering to abdicate?"

That was a possibility he had not given any serious thought; he had never believed Artil would ever consider giving up his position. The Council of Immortals had told the Chosen that a Dark Lord could choose to give up peacefully, and surrender all his magic in exchange for being permitted to live, and in fact three Dark Lords had done so in the centuries since the system was created, but Sword had never for a moment believed that Artil im Salthir might be the fourth. It just wasn't in his character as Sword knew it.

But then, this desperate, pleading coward before him was

not the man Sword thought he knew. Whatever had broken his spirit might have caused him to reconsider retiring.

"*Are* you?" Sword demanded.

"No, I . . . maybe, yes, we can discuss it. . . ."

Sword saw the disgust on the faces of some of the soldiers, but none of them turned, none of them spoke. They were still ready to face Sword's blade.

And that, Sword realized, was why he could not simply accept Artil's resignation, even if it was genuinely being offered. Even if he gave up the Eight—no, the *Nine* Great Talismans, Artil im Salthir would still have his army, he would still have a populace that adored him, and he would still be the man who had ordered the deaths of a dozen wizards and three of the Chosen.

"You would give up your position if I swore not to harm you?" Sword asked, as much to distract Artil and the others as because he really cared about the answer. He wanted to find some way to get at the Wizard Lord without hacking through those eight men; the guards were relatively innocent in this. Even if they had been involved in carrying out the murders Artil had ordered, they had been under his influence.

And it was Artil that Sword wanted dead. Artil was responsible for all this. The others were just an obstacle to be overcome.

And he needed to overcome them quickly, before the rest of the soldiers, or any of the Wizard Lord's other attendants, arrived to further complicate the situation.

"My *position*? No, no, I didn't mean that," the Wizard Lord said, glancing at the captain of the guard. "I meant that I would consider relinquishing my *magic*. After all, I don't need it, *Barokan* doesn't need it. The time for magic is past."

Artil was perhaps not so oblivious to the soldiers' reaction as Sword had hoped.

"It's not enough," Sword said.

"And of course, provision would be made for the remaining Chosen," Artil said quickly. "You seem to have found a place for yourself here in the Uplands, Sword—and magic!" He gestured at the fallen rocks behind him. "You have Uplander magic, as no one ever has before! I would be happy to aid you in claiming the role of Wizard Lord here, as a counterpart to my own role in Barokan. And your compatriots would be welcome to join you. I would give you the Summer Palace, if you like, as your own residence—"

"Because I've damaged it so badly you no longer want it? You offer me your cast-off rubbish?"

"Nonsense! You've barely touched it! A few ruined furnishings are nothing; they can easily be replaced." The Wizard Lord seemed to be regaining his composure, looking and sounding more like the man Sword remembered. "I'm sure it could be made quite comfortable, and suitable for year-round occupancy, with very little effort, and naturally I would provide the labor and materials in recompense for whatever wrongs I may have done you. When we find the Beauty, we would of course send her up to join you here." He smiled, a little unsteadily. "I know the two of you are good friends. And the Leader and the Scholar would be freed, of course."

Sword stared at the man in disgust. Artil was offering not just the palace, but things he had no claim to—the Uplands, and the Beauty—as bribes for sparing his life. Wealth, power, sex, he was willing to give Sword all of them.

Or so he said.

And Sword did not believe him for an instant. Artil would offer anything, promise anything, and then have him killed anyway, Sword was certain of it.

"You would give me all this?" he asked.

"I would," Artil lied, smiling.

"And you would give up the Great Talismans?"

The smile vanished. "I don't think that would be necessary. You would be safe from my magic up here—"

"*I* think it would be necessary," Sword interrupted, moving a little to his left, positioning himself for a charge.

"Perhaps I was hasty!" Artil said, raising his hands as if to fend something off, and his tone had changed again, shifting back toward the panic Sword had heard back in the dining hall.

"Or perhaps you knew there are some lies no one would believe," Sword suggested.

"All right, Sword, listen to me. What good would it do to kill me?" The panic was gone again. "We both know which of us is considered a hero in Barokan now, and it's the one who gave the people roads and trade and safety, not the man with a big knife who's said to have chopped off women's hands and mutilated petty criminals."

"Those stories are lies."

"Can you prove it? People believe them. And even if they didn't, what of it? *I* built the roads, not you, and you did cut up a dozen of my soldiers in Winterhome last year. There were witnesses to that, plenty of them."

Sword growled.

"So here's an agreement I will swear to, if you accept it, swear on my own soul and by my true name. If you go away, if you stay away from Barokan, I won't pursue you, I won't do anything to you. I really will give you the Summer Palace if that's what it takes to get rid of you, and I really will let the Beauty join you here, if she's still alive and chooses to. I don't care what you do to the Uplanders, I don't know whether you really have magic or if the rockslide was just a trick, and I don't care—just swear you'll leave me alone, and I'll swear to leave *you* alone. No one needs to die. We can each live our own lives. Please, be reasonable!"

"You would swear to this in Barokan? Swear by your soul and your true name?"

"Yes, I would."

This time, Sword believed him. He was not entirely sure why. An oath by his true name would be binding on Artil so long as he was in Barokan; to break it would be to cast himself outside all law, to make himself the enemy of all *ler,* all nature—if he even *could* break it; there were some who believed it was not physically possible to break such a vow.

So long as he was in Barokan. Sword was not sure any oath would be magically binding outside Barokan's borders, and Artil had already demonstrated that he was capable of getting around magical limitations by leaving his homeland. He had given the command to kill the Council of Immortals while he was at the Summer Palace, and the Seer, whose magic would ordinarily have alerted her to such murders, had therefore been unaware that any deaths had been ordered.

But Sword didn't think Artil intended any such treachery this time. He thought the Wizard Lord's offer was sincere. He was offering Sword his freedom, and peace between them.

It would leave Artil as undisputed master of Barokan, of course, while Sword would have to survive one hellish winter after another. Boss and Lore would presumably stay in Artil's dungeons, while Babble and Bow and Azir would definitely still be dead. There would be no check on what the Wizard Lord might do; if he wanted slaves, he would have all of Barokan under his thumb. If he wanted an enchanted harem, like the one Farash had kept in Doublefall, he could have it, and no one would object.

And Sword couldn't allow that, not even if it meant his own death. He had sworn to protect Barokan from any Wizard Lord who went bad.

"No," he said.

"What?" Artil blinked in surprise.

"No!" Sword repeated. "No oaths, no agreements, no compromises. You, guardsmen, step aside!"

"Kill him!" Artil shrieked, pointing at Sword as his calm vanished again.

One of the soldiers raised his spear and made a halfhearted rush; Sword knocked the weapon aside and drew a line of blood across the man's cheek—but his defense was sloppy, obviously not the effortless work of the Chosen Swordsman. He felt his gut tighten; if these soldiers had any sense at all, they would recognize that the Wizard Lord had told the truth, and Sword's Barokanese magic did not work here.

"There's no need to shed anyone's blood but his!" Sword called out, pointing at Artil with his free hand. "If you fight me, you may stop me, you may not, but either way, you can be sure that some of you would die in the process—is it worth your *lives* to defend this treacherous, lying wizard? You all heard us just now, his promises and deceit."

No one answered, but Sword saw hands tighten on weapons; swords were raised, spears hefted. Obviously, these men *did* consider it worth risking their lives. They had spent too much time in the presence of the Wizard Lord's power, his ability to sway the hearts and minds of those around him with the magic of the Talisman of Glory.

Some of these men would have to die.

Unfortunate, but unavoidable.

And it would need to be soon, before the other soldiers arrived and overwhelmed him with sheer numbers. Sword turned his wrist and braced his back foot, preparing to charge.

He might die as well, of course—in fact, it seemed very likely. He was tired and weak and outnumbered eight to one; a single lucky blow would bring him down, and once he was down, those spears would make short work of him. He had survived the Upland winter, but he would not survive this. He had accepted that.

He was about to launch himself at the Wizard Lord when a new voice spoke.

[22]

"Wait!" Farash called, raising his hands. "Everyone, wait! I have an idea!"

Startled, Artil turned to look at his advisor. Puzzled, Sword stood, waiting, still slightly crouched. The soldiers stopped advancing; some glanced at Farash, some at their captain, while others kept their eyes on Sword.

Sword wondered just what Farash had in mind; did he think he could persuade the two of them into some sort of agreement? Surely, Farash knew that of all the people in the world, he was the only one Sword trusted even less than he trusted Artil.

It might just be a ploy to delay Sword until the other guards arrived, but even Farash deserved a chance to speak; after all, if Sword did kill Artil and survived, and the guards continued to fight, he intended to kill Farash next. The man had a right to say a few last words, if only to further condemn himself.

"Captain!" Farash said, holding out a hand to the guard's commander, who happened to be the nearest of the soldiers. "Give me your sword!"

Artil threw Farash a final glance, then turned his attention back to Sword. "Give it to him," he said without looking at the captain.

"My lord, I—," the soldier began.

"Give it to him!" Artil interrupted. "I don't know what his idea is, but I trust him—give him your sword." He glanced sideways. "And you, give me that," he said, snatching a spear from the hand of another soldier.

The captain still hesitated.

"Hurry up," the Wizard Lord said. "His Uplander allies might be here at any moment."

"As will more of your own men, my lord," Farash said as the captain reluctantly handed over his sword, hilt-first. "Which is why I can wait no longer." He hefted the sword, adjusted his grip—and then swung around and plunged his blade into the Wizard Lord's back, thrusting it through him so that the point jabbed out of his belly.

Blood spurted. Artil's eyes flew wide, his hands flew up, and he let out a dull croak; if he had meant it to be words, Sword had no idea what those words might have been. He released the spear he had just grabbed, and it rattled to the stony ground.

Sword stared in incomprehension. He could see it all very clearly, see the bloody point of the borrowed sword thrusting out of Artil's chest, but his mind refused to accept what he saw.

And then, as Farash inith Kerra yanked the sword back out, Artil im Salthir crumpled, bending at the knees and waist, folding down and then sprawling to one side upon the rocky ground. Red blood poured from his pierced body, pooling beneath him.

As Sword and the stunned soldiers watched, Farash stepped forward and swung the sword like an ax, chopping through the

Wizard Lord's neck. The blow did not entirely sever his head, but did cut through the spine, leaving no possibility that Artil could still be alive—and incidentally, badly chipping the sword's blade.

For a moment, no one else moved; everyone simply stared at the bleeding corpse, and the man standing over it holding a bloody sword.

Then Sword recovered from his astonishment and strode swiftly forward, brushing aside the unresisting men and weapons who blocked his path, until he stood a few feet from Farash. There he stopped, and raised his sword to the other man's throat.

He did not understand what had just happened, but he intended to. The Wizard Lord was dead, and that was good—but *Farash* had done it, Farash the traitor, Farash, the monster who had so hideously abused his power as Leader of the Chosen. That could not be good, could it?

It had to be a trick, a trap of some sort, a deception.

A rush of anger swept through the Swordsman; killing Artil had been *his* duty! How dare Farash deprive him of it?

Then he recognized that as the insanity it was—Farash had very probably just saved Sword's life. Farash had told Sword long ago that he wanted to make amends for the evil he had done; did he think this was the way to do it?

Was it a way to do it?

"Sir . . . ," a guardsman began uncertainly.

The captain's hand fell to his empty scabbard, then away. He stared at his own sword in another man's hand, covered in his master's blood. The Chosen Swordsman had paid no attention whatsoever to the fact that the man he was confronting was armed; in the torrent of emotion, it hadn't seemed important.

Farash opened his hand and let the red blade dangle loosely. "Drop your weapons," he ordered. "All of you."

"Do as he says," Sword barked.

The captain nodded, one hand raised.

Reluctantly, most of the soldiers complied, in spirit, if not literally—spears were lowered carefully to the ground, and swords were sheathed, rather than dropped. Two or three men stubbornly held on to their arms, but did not approach the Swordsman or their late master's chief advisor.

Sword stared at Farash's familiar, hateful face, trying to read his expression, but he could make nothing of it. The man was not smiling, or frowning; he simply looked tired.

And perhaps, just perhaps, he was somehow relieved?

"I suppose you think I'll spare you now," Sword said, pressing the tip of his blade against the skin of Farash's throat.

"I don't know *what* you'll do," Farash said. "I *hope* you'll spare me."

He met Sword's gaze with no sign of fear.

"I assume you changed sides to encourage me in that?"

"No."

Sword waited a few seconds, to see whether Farash would explain himself further, but no explanation was forthcoming.

"You knew I would triumph, I take it? You saw something I've missed, perhaps? Recognized the Thief among these men?" He gestured at the surrounding soldiers.

Farash shook his head. "To the best of my knowledge, the Thief is still in Winterhome. If all has gone according to plan, he's in the Winter Palace at this very moment, trying to find a way to free Lore and your Leader from Artil's dungeons."

"You know that?" Sword asked sharply.

"I helped arrange it," Farash said. "I didn't change sides, Sword; I have been on your side since shortly after I gave up the role of Leader. If you will allow me, I will prove it."

"How?"

Farash gestured toward his throat. "If you will allow me?"

Reluctantly, Sword lowered his blade.

Farash said, "Thank you." Then he bent down and laid his bloody sword by the Wizard Lord's corpse. Straightening, he displayed his empty hands. "I am unarmed, as you see—and you are a far better swordsman than me even without your magic, I'm sure."

"I think so," Sword agreed.

"Then trust me for just a moment." He reached into his

tunic and drew out a small round object—a coin. "This," he said, holding it up, "is the Talisman of Treachery, which must be borne by the ninth Chosen Defender of Barokan, and no other."

Sword recognized that it was, indeed, the mate to the coin that the Wizard Lord had shown him and called the Talisman of Trust. The bearer of this talisman, if it was genuine, was indeed the ninth of the Chosen. Sword blinked. "You?"

Farash nodded. "I, my friend and erstwhile companion, am the Chosen Traitor. So long as I carried this, and so long as the Wizard Lord carried the Talisman of Trust, and so long as we were within the borders of Barokan, he could not mistrust me. That was my magic. No matter what you told him, no matter what I had done, no matter what I did, the Wizard Lord could not believe me capable of betraying him."

"But you *did* betray him," a new voice said. Sword turned.

The captain who had given Farash his sword was speaking. "You betrayed and murdered him!"

"Well, of *course* I did," Farash said. "He was a Dark Lord, and as one of the Chosen, under the oath I swore to the Council of Immortals, it was my duty to kill him."

"But he was the Wizard Lord! He wasn't a Dark Lord—he built the roads and canals, and slew the monsters and the evil wizards—"

"They weren't evil," Farash said, cutting him off. "They were just wizards. And he had them all killed for nothing—*they* were as bound by the Talisman of Treachery as *he* was, and could not reveal my identity or nature. He was demanding the impossible of them."

"He was the Wizard Lord, sworn to protect Barokan from rogue wizards!"

Farash sighed. "They weren't rogues. And the Chosen had done nothing to harm him, yet he took two of them prisoner and killed three of the others."

"Three?" Sword asked. "You're sure?"

Farash turned his attention back to the Swordsman. "Three," he said. "He tracked poor Bow down months ago. The hunt was long and bloody—Artil must have lost at least twenty men before they finally caught up with Bow and butchered him." He shook his head sadly. "I tried to distract him, get him to call off the pursuit, but I couldn't do it."

"Why didn't you just *kill* him?" Sword demanded. "If he trusted you, and you were right there beside him all this time, why didn't you simply borrow a sword and run him through, as you did just now?"

"I *couldn't*," Farash said. "Oh, believe me, I *wanted* to—I even tried, twice, to slip into his bedroom and cut his throat. But I couldn't. Just as the magic would not let the Council identify me, or let the Wizard Lord mistrust me, it would not let *me* harm him when acting alone." He grimaced. "Even though you never told the Council why you wanted me removed as Leader, they didn't entirely trust me, Sword. They knew you must have had reasons for demanding I give up my role as Leader, so they put strong restrictions on me. None of my magic was ever under my own control; it was all bindings. And the binding on *me* was that I could not harm the Wizard Lord unless he was under attack by others of the Chosen. I had to be in the presence of another of the Chosen, and that other had to be trying to kill him, before I could act against him openly."

"And *this* was your first opportunity? What about when he imprisoned Boss and Lore?"

"*He* was acting against *them*. They weren't trying to kill him. They didn't even defend themselves. And after that, poor Bow never got close enough; it wasn't Artil who killed him, but a band of soldiers. Beauty never even *tried* to do anything but hide, so far as I could tell, and I don't think Snatcher ever trusted me enough to make the attempt. I had hoped that after I began running messages to him from the prisoners he'd believe my story, but if he did, he never admitted it. No, Sword, my first chance was today, back in the palace. Perhaps I should have struck then and there, rather than fleeing here, but you caught me off guard, and there were so many of his soldiers there—"

"There are eight of them here," Sword pointed out, waving at them.

"Eight of them, yes. There were thirty more back in the palace."

"Captain?" a plaintive voice asked, interrupting their dialogue. "He killed the Wizard Lord; shouldn't we do something?"

"Let them talk," the captain replied. "I want to hear more. It's not as if we can do anything for the Wizard Lord, or as if any of us are going anywhere. And look up there." He pointed toward the head of the canyon, where the main body of soldiers had just now arrived. "I don't think even the Chosen Swordsman can stand against all of us, here outside Barokan's borders."

Sword threw the new arrivals a glance. "Several of you would die finding out," he said. "I think we would all prefer to avoid that."

"Indeed," the captain said. "But we may not have any other honorable choice."

"Honorable?" Sword cast a glance at the Wizard Lord's corpse. "There was little honor in any of this, on any side."

No one disputed that.

[23]

"What's happened?" a distant voice called from the head of the canyon.

The captain turned, and pointed at one of his men. "You, Earflap, go tell them to come down, but not to interfere until we straighten this out. Tell them the Wizard Lord is dead, and we're discussing what it means."

"Yes, sir." The soldier saluted, and then trotted quickly up the path.

Sword watched the messenger leave, then looked back at Farash. "Speaking of dishonor, Farash inith Kerra, I would like to know just how the Council of Immortals ever chose *you* to bear the ninth talisman."

"They knew no better," Farash said. "After all, you had refused to tell them why I was unfit for my role as Leader of the Chosen."

"But of all the people of Barokan—"

"They didn't *know* the people of Barokan, Sword," Farash interrupted. "They were wizards, outcasts—they didn't live among normal folk. What's more, they didn't trust one another—if one of them had nominated one of his own friends or family, none of the others would have ever agreed. Wizards don't choose the Chosen, you know that; each of us chooses his own successor."

"But there never was a ninth before," Sword objected. "And they must have chosen others sometimes, when one of the Chosen died without naming an heir."

"Oh, that's true, and I'm sure they would have found some way to agree eventually if I hadn't been available, but I *was* available." He sighed. "You understand, it was made more difficult because of the nature of my role. The Traitor was to be secret, even from the other Chosen, so they could not let it be known they were seeking volunteers. With that limitation, and the refusal to consider one another's nominations, there were only three or four people in all Barokan they seriously considered—me, and Merrilin who had been the Thief, and the old Seer, and Blade, the Old Swordsman. We were the ones who knew what it meant to be Chosen, people they had dealt with before, people whom the new Wizard Lord might take an interest in. After all, they needed someone who could get close to Artil."

Sword nodded reluctantly.

"Blade and Shal Doro Sheth were old and tired," Farash continued. "So Merrilin and I were their preferred candidates, and Merrilin had refused to join the fight against the Dark Lord of the Galbek Hills. That left me as their first choice."

"Why didn't they approach one of Artil im Salthir's friends, though?" the captain asked.

Farash shrugged. "I don't know," he said. "But he was a wizard—perhaps he *had* no friends. And assuming he *did* have any friends who weren't wizards, perhaps the Council feared those friends would side with him against the eight Chosen."

"What about his guards, then? Why not the captain, here?" Sword gestured at the soldier.

"He scarcely *had* any guards yet," Farash pointed out. "And they didn't know which ones would be close to him. They thought that he would be eager to accept me as an advisor, as his tame expert on the Chosen. They knew I had done a poor job as the Leader, but the Traitor is a very different role."

Sword could hardly argue with that. "So you accepted the role."

"Well, of *course* I did!" Farash snapped. "What else could I do? Everything I had done as an adult had been based on my magic as the Leader of the Chosen. You know what I did to Doublefall; I'm sure poor Zrisha oro Sal told you about it."

It took Sword a moment to recognize the Leader's true name. "Yes," he said. "Some of it."

"*I* don't know," the captain said.

Sword threw him a glance. "We'll tell you later," he said.

"You'll tell me now!"

Sword turned, sword in hand, then thought better of making threats; the captain was unarmed, and probably nowhere near as good with a sword in any case, but he was the commander of the soldiers that surrounded the two Chosen.

"Captain," Sword said, "you'll have all the time you need to hear the details. The essence of it is that this man used magic to enslave the town of Doublefall, and used its people as his personal playthings."

The captain stared at him for a few seconds, then turned to stare at Farash. "Is this true?"

"Oh, yes."

"And the Wizard Lord knew you had done this?"

"He knew," Sword said.

"Not at first," Farash said. "But yes, he knew."

"He trusted you."

"He *had* to," Farash said. He sighed, and turned back to Sword. "When I was the Leader, any time I wanted to be worshipped, to have my every whim catered to, I stayed in

Doublefall," he said. "Any time I wearied of the adoration, I could travel anywhere in Barokan and be accepted as an honored guest. Everyone was eager to befriend me, the Leader of the Chosen—not merely because I was one of the Chosen, but because of my magic. I held the Talisman of Command; everyone wanted to please me, even if I did nothing to ask for it."

"Yes?"

"Yes. And I accepted it as my due. But after you killed the Lord of the Galbek Hills and ordered me to give up the talisman, I knew that was over. I hurried to Doublefall and freed the townspeople from my spell, before anyone else could find out what I had done to them, and I chose Zrisha oro Sal as my successor."

"As a joke on the rest of us, she said," Sword remarked.

"Well, yes," Farash admitted. "I was bitter over the loss of everything I had planned, everything I had stolen, everything I had done, and I chose her because I could think of no one less appropriate. But I didn't intend it to be permanent. I told the two wizards who ensorcelled her talisman for me, the Cormorant and Filri Torn-Ear, as much—that I had chosen her because I had no faith in my own ability to find a fit successor, after my own failure, and that I picked her for her common sense. I didn't expect her to *stay* the Leader; I thought that once she was free of my spell she would recognize for herself that she was completely unfit, and that she would find an heir and pass the role along in short order. And after all, even if she didn't, how likely was it that there would be another Dark Lord in our lifetimes?"

Sword did not entirely believe this excuse, but neither could he rule it out. And really, given that Farash had utterly misjudged his successor, what did it matter? "Go on," he said.

"Filri and the Cormorant seemed impressed by my reasoning—but I sometimes think all wizards are fools, by their very nature."

"I think that may be something we can agree on," Sword replied dryly. "So did they offer you the new role on the spot?"

"No." Farash shook his head. "And if they had, I might well

have turned it down. No, I wandered off on my own, planning to start a new life as an ordinary man. I did not dare stay in Doublefall; there were too many memories there, both mine and others, and too many ways my deceptions might be exposed and my past brought to light. No, I headed eastward. I had always liked Winterhome, and I knew Artil was building his palace there; I thought I might find work as a carpenter."

"Did you?"

"No. I didn't find work. I found something else. I found myself, Sword. I visited inns and taverns all across the Midlands, the same places where a year before I would have been greeted as a hero, and I discovered that without my magic, people didn't much *like* me. Even when they knew I had been one of the Chosen who had brought down a Dark Lord, and had no idea that I had not done my share, they didn't like me once they got to know me. No one wanted to hear my stories; they all sounded like empty bragging or shallow whining. No one thought me good company. No one would buy me a drink; innkeepers who would have kept my mug brimming full before would now pour more foam than beer. Women scorned me—oh, I was still handsome enough, with a good strong form, but I had the manners of a mule, and invariably said the wrong thing, too blunt or too timid, when I tried to lure them to my bed. No one liked me—and I found, Sword, that I didn't like *myself*. I was alone often, and had time to think about what I had done, and to look at the people around me whom I had treated with such contempt, and I realized that I had been a beast, and that it was time to be a man."

Sword frowned.

"I told you I had reformed when we spoke in the Winter Palace years ago," Farash said. "I don't think you believed me."

"I'm not sure I believe you now, either."

Farash sighed. "I'm not surprised. But at any rate, I arrived in Winterhome determined to be a better man, and *that* was when three wizards approached me about taking on the role of the Chosen Traitor." He shook his head. "They didn't know I had *already* been a traitor among the Chosen, and I didn't tell them, but I accepted their offer. I thought that perhaps I could atone for one betrayal with another—though I did not really expect Artil to ever deserve such a betrayal. He seemed to be doing a fine job as Wizard Lord."

"He did," Sword agreed. "He did seem to be."

"Once I had the Talisman of Treachery, becoming his advisor was easy. He trusted me. He believed everything I told him about myself."

"And did you, then, drive him mad with fantasies about the Chosen plotting against him, so that you would have someone you could betray?"

"No!"

For the first time, Farash seemed genuinely upset.

He forced himself to calm somewhat, and said, "No. I didn't, I swear to you by all the *ler* of Barokan—at least, not as you mean. *After* he turned on us, when Babble and the Seer had been killed, when he had Bow hunted down, only then, I *did* try to keep him worried, to make him see threats everywhere, so that he would be too distracted to do any more harm. I used the threat of your return to keep him from ruling as fiercely as he wanted—he had intended, once you were gone, to track down the last few wizards, to depose priests wherever they weren't absolutely necessary, to force his beliefs on all Barokan, and I dissuaded him by telling him how that would make allies for you. I warned him of nonexistent plots and conspiracies against him. Yes, I did that *then,* and I don't apologize for it, but when all the Chosen were still alive, I tried to guide him wisely. I told him that the Chosen wouldn't act against him without reason. I tried to convince him the Chosen could be his friends. He believed that I sincerely meant every word I said, because he trusted me—but he thought I was simply wrong. The magic that forced him to trust me did not let me *control* him; that would hardly suit the Council of Immortals, to have one of the Chosen ordering the Wizard Lord about."

Much as he wanted to disbelieve Farash, Sword had to admit that the Council probably would have put exactly that restriction on their spell.

"I tried to tell him not to worry about the Chosen, but he

dismissed it as foolish loyalty to my old friends," Farash continued. He shook his head. "I don't know why he was so certain we would turn on him; yes, we killed Galbek Hills, but how many Wizard Lords had served out their lives without any trouble? I wanted to help him with his plans to make Barokan a better place. I thought he was right in wanting to do away with magic as the means of governing. I advised him to build roads and bridges and canals, and to find work for bored young men, and to remove hazards on the roads—but I thought the Summer Palace was a bad idea, intruding on the Uplanders, and I tried very hard to make him see that the Chosen could be his willing allies, and he never truly accepted that. Oh, sometimes he seemed to; he accepted Lore as an advisor, and tried to befriend you all, but he never *trusted* any of you. Anything less than wild enthusiasm for his every project he took for a warning that you were going to kill him. And then there was the ninth talisman—*my* talisman. No one could tell him what it meant, or how it worked, or who held it, because by its very nature that would defeat its purpose, and that, more than anything else, convinced him that the Council and the Chosen were both out to destroy him."

Sword stared at Farash for a moment, then said, "You know, I can see why he would think that."

"So can I," Farash said. "But what could we do? The spell was cast, and could not be changed."

"It was a stupid spell," the captain interjected. "If it really worked as you describe, it was *stupid*."

"I can't argue with you," Farash said.

"I can," Sword said. "Creating a traitor was clever. All of it was clever—except letting him know that there were nine Chosen."

"How could they avoid it?" Farash asked. "He had to have the Talisman of Trust in his possession."

"Did he? I wonder. What if your talisman hadn't been linked to anything?"

Farash paused, startled.

"I don't know," he admitted. "Could they *do* that? I don't know enough about magic to know whether it's possible."

"I doubt they ever considered it," Sword said. "They had always given the Chosen linked talismans; it wouldn't occur to them to use an unlinked one."

Farash nodded. "They were traditionalists. Unlike Artil." He glanced down at the corpse.

"They were wizards," Sword said. "And they thought like wizards. Look at what they made you! The captain here said something about honorable behavior—what kind of people would deliberately create a traitor?"

"Wizards," Farash said.

"Wizards," Sword agreed. "People who could not trust each other, so they created the Wizard Lord to force themselves to behave. People who could not trust the Wizard Lord, so they created the Chosen to control him. People who would not fight their own battles, but relied on the Chosen to do all their fighting for them. The Council knew the Lord of the Galbek Hills had gone mad, but did nothing to aid us when we went to stop him. They knew the Lord of Winterhome was murdering wizards, but did they join forces to defeat him? No, they left it to the Chosen, while they fled and hid. Cowardice and treachery come naturally to wizards. Look at some of the roles they give the Chosen! The *Thief*? The Beauty, whose role is to seduce and betray? They had no honor; they trusted no one. No wonder so many became Dark Lords! The whole system they created was wrong."

Startled by Sword's vehemence, Farash looked away, and Artil's corpse caught his eye.

"So the Wizard Lord is dead," he said. "Now what?"

"I don't know," Sword said. "*You* killed him; what were you expecting?"

"I thought you would have a plan," Farash said. "I hadn't thought past this." He gestured at the soldiers. "I didn't expect to survive."

Sword grimaced. "I can understand that. Neither did I." He turned to the captain. "What do *you* intend?"

"We need to clear the trail," a soldier called before the captain could reply.

"So we can get back to Barokan," added another.

"We don't belong up here!"

"Yes, right," the captain said. The other body of guards had arrived as they spoke, and he gestured to them. "All of you, we're clearing this path. You, Redhair, run back to the palace and make sure everyone's out—not just our men, but the kitchen staff the Wizard Lord brought, the bearers, everybody. I want us all safely back in Winterhome by nightfall. You four, start over there. And you, you, you men here, line up and step forward."

Sword and Farash watched as the soldiers did as directed, the messenger dashing back up the canyon, most of the others heading for the fallen rocks.

About a dozen had been selected out and lined up, though— all new arrivals, none of the handful who had been there when the Wizard Lord died. The captain beckoned these forward, then pointed at the two Chosen. "You men, take these two prisoner! We'll take them down to Winterhome for trial."

Farash and Sword exchanged glances; then Sword whirled, and the blade that had been at the Traitor's throat a moment before was at the captain's throat.

The soldiers froze, staring at this tableau. No one moved to interfere, but from the corner of his eye Sword could see hands closing on sword hilts or tightening on spearshafts.

"By whose authority do you order this?" Sword demanded. "We are two of the Chosen, and we have slain a Dark Lord— what right do you have to interfere with us?"

"You killed the Wizard Lord!" the captain protested.

"*I* didn't kill him," Sword pointed out. "*He* did."

"But the Wizard Lord had already sentenced you to death for killing those soldiers!"

"Soldiers who had just slain two of the Chosen. You know the old law, Captain—the Wizard Lord is forbidden to harm the Chosen. And his edict died with him; you have no claim on me."

Frustrated, the captain shouted, "Well, then what about *him*?" and pointed at Farash.

"Tempting as it might be to let you kill him," Sword said, "he, too, is one of the Chosen, carrying out his assigned duties. Furthermore, Captain, your power comes to you entirely from the Wizard Lord, and extends only so far as the Wizard Lord's rule; well, right now there *is* no Wizard Lord, and even if there were, you aren't in Barokan. You have no authority here."

"Besides," Farash added mildly, "if you did take us down to Winterhome, who would try us? The priests? The Wizard Lord is dead, and the Council of Immortals destroyed."

"Captain," a soldier called. "Why bother fighting? He's dead. There's nothing we can do about it, and *I* don't want to fight the Chosen Swordsman."

The captain frowned, and looked around at his men.

Their lack of enthusiasm was obvious. Their lord was dead, their road home was blocked, and the sun was well down the western sky. No one was in the mood for starting further trouble.

"All right," the captain said, giving in. "Let them go for now, then." He turned away from the two Chosen, ignoring the blade that still lingered by his neck. "Let's just get this rubble cleared away. You three, take that big stone there; Stubtoe, you and Nosebleed work on that pile over there."

Sword and Farash exchanged glances, then stepped aside, Sword lowering his blade. There might be peace for the moment, but neither man felt sure enough of his welcome to join in the digging. Instead, they ambled to one side and continued their conversation as the soldiers worked.

"Will you go back down to Winterhome?" Farash asked.

"I think so," Sword said.

"What will you do there?"

"Go home to Mad Oak, I suppose," Sword replied. "Grow barley."

"Sounds exciting."

Sword did not bother to respond to this bit of sarcasm.

"I meant," Farash said, "what are you going to do about the Wizard Lord?"

Sword threw him a startled glance. "Nothing," he said. "What is there to do?"

"Well, traditionally, at this point the Council of Immortals would gather, reclaim the dead man's talismans, and choose his successor. I wondered whether you intended to be involved in that."

"There isn't any Council of Immortals," Sword said. "If there were, they wouldn't even know he's dead—we're outside Barokan, beyond the limits of their magic. His talismans are just harmless trinkets."

"Here, perhaps. Carry them past that rockpile, though, and everything changes."

Sword shrugged. "Then let us not carry them past that rockpile."

"He didn't kill *all* the wizards, you know," Farash remarked. "We could find the survivors and make a new Wizard Lord."

"No. I've had enough of Wizard Lords. Artil was right about them—their time is past. Magic is fading, and good riddance to it. Magic gave us Dark Lords, and Bone Garden, and Redfield, and Drumhead, and your rule in Doublefall, and your role as the Chosen Traitor. Let it fade, and let us be done with it."

"You really think it's fading?"

"Oh, yes. Definitely." Sword hesitated, then added, "I even know *why* it's fading."

Farash cocked his head. "How could you know that?"

"*Ler* explained it to me."

"Which *ler*?"

"The *ler* of the Summer Palace."

"You talked to Upland *ler*?"

"Yes."

Farash considered that for a long moment, then asked, "That earthquake—you did that?"

"I asked for it. The *ler* were kind enough to oblige me."

"They do what you ask?"

"Sometimes."

"How did that happen?"

Sword shrugged. "I don't really know. Apparently simply staying here through the winter was enough. They don't . . ." He stopped. Did he really want to tell Farash anything about the Uplands?

No, he decided, he did not. Instead he asked, "What are *you* going to do now?"

"I don't know," Farash said. He glanced at the laboring soldiers; they had already cleared a path several yards into the debris. "I don't think I'd be welcome anywhere in Barokan—I betrayed and killed the Wizard Lord, after all. People loved him."

Sword studied Farash's face for a moment, then asked, "Why *did* you kill him?"

Startled, Farash looked Sword in the eye. "What?"

"Why did you kill him? No one would have known you were the Traitor if you had simply stayed out of it, and let me kill or be killed. Now you're going to be hated and reviled—and you knew it. I thought at first that you had believed you would be greeted as a hero for killing him, but no, you knew better than that. You could have gone on as his advisor if he defeated me, or if I slew him, you could have had me killed in his name and declared yourself his heir after he and I were both dead. So why did you kill him?"

"Because it was my duty," Farash said, meeting Sword's gaze. "When I was younger and foolish, I betrayed the Chosen and aided a Dark Lord. I did not want to do that again. I did nothing when the Lord of the Galbek Hills slaughtered everyone in Stoneslope, and I enslaved the people of Doublefall, but Sword, while I know it sounds stupid, I never wanted to hurt anyone. I wanted what I wanted, power and women and pleasure, but I took no delight in anyone's suffering."

"Never? I remember hearing you say once that you wanted to gut every priest in Deepwell."

Farash blushed. "I didn't *mean* it," he said. "I was just boasting, making empty threats, trying to make myself feel like a man."

Sword was not entirely convinced. "Go on," he said.

"I didn't want to hurt anyone," Farash said. "I didn't! I wanted to help. When I advised Artil to build roads and kill monsters, I did so because I genuinely wanted to make life better for Barokan—that my role as his advisor gave me power and prestige certainly didn't hurt me, but I enjoyed helping others. Remember, when I convinced the people of Doublefall to serve me, they *enjoyed* it—oh, not of their own will, and I'm not defending what I did, but I never saw them suffering, never felt their pain. When I heard about Stoneslope, I told myself it was too late, they were already dead, and there was nothing to be done; unlike you, I didn't visit there and hear their ghosts in anguish. But when those wizards were murdered, I knew it was wrong. When Babble and the new Seer were cut to pieces in the street, there was no way to lie to myself about it. When I saw Lore and the new Boss languishing in the dungeons, I could see their pain. Artil im Salthir was a Dark Lord, and I had sworn to slay any Dark Lord. I had broken that oath once, yes, but then I knowingly swore it anew, in a new role, and I could not live with myself if I broke it again. When you came here—you, the man who had spared my life once, against all reason—and I saw you were determined to kill the Dark Lord even if you died in the process, I could not refuse to do my job. Either there would be a battle in which some of these soldiers would die, along with you or Artil or both, or Artil alone would die, at the cost of my own place in Winterhome. I could choose which it would be. That wasn't a hard choice, not really. It might have been once, but not today."

Sword met his gaze for a moment more, then nodded. "I'm very glad now that I didn't kill you nine years ago," he said.

Farash smiled wryly. "I am, too," he said. "You gave me a chance to redeem myself."

"And you took it. Thank you."

Farash glanced at the laboring soldiers. "Perhaps we should give these fellows a hand."

Sword nodded, and the two men turned to join the soldiers in clearing the road.

"I think that should do it," the captain said, looking over the path his men had cut through the rockfall. It wasn't as wide or as smooth as the original trail, and both sides were lined with piles of rubble, but it was entirely serviceable for a party walking in single file.

Three dozen soldiers and at least a score of other workers had aided in the task, and were now spread along the length of the newly cleared route; the supplies the servants had carried, and most of the soldiers' spears, were stacked at the head of the canyon, out of the way. Artil im Salthir's body lay undisturbed where he had fallen, and his sedan chair had been unceremoniously dumped beside him.

Sword and Farash had done their share of hauling stone and were as dirty and sweaty as any of the others. They stood by a pile of rocks that had accumulated in a wide part of the trail, and watched as the captain passed a few more orders to his men.

Then the captain turned and looked at them.

Sword looked back.

The captain gave a signal, a gesture, and two dozen soldiers drew swords or raised spears as civilians hurried to get out of their way. Sword frowned, and let his hand fall to the hilt of his own weapon as the captain marched toward the two Chosen.

A moment later the captain faced the two of them from about six feet away, with his soldiers forming a half-circle behind him, their weapons ready.

"We need to decide what to do with you," the captain announced.

Sword and Farash exchanged glances. "Why?" Sword asked.

"You're responsible for the Wizard Lord's death. I can't just let you go as if nothing happened."

"Why not?" Sword asked.

Before the captain could reply, Farash asked, "What did you have in mind?"

"Even with the Wizard Lord dead, I could take you prisoner," the captain said. "Law and authority or no, my men will obey me."

"What would be the point in capturing us?" Sword asked. "What would you do with us?"

"I'll hold you until the new Wizard Lord can decide whether you acted properly," the captain replied. "I know you're two of the Chosen, and it's your duty to remove Dark Lords, but the Lord of Winterhome was no Dark Lord! He built roads, he brought trade, he created our army—that's not evil!"

"Indeed it was not," Sword agreed. "But killing my companions, and all those wizards, was."

"Captain," Farash said, "there will be no new Wizard Lord."

The captain looked uncertain. "Of course there will," he said. "There always is."

"Not this time," Sword told him. "Your late master did his best to kill all the candidates. The Council that chose the Wizard Lords is destroyed."

"Artil did that deliberately," Farash added. "He believed the system had outlived its purpose. He intended to be the last Wizard Lord, and he was."

"No Wizard Lord?" The captain appeared visibly shaken. "But . . . but the weather . . ."

"The weather can take care of itself," Sword said. "It did for centuries before the Wizard Lords took control of it."

"And criminals, and rogue wizards—"

"There are no more rogue wizards," Farash told him.

"And if there ever are," Sword said, "who was it actually killed the Blue Lady, and the Cormorant, and Kazram of the Bog, and the rest? It wasn't Artil im Salthir, Captain—it was ordinary men, soldiers like yourself. If there are rogue wizards, you could handle it without any magic."

"But there must be someone in authority." The captain sounded less certain now.

Sword and Farash exchanged glances.

"The roads and canals will need maintenance," Farash said.

"Keeping outlaws in check is useful," Sword agreed.

"Deposing the priests in Bone Garden and Drumhead would not upset me."

"The one in charge doesn't need to be a wizard for any of that."

"He doesn't need any magic at all."

"Magic might be useful, though. Boss could certainly use hers."

"I don't think anyone would trust the Chosen anymore, after this last year, even if one of us wanted the job. Besides, remember Doublefall? The temptation to do something like that would be great."

"You're probably right. Not Boss, then—at least, not her alone."

"Well, I'm *sure* no one would trust *me*. Taking the role through assassination would be a very bad precedent, in any case."

"Indeed."

Sword turned back to the soldier. "Captain," he said, "you command the army, do you not?"

"I . . . yes."

"Then, Captain, *you* are the man in charge, the person with authority."

"I . . . but that's not my role!"

"It is now," Sword said. "The roles have changed. If you aren't happy with your new position, you don't need to keep it, but for now, you *are* in charge."

"You did a fine job clearing this path," Farash said. "I'm sure you can handle maintaining order, and keeping the roads and canals functioning."

The captain looked from the Swordsman to the Traitor, and back.

"Now, if you want to take us prisoner, it's *your* decision," Sword said. "No one else's. You no longer serve anyone but your own conscience. You won't be delivering us to someone; you'll be taking us for yourself."

"But you *will* need to answer to the people of Barokan," Farash added. "You can rule harshly, and live in fear of the assassin's blade as the last Wizard Lord did, or you can rule generously, and be loved—as the last Wizard Lord *also* did."

The captain stared at them for a moment, then stepped nearer and asked quietly, "If I release you, what will you do?"

"I'll go home to Mad Oak and plant barley," Sword replied. "I've done what my role required of me, and with no more Wizard Lords, that role is done."

"And I don't know what I'll do," Farash said. "I have no place in Barokan, I know that."

"You'll stay in the Uplands, then?"

"Yes."

"And in the winter? Will you come down to Winterhome?" The captain watched Farash's face intently.

"Would I be welcome?"

"I don't know," the captain said. "Things can change in so many months. It's too soon to say."

"I will come if I am welcome. I will stay in the Uplands if not."

"If you stay in the Uplands through the winter, you'll die."

Farash glanced at Sword, then shrugged. "We'll see," he said.

"You are really one of the Chosen?"

Farash looked at Sword.

"He is," Sword said.

The captain straightened, and announced, "Then as Captain of Winterhome, I acknowledge that your killing of the Wizard Lord was not murder, but I must nonetheless sentence you to exile from Barokan, effective immediately. You may apply for a pardon in no less than six months' time." He turned to Sword. "And I recognize that your actions last year were in self-defense, and I grant you pardon now."

The watching soldiers greeted this decision with applause. Sword suspected this was as much at the promise of avoiding a fight as because they thought justice was being done.

"All right, men," the captain called. "Fall in, and let's see if we can get home before dark!"

A moment later the soldiers had marched down through the narrow gap they had made, and the civilians were hurrying to gather up the supplies and equipment they had set down.

No one touched the Wizard Lord's body; one of the bearers glanced at the abandoned chair, then shrugged and left it where it lay.

Sword and Farash stood silently amid the bustle, and watched them all go.

"You know, you don't need to go back to Mad Oak and be a farmer," Farash said as the last servant trotted down the path. "You could stay in the Uplands. You can talk to the *ler* here; you could be the first Uplander wizard. You could be the *only* Uplander wizard, and make yourself *their* wizard lord, just as Artil said."

"No," Sword replied immediately. "No more wizards, and no more wizard lords, here or anywhere. The Uplanders have done just fine for centuries without any wizards, and I see no need to change that. If it's time for Barokan to stop living with wizards, why would I want to see the Uplands start?"

"Because you *can*," Farash said, but then he held up a hand before Sword could reply. "I know, I know—that's not a good reason. You won't do it any more than I would let you charge into those spears trying to get at Artil."

"And because if I stayed in the Uplands, you wouldn't be alone?" Sword asked.

"Perhaps," Farash admitted.

Sword considered his reply for a moment before saying, "You know, we may agree on many things, and we were on the same side against the Wizard Lord this time, but I still don't *like* you. You did betray us nine years ago. You did enslave Doublefall. I don't *want* to like you, and I don't want to keep you company."

"I understand," Farash said sadly. "Believe me, I understand. I wish I had lived a better life and been a better man, and I am trying to become one, but I know what I was."

"I took pity on you once before, and came to regret it," Sword continued. "But today, you redeemed yourself, so I'm going to take pity on you again, and hope that this time I won't ever have cause to regret it."

"But the captain . . ."

"I don't mean that," Sword interrupted. "I mean you don't know anything about the Uplanders, do you?"

"Not very much. I spoke to a few of their clan leaders during the winter, but . . . why?"

"They don't allow Barokanese up here. If they find you, and you can't account for yourself, they'll either kill you or enslave you. I talked my way out of it, but that was because they respected me as the Chosen Swordsman."

"Oh," Farash said. He glanced after the retreating soldiery. "Perhaps I—"

"You might be able to convince them to let you live among them, as I did," Sword said, again cutting him off. "Find the Clan of the Golden Spear, and tell them that I sent you to them. Demand to talk to the Patriarch. Tell him you slew the Wizard Lord, that I sent you to him and that you want sanctuary for what you've done."

"Will that work?"

"It might. I can't promise. But he let *me* live because I intended to kill the Wizard Lord."

"Oh."

"Can you use a spear?"

"Uh . . . not really."

"You'll want to have one anyway; you aren't considered a man without one. Can you use a rope? Because the only way to live as a free man up here is to hunt *ara,* and the Uplanders hunt with ropes and spears."

"I'll learn," Farash said.

"I hope so." Sword hesitated, then said, "If you do spend the winter up here, you'll need to provision yourself well—I almost starved. You need more food because of the cold. It's *far* colder up here in winter than down in Barokan. You'll need to find or build a shelter."

"You stayed in the Summer Palace."

"In the cellars, yes." Again, Sword paused, then continued, "About the *ler*—they avoid the *ara,* and sleep when the *ara* are active. In the winter the *ara* migrate far to the south, and the *ler* awaken. They won't talk to you if you have any feathers or bones or *ara* hide anywhere near you, but if you don't, you may be able to bargain with them." He grimaced. "Maybe *you* can be the first Uplander wizard, if you survive."

"Thank you," Farash said. "Thank you."

"I need to fetch my pack," Sword said. "I left it by the palace wall." A thought struck him. "You can have my spear; I won't need it anymore."

"Thank you," Farash said again.

The two men walked up the canyon side by side, and then turned north, toward the palace. They spoke little.

They reached the outer end of the tunnel without incident, where Sword presented Farash with his bone-handled spear.

Farash accepted it solemnly, and watched as Sword fished his pack out of the tunnel entrance. "So that's how you got into the palace," he said.

"Yes," Sword said. "Digging it kept me warm and busy. I think I might have gone mad without something like that to do." He grimaced. "Perhaps I *did* go mad, a little."

By this time the sun was below the cliffs; Sword looked around at the fading light.

"I think I'll stay the night here, in the Summer Palace," he said.

Farash looked at the wall, and at the gold-streaked sky. "I prefer not to," he said. "I spent too many nights here."

"As you please, then." Sword debated whether to offer the other man his little tent, or any other supplies, but something in the Traitor's manner deterred him. "As you please."

Farash nodded. "I wish you well, Swordsman," he said. Then he turned and began marching out onto the plain, following the distant smoke of an Uplander campfire.

Sword stood where he was for a moment, and watched the other man trudging eastward.

He was, in truth, unsure whether he wanted Farash to survive or not. The man had been his ally, and had slain his enemy, but he had done much harm, as well. Twice a traitor, Farash could not be trusted, and the idea that he might be marching off to slavery or death did not trouble Sword's conscience—but Farash seemed to have a knack for survival. He really *might* become the first wizard of the Uplands.

And if he did, it was none of Sword's concern. Sword hoisted his pack onto his shoulder and turned toward the gate; there was no need to squirm through the tunnel again.

That night he made a point of sleeping naked in the kitchen, well away from his feathered clothing and other *ara*-fraught possessions, but when he woke he remembered no dreams.

He sat up in his bedding, still naked, and said, "I thought you might want to say goodbye."

There was no reply.

"I'm returning to Barokan," he said. "I won't be back."

Still, no response.

"The man who had this palace built is dead," he continued. "I don't know whether anyone will be using it again."

They will not.

He blinked. "Why . . . how can you be so certain?"

We will ensure it. You have inspired us. This intrusion is ended.

"I don't . . . how?"

Go. Now.

Sword did not like that message at all, but he didn't try to argue; he quickly gathered his belongings and headed for the trail.

He found the Wizard Lord's corpse still lying by the road in the canyon, beside the abandoned sedan chair; flies and other insects had discovered the remains. He debated whether he should provide some sort of burial, or try to cremate it, but decided against it. Really, he was surprised the soldiers had left the body lying there; it seemed disrespectful of the man they had served. Perhaps they would come back later to retrieve it.

And if they did, he realized, they might try to retrieve the Great Talismans, and Sword did not want that to happen. He paused long enough to search the body and systematically remove every amulet and talisman—not just the nine that had made Artil the Wizard Lord, but the dozens of lesser trinkets he still wore around his neck and wrists.

He knew he could not carry those safely into Barokan,

where their magic would return; instead he gathered them up and placed them on a flat stone.

Then he picked up another fallen rock and began smashing the talismans, shattering them, flattening them, grinding them. For a quarter of an hour he slammed the rock down on them, reducing them to harmless powder.

Then at last he straightened up, tossed the rock aside, gave the corpse a final glance, and continued down the defile.

The path through the canyon beyond the corpse, once straight and easy, was now rough and winding, but at last he emerged from the crumbled stone, and had gone only a single step farther when he reached the border of Barokan.

The magic hit him with the force of a great wave, and he fell to his knees. As before, he had forgotten how intense the experience was. Sensation swept over and through him, and for an instant he felt as if all of Barokan's life were flowing into him.

Then he thought that the feeling had passed, and he started to get to his feet, but he paused. The world around him was not yet steady; the earth was shaking, and a low rumble surrounded him.

For a moment he thought this was still some effect of his restored magic, but then the shaking grew worse, and a sharp crack sounded off to his right. He staggered, then fell back to his knees as the entire canyon seemed to writhe and twist.

Another earthquake. The *ler* of the Uplands were causing another quake.

The entire world seemed to jerk and shift, and then the movement stopped—but not the sound. Again, he heard a great cracking sound, somewhere to his right, to the north. He got unsteadily to his feet and stepped forward, to the mouth of the canyon. He braced himself against the north wall and peered cautiously out.

Barokan lay spread out before him, green and shining in the morning sun. The trail down the cliffs turned sharply; that was still in deep shadow, so that it almost seemed to vanish, but it was obviously still passable, since the soldiers had made their way down the day before.

But that had been before this new tremor; had the *ler* destroyed the trail, and trapped the Uplanders on the plateau?

The trail was in Barokan, where their power did not extend. Sword crept forward another few feet and looked down.

The trail was still there, zigzagging down the cliffs. Winterhome was visible far below, still deep in shadow, and the path down to it was unbroken.

He glimpsed movement somewhere to his right, and turned.

The cliff was splitting open, a mile or more away; a fissure had appeared, and was widening as he watched. *That* was where the deafening noise came from.

A great chunk of cliff broke free as he watched, and with a tremendous roar it tumbled, breaking apart as it fell, scattering earth and stone—and wood and cloth and glass. The entire piece of land on which the Summer Palace stood was falling down the cliff, shattering as it went, and the palace was being demolished in the process.

The *ler* had ended the intrusion of Barokan's people into Uplander territory.

Sword watched in awe as a thousand tons of stone crumbled. *This* was magic, Uplander magic! Surely, it was just as well that no man had ever learned to control Uplander *ler*.

When at last the rubble had come to rest, far, far below the top of the cliff, when the last stone had rattled to a stop, Sword let out his breath, picked up his pack, and started down the trail toward Winterhome.

[25]

Sword stepped cautiously through the gate into the plaza and looked around.

The gates were unguarded, which surprised him; he had expected the captain to post a few of his men there to ensure that Farash remained in exile. No soldiers stood within twenty feet of the arch, though.

The plaza beyond, however, was crowded with merchants, soldiers, and townspeople.

As he had half-expected, even now, hours after the quake, while most of the people in the plaza were going about their business, several Host People were simply standing in the square, talking and looking up at the break in the cliff where the Summer Palace had once stood. The palace itself had never been visible from Winterhome, but the gap where it had been was a bite from the familiar curve of the cliff-edge.

A pile of debris—mostly chunks of rock, but also a broken beam, shards of glass, and half an armchair—had been gathered in the center of the plaza, presumably cleaned from the streets. The main mass of stone and wreckage had come down well to the north of town, but outlying fragments had scattered on the way down and bounced into Winterhome.

"Sword," someone said.

He turned, unsure who was speaking, what sort of reception to expect, and found Boss, Lore, and Snatcher standing there, smiling at him. Boss and Lore looked thin and tired, but happy; Snatcher was wearing the black-and-red livery of the Wizard Lord's servants and had a bandage on his left forearm.

Sword felt himself break into a smile, as well; tired and confused as he was, his delight at seeing the three of them alive and free was still undeniable.

"I want to hear your version," Boss said, her smile vanishing.

"Of course," Sword told her. His own grin widened. Months of imprisonment had not softened her. "Right here and now, or is there someplace private we can talk?"

"I have a place," Snatcher said.

Ten minutes later the four of them were in the attic of a cabinetmaker's shop a few blocks west of the plaza—this, it seemed, was where the Thief had been living for some time. The furnishings were mostly rudimentary: a straw mattress, a chest of drawers, a single cushion, a pitcher and bowl. A lush carpet, thick and glossy, seemed out of place; Sword supposed it had been stolen somewhere, and was there as much to muffle sound as anything else. After all, it would not do to have the landlord downstairs getting curious about odd noises produced by his tenant's activities.

Sword was fascinated by Snatcher's wardrobe, hung from hooks set in the sloping ceiling, or stacked in neatly folded piles on the floor. There were the black garb of Host People of both sexes, the red-and-black of a soldier, the elaborate embroidered coat of a trader from the southern coast, the simple white cloak and hood of a Winterhome priest, and a dozen other garments from various regions of Barokan, including the appropriate hats, shoes, scarves, and jewelry for each role.

There was also a box of interesting tools just inside the door—knives, pry-bars, corkscrews, pliers, and several devices Sword did not recognize. Snatcher pushed it aside as they entered.

Lore settled on the mattress; Boss sat cross-legged on that surprisingly luxurious rug, and gestured for Sword to take the rather worn cushion. He obeyed.

"I'll fetch something to eat, shall I?" Snatcher said.

"Yes, please," Sword said. "And something to drink."

The Thief looked at Boss, who nodded and waved a dismissal.

When the door had closed behind their host, Boss demanded, "So Farash inith Kerra was the ninth of the Chosen?"

"Yes. The Chosen Traitor."

"He killed the Wizard Lord?"

"Yes."

"You did not?"

"I did not."

"And the captain of the Wizard Lord's guard released you, but sent the Traitor into exile in the Uplands?"

"Yes."

"What happened to the Summer Palace?"

"*Ler* of the Uplands destroyed it. They were tired of Barokanese intrusion into their land."

"Tell me everything, then—everything that you've done since Lore and I were first imprisoned."

Sword blinked, took a deep breath, and began.

He had scarcely finished describing his visit to Morning

Calm when Snatcher returned with a platter of bread and cheese and a large jug of ale; Boss allowed Sword to take a few bites and one long swig before demanding he continue his tale.

This was the first beer he had tasted in at least half a year; Sword savored every drop.

The light outside the attic's two small windows had faded, and four of Snatcher's candles had burned down to little more than stubs, by the time Sword finally finished his narrative. Every crumb of bread and cheese was gone, and the third pitcher of beer was empty. Lore was yawning visibly, and Snatcher had curled up on the mattress; Sword was unsure whether he was awake or asleep.

". . . and I heard someone say my name, and there you were," he concluded.

Boss nodded.

"Now I have questions for you," Sword said.

"Then ask them," Boss said.

"Where's Beauty? Is she still alive?"

"We don't know," Boss said. "She fled Winterhome after the battle, and we haven't heard from her since."

"Bow is really dead?"

"Yes."

"How did you get free? Does the captain of the guard know you're out of the dungeon?"

"Snatcher set us free while the Wizard Lord was on his way up the cliff, but yes, we spoke with Captain Azal when he returned with word of the Wizard Lord's death. He had no interest in imprisoning us; in fact, he suggested that once more immediate matters have been dealt with, he and I might do well to confer on how best to replace the Wizard Lord."

"Will you?"

"Oh, yes. I think the captain and I may work well together." She smiled, her expression almost smug.

Sword nodded. He knew how persuasive the Leader could be; whatever she wanted from the captain, she could probably get it.

He was too tired right now, though, to wonder what she

might want. "Is it true that Farash conspired with Snatcher during your captivity?" he asked.

Boss turned to the Thief. "Snatcher?"

The Thief raised his head; apparently he had not been asleep. "It's true," he said. "Though I never entirely trusted him, and I never really believed his story of being the ninth of the Chosen. Remember, the magic of the Chosen does not work on the other Chosen."

Sword turned back to Boss. "Has there been any word from the surviving wizards?"

"No, but I expect they'll turn up once they learn the Wizard Lord is dead. You left his body in the Uplands? With the nine Great Talismans?"

"I left his body," Sword said. He did not mention smashing the talismans.

"Something will have to be done about that, or someone may try to create a new Wizard Lord."

Sword met her gaze, but still did not admit what he had done. Instead he asked, "You agree, then, that we are to have no more Wizard Lords?"

"Oh, absolutely! Even if the remaining wizards are capable of creating one, think about who the candidates are—a handful of wizards who fled and hid, some of the same wizards who chose Artil im Salthir, and chose Laquar kellin Hario before him. We've had two bad Wizard Lords in a row; we don't need a third to know the system has failed."

Sword nodded. "Those were also the wizards who thought creating a Chosen Traitor, and not only not telling anyone, but making it *impossible* to tell anyone, was a good, smart idea," he said.

"Well, it worked, didn't it?" Boss said. "The Traitor did his job, and the Dark Lord is dead."

"Only after the secret got most of them killed," Sword pointed out. "None of the survivors are fit for the job. Artil was right about that much."

"Artil was right about a great many things. If he hadn't been such a ruthless, murderous bastard, he might have been the best thing Barokan ever saw." She shrugged. "I'm still glad he's dead." She glanced at the window. "You must be exhausted, after climbing down here and then talking for hours."

"I am," Sword admitted.

"Well, we can all sleep here tonight, and go our various ways in the morning. Those two have the bed, which leaves the rug for us." She slid to one side, unfolded her legs, and lay down, leaving room for Sword to lie beside her. "Good night."

"Good night," Sword echoed.

He thought, as he lay down, that he would have trouble getting to sleep. There was so much to absorb, so much to think about, so much to plan.

He was wrong; weariness outweighed thought, and he was sound asleep seconds after his head hit the rug.

He was the last of the four to wake in the morning. When he finally opened his eyes he found himself looking at a plate of freshly cooked sausages, their delightful odor filling his nostrils. He sat up quickly, and looked around.

Snatcher was gone. Lore was struggling to brush his hair, which had grown long and tangled during his captivity. Boss was sitting on the cushion, eating sausages.

"Good morning," she said. "Eat, and then we'll talk."

He ate, and they talked. Snatcher returned with more food and drink, then departed again.

Eventually, when they had asked each other all the questions that came to mind, and discussed every subject Sword could think of, they left the attic and strolled back to the Winter Palace.

They parted at the door, to Boss's annoyance.

"I would prefer that we present ourselves as a unified group," she said.

"But we aren't," Sword said. "Three of us are dead, one is missing, one is in exile, and I, Boss, want little more than to go home and see my family. You and Lore present yourselves as you please, I won't disagree. I'm no leader, nor a scholar; I'm only a swordsman, and the captain has dozens of swordsmen of his own."

"But—"

"Not to mention," Sword interrupted, "that Snatcher isn't here, either."

Boss started, and looked around. Sure enough, the Thief had vanished into the crowd. "That little—"

"Let them go," Lore said. "With the end of the Wizard Lords and the destruction of the Council of Immortals, the Chosen will be chosen no more. We are relics, Boss. Leftovers. We may find places for ourselves, but we are no longer a team with a unified purpose."

"And my purpose is to go home and grow barley," Sword said.

Boss glared at him. "Fine, then," she said. "Go."

Sword bowed to her, and turned to go. He had taken just three steps when she called again.

"Sword!"

He turned.

"Thank you," she said. "Be well, be safe, and live well."

"Thank you," he said in return, startled. "And best of luck in your dealings with the captain." Then he nodded, and turned his steps northward again.

[26]

 It was more than two years later when Erren Zal Tuyo, formerly called Sword, finally managed to track down the Beauty.

Captain Azal had long since taken the title King of Barokan, and Sword had been in attendance at his wedding to Zrisha oro Sal a month before. The Leader of the Chosen had been proud to exchange her former title for that of Queen.

No one called her Boss anymore.

No one mentioned the Chosen much.

And Erren carefully didn't mention to anyone that she still had the magical power to give orders that people obeyed without thinking, the ability to persuade people with sketchy arguments, and a knack for jumping to accurate conclusions from inadequate information. Those were useful abilities in a queen; why bring them to anyone's attention?

No one ever suggested openly that perhaps the marriage had been more Queen Zrisha's idea than King Azal's. The possibility that his fondness for her might owe something to magic never came up in conversation. Similarly, no one mentioned that one of her husband's advisors had once been the Chosen Scholar, or that the man who had once been the Chosen Thief seemed to have a curiously undefined position in the royal retinue.

And if anyone knew that Erren had been offered the post of commander of the royal guard and had turned it down, they kept it quiet. The wedding celebrations were unmarred by any awkward facts or disturbing questions.

It was at the wedding that Erren had heard rumors about a strange house somewhere in Shadowvale, and now he stood among the dripping trees, looking at the bizarre structure the rumors had described.

The day had been rainy, and everything was soaked, but the sun had just broken through the clouds, and now the still-wet house, standing in a little clearing in the woods, gleamed brilliantly in the sun.

It was a good-sized structure, larger than he had expected, two stories and an attic, easily fifty feet from one end to the other, and every inch of the walls and roof was covered in feathers—*ara* feathers, in intricate patterns of black, white, and pink. Black feathers lined the shutters, and where those shutters stood open he could see pink and white feathers woven into the curtains.

The effect was strange and beautiful; especially now, with wisps of steam curling off the shining black-and-white roof as the midday sun warmed the feathers, it hardly looked real.

It was now obvious why no magic had been able to locate the Beauty.

Erren strode up the flagstone path and knocked sharply on the front door; the sound was somewhat muffled by the layer of feathers. He stood, waiting politely, for what seemed like a very long time before the latch rattled and the door swung in.

An elderly man peered out through the crack at him—not a tottering ancient, by any means, but a sturdy gray-haired man with a lined face. "Yes?" he asked.

"I'm the Chosen Swordsman," Erren said. "I've come to see the Beauty."

"Who?"

The old man was a very poor liar; his feigned ignorance was utterly transparent. "I understand," Erren said. "Tell her I'm here, though. I think she'll want to talk to me."

The old man contemplated his guest for a moment, then nodded. "Just a moment." He closed the door.

Sword waited. He listened, but could not hear any voices; perhaps the feathers provided soundproofing, as well as warding off magic.

Then the faint sound of approaching footsteps reached him, and he straightened up just as Beauty opened the door. She peered out through the crack, just as the old man had, and Erren's breath stopped as he saw her face once again—she was not wearing a scarf or hood, as she always had before, but only a simple robe, leaving her face and hair exposed. She appeared to have aged a little, but she was still by far the most beautiful woman Sword had ever seen, and he had rarely had such an unobstructed view of her features.

Then she threw the door wide and flung herself at Erren, and he staggered back, finding himself holding her in his arms. "Sword!" she said. "It's so good to see you!"

"Hello," he said, too startled to come up with anything else. He returned her embrace, and realized that she did not seem to be wearing anything *except* the plain brown robe.

"Come in, come in!" she said, sliding out of his arms and taking him by the hand.

He followed her inside.

He had half-expected the interior of the house to be as bizarre as the outside, but it was not. Except for the feathered curtains at every window, it was a very traditional, if unusually large and luxurious, home.

Something felt very strange about it, though; the instant Erren crossed the threshold the world seemed to shift, much like the transition he had felt when passing a town's boundary marker, back before the roads connected everything. He realized immediately what it was—the feathered covering served to shut out *ler*. Inside the house was not completely dead, like the guesthouse in Seven Sides, or completely asleep, like the Uplands in summer, but it was supernaturally calm; the only *ler* here were the spirits of the house itself, its furnishings, its inhabitants, and the earth upon which it stood. All others were shut out by the feathers.

It was a place of peace and happiness, though; Erren could sense that. He looked around with something approaching reverence. This was a good place, a happy place. He was pleased to know that the Beauty had found such a home.

There was one mildly discordant note, though. The old man was standing in the central hallway, watching Beauty and Erren with concern.

Beauty pulled Erren to him. "Kiamar, this is Erren Zal Tuyo, the world's greatest swordsman," she said. "Sword, this is my husband, Kiamar fis Poririn ta Parum eza Shesir."

Erren blinked. "Husband?"

"I'm honored to meet you," Kiamar said, holding out a hand. Erren took it, and shook.

"Husband?" he said again.

"Oh, yes," Beauty said. "He took me in when I fled from Winterhome, and we fell in love, and we were married that winter."

"I fell in love with her the moment I first saw her, of course," Kiamar said, withdrawing his hand. He smiled apologetically.

Beauty smiled. "I'm afraid I wasn't that quick about it," she said. "But it came to me in time."

Erren stared at her, trying to think which of a million questions he should ask first—and besides, staring at her was easy, just as it had always been.

She turned her gaze from her guest to her husband. "Kiamar?" she said. "Could you—?"

The old man shook himself. "You two must have a great deal to catch up on," he said. "Why don't you talk in there, while I see about something to eat?" He gestured into one of the rooms opening off the hall.

Erren and Beauty followed his gesture, while Kiamar vanished in the opposite direction, into the depths of the house.

The two Chosen settled on either end of a velvet-upholstered couch, and for a moment simply looked at one another—which was surprisingly difficult for Erren. He had to struggle to resist reaching out for Beauty, to grab her, or to pull open her robe to see whether he was correct in his surmise that she was wearing nothing else.

"How did you find me?" she asked.

"I heard stories about a house covered in feathers," he said. "I guessed that it was your hiding place; why else would anyone want to cover a house with *ara* feathers?" He shook his head. "But you didn't need to, you know. With the Seer dead, the Wizard Lord didn't magically know our whereabouts. That talisman stopped working when she died."

"But he had other magic," she said. "I thought he might be able to find us somehow." She shuddered. "Is he really dead? I know that's what everyone said, but there are stories that his body was never found."

"He's really dead," Erren told her. "Farash inith Kerra, the Chosen Traitor, ran him through with a borrowed sword. I saw it. Last I saw, his body was lying beside the trail to the Uplands."

She blinked at him. "Farash inith Kerra? Old Boss?"

"Yes." Erren hesitated; he knew she wanted the entire story, and he intended to tell her all about it, but there were other things he wanted to say before her husband returned. "I'll explain, but first—how did you come here? Are you really married? Do you really love him?"

She smiled. "I really love him. Were you hoping you'd find me alone? I know you had hopes, despite our ages. . . ."

Erren shrugged. "Hopes, yes, but nothing more. I was alone for a long time, and I thought of you often. But if you're happy, then I won't intrude. How did it come about?"

"Well, when Boss and Lore were captured, they told us to scatter and flee, so I fled. I headed north, into Shadowvale—no particular reason, it just seemed as good a direction as any. When I got far enough from Winterhome that my normal attire as a Hostwoman began to seem out of place, I started finding men alone and asking them for help; as I'm sure you understand, most were eager to help me however they could, but were not entirely trustworthy. I didn't need to worry about being delivered into the Wizard Lord's hands, but I *did* need to worry about being imprisoned or raped. I managed, though, and changed my clothes around enough to disguise my origin, while still keeping my face hidden as much as possible."

"I see," Erren said.

"I hadn't used my magic, my beauty, like that in years. It felt very strange to be doing it again, as if I were once again that miserable young girl fleeing a hundred suitors, the girl who idiotically agreed to be the Chosen Beauty." She sighed. "And then I met Kiamar, who was on his way home from a trading expedition to the Soreen Coast, and he fell under my spell, but I liked him better than most. Even when almost overcome with lust, he was kind and considerate. He was strong enough to have done whatever he pleased with me while I slept, but he did not—his strength was not just in his body, but in his soul. So I took him as my protector, promising him endless delights if he would guide and shelter me. I hadn't initially intended to keep that promise, but by the time we had reached his home I was beginning to think I might—he was such a nice man! Honest and direct, with a cheerful laugh and a bright smile. But I told him that I did not dare take off my clothing, that my enemies would find me with their magic; I had intended that to be my excuse for breaking my word. He accepted it, but the next thing I knew he was down in Fernbridge, buying *ara* feathers." She laughed.

"Then it was his idea to cover the house?"

"Oh, yes. At first he merely made feather bedcurtains. Then he papered the entire bedchamber, and eventually, he set out to cover the entire house. Isn't it lovely?" She gestured at the curtains in the nearest window.

"In its own way, yes," Erren acknowledged. He did not mention that it must have been fantastically expensive; she surely knew that.

"Do you know, I spent most of my life wrapped in cloth, hiding my face? But here, in this house, there was no one to see me but Kiamar, and the feathers protected me from being found by anyone else, and he took such pleasure in seeing me unclothed. I'm sure you've noticed that my face and feet are bare, that I'm wearing only a robe—well, ordinarily I don't wear that much. I don't wear *anything*. It's such freedom!"

Erren swallowed, trying not to think too much about what she must look like without the robe.

"You don't need the feathers anymore, though," he said. "The Wizard Lord is dead. The Chosen have been pardoned by the new King—in fact, Boss has just married him and become his queen. Lore is an advisor to King Azal, and I think Snatcher is working for him as a spy."

"There's a *King*?"

Erren stared at her silently for a few seconds before saying, "You don't hear much news here, do you?"

"No." She smiled. "I like it that way. When I first came here, and Kiamar made those bedcurtains, I didn't want to get out of that bed at all for weeks. I knew I should be doing something to defeat the Wizard Lord and free our comrades, but I couldn't bring myself to do it. I was enjoying it here too much. I was enjoying Kiamar too much. By the time I finally began to feel guilty about it, and began planning what to do— well, that was when the first reports of the Wizard Lord's death reached us. So I stayed here and did nothing, and do you know something, Sword? I don't regret it. I spent thirty years of my life hiding away, waiting to play my role; I did my part against the Dark Lord of the Galbek Hills, and I tried to help against the Dark Lord of Winterhome, but that was enough. It's time for me to please *myself* now—myself and my husband. If I knew how to pass my role on to a new Chosen Beauty, I would, but all the wizards are gone. . . ."

"Not quite all," Erren said. "There are rumors of the last few still being out there. There might be as many as six of them, though most of us think it's probably only three or four. However many it is, they're still in hiding. The King has let it be known that he would prefer they *stay* in hiding."

"Well, if you ever find one—"

"We aren't passing on our roles," Erren interrupted. "We are the last of the Chosen, just as Artil im Salthir was the last of the Wizard Lords. The old system is broken forever."

She nodded. "Good," she said. "Now, tell me how it happened."

Erren saw Kiamar standing in the doorway, holding a tray, and beckoned for him to join them. Cakes and tea were distributed, the three settled in their seats, and Erren began the tale.

When he had finished, Kiamar asked, "What happened to this Farash? Did he survive the winter?"

"We don't know," Erren said. "The King agreed to pardon him, and let him stay in the guesthouse with the Clan of the Golden Spear, but he never appeared. The Patriarch said that Farash had gone off on his own some weeks before. He spoke highly of him; apparently Farash made a good impression during his stay with the clan. He hasn't been seen since, so far as we have heard."

"And you went home to Mad Oak?" Beauty asked.

Erren nodded. "I grow barley and beans there, and care for my mother, and try to keep my younger sisters out of trouble."

"That doesn't sound very exciting after all your adventures!" Kiamar exclaimed. "Surely, this King you say now rules Barokan could have found a use for the world's greatest swordsman!"

Erren smiled. "I'm sure he could," he said. "But I didn't ask. Farming is a good life. And it's the life *I* chose."

Beauty smiled, and looked at Kiamar. "Just as I chose *this* life, here with my husband."

Kiamar returned her smile, then gathered up the dishes. "I'm sure you two have more to discuss; let me just clear this away."

The two Chosen watched him go; then Beauty turned back to Erren, her smile fading.

"You said Boss is the Queen, now?"

"Yes."

Beauty frowned. "Sword," she said, "I didn't think about that at first, but . . . she still has her magic, doesn't she?"

"Yes," Erren said.

"Do you think . . . well, you remember . . ."

"I remember what Farash did to Doublefall when he was the Leader, yes. Do I think Boss may have . . . *encouraged* King Azal in some of his decisions?" He shrugged. "I don't know. I honestly don't know."

"But if she did—then she's just another Wizard Lord, isn't she?"

"Maybe."

"But *Sword*—then we *are* still the Chosen, and we have to defend Barokan!"

"From what? She may be using her magic to rule, yes. That might make her something like a Wizard Lord, yes. But she isn't a *Dark* Lord—or Dark Lady, I suppose it would be. So far, she and Azal have been doing just fine at running things. Remember, most Wizard Lords filled the role peacefully."

"But . . . but the system . . ."

"The old system is broken," Erren told her. "There are still vestiges of it, yes—we're two of them, and Queen Zrisha is another. But we're the last. None of us has the magic to choose a successor and pass on his or her role. Queen Zrisha is helping to establish a *new* system, one that will have to work without magic once she's gone. Let her have a chance to help."

"But what if she *does* turn dark?"

Erren shrugged. "I still have my sword," he said. "I'm immune to her magic, and she doesn't have anything like the same magical power the Wizard Lords had, in any case. She thinks of me as a friend. If I choose, I can kill her. Or Snatcher can. We don't need the entire Chosen."

"She's younger than you are," Beauty said.

"If she outlives me and then turns bad, then someone else can choose to remove her." Erren's hand fell to his pocket, where he could feel the silver talisman that made him the

Swordsman. "After all, we chose ourselves, really; other people can choose, too."

"But they won't have any magic."

"The soldiers who slaughtered the Council didn't have any magic, either." Erren sighed. "You know, Beauty, I noticed something a long time ago, back when we were fighting our way through rainstorms to get to the Galbek Hills, but I didn't really understand it until much later. We called ourselves the Chosen, but we *did* choose ourselves. Yes, we have the magic the Council gave us, but most of all, we *chose* to fight the Dark Lords. And other people chose *not* to. The wizards never fought; they left it to us. The townsfolk never fought, either; they, too, left it to us. Why? Because we were the Chosen. Everyone knew we were there, chosen to defend them—and because we were there, they didn't need to defend *themselves*. But we chose *ourselves*. When the Old Swordsman came to Mad Oak seeking his successor, I *chose* to speak up, when no one else would. No one came and told me I *must* be the Swordsman; I volunteered. I stepped forward because I thought *someone* had to. Later on, when we were fighting for our lives, no one else stepped forward to help us, because we were the Chosen, we had already been selected for the job and it wasn't anyone else's place to be involved—but if there hadn't *been* any Chosen, would anyone have stepped forward?"

"I don't know," she whispered. "Would they?"

"I hope so," Erren said. "I think there were probably dozens of people who might have thought, someone needs to do something, and no one else is, so I need to try. But they didn't; instead they thought, the Chosen will defend us, how fortunate, *I* don't need to do anything! Only now there are no Chosen. And I hope, I *hope,* that that means that when the day comes that Barokan has a bad king or an evil queen, ordinary people will step forward to deal with the problem. They won't wait for someone else to act. They won't rely on preselected heroes. They'll do what must be done. Farash didn't need to kill Artil, you know, but he did it anyway, because he knew it had to be done, even if it got him killed. I hope there will always be people who can do that."

Beauty glanced toward the door where Kiamar had vanished.

"I hope so, too," she said. "But Sword, I will tell you right now—if a time like that comes, I probably won't be one of them."

Erren shrugged. "You have your own life to live," he said. "And I have mine. And I don't think the present King or Queen will ever need to be removed. If they do, well, we can worry about it then."

At that point Kiamar reappeared, and the conversation turned to lighter topics.

A few hours later Erren took his leave. He shook Kiamar's hand, then gave the Beauty a final embrace in the doorway of her feathered home.

"Remember," he said as he turned away. "We choose what we want to be. Heroes choose themselves."

[EPILOGUE]

"THE BALLAD OF THE CHOSEN"
(as sung at the coronation of Queen Zrisha)

One day turned dark and shadows fell
Across this land of fools
As madness turned the old ways 'round
And shattered ancient rules
Then nine were called by wizards' schemes
To save us from our doom;
The Chosen came to guard us all
And lay evil in its tomb

Chorus: The Wizard Lord of Winterhome
            Betrayed his fellow man—
            These Chosen nine would bring him down,
            Bring peace to Barokan!

The Leader showed her bold resolve
Confronted every foe
Her words would guide the Chosen as
She told them how to go

The Seer sought her comrades out
And gathered them to fight
Nor could their foeman hide from her;
She had the second sight

Chorus

The Swordsman's blade was swift and sure
His skill was unsurpassed

If any stood against him, then
That stand would be his last

A lovely face the Beauty had,
And shapely legs and arms
She distracted evil men
And lured them with her charms

Chorus

There was no lock nor guarded door
That could stop the Thief
He could pierce the fortress walls
To bring our land relief

Every song and story told,
The Scholar knew them all
He knew the wizard's weaknesses
To hasten evil's fall

Chorus

The Archer's missiles never missed;
His arrows found their mark
He struck at evil from afar
To drive away the dark

The Speaker harked to every tongue,
Of stone and beast and man
She found the Dark Lord's secrets out
So no defense could stand

Chorus

When here in Winterhome our lord
Forgot his proper role
The Traitor struck the Dark Lord down
To save our nation's soul

And thus the last of magic's spawn
Was slain where he did stand
Never more will wizards rule
Our lovely Barokan

Chorus

And now a noble man has come
To keep and rule the land
And bring us all a better world
Safe from magic's hand

The Chosen we shall need no more
Their long service now is past
A better way to keep the peace
We all have found at last

Our noble King will never turn
Against the common man
The Chosen nine no longer need
Bring peace to Barokan—
Yes, our King, and now our Queen,
Bring peace to Barokan!

APPENDIX

The Dark Lords and the Chosen Defenders of Barokan

In the seven hundred years that the Council of Immortals maintained the system of Wizard Lords and Chosen, nine Wizard Lords were corrupted in one way or another, and declared to be Dark Lords.

Some eighty-eight years after the system was instituted, the third Wizard Lord, the Lord of the Midlands, became the first Dark Lord and was removed by three heroes chosen by the Council of Immortals. Those first three heroes, not yet called the Chosen, were given whatever magic the wizards were able to improvise—one was given skill with weapons, one gifts of persuasion and intuition, and the third magical senses, including awareness of the whereabouts of both his companions and the Wizard Lord.

Two of the three were killed before the third managed to dispatch the Dark Lord of the Midlands.

The Council of Immortals decided that such heroes should be maintained permanently, as a check on future Wizard Lords, and established the Chosen Defenders of Barokan. They recreated the same three roles, somewhat modified, and named them the Swordsman, the Leader, and the Seer; given the loss of two out of the three, they added a fourth, the Seducer, to improve their chances should they ever be needed again.

Almost fifty years later, the four Chosen were called upon to remove the Dark Lord of Tallowcrane. That Dark Lord's extensive use of locks and bars in his defenses led to the addition of the Thief, and it was decided that henceforth the

Seducer role should always be taken by a female, to be called the Beauty.

For more than eighty years thereafter, there were no Dark Lords. When at last another did arise, he resigned quietly, rather than face the Chosen. More than thirty years later, another did the same, and for the first time people began to think there might be an end to the matter.

Unfortunately, sixty years later, in the 305th year of the Council of Immortals, the Dark Lord of Kamith t'Daru demonstrated that Barokan was not safe. When Kamith t'Daru realized that he was likely to run afoul of the Chosen, he carefully studied the surviving records of how previous Dark Lords were defeated. This made him a difficult opponent, and after his death, the Council added the Chosen Scholar, so that the Chosen would always know at least as much about past encounters as their opponents did.

It was almost 170 years before another Wizard Lord dared to break his trust and became the Dark Lord of the Tsamas. His reliance on keeping his enemies at a distance led the Council to add the Archer.

The Dark Lord of Spider Marsh retired peacefully in the 511th year of the Council, rather than fight the Chosen to the death. About ninety years later, however, the Dark Lord of Goln Vleys put up a ferocious resistance before finally being brought down.

The Council added the Speaker of All Tongues after that.

The sorry end of the Dark Lord of the Galbek Hills came at the hands of the Last Swordsman, while the one and only Chosen Traitor, added after the defeat of Galbek Hills, brought down the tenth and last, the Dark Lord of Winterhome.

Turn the page for a preview of

—————— A ——————

YOUNG
MAN
WITHOUT
MAGIC

◆

LAWRENCE WATT-EVANS

Available November 2009
from Tom Doherty Associates

A TOR HARDCOVER   ISBN: 978-0-7653-2279-1

[1]

In Which Anrel Murau Returns
Home to an Uncertain Reception

The rain had finally stopped, and the public coach's sole occupant was able to roll up the blinds and look out the unglazed windows without getting soaked. The countryside was still green, even this late in the summer and in the gloom of a heavy overcast; the passenger wondered how that could be, when so much of the talk in Lume for the past few seasons had been of crop failures and famine.

The coach jolted over some unevenness in the road, and Anrel Murau braced himself against the window frame as he gazed out at a harvested field. He could not tell what had been grown there, or how much the land had yielded, but the rain-darkened earth certainly looked rich and fertile—as it should. After all, this was Aulix, one of the richest provinces in the Walasian Empire. A famine in Walasia, the heart of the Bound Lands—could that really be possible? This was the realm where the forces of nature had been brought under control, where the Mother and the Father looked kindly upon humanity and its sorceries. It wasn't some wild hinterland like the outer reaches of Quand, or the Ermetian mystery lands, where days might be different lengths from one to the next, or monsters might prowl the fields, or snow might fall in midsummer, if the seasons were even regular enough to *have* a summer. No, this was a land of order and stability, where farmers had been feeding the population reliably for centuries, where sorcerers regulated the weather, where most of the wild spirits and negative forces that plagued the Unbound Lands had long since been banished. What could have changed, to allow food shortages to occur?

Nothing he saw from the coach window gave him any hint. The fields rolling by, whether still green or stripped bare, all *looked* fertile enough.

They also looked simultaneously familiar and strange. He had spent his entire childhood in this region, but after his four years in the capital the countryside seemed vaguely unreal, like a nostalgic dream rather than a present reality. The placid, rain-washed green hills and brown fields, virtually empty of human life, were so very different from the crowded, stone-paved streets of Lume. Here there were no pleading beggars, no hungry men clustered around notice boards looking for work, no coachmen with whips clearing the way for their vehicles, no scowling watchmen patrolling their elevated walkways.

Here in the country sorcerers looked after their subjects, as they ought to—or at least, that was how he remembered it, and he hoped *that* had not changed while he was studying history and law in the court schools. The most powerful magicians were the landgraves who ruled the empire's sixteen provinces, but every town or village was under the benevolent rule of a burgrave, every border was guarded by a margrave, and lesser sorcerers served as magistrates and administrators, devoting their magic to the public good.

At least in theory. Anrel knew all too well that sorcerers were merely human.

Some of Anrel's fellow students had insisted that discontent was widespread throughout the empire, that high taxes and tariffs were ruining trade, that sorcerers were too caught up in their own magic and their intrigues to attend to their duties, but Anrel chose not to believe it. People had always complained, and young men, he knew from his history books, always thought they were coming of age in a time of crisis and impending collapse. They wanted to save the world, and that meant the world had to need saving.

Anrel had no interest in saving the world, and did not think anyone needed to. He merely wanted to find a place in it.

He *hoped* the world didn't need saving, but matters did seem to have deteriorated in Lume during his time there. The burgrave of Lume's guards and the Emperor's Watch had been called out to put down riots more in the past season than in the entire previous year, which had already been an unusually violent one.

Surely, though, that was a temporary aberration.

Temporary or not, it had nothing to do with matters here in Aulix. The coach had taken him from the unhappy ferment of Lume through Beynos, where the streets had been only slightly troubled, and then Orlias, and Kevár, and all the other villages along the route, each calmer than the town before, until finally Kuriel had appeared so placid that Anrel had wondered if the inhabitants might have been enchanted. It was as if the coach had been carrying him back into his childhood, when he was blithely unaware of any political issues or unrest at all.

Not that his childhood had been unmarked by tragedy. He remembered the first time he had ridden a coach along this road, eighteen years ago; he had been a child of only four, but the memory was indelibly fixed in his head. He had been newly orphaned, on his way to live with a widowed uncle he had never met; of course he remembered it! He had been frightened and lost and alone, mere days from the horror of discovering what was left of his parents after a spell had gone wrong, and he had known, even at that tender age, that the coach was taking him to a new and different life, that he would never return to the house where he was born.

That new life had been pleasant enough. Lord Dorias Adirane, burgrave of Alzur, had been kind to him, and Anrel had spent fourteen happy years in his uncle's home before being sent off to Lume to complete his education.

Now he was once again on his way to his uncle's mansion.

He wished he could be more certain of his reception. Uncle Dorias's letters had not seemed very enthusiastic about his nephew's plans—what few plans he had, as he had to admit he was somewhat vague about his future. Anrel hoped to find some employment appropriate for a young man of his station, a young man without magic but with the best education the court schools of Lume could provide. As for the precise *nature* of this employment—well, he had not satisfied his uncle on that account.

He had not satisfied himself, either.

In truth, it was unlikely he would find a suitable post in Alzur; the village had no use for a scholar. Anrel had the impression Lord Dorias had expected him to find a position in Lume, or perhaps one of the other cities of the empire, rather than returning to his uncle's estate, but the old man had not come out and said so, and no such employment had manifested itself, as yet.

Uncle Dorias had made plain that he had no intention of supporting Anrel's studies beyond the customary four years, and with no prospects in Lume Anrel had had little choice but to return to Alzur, but he did not regret that in the least. For one thing, he had a notion that his uncle's fosterling and former apprentice Valin—*Lord* Valin—might have found himself a position where a skilled clerk would be useful. Settling down as his childhood companion's aide had a great deal to recommend it, Anrel thought. A few quiet rooms somewhere working for his friend, and eventually a wife, perhaps children—that was a life that would suit Anrel well. He had no desire to change the world or achieve great things.

He looked out at the countryside, and hoped his modest ambitions could be realized. He could see from the scenery that the coach was nearing the village of Alzur; he leaned out the window and peered at the hills ahead, trying to make out his uncle's house.

He spotted it readily enough. Although Lord Dorias was

burgrave of Alzur, he did not actually live inside the village's iron pale as a burgrave should; his manor stood instead atop one of the higher hills in the vicinity, roughly two miles south of the village square.

Anrel recalled that he hadn't known that when he had first come to Alzur as a child. He had mistaken the far larger estate of Lord Allutar Hezir, a mile north of town, for his uncle's home, and had been confused when he was instead taken back across the bridge to the southern bank of the Raish River.

Even now, eighteen years later, he never had understood why Lord Allutar, the landgrave of Aulix, chose to make his seat at a village like Alzur, instead of at Naith, the provincial capital. Alzur was a modest collection of shops and homes stretching along half a mile of riverbank between the two sorcerers' mansions, while Naith, a dozen miles farther west, was a thriving city that seemed a far more sensible place for the landgrave to live. All the other provincial officials, from the lowliest clerk to the Lords Magistrate, lived in Naith, but the landgrave himself dwelt in Alzur.

Anrel would have much preferred Lord Allutar to live elsewhere, but it was not up to him. He pulled his head back in and settled down in his seat to wait, leaning back against the worn leather.

He hoped that his uncle would be there to meet him; Anrel had said, in his last letter, which coach he would be on. If Lord Dorias was waiting for him, that would be an indication that the coldness Anrel had thought he perceived in recent correspondence was merely a figment of his imagination.

Then the coach was across the bridge and rumbling up the streets into Alzur proper.

A moment later the coachman called to his team, and the vehicle rolled to a stop on the wet cobbles of the town's only square. "Alzur!" the driver called as he set the brake. "This is Alzur!"

Anrel sat up and fumbled with the latch, and the door banged open. He thrust out his head and looked around. "Indeed it *is* Alzur," he said aloud, addressing the air. "It hasn't changed a bit, has it?" The town was exactly as he remembered it. Just now everything was damp from the recent rain, water dripping from the eaves and trickling down the streets, but otherwise it could have been any day since he had first seen the place eighteen years before.

But then, why would a sleepy village in Aulix look any different? The rabble-rousers of Lume might claim great changes were afoot in the world, but Anrel thought they would hardly reach a place like this.

He looked around and saw no sign of his uncle. He did, however, see a young man in a green frock coat trotting across the cobbles and waving to him. "Anrel!" this person called. "You've made it!"

The traveler looked down at his dearest friend and smiled broadly. "Hello, Valin," he said, clambering quickly down from the coach. "It's good to see you!"

"Very good indeed!" Valin replied, stepping forward, his own grin as broad as the traveler's.

The two men embraced, and when they separated Anrel said, "You haven't changed any more than Alzur has, I see."

"Ah, so it might appear to the casual glance," Lord Valin said, clapping his friend on the back, "but I believe that when we have a chance to talk a little you'll see just how different I have become. When you left I was little more than a child, and I like to think I am rather more than that now."

Anrel's smile broadened. Valin was his senior by more than a year, but in truth, had never in Anrel's memory seemed the more mature of the pair. Perhaps, though, he really *had* changed during Anrel's absence this time; his sparse letters provided no compelling evidence either way. "I'm eager to hear all about it," he said.

"And *I* am eager to hear all the news from Lume," Valin answered. "What's happening there? Is there much excitement about the calling of the Grand Council?"

Anrel's smile dimmed. Not two minutes out of the coach, and Valin was asking him about political affairs. Pleased as he was to see him apparently unchanged, Anrel had hoped that Valin's obsession with wild schemes to change the world had faded. He was as bad as the firebrands of Lume, and with far less justification.

Indeed, it was largely his familiarity with Valin that had led him to dismiss the beliefs of the agitators, idealists, and theorists of the court schools as unfounded.

"I am not sure I would call it excitement so much as uncertainty," Anrel said. He glanced over to see that the coachman had already exchanged the day's incoming and outgoing mail with Alzur's postmistress, the same plump little woman who had held the post when Anrel departed four years before— Oria Neynar, was it? Yes, that was her name. She was trotting off with the dispatch case in hand while the driver proceeded around toward the back of the coach. "But let us retrieve my baggage and be on our way, so that this good man can get on with his business."

"Yes, to be sure," Valin agreed.

A few fresh raindrops spattered the pavement just then, and Anrel glanced at the sky. He hoped it was just a final sprinkle, and not the start of a fresh downpour. "I think we should make haste," he said. He turned to the driver, who had untied the protective canvas and was heaving a leather-bound traveling case to the cobbles.

"Of course!" Valin said, hurrying to snatch up the first bag.

The coachman handed the next bag, a battered valise, directly to Anrel, who nodded, and passed the man a coin in exchange—a sixpence, one-tenth of a guilder, which was generous, but the man had made good time and kept the ride reasonably smooth, and there were no other passengers to contribute to his pay.

The coachman smiled and tipped his hat, then turned to secure the coach for the next leg of his run. Fat drops began to darken the canvas as the driver tied it back in place, and Anrel looked up again. The sky did not look promising.

"Is this everything?" Valin asked, hefting the traveling case.

"Indeed it is," Anrel said, turning his attention to his friend. "I am, after all, only a poor student, not a mighty sorcerer like yourself." The statement was made in jest, but it was also the simple truth—Valin *was* a sorcerer, where Anrel was not.

Valin punched him lightly on the shoulder. "Sorcerer, pfah! I am a man like yourself, Anrel. Are we not all the children of the Father and the Mother, and heirs of the Old Empire?" He began marching south across the square.

"Some of us are the more favored heirs, Valin, while others are but despised cousins," Anrel said, following his companion. "Your magic gives you a status most of us can never aspire to."

Lord Valin glanced back over his shoulder. "*Never* aspire to? I think you may misjudge the situation, my friend. What our fathers dared not dream of, our sons may take for granted. Changes are coming, Anrel! Surely, if I have heard as much in the taverns of Naith, you have heard it in the capital!"

Anrel did not need to ask what he meant, since he had indeed heard these utopian schemes bruited about in Lume. He did not put much stock in them himself, but kept his opinion to himself. Instead, hoping to divert the discussion away from the capital and toward Valin's own situation, he said, "You have certainly achieved what *your* father did not."

"Pfah!" Valin waved his free hand in dismissal. "I can take little pleasure in a fortunate accident of birth. I was merely . . ."

At that point, with no further warning, the skies opened anew, and rain deluged upon the pair, turning the world gray and wet. Water poured from the eaves on every side, and the spaces between cobbles all seemed to fill instantly.

"Over there!" Anrel shouted over the drumming of the torrent, as he pointed toward a pair of small tables set beneath a broad sky blue awning. The awning was already soaked, but it was still the closest shelter; the two men ran for it.

A moment later the two of them had ducked beneath the sagging awning, and turned to stare out at the downpour.

"It would seem that the spirits of air and water do not want me to rush to my uncle's hearth," Anrel said.

"Indeed," Valin agreed.

"This is not the homecoming I had hoped for," Anrel said. He meant not merely the weather, but the fact that Valin had come alone to meet him. His uncle's presence would have been very welcome, or that of Anrel's cousin, Lady Saria. Lord Dorias's only child had been a baby when Anrel first came to Alzur, and only just blossoming into womanhood when he left for Lume. He wondered what she looked like now; she had shown signs of becoming a beauty. How much had she changed in his absence?

He would see her soon enough, he supposed, but he wished she had come to meet him and welcome him home. He would have found it reassuring.

But at least someone from the Adirane household was here, even if Valin was not actually a member of the family. It was very good to see Valin again, and to know at least *someone* welcomed his return.